D1521746

Stolen Memories

Mary Miley

Other books by Mary Miley

The Impersonator

Silent Murders

Renting Silence

ISBN: 151-8883702
ISBN-13: 978-151-8883705

Stolen Memories

Mary Miley

PROLOGUE

They say Paris is for lovers, but Tadeuz Zdrojewski hadn't found one yet.

Still unaccompanied after two bars and one jazz hall, he and his shipmate tried to overcome the communication barrier with a middle finger gesture they'd learned during the Great War, but the move only landed them in the stone gutter outside the Bar d'Austerlitz. Swearing at their wretched luck and dwindling shore leave, the two sailors were untangling their legs when something caught Zdrojewski's eye. He squinted toward the darkened banks of the Seine, forty meters from the bar. There had been a sudden movement, a sharp cry. Or maybe not. He blinked to focus. The air stilled, and in the shadows cast by a feeble gaslight, he made out several pedestrians walking along the quay. He turned to give his mate a hand up. Something made him look again. Three or four people moving furtively, all dressed in dark clothing except one. Somehow he knew the light one was a woman. In the time it took him to assemble that thought, she had gone limp as a sack of grain.

Without thinking, he lunged forward. No French came to mind, but his tone of alarm cut through the twilight as he cried out for the figures to stop. They heard him shout, and they moved faster, dragging the body to the edge of the quay and heaving it into the dark strong current of the Seine.

1

Mary Miley

1 THE HOSPITAL

At first, I thought I was watching a motion picture. Flat figures in white and black and pewter grey glided in silence across the screen before my eyes. The story had something to do with a hospital—solemn men wearing white coats and sisters in grey habits and crisp white wimples made that plain—but I could not follow their conversation for there were no subtitles, nor was there any music to set the mood.

Someone was dying and I was not keen on watching. I closed my eyes and left the theatre.

A moment later—an hour, a week, a month—I opened my eyes again.

I had moved from audience to centre stage. Actors stood on either side of me. They looked at me and spoke, but no sound came from their mouths. They wanted me to say something; it was my turn, but I had forgotten the lines. My head was empty. My mouth was closed.

One doctor smiled reassuringly; the other gave a black scowl.

I did not want to think. I wanted the darkness. I wanted to *be* the darkness, away from the blinding stage lights, somewhere safe and warm. I closed the curtains and escaped into the shadowy wings of the theatre.

I have no idea how many times I came and went. I could not sift dreams from reality or day from night. Demons tormented me, pushing me, pinching me until I cried out in pain. Sisters dribbled water and syrup down my parched throat with a spoon and wiped

3

my limbs with a cool wet rag; the kind doctor felt my wrist, took my temperature, listened to my chest with his stethoscope. I tried to hide behind closed eyelids when the other doctor was beside the bed, looming over me. Once he said angry things to me. I could not hear him, but his twisted lips and the ugliness on his face told me more than I wanted to know. Or perhaps it was all a dream, or another motion picture.

It was the noise that finally dragged me out of my soft hiding place, back into the harsh world. The noise came on suddenly, like radio static when you twist the dial to find a clear signal, unfocused at first, then sharpening into words and sounds.

"Ah, *madame*, can you hear me now?" It was the kind doctor, alone. He held his pocket watch in one hand and my wrist in his other, and his eyes smiled at me through thick spectacles. His coat was rumpled and none too clean. He spoke with an accent. A foreigner.

Yes, I answered him. *Where am I?* My brain phrased the question clearly but there was no sound. My lips did not move. I thought they moved. I was quite certain of it, but the doctor continued to nod encouragingly, like a teacher waiting for the correct response from a slow pupil.

"Can you hear me now?" he asked again.

Panic welled up inside me and spilled out my eyes. I tried to nod a little to show I understood aright. The motion brought an explosion of pain into my head, sharp as a hammer on steel, and I gave a silent cry.

"No, no, do not move, madame. You have a big accident. One moment."

He left.

A big accident? What had happened? In alarm, I took stock of my body. My left hand was bound tight in a splint to the elbow, but I flexed the fingers on the other hand and wiggled my toes, thankful for the pain that told me my legs were still connected. Without moving my head, I let my eyes search the room. The window was shuttered with heavy wooden panels—I supposed it to be night. No sounds filtered in from the outside world. Enough light shone from the single electric bulb on the ceiling to reveal a small room with three wooden chairs and as many beds, all unoccupied save mine. A *prie-dieu* stood in one corner facing a crucifix. The walls could have used a fresh coat of paint. Once white, they had faded to yellow as white paint always does, and the plaster surrounding the doorway had chipped away, giving the room a shabbiness one feels in a boarding house. The cracks in the ceiling flowed like rivers on a map. My eyes followed the Danube east to the Black Sea.

The doctor returned with a sister who gave me laudanum for the pain and began spooning tepid water between my lips, moistening my swollen tongue enough to speak.

"What . . . ?" This time I heard my voice, a whisper as scratchy as an old record.

"Bad men rob you and hit your head and push you in the Seine." With his hands he re-enacted the event. "You remember this?"

My lips shaped a soundless No. Thinking hurt. I didn't plan on doing much of it.

"You are in hospital. *Notre Dame du Bon Secours.*" I suppose I looked blank because he added, "In Paris."

The Seine. Paris . . . Paris, France? Then I was the foreigner, not he.

"You are here five days." He held up all five fingers.

Five days! Instinctively I reached up to rub my pounding temples and touched more bandages. It was then that I realized I had only one eye. I cried out in alarm as my fingers grazed the gauze.

"*Ne vous en faîtes pas, madame.* Do not worry. We sew the cut in the skin. The eye is—" he groped unsuccessfully for the word— "closed." I prayed he meant it was merely swollen shut, not missing. Now I understood the reason for the celluloid flatness of the view. With only one eye, I had no sense of perspective.

"You remember the men that do this?"

I considered the question gingerly. "N-n-n-no," I stuttered. The word in my head couldn't push past my tongue. Finally I managed a weak reply. "I-I-I d-d-d-don't remember a-a-a-anything."

He gave me a speculative look and fingered his stethoscope. "What is your name, madame?"

I had no idea.

Sensing the panic that threatened to overwhelm me, the doctor reached over and patted my hand in a fatherly manner. His thin grey hair stood up in disarray and his eyes drooped with fatigue, but he pulled up one of the stiff oak chairs and made himself as comfortable as possible.

"*Eh bien.* What is the year?"

It was a difficult question. After long, painful thought, a likely possibility emerged from the depths of my consciousness. I forced my tongue to shape the difficult sounds.

"N-N-Nineteen t-twenty-eight?"

"*Bien sûr.* And the month?"

More thinking. "M-M-May?"

He nodded. "And your King of England?"

"George V."

"Very good," he smiled, patronizing me as one does a dutiful six-year-old. "And how many is seven times six?"

I turned my efforts inward. The numbers reluctantly assumed their shapes in my head, a fat round six and a sharp seven. When they mated, sparks flew, but no progeny stepped forward. I could only stutter helplessly.

The doctor took a pencil from his breast pocket and wrote something on a piece of paper. "Can you read this?" The marks bobbled disobediently about the page, mocking all efforts to sort them out. Once again, tears stung my eyes. I couldn't talk; I couldn't read. My heart pounded in fear.

"Do not worry, madame. The head is very hard hit. The brain cannot think. It is not normal to remember all things. You remember some now. After rest you will remember more." He continued to smile and pat my hand. "And we know your name, from the passport. You are Eva Johnson." He watched me, his eyebrows arched expectantly, hoping this revelation would unlock the door to further memories, but the name slid past me like an introduction at a noisy party. "You are a English lady. Your husband will come soon. He will help you to remember."

Instead of reassuring me, the information brought only confusion. Eva Johnson? It was a name I had never heard before. How could that be me? There must be some mistake. Surely I would recognize my own name. I would remember everything later? When was later? I wanted to know at once.

A sister bustled in with a tray and the doctor took his leave. Gently, as if she knew how much the slightest movement hurt, she eased another pillow under my head and began spooning warm beef broth into my mouth. She didn't speak—either she knew no

English or had taken a vow of silence.

Eva Johnson? And I was married? Impossible. I looked at my fingers to see if I wore a wedding band, but my left hand was swathed in bandages. And no images came to mind. No names, no family, no faces. Did I have children? It was all too unimaginable. Eva Johnson was someone else, not me.

I noticed the sister's capable hands. Rough from scrubbing, they smelt of ammonia. She wore a wedding band. Brides of Christ, they called them. It was hard to tell them apart, these nuns—one saw so little of their faces or shapes—but I noticed her name embroidered on the top corner of her apron: *Soeur Genevieve*. She hummed tunelessly as she smoothed the covers and tucked them in at the sides, pinning me securely between the sheets. It did not occur to me until long after she had gone that the embroidered letters had not done their weird dance. I had read her name. Maybe the doctor was right. I was already regaining my memory. Comforted, I slept.

My fever returned that night, robbing me of reality. The shutters stayed closed so I could not tell daylight from darkness. Sisters and doctors came and went, united in their insistence that I consume liquids and fever powders and unpleasant tasting potions. My body burnt hot enough to set the sheets ablaze. Dreams came and went as well, frightening, vivid scenes that fled to the corners of my mind the moment my eyes opened only to creep out of hiding when my temperature climbed. A long corridor, paintings hanging high above my head, falling silently off the walls . . . the paintings were lost. I was lost. A little boy was lost. A scream—one long scream—echoed inside my head, again and again, ricocheting through the empty hall like a bullet off stone walls.

I dreaded seeing the angry doctor by my bed, his steely eyes boring into me, asking question after question that I could neither understand nor answer. Once the kind doctor sat beside my bed, reciting the alphabet and counting numbers. I heard voices—calm, uncaring voices—saying there were rats on my bed, and I felt them crawling over my legs and I screamed and tried to push them onto the floor, but the sisters were there in the way, changing my bed sheets. When at last the fever broke, I was weak as a newborn. Sister Genevieve bathed the sweat off my bruised limbs, humming as she worked.

When she had finished, the kind doctor came in with another sister. As he made notes on a chart, she began replacing the gauze that bound my hand with fresh cloth. She was younger than Sister Genevieve and shorter, with large grey eyes that matched the colour of her habit, and she smelt of bleach. My eyes fell on the name embroidered onto her apron: *Soeur Marie Claire*.

My heart nearly stopped beating. Sister Marie Claire. Marie Claire. The name galloped around in circles inside my head. Marie Claire. Marie Claire. I looked again at her stitchery. The second name seemed to leap off the fabric. Claire. It was my name. Claire.

I cried out at the discovery and the little nun abruptly stopped what she was doing, thinking she had hurt me. The doctor glanced up from his scribbling. "Th-th-that's my name!" I cried, agitated beyond anything they had previously seen. "My name is Claire!" And then the rest burst out like a cork from a champagne bottle. "Claire Smith! That's it! I'm Claire Smith!"

The excitement had me almost sitting up in bed, and Sister Marie Claire gently pushed me back onto the pillow. "*Mais non, mais non*," the doctor humoured me. His glance at Sister's embroidered name told me he understood the origin of my recollection. "We have your passport, madame. Your name is Eva Johnson. Your purse, your hotel key. All is here. Your husband will tell you."

The name was so clear, I would not be dissuaded. I felt like Claire. I didn't feel like Eva. And I didn't feel married.

"Perhaps this Claire Smith is your friend or your sister. A person from a book you have read or from the cinema."

"B-B-But—"

"The concussion has confused you."

"That passport, m-maybe it isn't mine."

"The blue passport is English. It writes how high you are and how your eyes are green, your hair brown. It has a little photograph."

There was not much to be said to that.

"This is good news, madame. You understand? You can read again. You read the name on Sister's apron, yes?"

"Yes. I . . . the letters are s-steady now. I fancy it was your alphabet recitation that did it. Thank you." He looked so puzzled, I had to explain. "When you sat by my b-bed and counted the numbers and said the alphabet for me."

"But I never did such a thing, madame."

"But I remember you sitting there and . . . "

"Fever gives a person many dreams. Some good, some bad. This is a dream. A good dream, yes?"

What was wrong with me? Reality seemed like a dream and my dreams seemed real. How was I to know what to believe? Hot tears slid down my cheeks.

"*Tenez*, do not worry, madame. There is not one chance in a million that you will remain like this. Your husband is here. He eats his dinner; he will return soon. A strong blow to the head—it is often like this. You are fortunate. Very fortunate. You can talk. Many stutter. You do not stutter very much and it gets better, eh? You are confused in the head but you will remember everything soon. Be calm."

At that moment, the mean doctor walked through the door, his scowl so fierce it drew his eyebrows together. Only this time, I was lucid enough to notice that his white coat was not a medical jacket, but a starched white cotton shirt with no name embroidered above the pocket, and he didn't wear a stethoscope around his neck or carry a notebook like the old doctor.

Because he was not a doctor. This was my husband.

Two gendarmes who had been waiting in the passageway followed my husband into the room. The men had come every day, hoping to question me, and at last the doctor admitted them. They had found one who spoke English to send along with the one who had arrived first at the scene of the crime. The doctor remained in the room, thinking no doubt to protect his patient from over-exertion. The man who claimed to be my husband moved to the head of my bed on the left side where the bandages prevented me from seeing him without turning. And turning was not something I planned to do soon.

"We are very happy you are mending, madame," the older, well-fed policeman began. His voice was gravely, his manner gruff, as if he were embarrassed to be standing by the bed of a battered woman wearing nothing but a hospital gown. "We are sorry to have such a crime in Paris. It is our hope you can tell us something to help catch these bad men."

"I'm afraid I d-don't r-r-remember anything about them." My head throbbed and my hand hurt even more. The silent presence of the man behind me flustered me beyond all reason and made my stutter more pronounced. All I wanted was to be left alone to go back to sleep, to deal with all this later.

"So said the doctor. Perhaps we can help you remember. You were walking along the Quai de la Tournelle, on the Left Bank. What were you doing there?"

"I don't know."

"It is some distance from your hotel. We questioned all the taxis. No one remembers taking you to the *Quartier Latin*. You walked, perhaps, or met a friend?"

"I d-don't remember."

"It was almost ten o'clock. Still some light this time of year. You were returning to your hotel, perhaps? Do you remember your hotel?"

"No."

"It was *L'Hotel de Crillon*. A very fine hotel. Do you remember your room?"

"No. I'm sorry." I began nibbling on my fingernails.

"Why were you in Paris? To meet someone, perhaps?"

I thought of the man who claimed to be my husband. If he was my husband, why didn't he answer? Surely he knew why we had come to Paris.

"I don't remember." This was a useless exercise, and I could feel my head pounding all the way down in my feet. The gendarmes exchanged glances. Even the younger man knew enough English to understand these broken record responses. But they were not going to leave until they had something of substance to report.

"Tell me what happened," I asked wearily. "M-Maybe it will make me remember."

The gendarme nodded. "There are two men. Poles. Sailors of a merchant ship. They come out of the Bar d'Austerlitz. They see nothing clearly. There are shadows. We—Laurens and I—return to the Bar the next night at the same time and we understand why the Poles cannot see. Two men or three men come out of the shadows and hit you. They take your purse and take the money, then they throw the purse away. You fall down. They drag you to the river and push you in. The Poles shout and run but are too late. One jumps into the water. This is very brave. The Seine is dark and the current is strong, but you wear a yellow dress, and this he can see. It is very difficult, but he pulls you to the side, where the current is not so fast and there are stone steps, and his friend pulls you out. Another man, a Parisian who walks his dog, calls the police. He sees your purse. Laurens is near and calls the ambulance. The ambulance bring you to this hospital. You are very lucky, madame."

"The Polish sailors came here the next day to see you," said the doctor. "Their shore leave is finish and they could return no more. I said I believe you will survive and thanked them for you for saving your life. They were sorry for your broken hand and bruises, perhaps caused by themselves, perhaps by the thieves. A small price to pay for a life, eh?"

"I am sorry I cannot thank them myself. Did you get their names?"

"We did, madame. And the name of their ship, in case we would need them for a trial." The gendarme frowned and looked down, disappointed, thinking no doubt that a trial was highly unlikely now that the victim was proving so uncooperative.

"Perhaps I can write to them later, when I'm able . . ." I looked at my disabled left hand, aware somehow that I was left-handed. "The man with the dog, he was certain the purse was mine?"

"Not he, no, but the sailors, yes. They see the bad men throw it on the street."

The doctor assured the gendarmes that Madame's amnesia was temporary and promised to call them as soon as I regained my memory. They had to be satisfied with that. When the doctor escorted them into the hall, I was left alone to study the rivers on the ceiling.

I felt as if I had just been born. What did I know for certain? I must be English because my thoughts were English and my passport was English. My name was Eva Johnson. Someone was named Claire Smith; surely I would soon remember who. I had an angry husband. I was left-handed. My hair was brown and my eyes were green. Oddly enough, I could not picture myself.

There is something I believe few people understand about amnesia. It means the loss of more than one's memories. A person who loses all memory also loses his personality. I realized with dismay that I did not know myself, whether I was shy or outgoing, kind or cruel, friendly or aloof, lazy or hard-working. I was a stranger. I would have to observe myself, judge by my actions what sort of person I was, just as I would with anyone I happened to meet for the first time. When the doctor stepped back into the room, I asked him for a mirror.

"*Bon dieu, madame*, for why do you want a mirror?"

Was that not obvious?

"*Ah, non, madame*, it is not a good idea. You are a very beautiful woman but you do not look so beautiful at this moment. It would be better to wait a day or two."

My banged-up face must look worse than I supposed. Still, the sight of a few stitches and bruises was not going to send a modern English girl swooning. No matter if it did, I was already lying down.

"If you please, I'd like to see for myself."

He looked at a point on the wall behind my bed and shrugged in that expressive way Frenchmen have, and I realized with a jolt that the man who claimed to be my husband was still behind me. He hadn't left during the general exodus. He hadn't made a sound and I'd forgotten he was there. Ice slithered down my spine and my pulse raced.

"Bring her a mirror," he said curtly, and I started again at the sound of his voice. It was deep and rich and bore traces of an accent. Instinctively I knew that he had sided with me out of cruelty, not kindness. He wanted me to see my ruined face. He wanted to watch me suffer. I braced myself to show no reaction, no matter what I saw.

The image that stared back at me would have made a prizefighter flinch. I did indeed have green eyes—one, at least. The other was not completely covered by bandages as I had thought; rather it had swollen shut, a nasty purplish bulge streaked with yellow. My cheek was similarly bruised. The stitches above my eye were covered by the bandage that wrapped my forehead. Wisps of short brown hair stuck up every which way from beneath the gauze, like dirty broom straw. My lips were puffy and cracked. A slight gap separated my front teeth.

The doctor had called me beautiful, something I took for Gallic gallantry. Neither he nor I could tell what I looked like under normal circumstances. He took the mirror away and left the room.

I was alone with my husband at last. He wasted no time.

"You can stop pretending now, Eva. Your games don't work on me any longer. And for God's sake, quit that damned stutter! It's driving me mad."

The stutter only got worse. Every word had to fight its way out. "I . . . I don't know what y-you mean. I assure you, I'm not p-pretending anything. I cannot remember anything about the v-violence or about myself. I wish to heaven it wasn't true, but it is."

Hard eyes examined my face without blinking. "Your latest lover seems to have been a brutal sort. A poor choice, Eva. Though I can't say that I blame him. I have often wanted to do the same thing."

I winced. "Y-You heard the police. This was a robbery, not a lovers' quarrel. There were two or three of them and they took m-m-money."

"Perhaps a jealous wife hired thugs to do away with the competition and make it look like robbery. What does it matter, as long as it brings us together again, dear wife."

My head was swimming. Everything was wrong and I couldn't explain it to myself, let alone to this horrid man who claimed to be my husband. The only thing that kept me from bursting into tears was the certainty that he would enjoy my distress. I took a shaky breath.

"Look here, mightn't there be some m-mistake? Perhaps in a few days, when my bruises and swelling are gone and the b-bandages off, you'll see I'm not your wife, just someone who resembles her. Perhaps she was brought into the hospital at the same time as I was and the records were switched, and she is lying right now in another b-bed down the hall."

His look was pure disgust.

"What did you do with the paintings?"

"I d-don't know what you're talking about." Then I paused. A tiny fragment of memory teased its way forward in my head. Hadn't there been something about paintings in my hallucinations? What was it? My hesitation was a mistake, for he took it as confession.

"Where are they?"

"I p-p-promise you, I d-don't know."

"You know. I could see it in your eyes."

I shook my head helplessly and repeated myself. "I don't know."

"Technically, you could be telling the truth. You surely would have sold them by now. Just tell me where you sold them. Save me the trouble of beating it out of you."

"You don't f-frighten me," I said, hoping I didn't look as frightened as I felt. Here in the hospital, I told myself, surrounded as I was by nuns and doctors, I was quite safe from this beastly man. I told that to myself over and over.

The gendarmes returned the next day, but I did not see them. The man who claimed to be my husband intercepted them in the courtyard, told them that I had no new recollections to share, and that he preferred I not be disturbed. The doctor joined them, and the four fell to discussing the peculiarities of my case until the doctor left the group and came to my room.

"I said I would call them as soon as your memory was improved," he told me. "It will be soon, never fear, *ma petite*," and he smiled like an indulgent uncle bestowing a birthday gift. "Look how your stutter has almost gone." He was right. It was much better, but for some reason, only when I talked with him. He patted my hand and sat on the bed beside my legs. "The police are in the courtyard still, talking with your husband."

Usually he was rushing to the next patient—it was a busy hospital with many beds and the hallway bustled with activity—but this morning, it seemed there was time to talk.

"Doctor, you believe me, don't you? That I am not shamming? I really can't remember."

"Of course, madame. Why should you ask such a thing?"

"I . . . I don't believe that man is my husband. He doesn't believe me. He hates me."

He shook his head in disagreement. "No doubt it feels peculiar not to remember one's family, but I assure you, madame, it will not last. And you are very wrong. The fever has confused you between dreams and truth. Remember, you thought I had recited the alphabet at your bedside? More likely it was your husband who did so. He does not hate you, *au contraire,* he is most concerned about you. No one could have been more diligent. He has spent every night by your bed, to calm you from your feverish delirium. Only now that you are quiet at night does he go to the hotel to sleep."

The man who envied my assailants their fun was playing the attentive nursemaid? I thought not. Something else kept him tied to my bed at night. As I remembered snatches of my hallucinations, jumbled impressions of pursuit and denial, it came to me: he was waiting for me to reveal some vital information. The name of my supposed lover? The paintings? Something else?

"Are there any unidentified female patients in the hospital?"

"No, of course not, madame. Every one is known to us."

"Any English patients?"

He nodded. "*Oui,* another English woman is down the hall."

"Oh! Perhaps she is—"

"*Non, non, non, madame.* She is a lady of middle years who visits Paris with her sister. She recovers from the remove of appendix and will leave soon."

"Could you inquire at the other hospitals in Paris? Perhaps even . . . the morgue?"

He shook his head. "No, madame. The police would know if such a thing happened. They investigate thoroughly. That is why they talk with your husband now. The police, they recognize him when they came yesterday to your room. They recognize him from the newspapers. I am afraid I did not know, only when I heard the name did I know who he is. The police did not know he is married, and they ask why the passport of his wife carries a different name. He tells them your maiden name avoids notice."

This was far too complicated for me to absorb. I help up my hand to slow him down. "Wait a moment. His name is not Johnson?"

"*Ahhhh, non. Pauvre petite*, I am forgetting. You assume, of course, his name is Johnson, but no, your *nom de famille* is DeSequeyra.*" As he did when he told me the name on the passport, he watched to see whether this information would fire up any brain cells. But the name meant nothing to me, and I said so. I doubt I could have repeated such an odd-sounding word had I tried.

"But he is a man well known throughout France, throughout Europe." And he went on to sketch an outline of what he knew. It seemed that Monsieur DeSequeyra's father was Portuguese, which explained his strange name and dark countenance, but his mother was French. He was one of those for whom the phrase "life in the fast lane" was coined. When he was not behind the wheels of a sports car—he had won at Le Mans in 1923 and again in 1925—he was making the rounds of the casinos, spas, and resorts popular with the idle rich. It was not clear to me whether Monsieur himself came from a wealthy family or whether he was among the parasites who learn at an early age how to latch onto the moneyed set, but I could read between the lines well enough to understand that he was what we English call a playboy. No wonder he didn't want it known he was married. And he called *me* unfaithful! The hypocrite.

"Your husband tells the police that you come to Paris to shop." The doctor was no one's fool; he said this with a raise of the eyebrows that gave me to understand he saw through the statement. So did I. I shrugged. I couldn't help what he told the police. "They wish to see you again, so I said return Wednesday. Perhaps by Wednesday . . ." He pouted with his lips, which in French means, Who knows?

Two young novices came in to give me a wash in bed before changing the linens. I smelt the rubbing alcohol in the warm water they carried. The doctor mumbled something about reports to write and excused himself. I asked him to close the door as he left. I did not want Monsieur DeSequeyra walking in while I was lying naked on the sheets. Although on reflection, I did not think a closed door would give him pause.

When the sheets were pulled back, the novices sighed and made tsk-tsk noises with their tongues. No wonder! My legs showed evidence of having been dragged across jagged stone; one hip was mottled with purple and greenish-yellow blotches and tender to the least movement. My rib cage ached whenever I took a breath. I hoped nothing was cracked there but it wouldn't have surprised me. The novices were gentle with their sponges and towels, but a gust of wind would have pained me.

I had heard the doctor say how full the ward was, yet I was alone in this room. Had Monsieur DeSequeyra demanded privacy? So no one would hear my feverish ravings except him? I chewed on my nails, noticed I was doing it, and stopped. I had some notion that I would improve myself during my recovery by undoing this nervous habit. One hand was immobilized, and through force of will I would control the other. Something positive would come of this accident.

Could this not be a case of mistaken identity? The gendarmes had discovered his wife's handbag near the place I had been assaulted. Perhaps she had been similarly assaulted moments earlier, and her body thrown in the Seine as well. The authorities had contacted him based on the contents of the handbag. I bore a superficial resemblance to her and he had identified me through the bandages and in spite of my swollen face. When my body healed, he would recognize his error. And apologize. No, he was not the sort to admit he was wrong. Or perhaps, before any of that occurred, I would regain my memory and contact my friends and my family, who were no doubt frantic with worry by now. He would have to search elsewhere for his faithless wife.

Unless that faithless wife was lying here in my bed.

There is nothing like French bread warm from the oven to tease an appetite. That afternoon, Sister Marie Claire brought me the end of a fresh baguette with the usual beef broth—this time there were a few grains of rice swimming about the bowl—and allowed me to feed myself. With a hard pillow behind my back, I accomplished the feat, using my awkward right hand. The effort exhausted me. She was clearing the tray when Sister Genevieve came to check my temperature and feel my racing pulse.

As she was recording her observations, Monsieur DeSequeyra entered the room. With lowered eyes and a quiet *Bonjour, monsieur,* the women slid past him and out the door, like guilty girls caught playing a kissing game. He ignored them. I suspected he ignored most people. He was wearing his usual white shirt and black scowl. His eyebrows were drawn hard and sharp against his skin, as though an artist had brushed them in India ink. Without the frown, he might have been called handsome . . . by some women, perhaps, certainly not by me.

Seeing me propped up in bed only deepened the creases in his forehead. "You are better today?"

"I can see you are overjoyed at the prospect."

"I assure you, no one has prayed for your recovery more ardently than I. Dead you are no use to me." He looked at the chart at the foot of the bed and pursed his lips with satisfaction. "This is good. *Bon*, I cannot wait any longer. We must leave here."

"L-L-Leave? You m-must be joking! The doctor said it would be several weeks before I could—"

"You do not have several weeks. You do not have several days. We go tomorrow. And stop that damned stuttering!"

He was serious. Horrified, I tried to make him see reason. "But I can barely move. And . . . and the f-fever—"

"The fever is gone. You have not hallucinated for two days."

"The doctor said I must lie quietly until the concussion heals."

He brushed aside my protestations with a wave of his hand and the arrogance of one whose wishes are never denied. "You can lie quietly elsewhere. My mind is made up. There is no time to waste."

"B-B-But monsieur, the stitches in my head and hand are not ready to be removed—"

"Shut up!" He swore in some language I didn't recognize. "Do you think I care about your stitches? Do you think I care if you scar your pretty face? No doubt you'd rather take your chances with the police than with me. *Tant pis.* We must be gone before the police return. Or . . . " he paused dramatically and waited for me to meet his eyes. "Or, if you choose to tell me where the paintings are, you can stay here until the end of time with my blessings."

"Look, I am telling you the truth. I don't know anything about your paintings!"

"As you wish. Tomorrow I'll bring your clothes from the hotel."

Instinctively I looked toward the door, thinking of the doctor. He would surely have something to say about any premature discharge from the hospital. Monsieur DeSequeyra followed my eyes and my thoughts with an ease I found unsettling.

"You are my wife. It is for me to decide, not the hospital staff."

I discovered I was a persistent woman. "Monsieur, please, I only need—"

"For heaven's sake, quit calling me Monsieur! It sounds ridiculous."

"DeSequeyra is a bit of a stumble. And I don't know your given name. No one has dared use it at the hospital; they are all in such awe of your reputation. I only learned yesterday that your family name was not Johnson."

He glared at me for so long, debating whether or not to play along with my game of amnesia by telling me something he was sure I already knew, that I thought he was going to refuse. Grudgingly, he gave in. "Alexander."

Alexander. As in Alexander the Great. It fit him. He certainly gave himself royal airs. An image came to my head of a pack of cards. The royal cards.

"The King of Clubs," I murmured absently, chasing a thought just out of reach.

"What was that?"

His unexpected thrust startled me into a defensive posture. "Nothing," I parried.

"Tell me!"

"I-I-I was . . . It was just . . . nothing important. I thought of the K-King of Clubs. Legend says he is Alexander the G-G-Great. All the court cards are based on real figures." I closed my eyes to see better, trying to remember the others now. A silly bit of trivia but it seemed important at this moment. "The King of Hearts is Charlemagne; the King of Spades is King David from the Bible, and the King of Diamonds is . . . I can't recall. Oh yes, Julius Caesar!" I was absurdly pleased to have remembered all this. As trifling as it was, it represented a recaptured memory and encouraged me to hope for more. Buoyed by this small success, I met his eyes. He was staring at me intently, boring a deep hole into my head.

"Alexander," I repeated thoughtfully. Did anyone call him Al, I wondered? No, too working class. Alex, perhaps? Or Alec? He seemed to hear my unspoken question.

"My friends call me Alex," he admitted, clearly preoccupied

with another line of thought.

"Well, I have surmised that I am *not* one of your friends, however, I shall call you Alex for form's sake."

At that moment, the doctor passed by my room. Seeing Monsieur DeSequeyra, he paused. "The police have left," he told him.

In the blink of an eye, my husband spun around, wiping the tense expression from his face and presenting the doctor with a guileless smile. The change astonished me. Mr. Hyde to Dr. Jekyll.

"Yes," he said, "disappointed, to be sure, but I am afraid that even when my dear wife regains her memory, she will not be able to describe her assailants. It was, after all, almost dark. Sadly, ours is likely to remain an unsolved crime."

I seized my chance. "Doctor, Monsieur DeSequeyra wants to leave tomorrow."

"Ah? You have business to attend? *Je comprends, monsieur.* Never fear, we will take good care of *madame* until you can return."

The doctor did not see the glare my husband shot in my direction. He recovered smoothly. "My wife means to say that I wish to remove her from the hospital tomorrow. I was planning to discuss it with you this evening."

The doctor ran his fingers through his thin hair, making it stand up straight from his head like a mad scientist. "*Ah, mais non, mais non,* it is too soon. It would be dangerous to move her now. The stitches have not been removed. There is a chance of infection we must not risk. And the fever . . . Perhaps in a few weeks . . ." I held my breath.

"I only plan to go as far as our hotel, *L'Hotel de Crillon.* It is very comfortable there."

"*Oui,* I know this hotel. But—"

"And I shall engage a private nurse who will follow all the instructions from you and the sisters."

"But if the fever returns . . ."

"Of course, if the fever returns, or if any problems develop, I shall call you and bring her directly back to the hospital."

It was useless to hope. I knew how it would go. He wanted the doctor to agree with his decision, but he was going to move me whatever the man said. That was as clear to the doctor as it was to me. A husband's authority over his wife was sacrosanct; no one would presume to stand between us. The doctor was saving face, following an unwritten script where he would put up all the objections he could think of, then pretend to be persuaded.

"I do not think it a good idea. The danger of infection cannot be ignored."

"The Crillon is close, just across the Pont de la Concorde. We will both be more comfortable there. A dose of laudanum will ease the ride."

"Well, if there is to be a nurse . . ."

"Perhaps you can recommend one?"

I could see the doctor mentally paging through his list of private nurses and I knew the game was over. They left together, two men making decisions for a grown woman as if she were a child. He was taking me away from the safety of the hospital ward, this man who cared nothing about my recovery.

I had finished crying by the time the doctor returned. I would not give up without one more try, and now I had him alone. I told him I was afraid to leave the hospital, that I was too weak for the hotel, but he countered each of my objections as my husband had countered his. At last I reached one he had not heard.

"Monsieur DeSequeyra thinks I am a fake. He thinks the amnesia is not real."

"*Mais non, mais non, madame.* Why would you pretend such a thing? You are mistaken. You are confused in the head. He is very concerned about the amnesia. He asked for more information about this: how long it usually lasts, how best to help the patient remember. I give him a recent article from a medical journal and some books on the work of Doctor Pierre Janet and Dr. Sigmund Freud, and he reads them. Perhaps he was sceptical at first—who is not?—but now I am sure he understands. He will learn and soon he will know as much as a doctor."

I wanted to know as much as a doctor too, but when I asked him what the books said about amnesia, he hedged. I wasn't to worry about such matters. It was over my head. I insisted and in the end, he gave me a brief summary.

Severe head injuries occasionally caused temporary amnesia, he said, usually lasting no more than a few hours or days. There were many instances of such injuries during the Great War and most of the current information had come from studies of wounded soldiers. The injured person usually regained his memory in pieces, randomly, over a period of days or weeks. Pressuring the patient to try harder to remember was counter-productive; it only brought on headaches and discouragement. Most doctors today thought it better to expose the patient gently to different people, objects, and experiences, one of which would trigger an association with a memory and stimulate the brain.

"That is how you thought of the name Claire, was it not? From the apron of *Soeur Marie Claire?*"

It was. And that was how he expected I would come to remember the rest. My husband, my home, my family, my past. "There is so little stimulation here," he said, his eyes taking in the bleak, bare room as if for the first time. "The hotel will be better." He could read the fear on my face, the worry that I would never recover my mind and have to live the rest of my life as if I had been born in May of 1928. He patted my hand again. "I assure you, madame, amnesia patients always recover."

"Always?"

He looked out the window for a few moments and did not turn toward me as he answered softly, "Almost always."

Anxiety throbbed through every part of my body, making the pains in my chest and arm increase alarmingly as the afternoon hours crept by. My head ached so badly I could hardly think what to do. Tomorrow he was coming to take me away. To some hotel. A nice hotel, the doctor had said, but what did that matter? It would be a hotel where everyone was in my husband's pay. Alone and friendless, I would be entirely in his power. No one would know what he did to me, or what he didn't do. Any help I got would come only from myself.

Calm down, I told myself sternly. Your imagination is running away with you. He won't let you die. He'd never learn the whereabouts of his paintings if he did. Hadn't he said just that a day or two earlier? "You're no good to me dead."

A sister interrupted my conversation with myself to deliver a dose of laudanum. I hated to accept it—the medicine left me feeling as if I were swimming through thick fog—but I hated the pain more. She spooned some broth into my mouth before leaving me to drift off.

The hospital was quiet. Through the open door I could see sisters pass by on their way to other rooms, I could hear their soft French murmurings and catch glimpses of patients in hospital gowns moving back and forth on tottering legs or being pushed in Bath chairs. All at once I realized I could understand some of the words. As I watched, two stout English women slowly made their way past my door, deep in conversation. The appendix patient and her sister. The doctor was right, in no way could this patient have been mistaken for me.

I fancied calling out to them, saying that I was an Englishwoman too, but the medicine had already robbed me of any initiative. I listened as one said to the other, ". . . and it was the same man . . . that racing car driver with the . . ."

They were talking about my husband, Alexander DeSequeyra. Blinking back the wooziness, I strained for every word.

"I saw him again when I came in this afternoon. You remember, don't you, Maud? That awful murder?"

Murder? I stopped breathing to hear better. They were moving past my door now, away from me and their voices faded slightly. Maud said something I couldn't hear.

Her sister replied, "Yes, you do. It was some years ago . . . made all the papers, even in London . . . some sort of revenge murder for his brother's death. Got off scot-free, he did, and walking around today like he never killed a man in his life. Jury wouldn't convict . . . . different laws for the rich and famous, you know."

Maud said something else. They had turned and were headed in my direction again. I fought against the muzzy effects of the medicine, struggling to hear the louder sister's reply.

"Is that so? Well, if not juries, it must've been judges. Who knows how Frenchmen do these things? He'd've had a proper trial in England, I can promise you that. They'd've hanged him in England."

The laudanum won in the end, and I heard no more.

A tense Alexander DeSequeyra arrived at midday sporting a leather driving jacket *à la Lindbergh* and a jaunty cap, and carrying a calfskin valise. I had expected to wear my own clothes when I left, but even the skilled fingers of the nuns could not mend the rents in my yellow dress, or remove the stains from the river. Sister Genevieve brought the damaged dress to me with my handbag and an apologetic shake of the head just as Alexander DeSequeyra strode into the room. He reached for them both, and she complied.

The man was a water faucet, turning on a strong flow of charm for the nuns who obeyed him as quickly as they did the doctors and the priests, and shutting it off abruptly for me. He was eager to collect me and go. He said something I couldn't hear to Sister Genevieve, who glided away, returning moments later with a dose of laudanum. Cynical as I had become about DeSequeyra's motives, I suspected it was meant less to ease my pain during the transfer than to keep me quiet and biddable.

My heart began pounding with the anxiety of a youth leaving home for the first time. The austere little hospital room was the only home I could remember, the doctor and the nuns my only family. I didn't want to go. It all felt so wrong. I couldn't be his wife. I couldn't be Eva Johnson.

The man who claimed to be my husband examined my yellow dress with ill-concealed disdain, holding it between his fingers as if it had come from the back of a leper, then dropped it in the rubbish bin. A cry of protest escaped my lips. "No!"

He ignored me.

"G-Give it to me!"

"Whatever can you want with it? Even in its prime, it was a shop girl's rag. You must have been in disguise to wear such a thing." Grudgingly he retrieved it from the bin and tossed it on the bed.

"I don't care. It saved my life. Throwing it out seems ungrateful." It was my only connection to the accident, something that just might hold a clue to what happened on that awful night. And, although I didn't recognize it, this poor garment was the only thing in the world I was certain was mine.

The leather valise lay at the foot of the bed. "This is yours," he snapped, opening open the brass latch with a sharp click and pulled out a handful of clothing. "And these."

Credit where credit is due—the bastard had chosen well. The costume he brought from the hotel was soft and easy to slip on and he had not forgotten the appropriate undergarments, or a pair of stockings—silk, not rayon! My cold toes would have preferred thick socks but I would have to wait until I was back at the hotel to see whether I had any. He had not included shoes, gloves, or a hat, but I would not be walking anywhere, and my bandaged head and messy hair precluded a hat. The labels boasted the name of one of Paris' leading couturiers, Coco Chanel, and there was a script monogram: EJDeS. But none of it—not a single item—looked familiar.

"I don't recognize any of this. I can't be your wife."

"Come now, Eva, don't start—"

None of this was right. I couldn't be the woman who wore these clothes, I couldn't have a husband, I couldn't go away with this stranger. Something inside me snapped. "D-Don't call me that. I'm not Eva. I am C-Claire S-Smith from . . . from . . ." The name was just out of reach.

He gave me a measured stare. "You are out of your head. There is no doubt—none whatever—that you are Eva Johnson DeSequeyra. My legal wife." He reached into his shirt pocket. "This is your ring, the one I gave you on our wedding day that was taken from your finger by the doctor. Look at the inscription." I hesitated. "Read it!"

It was a thin gold band enamelled with scrolls and hearts in the Art Nouveau style. *Eva ~ Alexander* it said inside.

"The doctor thinks the men broke your finger trying to get it off. They probably succeeded in removing the four-carat diamond ring you wore in front of this—*if* you hadn't pawned it long ago—but could not get this off before the Polish sailors interrupted. Do you want to see your purse?" I shook my head no, preferring to cling to my illusions rather than admit the obvious, but he dumped the contents onto my lap anyway. "Here is the key to your room at the Hotel de Crillon. It is registered to Eva Johnson. Several clerks and the concierge identified you from your passport photograph. More to the point, *I* recognize you, and your bruises do not disguise your looks as much as you think."

Tears blurred my vision. I picked up a tortoiseshell comb with a silver back, a platinum cigarette case floridly engraved EJDeS, a lipstick and some rouge, a handsome gold fountain pen, a round mirror in a filigree case, a few loose francs, some French postage stamps, a small English-French phrase book, a couple of keys, and a fine lawn handkerchief beautifully embroidered with fleurs-de-lis around the edges and "deS" in one corner. I had to admit it, the comb looked familiar, and I did favour that colour lipstick.

I picked up the wedding ring again. *Eva ~ Alexander.* How utterly unromantic! Where was the "with love" or "forever yours," or even "To Eva from Alexander?" There wasn't even an "and" to link our names, just a scroll that seemed to push them apart. Had there ever been any romance in this bitter marriage? Then I saw the date I had missed earlier. "19 June 1923." I had been married for five years.

The idea staggered me. Five years was a long time. For some reason, I had assumed it was much less than that. After five years of marriage, a man would recognize his wife, even through the gauze and bruises.

It was as the doctor had said. Association. Thinking of dates and years made me aware that I knew my age and my birth date. "I remembered something!" My husband looked at me with interest. "10th May, 1904. The date of my birth."

Without comment he reached into an inside coat pocket, pulled out my passport, and tossed in into my lap. Under Date of Birth, it contradicted me. In neat blue ink, the passport officer had penned, 10 May, 1900. I looked at the tiny photograph for the first time. The light had been too strong and the features on the face had washed out. One might argue that it could have been any young woman of average appearance, but it was clearly my picture. I was Eva Johnson. Eva Johnson DeSequeyra. Who, then, was Claire Smith?

"Four years off," he said. "You're twenty-eight. The same age as the century, as you liked to point out. Dropping years is a woman's prerogative, I suppose, but you've gone a bit hard to pass for twenty-four."

Only pride prevented me from abandoning myself up to a great sobbing fit. The evidence was overwhelming, the circumstances incontrovertible. "Claire Smith . . . it seems so familiar."

"Probably the alias you've been using. Not very imaginative, choosing the commonest surname in the English language. Or perhaps that's why you chose it."

Yes, that's why I chose it. Ordinary, unremarkable Smith. It was an alias. I remembered now. I was Claire Smith. At least, I had been for a while.

"Then you believe me? You think the amnesia is real?"

"Let's say I'm willing to take a gamble on the possibility. You're such an accomplished liar, I can't credit anything that comes out of your mouth, but the doctor assures me your amnesia is genuine. The lump on your head is certainly genuine and so are your injuries. But if I ever find you are making a fool of me—again—I promise you, I shall finish the murder your lover started."

Murder. The way he said it, softly and without any trace of emotion, frightened me more than the actual words. A chill washed through me and I shivered. But the word loosened a memory, and only at that moment did I recall the Englishwoman from the previous afternoon. What had she said about murder? I groped toward the memory, just out of reach. My husband, revenge, murder. My husband was a murderer? Yes, that was it. A proven murderer whose wealth and fame had kept him from the guillotine.

Shocked, I gasped, and my hand instinctively flew to my throat.

"What is it?" he demanded, examining me sharply. I dared not meet his eye.

"N-Nothing."

"You remembered something."

I shook my head. "No."

"Out with it!"

"I . . . You . . ." I swallowed hard. "You murdered a man . . ."

"Ah, so you remembered that little incident, did you?"

"I overheard . . ."

"Then you also overheard that I got off. If you remember nothing else, dear wife, remember that. They say murder becomes easier each time."

I struck back with a display of bravado I didn't feel. "What a pity it is for you that I can't remember anything! I expect vengeance tastes a bit bland when the victim doesn't remember you, let alone her transgressions. You may as well choose some random pedestrian to terrorize for all the satisfaction you'll get here."

"Revenge? You think that's what I'm after? I admit the prospect is sweet, but all I came for is justice. I want information and I want my paintings, and I'll do whatever it takes to get them. I had hoped the fever would loosen your tongue, that I could find out what I wanted to know and then leave you here for the police to deal with. As it turns out, I'll have to wait for the amnesia to wear off, or, if you're shamming, God help you, I'll wring the truth out of you and take great pleasure doing it."

I was saved from further threats by the appearance of a novice who had come to help me change clothes. I could have continued the conversation—she spoke no English—but decided to wait until we were alone before asking what information he was seeking and what he could tell me about these missing paintings. How many were there, and what exactly did they look like? Were they the ones in my feverish dreams? If remembering where they were was my only chance of extricating myself from this nightmare, then remember them I would.

The novice lifted up a two-piece dress with crisp pleats in both the knee-length skirt and hip-length blouse and held them up for inspection. I looked pointedly in the direction of Alexander DeSequeyra who was showing no signs of leaving. "Monsieur, if you please, some privacy?"

"How amusing. I wasn't aware that modesty was a side effect of amnesia."

"I prefer to dress alone."

"Do you think the sight of your body after all this time will inflame my passions beyond my control?" he sneered. "Never fear, my dear."

My face burned as if I'd been slapped. The little novice stood patiently beside me, somewhat perplexed at the exchange, until I turned to her with a feeble smile and indicated she should remove my hospital gown. I believe she was more embarrassed at my nudity than I.

The novice eased my bandaged arm into a soft jade green jacket with a high collar and wide cuffs to protect against the chill of the air. The ensemble looked to be rather small in size, but everything fit perfectly.

Sister Marie Claire wheeled a Bath chair into my room but my husband waved her off. Lifting me in his arms like a sack of potatoes, he carried me out of the room, down a long passageway past a dozen other rooms identical to mine but with all beds full, down a flight of worn sandstone stairs and into the courtyard where his automobile and the doctor waited. I had nowhere to put my arms but around his neck. It was the first time I had touched him, and I hated it.

"*Au revoir, madame*," the doctor said with an anxious expression that did nothing to calm my fears. Clearly he expected to see me again within a matter of hours. But the face he turned to Alexander DeSequeyra showed no disapproval, and when he thanked Alex for his generosity, I understood that a substantial donation to the hospital had assuaged any concerns about my welfare. Ah, money. It had chased away his murder charge. It worked again today.

I wanted to plead, "Don't let him take me! He's a murderer, and he's threatening me!" but I knew all too well how futile that would be. "No, no, madame," the doctor would only say. "You are confused in the head."

Without further ado, my husband deposited me in the back seat of an enormous Peugeot touring car and climbed behind the wheel.

Most rich men employ drivers. The roads are hazardous, especially outside the cities where there is little pavement, and the changing of tyres is hard work for soft hands. Far more pleasant to relax in a pub or café while the driver borrows oxen to pull the vehicle from the mud or raises the bonnet to repair the engine. There would have been no shortage of young men queuing up for the chance to drive Peugeot's newest luxury car, but Alexander DeSequeyra drove himself, at Le Mans and at home. Perversely I hoped for an embarrassing breakdown in the middle of the Champs-Elysées.

Sitting upright made me dizzy; the laudanum made me sleepy. My arm hurt. The Peugeot's back seat was as large as a bed but there was no point in lying down for such a short ride. I ran my fingers over the cream-colored upholstery, soft as glove leather, feeling the car's powerful engine humming along on one note like Sister Genevieve was wont to do. People along the sidewalks stopped to stare. Vehicles such as this exist for no reason other than to call attention to its owner.

The narrow streets and wide boulevards of the Latin Quarter were crowded with cars, carts, motorbikes, lorries, and bicycles, but Alex drove carelessly, his right arm draped across the back of his seat, like royalty expecting the courtiers to make way. Make way for the King of Clubs. Mostly they did.

Within minutes we had crossed the short bridge to the Ile de la Cité and passed the Palais de Justice and the massive Conciergerie on the left. Thoughts of Marie Antoinette flickered through my head, she and the countless others who were held prisoner there before being taken in tumbrels to meet Madame la Guillotine. I thought of Dickens' *Tale of Two Cities* and Baroness Orczy's *Scarlet Pimpernel* and all the marvellously heroic Englishmen and villainous Frenchmen as we drove over the Pont au Change onto the Right Bank and down the arrow-straight Boulevard Sebastopol. It seems I had spent enough time in Paris to know its main features.

The city exploded with colour and light. In the distance on my left, the graceful Sacré Cœur perched atop the hill of Montmartre, its white dome and bell tower gleaming like mother-of-pearl in the afternoon sun. All Paris bustled past my window in its inimitable way, with flower vendors on the corners, bicyclists with baguettes strapped to their baskets, old men in berets playing boules in the park, young lovers holding hands beneath a café table, and a gaggle of schoolgirls in blue pinafores skipping home for the midday meal. It all seemed quite familiar. I could only wonder why.

Why had I married this vulgar Frenchman? Had I fallen in love with France and settled for a Frenchman?

I had done a lot of thinking in the clear morning light. The rudiments of a plan had grown in my head. As loudly as my instincts protested, logic beat them back. I, Eva Johnson, was unhappily—and secretly—married to an arrogant playboy whose only attraction I could see was his wealth. We had both taken lovers, or at least we were sure the other had. I had taken some paintings of his—idly I wondered whether he was the artist or the owner—and he wanted them back. Not unreasonably, perhaps. He was a violent man, having committed one murder already. Heaven knows what had attracted me to him five years ago. I was a sadly shallow person who had married for nothing more than a handsome face and money.

I had no other choice but to jolly him along as best I could while I recovered my memory at the hotel. As soon as I remembered where his paintings were, I would swap the information for his signature on divorce papers. If divorce was not possible in Catholic France, it was growing more common in England where it no longer blighted one's social life beyond all redemption. I could then return to my family in England.

I gasped. My family! Of course my husband would know my family. Relatives would have attended our wedding. Why had he not mentioned them earlier? Surely their names would hasten the return of my memory. Surely, if he would let me go home to England, someone there would let me stay while I recovered my health.

But I couldn't ask. I tried, but my body refused to obey my commands. The medicine and the gentle vibrations of the automobile combined to blur all the colours and overpower my consciousness, and I nodded off.

Some time later, the tyres hit a rough patch in the road, jostling me painfully out of my stupor. I straightened up to see if we had arrived. We were moving faster now that the road was nearly empty of vehicles. In a field on the right an overloaded hay wagon was being hitched to a pair of mules. Closer, at the edge of the road, goats grazed behind a fence that was collapsing into brambles. Where was the city?

"Where are we?" I demanded sharply, jolting forward toward the front seat. "Where is the hotel?"

He said nothing.

How could we have come so far so fast? How long had I been asleep? Where was this man taking me? Fear burned from my throat down to my stomach until I thought I'd be sick.

Finally, in a lazy drawl he answered without turning around. "We are not going to the hotel."

"Wh-Where are you taking me?"

He did not reply.

Mary Miley

2 THE CHAMBER

The ticking sound grew loud beside me as I struggled up from drugged oblivion only to find myself trapped inside my own empty head. Then I heard quiet voices. First a man's, deep and familiar, then another softer one, the two talking so close to where I lay that if I could have stretched out my arm, I might have touched one of them. I tried to open my eyes to see where I was; I tried to speak, but my body seemed to have turned to wood. I wondered, without much concern, whether I was dying. Those thoughts were diverted by the appearance of fragments of the recent past that began floating home for inspection. A long ride in an automobile . . . an accident. I had been in an automobile accident. No, the accident had come earlier. I had been injured somehow. A hospital . . . nuns . . . a doctor . . . police. A crime had been committed. Murder. I was a murderer. No, I was a victim. Someone else was a murderer. My husband. Everyone said he was my husband. It was he who had taken me away from the hospital where I was safe and brought me to this place, where I was not. His was the familiar voice.

Although I strained my ears, the sounds were hollow and quivering and I could hear only snatches of the conversation. The fact that they were speaking in French added to the difficulty.

"You can't keep her prisoner in the chateau," said the soft voice with a strange accent.

The familiar voice was sharper and easier to understand. My husband replied, "Of course not. But if no one tells her . . . (and there was something I missed) . . . she won't get that far."

After an ominous silence, the soft voice gave a sigh and took a few steps as she replied, making it harder to catch her words. "I don' t like it . . . drowning is too cruel . . ."

"She'll never know."

The soft voice said something unintelligible.

"Unless you can think of some other . . . In any case, Madame must get well before I can learn what I need to know, so spare no expense on medicine or supplies."

The other said something about food and "cuisine." The kitchen.

"Prepare whatever you think best. Also, Madame does not speak French. If you need me to translate, I'll be in the library . . ." Two sets of footsteps and the close of a door, and all was silence.

Well, he was wrong about one thing, wasn't he? I derived some small satisfaction knowing that Madame did, indeed, speak French, not fluently perhaps, and not the local dialect, but she could understand much of what was said. As to the rest, any doubts I may have had about the truth of the story told by that middle-aged Englishwoman to her sister at the hospital were put to rest.

The ticking sound intruded on my thoughts. Time passing. More time passed, and I finally opened my eyes. A pocket watch lay on the bedside table. It was a while before I could make my good right hand reach across for it. Knowing the time seemed very important in view of the fact that I knew nothing else about my surroundings. Half five, it said. Not very revealing when one doesn't know the day, month, or year. It could just as easily have been early morning as afternoon, judging by the light seeping through the edges of the draperies. My reward for all this thinking was a pounding headache.

The watch provided the single touch of modernity to a bedchamber richly furnished in the old-fashioned manner. I was lying on a massive bit of Louis XVI splendour topped by a canopy hung with generous folds of fringed toile that had been caught up to each post with tasselled tiebacks. The bed sheets were fine linen. A mammoth pair of mahogany armoires flanked the stone fireplace where a chimney stretched up sixteen feet or more toward gaily-painted ceiling beams. I might be imprisoned here, but it clearly wasn't a prison.

It was warm in bed. I hated to get up, but I had an urgent need to find a toilet. I pulled myself to the edge of the mattress where I waited until the room stopped spinning, then eased my bare feet down to the rug. I crossed the room with tottering steps and opened the doors to two storage closets before I found one with a water closet behind it. I was shivering now and weak with wobbly legs. The nuns at the hospital had not allowed me to move about on my own, for good reason, it seemed.

As I made my way back to my bed, the dizziness escalated with a vengeance. My vision went black at the edges and the carpet rose up and struck me in the face. My absurd last thought was: Aubusson, Directoire period, circa 1790.

Like the replay of a familiar film, I woke up in bed with an angry husband on my left and a stern nurse on my right. Thankfully, this time I was lucid. The laudanum must have worn off. I swore I would swallow no more of it, not if I had any say in the matter. Pain would be preferable to confusion.

"It seems I was mistaken about your need for a nurse," he snapped, angry at *me* because *he* had been wrong. "I have engaged Madame Renaud from the village. She does not speak English, but she will look after you well enough and help you regain your strength. And your memory."

An examination of Madame Renaud revealed a sturdy woman in her forties, with grey hair pulled so tight in a knot on top of her head that it looked like it hurt. She seemed capable of lifting two of me with strength left over for a load of firewood. It was not reassuring.

"Why have you not drunk your medicine?" he demanded.

"Wh--what?" I followed his gaze to a short glass beside my bed that seemed to have been conjured out of the shadows. "Oh . . . I hadn't noticed . . . What is it?"

"Medicine. Drink."

"What sort of medicine?"

"We talked about this yesterday," he said impatiently.

Bewildered and discouraged, I had to confess that I didn't remember much of yesterday. Instead of getting better, I was getting worse, unable now to recall even recent events.

"It is a restorative," he said, handing me the glass. "The doctor said you were to drink some every day. He told you this at the hospital before we left. You cannot remember that?"

I took a sip. It didn't taste like laudanum. "It tastes like cider."

"To mask the bitterness. Drink."

When I looked up from the empty glass, he had gone.

Without a word, Madame Renaud went to work carrying coal to the fireplace grate, then she disappeared into the adjacent lavatory. I heard the groaning protest of pipes and realized she was running me a bath. I nearly cried with happiness.

My jailor's given name was Cécile. Her thick arms and rough hands were gentle as she helped me out of my rumpled clothes and up the three steps to the porcelain tub, propping my left arm out of the water with a folded towel. She had hung a gauze bag stuffed with herbs in the bath, permeating the room with fragrant bee balm. I sighed deeply and closed my eyes.

My knowledge of the French language puzzled me. At first I assumed I had regained it all at once today, the way my hearing returned shortly after I woke up in hospital. But on further reflection I realized that today was the first time I had actually heard spoken French. No one at the hospital had used it in my presence, all presuming from what my husband told them that I understood none of it. The doctor and Alex spoke in English to me. So did the gendarmes. The nuns occasionally whispered to one another in French, but so softly it could have been Arabic for all I knew. I decided I had not remembered my French—it had never left me in the first place.

It seemed best for the time being if no one knew about this. If they all thought I could not speak French, they would assume I was more isolated than I was, and they would be less vigilant about guarding me. Perhaps I could overhear things no one would otherwise tell me, like where I was being held. But it is hard pretending not to understand when you do.

Evidently Cécile shared the doctor's opinion about battered women and mirrors for she made sure I had no chance to catch a glimpse of my reflection in the looking glass that hung over the marble basin. Pulling up a wooden stool, she sat beside the tub to wash my sticky hair, taking care not to disturb the stitches in my skull and forehead. In no time I was clean and dry and perched on a padded bench with my back to the glowing coals. She combed my hair until it was fluffy. Since Cécile couldn't talk to me, she sang, with a mellow, mannish voice that carried the full weight of emotion. I recognized "*Avec mes sabots*" and several other old French folk tunes, and imagined these were the songs she sang to her children when they were little. It made me long to be a child again, safe and protected.

As I soaked up heat from the fireplace, Cécile busied herself emptying my valises and hanging the dresses in one of the wardrobes or folding the silk undergarments into drawers. From the labels, it appeared I had a preference for the austerity of Coco Chanel, for much of my daywear came from her *atelier* on the Rue Cambon, but there were also filmy evening dresses bearing tags from Worth and Molyneux, and several dresses, coats, and wraps designed by Paul Poiret. Evidently green was my favourite colour, no doubt because it accentuated my eyes. She found a profusion of vials and bottles, which she showed me, asking in pantomime where they should be stored. Not sure if they were medicine or cosmetics, I indicated the dressing table near the window. Like most of the furniture, it was Louis XVI, but with its graceful legs and stunning rosewood marquetry, this was easily the finest piece in the room. All at once I wondered how I knew such things. Had I grown up in a stately mansion filled with valuable antiquities like these? Was I a nobleman's daughter? I almost smiled at the preposterous idea.

When Cécile came to a jewellery case, I motioned for her to open it but it proved to be locked and neither of us knew where to find the key. Then I remembered my handbag. The first key we tried fit the lock. Like children with a Christmas present, we opened the box and marvelled at the profusion of necklaces, brooches, and bracelets jumbled carelessly together like so much costume jewellery. Given the quality of my clothes, I didn't think it likely that they were imitation.

The shadows were growing longer. I pointed to the only lamp, an electrified urn on the far side of my bed whose cord ran down the stone wall, around the edge of the room, and out the door. Cécile turned on the light and patted her stomach, saying, "*Vous avez faim?*"

The thought of food made me realize how empty my stomach

was. It ached, probably from the medicine and lack of food, and without thinking, I replied, "*Oui, je meurs de faim.*"

She pounced. "Ahhhhhh, madame knows a little French?"

Too late to deny, I prevaricated. "Only a few words."

Accepting that at face value, she left for the kitchen.

Furious at my carelessness at having thrown away my only advantage, I consoled myself that it was better this way; perhaps I could get some information from her. If only she did not tell Alex! I had been uneasy in his presence at the hospital where I had been surrounded by kindness, but here where his power was absolute, I was more afraid than I wanted to admit. The man was unquestionably violent, and he hated me and would stop at nothing to get the information he wanted. Information I didn't have.

In a few moments Cécile returned with a bowl of pureed vegetable soup and a glass of red wine. For the blood, she said. As I ate, she talked.

I started off by asking, in French, "Are you a nurse?"

Her speech was slow and accompanied by pantomime as she tested my comprehension and found it wanting. Her accent and the local dialect made understanding difficult, or perhaps my hearing wasn't as good as it should have been, but it seems for all that, that I was good at listening. She poured out her life story in words and gestures, and I managed to make sense of most of what she said.

When her husband was killed at Verdun, God rest his soul, grief sent her walking east toward the front until she came upon a unit that needed her help. She had been born knowing herbs, but what she knew about healing had been learned on the battlefield where necessity promoted her from orderly to nurse to surgeon. She had not attended nursing school but plainly considered herself the equal of any trained physician. She had seen some amnesia, brought on mostly by head injuries but sometimes by the shock of battlefield carnage.

After the war, she returned home to live with her widowed sister and nephews. They farmed; she kept an herb garden. They managed well enough, living heads high and wallets tight. Since the nearest doctor was in Troyes, she functioned as the town's nurse, doctor, pharmacist, herbalist, and midwife.

"And what town is this?" I interrupted, as if the name were a minor casualty of my amnesia.

It was Ranton-sur-Marne, a *petite village,* not a town, located at the foot of an ancient fortification that the schoolmaster said dated back to Roman times. She was optimistic about my prospects, now that she had seen me. Thumping her chest for emphasis, she boasted that she had better success than any doctor. She had not abandoned the old ways for the new as they had, but added them together and used the best of both. My bathwater herbs included marigold to aid healing and reduce scars, so I was not to worry about disfigurement. A daily dose of valerian, much used during the war for shell shock, would calm me.

By the time I had finished my soup, I did indeed feel relaxed. Cécile was a natural healer. She seemed a decent enough sort, a village woman hired to nurse an invalid. After all, it was she who had voiced her objection when Alex proposed to stage a drowning accident. If I played my cards well and engaged her affection, she might become my ally instead of his.

Cécile rose to return the tray to the kitchen. "I say goodnight now, madame, and come tomorrow morning. You wish me to turn out the light?"

"Yes, please. But first, will you look into the chambers near by and see if there is a clock you could bring in here?" The pocket watch had disappeared and knowing the time was somehow calming.

I closed my eyes. It was probably only about 8 or 9 o'clock, but I was exhausted. Back at the hospital, the sisters would be gliding in and out of the rooms on silent cat feet, checking the beds, taking temperatures, and dispensing those last doses of medicine before turning out the lights. The novices would be closing the shutters and bringing fresh water to each bedside. My room was probably already occupied by three people who were watching the Danube River flow along the ceiling. What had been the doctor's reaction when he learned I was not at the hotel? The nurse he sent would have returned to him, perplexed, thinking perhaps she had made a mistake. "Monsieur DeSequeyra checked out of the hotel that very morning," she would tell him and he would frown, realizing he had been misled. He would think of notifying the police but would reconsider. After all, what could he say? A husband had decided to take his wife to a different hotel? This was no crime. When the gendarmes came again, he would tell them the English lady had left without remembering anything more. If they chose to trace her, it was their affair. A husband had his rights. It was not for others to interfere.

Cécile returned with a pewter mantel clock of the Art Nouveau persuasion, gracefully asymmetric, and since there was no mantel above my fireplace, she set it on the bureau where it was visible from the bed. She helped me in the lavatory, then moved to the far side of the bed to pull the light cord.

The voice from the doorway startled us both. I hadn't thought he would return this evening.

"I'll see to it, Cécile," said Alex. "You can leave now. Thank you for coming."

I breathed a sigh of relief that she had not thought to mention my newly acquired French but my satisfaction was short-lived. As soon as she had departed, Alex walked toward the wardrobe and began unbuckling his belt.

"What the d-devil are you doing?" I blurted.

He tossed a disgusted look over his shoulder, pulled off the belt, and stepped out of his trousers. Slapping the leather against his palm, he surveyed what I suddenly realized was *his* room. How had I missed that? My toiletries may have been piled on the dressing table, my clothes may have occupied one of the twin wardrobes, but it was clearly his room. His eyes fell on the clock and I could feel him bristle at my effrontery in having had it moved from one room to another.

"You aren't s-sleeping in here!"

"*Au contraire, madame.* I am sleeping where I always sleep. In my room, in my bed."

"Very well, then, I'll m-move to another room."

He stared at me, letting the belt slap, slap idly against his palm. "I see Cécile earned her pay this evening. Cleaned up and combed, you look almost presentable. Too bad you dyed your hair; it looked better red." He hung up the belt and unbuttoned his shirt.

"S-See here, n-neither of us will get any sleep this way—"

"If you imagine that I have any interest in your body, allow me to reassure you. You have all the appeal of a diseased whore. I am sleeping beside you and will continue to do so in the event that you say something of interest in your sleep. You talked a good deal at the hospital and I have hopes you will continue. The war taught me to be a light sleeper. I will hear every sound you make."

"I'm not feverish any longer. You said so yourself. I shan't be talking in my sleep."

It was the Gallic shrug again, the combination of lips and shoulders that says, Who cares? with the eloquence of a whole page of Proust. Then, because he knew it made me uncomfortable, he stripped naked and walked past me into the bathroom.

Fighting back the panic that threatened to overwhelm me, I considered my options. I was too weak to move to another room by myself and powerless to do so in any case without permission. I'd only aggravate him further by arguing, perhaps even provoke him to violence. A man who had killed before wasn't going to flinch at striking his wife, invalid or not. Telling myself not to worry, he wasn't going to murder me in my sleep before I'd divulged the whereabouts of his paintings, I moved to the farthest edge of the bed, closed my eyes, and listened to his progress as he walked about the chamber, putting away his shoes, closing the wardrobe doors, filling the grate, pulling the draperies. I felt the bed sag with his weight as he sat to wind his watch and turn off the lamp. I did not breathe as he played with the pillow and threw back one of the blankets.

"Good night, Eva dear."

I said nothing. I was supposed to be sound asleep. I heard a soft, cynical laugh.

Alex rose early. Careless of his noise, he showered, shaved, dressed, and left the bedroom. Before I had time to stir from beneath the covers, I heard the door open again. I buried my face in the pillow and kept my eyes shut tight as he moved about in the darkened room, opening the armoires in the back, then some drawers nearer the window, searching for whatever he had forgotten. It wasn't in the bureau, so he moved on to the dressing table where I could hear him for several minutes going through the jewellery box that Cécile had left sitting out. Finally I risked opening one eye.

I opened the other, and pulled up. "What are you doing?"

A podgy girl of about fourteen or fifteen turned sharply, bouncing her long braid over the front of her shoulder. "I'm looking for what's mine!" she spat, and turned a defiant back on me.

"Very well then, why don't you pull open the draperies so you can see better? No need to sneak about like a thief." With a snort, she did as I suggested, then returned to the jewellery. In the morning light, I could see her face. The resemblance was strong. "What's your name?"

"I don't believe your amnesia story and neither does my father!"

"I can't help what you believe, it's the truth. Not for long, I hope. I have been remembering snippets for days now, inconsequential things, but welcome nonetheless. I have not remembered your name, however."

The girl was far too old to be a child of mine, but there was no denying her paternity. She and Alex shared the same accent, the same thick, dark hair and eyes, identical aristocratic cheekbones, and a haughty Andalusian stare. Her mother must have been Spanish or Italian. And very beautiful.

"My father said there was nothing here but I had to see for myself. I thought maybe there would be one left, one you forgot." She slammed the lid shut and stood with her hands on her hips in a radiant fury worthy of Garbo. "I hate you! We all hate you! I hope you die and go to Hell!"

"That's all very pleasant for you, but it won't get you what you want."

"What do you mean?"

"Shutting me up in a room to wait for my memory to come back is foolishness. If I had some information, someone to talk to about the past, I expect I would remember much faster." I could see this made sense, even to a girl who doubted my amnesia. I tried again. "What is your name?"

"Lianne."

"Lianne," I repeated. "How very pretty. And how old are you?"

"Sixteen."

The braids and the schoolgirl clothing made her appear younger. Alex must be in his late thirties, I calculated. "And you think I might have some of your jewellery?"

"Father said you wouldn't have it anymore, that you'd have sold it the moment you left."

"What did it look like?"

"It wasn't one piece; it was all of it. My mother's jewellery. Brazilian emeralds in a necklace, diamonds, and ruby rings. Earrings and bracelets too. I don't remember them all. But they were mine! She meant me to have them. And you stole them all!"

Dismayed, I chewed on my nails. Was this true? Stealing from a child sounded far worse than taking a few paintings.

"Your mother is dead?"

"Of course she is dead! She died ages ago, of the influenza. How else would Father have married *you?*"

I felt sick to my stomach. I was a horrible person, a common thief. Whatever Alex had done to make me leave with his paintings might have been justified, but taking a dead woman's legacy to her daughter? There was no defence for that.

"You sold my mother's jewellery first, Father said." She flung the words at me like sharp stones. "The paintings took longer to sell so you sold my mother's jewellery first."

"I'm very sorry, Lianne. Are you certain nothing in the box looks like your mother's?"

She looked again and answered wistfully, "I don't remember all of it, just the emeralds. I was only eleven."

"When she died?"

"When you stole them."

"I stole the jewellery when you were eleven?" Lianne nodded.

Five years ago? I was astounded Alex hadn't applied thumbscrews to wrench the information out of me at once. "And in all that time, I never told your father what I had done with them?"

"How could you? He only just found you last week!" she said, the exasperation in her voice telling me how slow witted I was.

"I took the paintings and the jewellery *five years ago?*"

"Of course."

"I've been missing for *five years?*"

"Father has had people looking for you all that time."

"Then you haven't seen me for *five years?*" She looked nervous now, as if I'd accused her of something terrible, and didn't respond. "How can you be sure I'm Eva after *five years?*" I pressed.

"Oh, you're Eva. I remember you," she said, her lips pressed in a grim line.

"But if you couldn't remember the jewellery very clearly, how can you—"

Her eyes widened as she looked past me to the bureau. "My clock!" she gasped. "Already you've stolen my clock!"

Dazed, I followed her pointed finger. "Oh, the clock . . . I'm sorry, I didn't realize it came from—"

She snatched the timepiece with both hands and stormed out of the room.

Burning with questions, I sent Cécile to find Alex the moment she arrived. She returned with my breakfast tray and the reply that he would be along when it was convenient. The underlying message was plain enough.

Food was a welcome distraction: Cécile had prepared a fluffy omelette with herbs from her garden. "And tea!" I exclaimed with delight.

"An English lady will want tea," she said, pulling up a small table to the side of my bed where I could reach it for refills. "It is good for you." She had brought lumps of white sugar and brown and a small pitcher of hot milk so I could prepare the tea just as I liked. I demolished the omelette and polished off the entire pot of tea so quickly she asked if I wanted more.

"Yes, but later this afternoon, please."

"Now this." She handed me a glass with the cider medicine. The restorative, Alex had called it. The medicine the doctor had prescribed.

"What is in it?"

"The Parisian doctor said it will make you strong."

"I know, but what is it?"

"A restorative."

I didn't want to drink it. It made me feel worse, not better, and I said as much, but Cécile was having none of it. Monsieur DeSequeyra had said I was to drink it, and drink it I would. I gave in. The unpleasant aftertaste was not something I remembered from the hospital. Perhaps the sisters there had mixed it with something other than cider. Perhaps my memory was at fault, as Alex had said, and I had forgotten the doctor telling me about this medicine. Or perhaps the doctor had never prescribed anything. It is frightening to trust no one. It is even worse when you can't trust yourself. I looked at the bottom of the glass and decided, come what may, I would not drink any more. Somehow I would dispose of this so-called medicine without their knowing.

Cécile took up her satchel and stirred around inside until she found what she was searching for—a pair of surgical scissors.

"Now lie still," she said. Within minutes, the stitches in my head and hand were ancient history. "Hmmm. It looks good. That doctor knew how to sew a good seam, for a man." She made no objection when I went to the bathroom and examined myself in the mirror.

I didn't think of myself as a vain person, but everyone—or every woman, at least—would be concerned about scars. The marks on my skull would be hidden as soon as my hair grew back, but the gash above my left eye looked wicked. I knew it would fade with time, but I had to acknowledge that it was unlikely to disappear completely. Never mind, I told myself firmly, there were much worse things. One had only to scan the streets of Europe to see wheelchairs, crutches, missing eyes, and empty sleeves. *Mutilés de guerre*, they called them in France, and saved the front seat for them on all the buses and trains.

At that moment, Alex walked into the room. Cécile took the opportunity to return my tray to the kitchen and we were alone at last.

"What have you remembered?"

I looked at him blankly. "Nothing of importance. That's not why I asked for you, I should like to—"

"I shall decide what is important. Tell me what you have remembered."

"N-Nothing!"

"Lianne told me you said you had remembered many things over the past few days."

"Oh, that. I d-didn't mean . . . yes, I have remembered some small things, but nothing to do with your paintings. I wanted to ask you some questions about—"

"First you will answer my questions." He sat down and took a small notepad from his pocket. "Everything you remember, I will write down. No matter how small. It will perhaps lead to something else, or have importance later." And he waited, pen poised. Plainly we were going nowhere until I gave him something to write down. With a sigh of resignation, I related a few of my recent recollections. Riding a pony across a grassy meadow. A blue ribbon prize. Sitting in the front row of a classroom in a scratched wooden desk. A new cloche hat that was red and white. Wading in a clear pond. And a child's bedroom.

"There, you see? Nothing to help you locate your p-p-paintings. Or your d-daughter's jewellery." I know my stutter irked him, and I tried to control it, but the harder I tried, the worse it got.

He waved his hand dismissively. "That is gone forever. The fence breaks apart stolen jewellery the moment he gets it so the pieces can never be traced. But my p-p-p-paintings," he mocked my stutter, "are another matter. Let us explore this—"

"I have done as you asked. Now it is your turn. I want to know about the Johnsons. My family. Surely you have met them. They must have come to our wedding."

His eyes bored into my head, and I knew he was struggling with himself, calculating whether there was anything to be lost by answering my questions. Did he want me to know more? Did he believe my amnesia? He succumbed with a reluctant sigh.

"You have no family. You were raised in a London orphanage." He went on, watching me closely, thinking no doubt how he could trick me. I wondered if he was feeding me lies to test my reaction. "I know nothing of the details. You told me very little. When we met, you were playing the part of the daughter of an English industrialist, and it was only after we were married, when you were very drunk one night, that you let slip your humble past. You were adopted at an early age but returned to the orphanage when the adoptive mother died."

I felt as if I had been kicked in the stomach. I had no family. But I remembered a school—well, of course, orphans went to school until they were fourteen. And I remembered a bedroom, with green curtains, a washstand with a pitcher and basin with white roses painted on it, and a small bed with a faded green spread. An orphan's room? A feeling of desolation crept over me like a winter chill. If Alex should ultimately decide to stage a deadly accident, no one would ask questions. No one would miss me.

"I want to know about these paintings I have been accused of stealing."

"Do you deny it?"

"No, I merely ask for details to help me remember."

Cécile returned and he used the interruption to take his leave. For whatever reason, he would not talk about the paintings. He did not completely trust my amnesia, I knew that, but I also suspected he did not want to give me any information I could later twist and feed back to him as regained memories. His plan was for me to talk and for him to listen.

I spent most of that day sleeping and eating. The previous night had left me exhausted—my nerves had kept me awake for hours as I lay stiff as a couturier's mannequin for fear of accidentally touching Alex in my sleep. Cécile kept the tea hot all day and brought me egg custards and bowls of thick vegetable soup, made orange with puréed carrots. The food tasted divine. So did the glass of hearty red wine I drank twice a day like medicine. "A glass of wine each day steals a franc from the doctor," she was fond of saying. I told her the English version: "Eat an apple before going to bed; make the doctor beg his bread," and she promised me fruit the next day. When I was asleep, she sat in a comfortable chair and knitted. The sweater was for her oldest nephew, Jules, who was soon off to Paris to seek his fortune.

From her, I learned something about Alex's family. The house I was in—she called it Chateau Denon—belonged not to Alex but to his grandmother, Madame Denon, who lived in the opposite wing with her spinster cousin, Pauline. Both women were in their eighties: Pauline spry but not very alert; Madame Denon the opposite. There had been another, larger residence somewhere to the east but the filthy Bosch had destroyed it during the Great War.

Madame Denon had borne but one child and that was Madeleine. Here Cécile's lips tightened in disapproval. Madeleine had exhibited artistic talent at a young age and had been sent to Paris to study. There the obedient child had been corrupted, falling under the influence of wicked artists and atheists who encouraged her to flout her parents' authority in matters of marriage and domicile. She took lovers and painted pictures and never even returned home for her father's funeral. Then without warning she married Paulo DeSequeyra, a foreigner with estates in Portugal and Brazil. Some claimed he was nobility, but from the way Cécile wrinkled her nose, I gathered she was not among them. After bearing two sons, the DeSequeyras moved to Brazil where another son and daughter were born.

When Paulo DeSequeyra died in Brazil, Madeleine wasted no time in moving back to France with her brood, back to her mother. But her maternal instincts were no match for the lure of Paris, and she abandoned the children to their grandmother to pursue a hedonistic life of art and artists, cafés and salons, producing sloppy, immoral paintings that affronted decent citizens. Cécile sniffed. She had seen art, mind you, *real* art, in churches and in picture books, and the kindest thing one could say for those Impressionists was that they were near-sighted.

When the Great War broke out, Philippe and Alexander, having been born in France, felt it their duty to defend their native land from the Huns. Philippe, like her own dear husband, God rest his soul, had paid the supreme price, but at least Alexander had avenged his older brother's death.

This, then, was the murder that the English ladies had been talking about back in Paris. I risked interrupting her to ask, "Avenged? How?"

Here Cécile seemed vague about the details. Alex, she said, had spent some time trying to discover which deskbound army officer had signed the order that sent Philippe to the most dangerous part of the front, had somehow tracked the man down and shot him dead. It happened at Le Mans some years ago. Maybe in '21. Her mouth tightened with grim satisfaction, and she continued where she had left off.

The youngest son, Manuel, had always looked upon Brazil as his home since he and his sister Danielle were born there. Manuel returned to São Paulo as soon as he reached his majority, and it was he who managed the DeSequeyra coffee plantations and mines there. Cécile believed Manuel and Danielle were both married, but no one in Ranton-sur-Marne had seen them in years.

"So Alex is the head of the family now?"

"*En effet,* but Madame Denon is much respected still."

Perhaps I could expect some sympathy from the grandmother, I thought. Where I would not find sympathy was with my ruthless husband. I wished Cécile had divulged more about the murder at Le Mans, but it didn't sound as if she knew much more. How had he gotten away with murder? Had there been no trial? The story contained some similarities to my own circumstance: a dogged pursuit lasting several years, the quest for ultimate revenge, a murder to settle the score. There was a lesson for me there.

When Alex again produced his notebook on the second night and commenced to question me like a prisoner of war, I took refuge in a throbbing headache. It stayed with me even after I had fallen asleep and brought disturbing dreams. In the middle of the night, I jolted awake.

Alex was instantly alert. "What is it? What did you remember?"

I could hardly speak, my heart was pounding so hard in my throat. "Nothing."

"Something frightened you."

"A nightmare. It wasn't real." I drank some water and breathed deeply, wishing I had strong arms around me to stop the trembling. He was very close.

"Tell me."

"I dreamt of stairs. I w-went down them, into a cavernous room full of huge furniture, like a giant's house. It was dark, and it scared me. I tried to push past it toward the door but the furniture moved closer together, to block my way, to squash me. Monstrous tables, chairs, chests, pressing in at me. Suffocating me." All I had of my past were my dreams, and they were as solid as smoke.

"No paintings?" I shook my head. He lay down again, settling himself beneath the covers with his back turned toward me. "Go back to sleep," he commanded tersely.

I stifled a strong urge to kick him.

Mary Miley

3 THE CHATEAU

The following day, Cécile decided I should spend some time in the garden before the sun grew too strong for my pale English complexion. Delighted to be free of my quarters even for an hour, I agreed. Nothing in my imagination could have prepared me for the reality of Chateau Denon.

Outside the island of luxury I occupied with Alex, not a corner looked as if it had progressed past the nineteenth century. Whether the Denon family had fallen on hard times or Madame was simply penurious was impossible to say, but the part of the chateau I saw on my way to the courtyard was shabby beyond words. Once lovely carpets were frayed with wear, rich upholstery was threadbare from decades of hard use; uncounted summers of sunlight had bleached silk curtains and tapestries until the rich colours ran together in watery pastels. Astonished, I kept my thoughts firmly in my head as I walked through the upstairs passageway with Cécile holding my arm.

When we reached the top of the curving travertine staircase, I began to sneeze. Everywhere about me hung dusty dead animals gruesomely posed. Wild boars' heads with curling tusks charged at hunters long vanished. Fierce wild cats baring razor sharp teeth snarled from wooden escutcheons suspended on the walls between frescoed angels on the ceiling and the black and white chessboard floor. Interspersed among them were hundreds of antlers, many with deer's heads still attached—one with the whole deer posed in his death leap—and dozens of birds of prey that looked to have been stuffed in mid-attack. And in a macabre touch worthy of Edgar Alan Poe, portraits of dead Denons hung amongst the animal trophies, staring ahead with the same vacant look as the beasts beside them. With a shudder and another sneeze, I ran the gauntlet of a thousand glass eyes and exited into the fresh air.

Chateau Denon had been constructed centuries ago, atop a bluff where the river Marne makes a jagged detour north before continuing on its westerly way toward Paris. Atop massive medieval foundations sat a newer portion, constructed of tufa limestone during the seventeenth century when graceful ornamentation set the standard and symmetry ruled the land. It had come into the possession of the Denon family during Napoleon's reign, thanks to the acquisitiveness of Vivant Denon, an artist who became the emperor's confidant and who had been placed in charge of confiscating art and sculpture from all the lands Napoleon conquered. It seems he had not hesitated to collect a little on the side for himself.

Built in a square with the side facing the river left open, Chateau Denon's three slate-roofed wings surrounded the gardens of a central courtyard like loving arms cradling a bouquet of flowers. I looked about with prisoner's eyes, taking in the forty-foot drop to the Marne and the single Romanesque arch on the opposite side that led to the world beyond. In the old days there would have been a portcullis and a drawbridge over the moat to keep invaders out; today there was a gatekeeper stationed at the arch to keep me in.

"*Voilà,*" said Cécile, dusting off two wicker chairs she had fetched from the orangerie and placing them in the sun where we could overlook the river. But the river reminded me too much of the Seine, and it frightened me to look at its powerful current far below. I turned the chairs around to face the courtyard where there was more activity.

Cécile settled in beside me, knitting needles clicking like Spanish castanets. Jules' sweater was finished—this was a simple blanket for the baker's new grandson. Which was fortuitous, because the baker arrived at that very moment with a mountain of baguettes strapped to the back of his bicycle.

"*Bonjour, Madame Renaud,*" he began in that formal manner Frenchmen often adopt toward women. He doffed his beret as she introduced me, and kissed the hand I offered for shaking. Cécile remarked on the weather and a lively discussion ensued about the probable forecast for the upcoming week. Cécile held for light rain, based on her reading of the insect activity. The baker was equally certain of a deluge because of the way his yeast had risen that morning.

Alex came out of a door in the central wing and crossed to the kitchen wing, his heels crunching sharply into the crushed shell walkway. He spared a glance in my direction but did not alter his steps or make any greeting. A servant girl in clogs hurried out to the herb garden with a pair of scissors; another servant nodded to me as she carried a pile of folded laundry out of one door and into another. Among the vegetables, a white-haired gardener threw weeds into a wheelbarrow with his left hand and strawberries into a basket with his right. Bees danced among roses that preened themselves in the sun. Swallows gave their faint, high-pitched cries as they swooped endlessly over the courtyard, now and then darting into an opening high in the corner turret. At the small fountain in the middle of the flower garden, four stone dolphins spouted four thin streams of water, a soothing trickle that was momentarily joined by the sound of a nearby church bell. It was a lot of excitement for an invalid who had spent the better part of a fortnight staring at ceiling cracks.

Alex came out again, and this time he approached us. "You are feeling stronger today." It wasn't a question, but I answered as if it were.

"Yes, thank you. It is lovely to be outdoors. And such beautiful flowers!"

His eyes shifted to the elderly man kneeling in the dirt. "Henri has the gardener's magic in his hands. He has been tending this—" and his arm swept the entire courtyard, "for fifty years."

"Alone?"

"For the past few years, I'm afraid so. *Grand-mère* used to have three or four gardeners, but since the war, servants have been hard to find. The flowers and *parterres* were impressive in the old days. Now Henri relies on the occasional village lad for help."

It was such a pleasant, ordinary exchange, I should have known to be on guard.

"If you care to join us for dinner this evening, I shall have another place laid at the table."

I debated the offer briefly. He was clearly going out of his way to be agreeable, so why should I not match him? If I felt well enough to sit in the courtyard, certainly I could sit at the dining table for the family meal with two elderly ladies and young Lianne. "Why, yes, thank you. I'd like that."

"The rest of your clothes should arrive today." My astonishment must have shown plainly on my face for he continued, "Surely you didn't think those few valises contained everything? The Peugeot would not hold your trunks, so I engaged the hotel to send along the contents of your room as soon as possible. Their man has been instructed to carry your belongings to one of the guest rooms where you can go through them at your leisure." I nodded my thanks, still rather flummoxed at the thought of *more* garments when I already had a dozen chic ensembles hanging in the wardrobe. I dared to hope there would be some everyday wear in the trunks.

He pulled out his pocket watch and snapped open the cover. Alexander DeSequeyra was not the sort of man to wear a wristwatch, I realized, even though the Great War and Cartier had transformed them from feminine jewellery into acceptable men's wear. I sensed in him an uneasy alliance between modernity and tradition, one that required constant vigilance to guard against either philosophy gaining the upper hand.

"Dinner will be served at seven o'clock. It is usually served at midday in the traditional manner, but *Grand-mère* and Pauline have gone to town for the day and will not be back until five." He turned to Cécile and told her in French to see that I was dressed suitably and shown to the drawing room by half six. "And stay until after dinner, if you please," he added. "Madame DeSequeyra may need your help getting ready for bed."

Fatigued from the excursion outdoors, I returned to my room for a long nap. Afterwards, Cécile helped me with a bath and made my hair presentable. I chose one of Poiret's simple evening dresses—a stunning knee-length beaded gown with a straight profile and jagged hemline—then spent some time at the dressing table examining the infinite bottles of face cream, the cakes of colour, the tiny pots of kohl, and the nail lacquers before settling on some dark red lipstick that matched the shade of my dress. Cécile found a pair of shoes, lizard skin with pointed toes dyed the same red that looked perfect but fit poorly . . . unless I stepped carefully, I walked right out of them. Fashion before fit, I thought, admiring the total effect in the full-length glass.

With an awkward right hand, I outlined my lips in a pert bow and rubbed a bit of rouge on my cheeks. The transformation was remarkable. I added some kohl to shadow my eyes. I couldn't imagine what I had ever done with so many bottles of nail lacquer—any treatment would only call attention to my ragged fingernails. I vowed I would never bite them again.

With mounting trepidation, I followed Cécile down the *grand escalier* and across the chequerboard marble of the hall floor.

The drawing room of Chateau Denon had been grandly furnished at one time, but that time was long past. Two white-haired ladies sat together on a sofa upholstered in faded but still exquisite blue-green brocade. I guessed it was not penury that caused them to dress in a style popular twenty years ago—floor-length gowns, covered sleeves, high necklines—but rather a disdain for the short skirts and straight lines of contemporary fashion. It was immediately clear which was Madame Denon and which Cousin Pauline. Madame's erect posture and the careful placement of her hands—one in her lap and one on an ivory walking stick—announced her authority to anyone who presumed to question it.

Alex stood beside them, listening with rapt attention to Cousin Pauline's querulous wanderings and looking for all the world like a pirate who would as soon run you through with a cutlass as light a cigarette. I faltered at the door, wondering if my decision to join them for dinner would prove a mistake. Alex acknowledged my appearance with a cool, fleeting glance. Dressed in a smashing dinner jacket, he was standing on the largest antique Savonnerie carpet I had ever seen—obviously made to order for the room eons ago, now worn through to the warp in several places. Soft light spilt from gasoliers and from the lone electric lamp on the grand piano. Caruso sang from a gramophone. Lianne sat across the room kicking her foot against the chair leg as if bored silly by both the music and the company. Her face lit up when she saw me. Not from affection but from the expectation that now, at last, things would get interesting.

The fifth occupant of the room trotted up to greet me in a most friendly fashion. A simple hound he was, tan coloured with brown ears. All eyes turned in my direction as I patted his head. No one spoke.

"Hullo, boy," I said to fill the awkward silence. Had Alex not told the family he had invited me to dinner? "What's your name?" I dropped to my knees to scratch under his chin and stroke his neck. He sniffed at me, decided I smelt fine, and sat down to enjoy the caress. "What a nice gentleman you are, so friendly. D'you remember me?"

"That's Charlot." Lianne spoke up. "He's friendly to *everyone*." Touché.

"I think he remembers me."

Alex snapped his fingers and Charlot removed himself from my side and went to sit at Alex's feet. I had a feeling Alex expected the world to respond in the same way. "He's only three years old," he said, ending that happy speculation.

"Oh. Well, shame on you, Charlot, for being so welcoming. You'll give the place a bad name."

"As you may or may not recall, *Grand-mère* speaks no English. Nor does Cousin Pauline. She wants me to welcome you to Chateau Denon and tell you that she is glad you are feeling well enough to join us tonight. She hopes you are comfortable in the room and will feel free to make use of any other part of the chateau that pleases you."

I nodded to *Grand-mère* and thanked her in French. A simple "*merci*" and "*s'il vous plaît*" would not jeopardize my pretence of knowing none of that language.

"Good evening, Lianne," I said. She gave me a sullen stare and continued to kick the chair leg.

"Lianne!" Alex warned. Interesting, I thought, that he expected better manners from his daughter than he was willing to extend himself.

"Good evening, Eva," she said. Hearing that name made me wince. No matter how many times I heard it, the name grated on my nerves. I must have used my alias, Claire, for so long that I preferred it.

"Is Charlot yours?"

"He belongs to *Grand-mère*. Come here, Charlot," she called softly and he came. "But I named him. And he likes me best."

"Charlot is multi-lingual too, isn't he," I noted. "He responds as easily in English as in French."

"He's very intelligent," agreed Lianne, happy as a mother boasting about her child. "He was the smartest puppy I ever saw. He looked so funny when he was learning to walk that I thought of Charlie Chaplin, the way he walks so crooked, and I thought of naming him Charlot. It's what we call Chaplin."

I knew that. Amazing what trivia I remembered, when I recalled none of the important aspects of my life.

"D'you like the flicks, then, Lianne?"

She looked blank at the slang, then caught my meaning. "Oh, the pictures. I love them all. I've seen every one of Chaplin's. There is a cinema near my school in Lausanne. We go as often as we're allowed."

"Did you see Lon Chaney in *Phantom of the Opera*? That was one of my favourites. That and *Son of the Sheik*." Evidently Alex had the ability to listen to two conversations simultaneously because at that moment, he shot me a stern look from across the room that let me know I'd blundered into harm's way.

"I'm not allowed to see Valentino's pictures," Lianne said with a sullen glance in Alex's direction. "Father says I'm not old enough."

"Oh, I see. Well, perhaps he's right. Those are a bit . . . um . . . never mind, you'll be old enough in no time. What about actresses? Which ones do you like?" I seemed to have no trouble recalling Mary Pickford's films or the latest Greta Garbo pictures.

Lianne was peering at me thoughtfully. "You know," she began, "you look like that actress—Clara Bow."

In a flash, I knew I had heard it before and that it was true. I had consciously mimicked the hair cut and colour, the delicately drawn bow lips, and the heavy eye shadow of the actress known everywhere as "the It girl." I was hardly alone. She had set off a firestorm of imitation, and it was the goal of half the women in the Western world to look like Clara Bow. I was flattered by the comparison but well aware that I fell a few screen tests short of the glamorous film star.

"Doesn't she, Father? Look like Clara Bow?"

It was a compliment he was not prepared to make, so he pretended he didn't know who we were talking about. "Claire Bow? An actress, you say? I don't know her." But he did. He looked me squarely in the eyes to let me know that he knew. And he knew where I had gotten my alias.

"No, Father, it's *Clara* Bow, not *Claire*."

He gave his what-does-it-matter shrug. Still, I imagined he was right. I admired the famous film star. I copied her makeup, I dyed my red hair brown like hers, I borrowed her first name and paired it with Smith when I needed an alias. There wasn't much original about me, it seemed.

"Did you see her film about the girl at boarding school," asked Lianne, "who has a horse and wins the prize in a show? And she nearly drowns and the boy saves her?"

Horrified, I could only stare at Lianne while she prattled on about the film. A school room, a horse, a blue ribbon, a pond—incidents that were all mirrored my new-found memories. The appalling notion that these, and perhaps others of my regained memories, were nothing more than snatches of films I had seen instead of my own life filled me with horror. Were they my own memories or not? And how was I to know the difference?

I was saved from reply by a butler who entered and stood silently near the door in his white gloves and black attire, his presence asking the question.

"An apéritif, Eva?" said Alex.

"No, thank you." My head was muddled enough without bringing alcohol into the picture.

"We are having champagne. Our own vintage."

My hunch was right. I was east of Paris, in the province of Champagne, where the bubbly wine of the same name originated. "Perhaps another time."

Alex placed the order and the white-gloved servant bowed. He offered me a cigarette, right in front of Cousin Pauline and *Grand-mère*. When I declined, he raised one dark eyebrow and would have made some comment had not *Grand-mère* spoken first. I think she said to tell me about the vineyards. Her accent was unfamiliar, not like Madame Renaud's vernacular, but not Parisian either. Perhaps it was the more formal speech of an era long past.

Alex complied with her request. "Chateau Denon grows it own grapes and produces its own champagne. It is not a large operation, but it is a respectable house."

I looked at Madame Denon and wondered who oversaw the work. Certainly not an old woman, nor a playboy like Alex. "How interesting," I said politely. She returned my nod.

Age had made Madame and her cousin as alike as sisters. Close in years, they wore their white hair piled high and enough jewels at their throats to turn Queen Mary green with envy. The stones on their gnarled fingers were so large I wondered that they could lift their hands to eat. I glanced at Alex. A sneer curled his lips. Don't even think it, he seemed to say. I blushed—I was *not* a thief, I was *not* thinking of stealing them—but my red cheeks only confirmed his suspicions.

The servant interrupted our silent battle with a silver tray, a bottle of champagne, and glasses. Alex popped the cork and devoted himself to the two elderly ladies who were, I think, talking about repairs to a fishpond outside the chateau walls, so I turned to Lianne. My stepdaughter, I reminded myself.

"Your English is very good, Lianne." In spite of her dislike for me, she responded to the compliment with an eagerness that made me think she didn't get many. "Did you learn it in school?"

"Yes. I already knew French and Portuguese from birth, and Father thought English lessons would be best. But I learn more from my roommate, Helen. She is from Canterbury."

"So you speak English with her?"

"On even days. Helen is trying to learn French so we speak French on odd days. Our teacher says we learn as much from one another as in the classroom."

"The teacher sounds very wise. What other subjects d'you study?"

Lianne was at that age girls reach when they feel the world revolves around them, so she had no hesitation relating all the details about her exclusive Swiss boarding school. I enjoyed hearing about the girls and their ski lessons, their musical recitals, their drawing teacher, and their singing lessons, until I began to wonder if this school was nothing more than a farm for growing placid wives and mothers supervised by a hidebound headmaster who thought academics unsuited to the female temperament. But no, Lianne also studied botany, European history, geometry, and French literature. Judging from her comments, she was neither first nor last in her class. I knew instinctively that boarding school had not figured in my past. Of course not, orphans attended school only to age fourteen as the law required, and they most assuredly did not have ski lessons or piano recitals.

The butler, who seemed to have no name, announced dinner.

Because it was just family, we dined simply that night on trout cooked in dilled cheese, pigeon pâté, and roast lamb with artichoke sauce. *Grand-mère* sat on one side of the table with Cousin Pauline on her right; Alex was seated opposite her. A footman hovered to make sure no one strained a muscle reaching for the salt. *Grand-mère* may have had difficulty finding house and garden servants but she had put her money where her mouth was. The cook was superb. It was a little difficult to eat with one hand, and for me, the wrong hand, but before I could falter over the lamb, the butler stepped wordlessly to my side and cut it for me. I gave him a grateful smile that he did not acknowledge.

A fortnight without solid food meant I filled up quickly. I thought I could not eat another bite until a dish of strawberries was set before each of us—tiny, fresh, plump, blood red, and topped with *crème fraîche*. They looked heavenly. They tasted divine. I ate them slowly, savouring their sweetness.

The table grew quiet. Every time I looked up, Alex looked away. I checked to make sure I was using the dessert spoon and not the teaspoon, and I dabbed my mouth with the monogrammed *serviette* in case I was wearing a bit of cream. But he continued to watch me closely, his eyes not leaving my face until at last I challenged his stare with one of my own and he looked away.

I had finished half my bowl when Lianne dropped her spoon with a clatter and gave a shriek. "No—stop!" she sputtered. She lunged out of her seat, pointing at me. In her panic, her English deserted her. "*Les fraises*—stop!"

Startled, I set down my spoon. "What?"

"*Les fraises*! The strawberries. Do not eat them! They are sick for you! You . . . you . . . red all over and—" She puffed out her cheeks like a blowfish.

I turned to Alex. "I'm allergic to strawberries?" He said nothing. "That's it, isn't it? I'm allergic to s-s-strawberries!" Like a crash of thunder, I understood everything. I came out of my chair shaking so hard I couldn't control my voice. "And you knew it. This is some sort of sick t-t-test, isn't it? Isn't it? To see if the amnesia is real? You filthy b-bastard!"

The shocked faces of *Grand-mère* and Cousin Pauline told me they understood at least one of the English words I flung at him before I fled the room. I didn't care what they thought. They were horrible people, treating me as if I were some sort of a criminal. Yes, I had made some mistakes in the past, but I was trying to put them right. I was trying to remember! It didn't give them reason to try to poison me!

"*Madame, madame, qu'est-ce qui se passe?*" Cécile dropped her knitting as I rushed into the room, past her chair, and into the bathroom. No time to answer, I was going to do the only thing I could think of—stick my finger down my throat.

As soon as she understood my purpose, she rummaged around in the knitting bag that doubled as her medical kit and produced a small bottle. "*Non, madame, voici. C'est mieux.*" Grateful, I swallowed the bitter dose of gentian she gave me. Almost at once, my stomach heaved and the meal I had so enjoyed began to come up.

"Strawberries," I gasped in between heaves. "I am allergic to them."

"Ahhh." She shook her head with remorse. "Pierre Lebrun in the village, he too is allergic to strawberries. If one bite even touches his tongue, his face turns red and his whole body swells with hives. His daughter too. Did you eat one?"

"Half a bowl," I replied miserably. She looked closely at my face and frowned. I turned to the mirror. My face was as red as the strawberries and hot enough to light a fire, but it had not puffed up yet. I was trembling so hard from the vomiting and the anger that Cécile had to help me out of my clothes and into bed. I lay back on the pillows, taking deep breaths. She gave me a cold wet compress for my eyes.

"I would give you some chamomile tea to help you relax, but your stomach would give it back at once. You must sip some water, very slowly, but you cannot take anything else until tomorrow morning."

Alex sauntered into the room. He stood by the bed and looked over the goods like an auctioneer evaluating the next item up for bid. At that moment, I could have cheerfully piled faggots at his feet and lit the fire myself.

"I am sorry I had to do that," he said. I snorted—never did a man sound less sorry in his life. "I did not act out of malice, I assure you. I had to know for certain if the amnesia was real. Now I know it is. If you had been shamming, you'd have made some excuse to avoid eating the strawberries rather than endure the reaction. Hmm. You do not look very red."

He was right, thank God. Cécile brought me an ivory hand mirror and I saw my face. "I rid my stomach of the berries before they could act. Thanks to Lianne. If she had not remembered, you would have waited until it was too late."

"It may seem drastic to you, but I had to know for certain."

"You risk my life so you could be certain!"

"Your life was never at risk. When this happened five years ago, you were fine after a week or two."

"When it happened five years ago, I was not suffering from a concussion, broken bones, amnesia, and malnourishment!"

His careless shrug said it all. I despised him. I despised myself even more for having thought, however briefly, that there might be a gentler side to his personality. How could I have been so gullible? Was I so starved for kindness that I could allow those few cordial moments in the courtyard to blind me to his true character? I'd not make that mistake again.

"Now that I know the truth, we can come to certain conclusions about your mental problem. Have you heard of schizophrenia? People who suffer from schizophrenia hear voices and believe they are someone else, like Napoleon or Joan of Arc. You believe you are Claire Smith and the actress Clara Bow."

"That's highly offensive and quite untrue."

He shook his head regretfully. "I am only saying that what we thought was simple amnesia is looking more and more like symptoms of schizophrenia."

"I am not insane!"

"Not insane, merely suffering from delusions. Although in the old days, you're quite right, such people might have been called insane or mad or possessed or even labelled witches. I've been in contact with the director of the Kreutzer Institute in Switzerland where they specialize in treatment of psychiatric illnesses such as this. He said that they could very likely help you regain your memories and even do away with your delusions if you were to—"

"No!"

All this time, without my knowledge, he had been researching these horrible subjects. For days now he had been theorizing . . . planning my future as if I were mentally incompetent. The sound of the sea in my ears grew louder until it drowned out his voice and left my own raw fears exposed. I knew what happened to people who suffered from delusions. They were put away in asylums, forced into straight jackets, and fed mush with a spoon twice a day. If Alex prevailed, I would end up in some Swiss version of Bedlam, strapped to a cot in an empty cell, staring at the cracks in the ceiling forever.

As long as he thought I might regain my memory and help him get his paintings, I was relatively safe. The moment he lost that hope, I was doomed. He wouldn't have to stage an accident to rid himself of me. He could commit me to some asylum forever with no risk to himself at all. Come what may, I had to get out of here before he decided I was no longer of use.

Cécile stood apart from us with a puzzled expression on her face, thinking her own thoughts, understanding none of what we were saying. "Last summer," she said thoughtfully, "when Pierre Lebrun accidentally ate a strawberry in a fruit tart, he turned red as a beet. He vomited at once, but he still got the rash and the swelling."

She was talking to me, but Alex assumed otherwise and answered her in French. "No doubt he had a stronger allergy than Madame. You may go now, Cécile. Thank you for your help."

He lit a cigarette and stood by the open window looking out. I know what he saw, I had looked out the window the first day, at the orange-tiled rooftops of the dun-coloured village that tumbled down the hill from the chateau like a child's blocks thrown out the window and left to lie where they fell. Where the narrow streets converged at the community water fountain stood the monument that honoured the village sons who had died in the Great War. Every village in France had one. *Morts pour la patrie.* Alex did not turn to look at me until he had finished his cigarette. I hated him.

"*Alors,* now I shall tell you about the paintings."

Now that he was satisfied that my amnesia was genuine, he would open up about the past. Our past. Crushing the cigarette in a porcelain dish, he paced the room as he talked, avoiding looking at me as he told his story.

"My mother was an artist," he began, "and better at art than

63

motherhood. When she lived in Paris before her marriage, she fell in with the *avant-guard*, those who are now called *Impressionistes*, and was influenced by their styles, their lives, their *absinthe*. She became good friends with the American Mary Cassatt and others who were more her own age like Toulouse-Lautrec and Henri Matisse. Her paintings, like theirs, were unpopular with the critics and with the public, which follows the critics like sheep. But unlike most artists, Madeleine Denon had money. Although *Grand-père* did not approve of her lifestyle—he believed artists were immoral—*Grand-mère* defied him and sent whatever she asked for. With this money she supported herself and her friends by buying their paintings.

"She met my father in 1887. They were wholly unsuited and would never have married had it not been for the advent of my eldest brother. They married at once—there are no bastards in the DeSequeyra family. Philippe was born a few months later, and I the next year, but my father longed for his home in São Paulo. A wife must follow her husband, so they moved. When I was twelve, my father died and Mother seized the chance to come home to France. Leaving the four of us in the care of *Grand-mère,* she returned to the Paris art world where she was welcomed like a prodigal daughter.

"Do not think we were neglected—she visited us twice a year. She loved her children; she just loved painting more. She died a few years before the war began, leaving us her collection of several hundred paintings—her own work and that of her friends, plus some older, more valuable ones by noted traditionalists. Some were sent to our home in São Paulo, some were brought to *Grand-mère*'s chateau on the Aisne River. When the Germans invaded, they destroyed that chateau and its contents."

He paused to close the draperies, then turned on the bedside lamp and stood there in its feeble light, his hands on his hips, glaring at me as if I had caused some natural disaster.

"When you left Brazil, you took four paintings from their frames."

"Wait! I was in Brazil?" I couldn't call up a wisp of memory about such a foreign place.

"For some months only, until you ran back to Europe with your lover and my paintings. You knew little about art, but you knew enough to leave the Impressionists which would never have brought more than a few hundred pounds and to help yourself to the more valuable canvases: a Delacroix, a Géricault, and a Goya. The fourth was one of my mother's own paintings and of little commercial value. She called it "Memories." I expect you took it by mistake, thinking it was something else."

"Why are you telling me all this now?"

"I am hoping that talking about the paintings will cause you to remember where they are."

What he meant was, now that he felt confident I was not playing him for the fool, he would work with me. He had been afraid that I was manipulating him with my story of amnesia, laughing at his gullibility behind his back, and he was a man who could not bear the thought of being bested by a woman. At last he had the upper hand. I feared this was not good news for me.

"But it's been five years. Surely I sold them long ago."

"It was impossible for you to sell them through normal channels. I notified Sotheby's, Duveen's, and Christie's in London and every auction house in Europe to be alert for stolen property. Also most active collectors. You had to sell them carefully, to find people rich enough to pay your price and unscrupulous enough to turn a blind eye to questionable provenance."

He had numerous copies made of the four paintings, crude copies, done from memory, but useful nonetheless to send to auction houses. He kept one set for himself, and he showed them to me now. There was a depiction of a strong, spirited white horse fighting against restraining ropes that Gericault had painted and a dramatic battle scene that showed the free brushstrokes and brilliant colours so typical of Goya. The radiant light and the exotic subject matter of the third canvas made me certain that Delacroix had painted it during his sojourn into North Africa a hundred years earlier. The fourth I did not recognize. It was, of course, the work of Madeleine Denon, an impressionistic beach scene she had titled "Memories," showing a woman in white dress in the foreground holding a parasol and two children playing in the distance. But they released no memories from the locked rooms of my brain. It was not lost on me that both Madeleine's "Memories" and my own were missing.

"Surely the originals were not this small?" Madeleine's was, perhaps—I knew nothing of her artistic style—but the three romanticists generally favoured larger canvases. For a fleeting moment, I wondered how an ill-educated orphan had learned such things.

"You remember them as larger? Yes, they were."

"I don't know that I remember them, but I recognize them for what they are," I tried to explain. They were familiar, but only in a general sense that anyone who understood a little about the art world would understand. I grimaced a little, frustrated that I knew more about Delacroix's life history than my own. And where had I learned about art? Certainly not from the rudimentary education dished out to orphans. "Why didn't you notify the police?"

"I did. In France, Brazil, Italy, and England. They were not interested in domestic disputes."

"And you think I've been living off the sale of Lianne's jewellery for five years, with the paintings in a bank vault somewhere?"

"The money from the jewellery would not have kept you and your stable of stallions for more than a year. You have expensive tastes, my dear, and no self-control. I expect to learn that one or more paintings have been sold. If I can locate the buyer and prove he knew he was accepting stolen goods, I can recover them. The others are probably hidden. Soon you will remember where." He glanced at the glass of cider medicine on the table beside the bed. "Ah, you haven't had your restorative. Here."

He watched until I had finished every drop, giving me no opportunity to pour it down the sink. I began to feel sick almost at once, but I told myself this could not be poison. He might be planning to kill me, but murder by strawberries or drowning or poison seemed premature—at least until after I had disgorged the whereabouts of his precious paintings. Once he had those, my life would not be worth a *sou*. And if I couldn't remember soon, he would surely tire of the wait and pack me off to the Swiss asylum for the good doctors to work on me.

I began thinking about how I could escape from Chateau Denon.

"*Entrez!*" I called, sitting up in bed and running my fingers through my hair. My stomach was empty as a beggar's cup and I hoped it was Cécile with some breakfast.

The heavy wooden door swung inward and Lianne entered, looking about the darkened room as if to reassure herself that I was alone. Evidently she could not stay away—no doubt she couldn't bear to miss the chance of finding more to despise in me.

"Oh, good morning, Lianne. Open the draperies so we can see."

She came in furtively, like a child sneaking into a forbidden room. "I brought you this," she said as she set her Art Nouveau clock on the dresser.

"How kind of you! I feel so lost without knowing the time. I hope you understand that I didn't know it was yours when I asked for—"

"I know. Nurse Renaud told me she borrowed it from my room. I don't need it. I took another from one of the guest rooms."

"Thank you so very much. I've been relying on the sound of the church bell in the *place de l'Eglise* but it's so erratic, I've concluded that the priest has a memory as unreliable as mine!"

She stood a moment, awkwardly, so I invited her to sit down. "I wanted to thank you also for last night. I am so grateful you remembered about the strawberries in time to save me from the reaction."

"I thought you would be all . . ." she groped for the words, ". . . all blown out. Last time, you looked horrible. You itched like mosquito bites everywhere."

"Thanks to you, I threw up so quickly the allergy didn't have time to do its worst. Tell me about the other time."

"There was some cake. You didn't know there were strawberries in it. No one knew. You were very angry. You screamed and smashed some vases."

"Where was this?"

"In Brazil. We live there. You thought we lived here? *Non.* Oh, I am at school part of the year, but when the term is finished, Father comes to bring me home. We visit *Grand-mère* here for a while, then sail for São Paulo for the summer, but it is winter there of course, then we return in September to see *Grand-mère* again and go back to school. We will be going home after the midsummer festival, *les feux de la Sainte-Jean.*"

Without me, I fervently prayed.

"Father comes to Lausanne for end-of-term ceremonies. We have concerts, poetry recitals, and dances for the parents. He had a telegram about you in the hospital and left right away. He missed my piano recital."

"I am sorry." I *was* sorry, but I was also getting tired of apologizing for having caused every disaster since Noah's Flood.

"It doesn't matter. I played my piece for them on the piano here—*Für Elise*—and *Grand-mère* and *Tante Pauline* and Jean-Claude got to hear it too."

"Jean-Claude?"

"Another cousin. He lives . . ." she pointed carelessly toward the south.

"So the police notified your father?" How on earth had they traced him when I was using the name Claire Smith? The key in my purse would have led them to the hotel room but there had surely been no note in my luggage saying "In case of assault, please notify Alexandre DeSequeyra." Even if there had been, who was to know he was in Lausanne?

Cécile Renaud arrived. She greeted me and Lianne fondly and left to get my breakfast. Lianne prattled on about their home in Brazil and the coffee *fazendas* that were, I gathered, the source of the DeSequeyra fortune. She was a sweet girl, immature for her age, and her conversation jumped erratically from one thing to another. I soon knew the names of her horses, her pet parrots, and her girlfriends. The lack of any mention of boys confirmed my suspicion that Lianne lived in a gossamer cocoon, both in Brazil and in Lausanne, with a highly protective parent to make sure she remained as sheltered from the world as possible. I knew this was common amongst the upper classes, keeping their daughters youthful and naïve for as long as possible by sequestering them in convent schools or strict boarding schools until a suitable marriage had been arranged. I also knew instinctively that it was not my own experience. I had been independent at a young age. Orphans quickly learn to take care of themselves.

When Cécile came back with my breakfast, Lianne jumped up guiltily. "I must go now. I am riding with Father this morning."

"I'm sure you will have a lovely ride. It looks like a very pleasant day."

She chewed her bottom lip. "I wanted to tell you . . . I am sorry for your strawberries last night. I am sorry for my father. He should not have done such a thing." And before I could reply, she turned and slipped out the door.

I spent the next few days in bed sleeping, eating, and drinking so much of Cécile's tea that I nearly floated out of the room and into the Marne. Chamomile was best for me, she maintained stoutly, but I consumed rivers of Earl Grey and Bohea along with the chamomile and, for a treat, a tisane brewed with mint she picked from the courtyard garden. Sweetened with heaping spoons of sugar, it tasted like liquid peppermint drops. My intent was to regain my strength while seeming to remain weak.

Memories were returning like bees to the hive. One night as I slept, most of my childhood seeped back into my head—it was there when I woke in the morning as if it had never left: the row of dolls in my bedroom, the faces at school, my mother and father, no brothers or sisters. They called me Claire. Nothing I recalled overlapped with life in an orphanage. The more time passed, the more I doubted I was an orphan. I had a father who was tall and thin and wore spectacles, and a mother who smelt of rosewater.

Alex would have none of it. "Those could be your adoptive parents, the ones who returned you to the orphanage when the mother died."

I shook my head. They didn't feel like adoptive parents. They weren't dead. They were worried about me. I wanted to contact them right away, to ease their distress. I wanted Alex to try to find them.

"What are their given names, these Smiths?"

I thought so hard I brought on a splitting headache, but the harder I tried, the more they receded into obscurity, like white stones at the bottom of a murky pond. I could almost make them out until I reached for them, then my hand stirred up the silt and they were gone. My parents' names were Dad and Mum, of course.

"The Smiths, somewhere in England. That will be easy to trace," he said sardonically.

"I'm not making them up!"

"I didn't accuse you of that," he said, "but obviously one of your accounts is a lie. Perhaps the orphan story is the lie, one you fed to me so I wouldn't try to contact your family. Or possibly they are both lies." I could almost read the word schizophrenia on his forehead.

Well, the orphan story certainly felt false, at least until the next night when I woke up with a start, sobbing with grief. Alex was alert at once, demanding to know what I had been dreaming. Images fleeting and ephemeral echoed inside my head, too faint to sustain but strong enough for their sorrow to linger. Somehow I knew my mother had died and the sorrow I felt was as fresh as if she had passed away yesterday. Maybe she *was* an adoptive mother and somehow I'd become confused about how long I'd lived there. Suddenly the orphan story didn't seem so preposterous.

"It would be more productive if you would try to remember more recent history," was all Alex said.

Lianne came to see me again the next morning just as I was finishing my medicine. She must have been bored indeed if she had been reduced to stopping by my room, but there she was, eager to talk about the cinema. No, I had not seen the talking picture that had come out last year in America. Lianne was desperate to see it, but she had just received a letter from her roommate Helen who told her it was not coming to France because none of the theatres in France could afford the expense of installing sound equipment. Lianne was devastated.

"No one will see these talking pictures except in America," she wailed, and let loose that eternal cry of youth: "It isn't fair!"

To divert her I talked of film stars, and soon we were discussing Clara Bow's lips. I opened up the dressing table with all my makeup to show her how the Cupid's bow effect was achieved. Then we experimented with the eyes, which were harder and required globs of cold cream to remove the blotches. Cécile watched from behind her knitting needles with a suspicious frown, unsure where all this hedonism was heading.

"Your hair looks so *chic*," Lianne sighed. "Father will never let me bob my hair." What a hypocrite he was, this international playboy who lived in the centre of the fashionable world, shielding his daughter from his own lifestyle.

"But there are other popular styles for long hair," I said carefully. "Like earphones. Pauline Frederick wears them." Not as big a star as Mary Pickford or Clara Bow, Pauline Frederick had not yet bobbed her hair, although I suspected it was inevitable. Meanwhile, perhaps Lianne could be happy with her hair wrapped around her ears like earmuffs. We worked at it for a while, and the result, if I do say so, did me proud. After I had plucked her thick eyebrows back to a fashionable thin arch, darkened her eyelids with kohl, and rouged her cheeks, she looked more mature, yet still the *ingénue*.

She preened a bit, then gave a gasp. "Wait here," she commanded and dashed out of the room. I hoped she was not going to show her father. I was in no mood to tangle with Alex again so soon. She returned in a moment with a photograph framed in silver gilt.

"Look," she said. Cécile and I looked. There was a beautiful young woman, standing next to a chubby little girl dressed in white. "Don't you see? I look like *Maman*. I never thought so before, but I see it now, with my hair and the makeup."

I examined the photo carefully. "You're right, you do look like her. You're getting older now, and the resemblance becomes stronger as you approach her own age. She was very beautiful. You will be too."

Lianne's eyes opened wide. "You think so? You told me—"

"What?"

She looked at her feet, like a naughty child caught in a prank. "You told me once I was fat."

Dear God, what a prize I was, insulting children. "How rude of me! But, you know, children are often chubby. They grow out of it as they grow up."

"You're very thin."

"I've been at Death's front door for more than a fortnight—I expect emaciated is the better word. Oh, yes, it's fashionable for flappers to be straight as a stick, but I think that's a bit extreme, don't you?"

If I did, she did.

"You were thin *before*," she said, meaning when she knew me in Brazil.

"Are there any photos of me in the house?" I asked. "I'm

wondering what I looked like, before." I was pestered by doubts of who I really was, and how I could possibly have lived this other life when my memories were revealing something entirely different. But every time I sank into serious disbelief, I was pulled to the surface with the incontrovertible proof of wedding rings, handbags, and hotel keys. How could I *not* be Eva?

Lianne shook her head, then had a brain wave and ran off. She returned after some time with a photograph that showed Alex and me sitting in a lush garden. It was an amateur shot and my hunch was right. "I took this when Father gave me a camera for my eleventh birthday," she said. "It isn't very good."

No, it wasn't. The subjects were off-centre and Alex's face was shaded by a large tree. But I was in full sun, front and centre, hair shorter and straighter then, and a little lighter, makeup heavier than I like now. But it was my face that smiled into Lianne's birthday present, no mistake about it. I scrutinized the background, looking for anything familiar. Nothing.

"Why don't we remove the makeup for now, and leave your hair this way for dinner? See how your grandmother and father like it?"

"Are you coming to dinner this afternoon?"

I hadn't been asked to come, and after the strawberry sabotage, I thought we would all be better served if I continued to take my meals in my room. "I'm not strong enough to venture downstairs. Perhaps another day."

"Jean-Claude is coming today. He's back from Dijon."

"Is he your age?" I asked, scenting romance.

"Oh, no! He's quite old. He lives in a house in the village, and comes for dinner often."

"And have I met him before, on another visit here?"

She wrinkled her nose. "You've never been here before. The only people you know from the other time is *Grand-mère* because she was visiting us in Brazil when you were there with Father." That put me in mind of something that was bothering me. Just how long had Alex and I been together, if I had left him five years ago?

"I see. How long was I in Brazil?"

"Oh, I don't remember. Just a short while. Then you lost the baby and ran off."

"I *what?*"

Cécile chose that moment to complete the casting off of her

final row and hold her blanket up for admiration. Lianne, after indicating she knew nothing more about the subject, remembered there were newborn kittens to visit in the barn, and left. I was so shaken, I felt sick to my stomach. A baby? I had a baby, or almost had a baby? It seemed impossible that I could forget something like that. I drifted miles away, unable to focus my attention on Cécile who was rattling on about village preparations for Midsummer's Eve. *Les feux de la Saint-Jean,* the locals called it. The fires of Saint John. An ancient holiday with its roots in pagan rites. A baby. ". . . and I will go home for dinner and check on old Madame Flohr, then return afterwards," she was saying.

"Oh, if you have other patients to see, please go. I really don't need you all day any longer, you should feel free to come and go as you need to."

"I will ask Monsieur DeSequeyra."

"If you like, tell him that I really only need your help for a few hours a day, for bathing and meals. Perhaps tomorrow I should start going down for dinner."

"I'll tell him."

"Oh—and, Cécile? Perhaps you shouldn't mention my French, I'd rather Monsieur did not know just yet—"

"Because he would do what?" Alex's voice came from the open doorway. In French.

My heart plunged to my toes.

"Because it would spoil the grand surprise, would it not?" he continued, smooth as oil for Cécile's benefit. The sharp, I'll-deal-with-you-later look was mine alone. "Go ahead, Cécile. I have complete faith in your judgment. Adjust your hours any way you see fit. I came upstairs to invite my wife to join us for dinner— Lianne asked me a moment ago, and it seems you both think Madame is well enough to come. Dinner is at one o'clock. We'll promise not to serve strawberries today!" He laughed, as if it had all been a good joke.

I wanted to tell Cécile not to close the door behind her, but showing any sign of weakness would only give Alex another weapon to use against me. He wasn't going to beat me here among witnesses, although with his clenched fists and hostile stare, he looked as if it would give him great satisfaction. I had committed the unpardonable sin. I had tricked him, made a fool of him. His fury was all the stronger for its silence.

"You will pay for that," he said quietly, then turned his back on me and left the room. I expected he was right. I had just lost my only advantage, and probably my best chance of escape. I had already paid a high price.

At half twelve I descended the bare stone treads of the *grand escalier* and sneezed my way through the reception hall with its pathetic stuffed heads to the drawing room where the family gathered before meals. There was no one there. The prospect from the window on this side of the chateau drew me like a magnet, and I settled into a window seat to examine the view. I jumped when I heard a man's footstep cross the threshold.

"Ah, *pardon*, I am early," said a pleasant-looking man dressed in a casual house suit only slightly behind the style. "You must be Madame DeSequeyra, Alex's wife. Jean-Claude Denon, *à votre service, madame.*"

I burst out laughing. The sound surprised me. I'd never heard my laughter before. And once I'd started, I couldn't stop.

"I'm sorry," I gasped. "I don't mean to embarrass you, it's just that I was expecting someone much older. Lianne told me about you, you see. A cousin, she said. Quite old."

He grinned. "And you pictured a white-haired ancient. Well, compared to Lianne, I am very old indeed—twice her age. She told me about you as well, but not that you were such a beautiful young woman." He bowed over my hand and kissed it, brushing the skin with his soft moustache, and only then did I notice he was missing an arm. He had an easy way about him, thick curly hair and a quick smile, not as handsome as Alex but far more appealing, and I liked him at once. "She did tell me," he continued more seriously, "that you were very nearly murdered a few weeks ago in Paris and have lost your memory. You have made an excellent physical recovery."

"This is only my second time downstairs," I explained, "and I'm afraid I'm better at sitting than standing. There are still large gaps in my memory, but I am pleased to say they are shrinking every day."

"Please, sit," he urged, probably worried I would crumple to the floor at any moment. "I had a comrade during the war who suffered from amnesia. Like you, he had a head wound. There were others whose injuries left no visible marks. It was harder for them. Some of the doctors said they were cowards, only pretending, but I think it wasn't true. The wound was there, inside the head, caused by fear or shock."

"But your friend, he recovered, I hope?"

"After a few days. But he said the emptiness was frightening." I certainly agreed with that sentiment. "It was not much use, in the end. He was killed the next month."

"How sad!" I said weakly.

"Indeed. Well. But tonight is not for sadness. Lianne tells me you are responsible for her new hair arrangement?"

"Guilty as charged. What did you think?"

"I told her that she looked lovely, and more grown up. She liked that."

I winced. "Yes, but will her father?"

"I have no children myself, but I imagine it is hard for fathers to accept that their little girls turn into young women."

As we talked of this and that, I learned Jean-Claude was the chateau's vintner, the man who oversaw the wine production from vines to corks. His father was another of *grand-mère 's* cousins, and he had grown up on the property, learning the art of making champagne from his father and uncle. His own house at the vineyard edge of Ranton-sur-Marne was convenient to his fields, "so I can run see my vines whenever they call to me," he said.

"It's strange," I said, "but I feel as if I know you."

He shook his head. "We have never met before today. You have never been to Chateau Denon, and I seldom leave it."

"Still, it's perverse of me, isn't it? To think I remember people I don't, and not remember people I should." As we laughed, Alex came into the room with Cousin Pauline and *Grand-mère* on his arm, both dressed in full Edwardian splendour. Lianne trailed behind them. Alex glared at me, no doubt annoyed that I sounded happy. Jean-Claude greeted the ladies with kisses and shook hands with Alex.

I saw little resemblance between the two cousins. Alex, half a dozen years older than Jean-Claude, was slightly taller and he had a

lithe, athletic build that reminded me of film star Douglas
Fairbanks. All he lacked to double as Zorro was a black mask, a
swirling cape, and a ledge to leap from. Jean-Claude brought an
element of innocence into the room with eyes that gazed
unflinchingly at the world and saw only what was decent. It was
perhaps his boyish charm that put me in mind of Chaplin, although
they had the same high forehead topped with curly hair and the
same impossibly sad eyes. He said something quick to Alex in an
argot I could not catch, and both men chuckled. Jean-Claude was
not intimidated by his famous, older cousin.

As he gently seated his grandmother in her usual place on the
brocade sofa, Alex said quietly, "I have business to attend to in
Reims and will be leaving after dinner . . . is there anything I can
do for you there?" The old lady gave an imperceptible shake of her
head, and he continued in a stronger voice meant to include
everyone. "There is good news today. We will be able to share our
conversation from now on. I am pleased to say that Eva has
remembered some French."

He took out his cigarette case and offered me one before
lighting his own. I shook my head.

"My word," said *Grand-mère*. "How fortunate! But you did not
speak French when I knew you in Brazil. Have you recently
learned?"

Before I could respond, Alex answered for me. I dislike that in a
man, but then, I disliked most things about my husband. "She
doesn't recall, but she must have picked up some French after she
left Brazil."

"I see." *Grand-mère* looked as if she did not see at all, and
wasn't sure whether she should speak directly to me or not. Finally
she asked how I was feeling. I presumed she referred to the
strawberries. She probably blamed the incident on me.

"Better, thank you, *madame*."

"You have met our cousin Jean-Claude Denon?"

"Yes, *madame*, he was just telling me about the vineyards when
you came in."

She looked at him fondly. "Ah, yes. Sometimes I think
champagne flows through Jean-Claude's veins. *Un apéritif, s'il
vous plaît,* Jean-Claude?"

During dinner the conversation moved to the subject of Paris, where a crowd of women had gathered to petition the Poincaré government for the right to vote. Jean-Claude had brought a Dijon newspaper with him, but *Grand-mère* and Alex had already read the news in *Le Figaro,* the Paris daily delivered to the chateau a day late by mail. It was the largest demonstration thus far in the French women's suffrage movement and several people had been trampled in the crush.

I pictured a crowd of French women, young and old, some carrying children, others waving with placards and banners. My imagination took on a life of its own as I fancied I could hear the songs they sang and the instruments they played—more for noise than music—and I could feel the vibrations of hundreds of feet on the ground as they marched through the streets. And the shrill whistles of the bobbies trying to break up the demonstration—but no, that wasn't right. The French didn't have bobbies.

"If the police had left them alone, no one would have been hurt," Alex was saying in that patronizing manner men so often take when it comes to women's suffrage. "The women were doing no harm. If they'd been ignored, they would have tired and gone back to their kitchens."

"Poincaré would be the last to support their wish for the vote," said *Grand-mère*. "He knows they would all vote against him. The devaluation of the franc has made him very unpopular."

"I take it you disapprove of women's suffrage," I asked Alex, unable to keep the tartness out of my voice. His eyebrows lifted. Alex disapproved of women asking impertinent questions as well.

"And with good reason. Women's votes are likely to push politics to the far right which will not benefit this country. And many legitimate industries such as breweries and wineries fear their prohibitionist agenda. I am hardly alone in my opinions, the Church fears the weakening of marriage and the family if women engage in politics." That last point was rich—a playboy with as many conquests as Don Juan upholding the sanctity of marriage.

"Women have been voting in Canada and the United States for eight or ten years now and those countries have yet to fall into the sea," I said.

"And the prohibition folly brought on by American women has ruined legal breweries, wineries, and importers around the world, only to bring illegal alcohol and black-market crime to the fore. A high price to pay for the vanity of voting."

"So it is vanity for women to want to vote, but for men, it is good citizenship?" I asked in a biting tone.

"I don't believe Europeans are prone to the same mistake the Americans made," said Jean-Claude, before Alex could respond. "Women vote in Great Britain, do they not? You lived there, did you not, *madame*? Have you voted?"

I don't know how I knew, but I shook my head. "No, I don't believe so. However, there is a bill before Parliament to allow universal female suffrage at twenty-one, the same as men." It seemed I knew a good deal about women's suffrage, and at last the obvious became obvious even to me. The excitement of the memories must have lit up my face for all eyes were on me as I came out of my seat. "I've worked for the passage of this bill! I've written letters to MPs and gone to meetings and marched with Mrs. Pankhurst in London for women's rights! That's why your newspaper article seemed so familiar!"

"Most commendable, *madame*," said Jean-Claude with an arch look at Alex. "Not all men oppose the women's vote. Perhaps you will vote in the next election."

I had only to look at Alex to know how unlikely that was. Until he had his paintings, I was as much a prisoner at Chateau Denon as if I had been tossed down into a dark *oubliette*.

I retreated into myself to contemplate this new revelation. So I had been in London for some part of the past five years. Living with a lover off the proceeds of stolen goods, according to Alex. I concentrated hard, but it was like listening for an echo that had long since passed away.

"*Tiens, Alexandre,*" Grand-mère began. She was the only person I ever heard use his complete name. "You would deny your grandmother the vote?"

"I wouldn't dare." He gave her a warm smile that made me wish he would turn a little of that charm in my direction. "But seriously, not every woman is as educated as you, *Grand-mère,* nor blessed with such good judgment."

"Nor are all men educated or thoughtful," she replied. "Many fools vote. It is for the state to educate its citizens so that there are fewer fools, men or women. As for the Church--*bah!* The Church is made up of unmarried men who know as much about families as they do about racing cars. Priests should stay out of politics and stick to their prayers." She turned to me. "Do you know the story of the Widow Clicquot?"

"I don't believe so."

"Tell her, Jean-Claude."

"A woman by the name of Madame Clicquot was widowed at the young age of twenty-seven—about your age. This was around 1825, isn't that so, *Grand-mère?* Although everyone told her it was unsuitable for a woman, she took over her husband's winery and managed it herself. She bottled her champagne under the label of *la Veuve Clicquot*, the Widow Clicquot, flaunting the fact that a woman now owned and ran the business. She could have hidden behind her husband's name, of course, and few would have known. But the widow built up the winery until it became one of the major producers in all of France, sending her wines throughout the world and spreading the popularity of champagne to all corners of the globe. All of Champagne owes a debt of gratitude to the widow but Chateau Denon in particular. It was Madame Clicquot who gave *Grand-mère* the confidence to carry on the family business when she herself was widowed."

"She was my friend," said *Grand-mère*. "I was far younger than she, but she encouraged me after my own husband died. I directed the winery myself until Jean-Claude's father took over. There is very little men can do that women cannot," she concluded with a sharp look in Alex's direction that had probably made him quail when he was younger.

"I yield to your greater wisdom and experience, *Grand-mère,*" said Alex formally, and he illustrated his concession with a flourishing bow from the waist. Mollified, she nodded graciously. My satisfaction at seeing his retreat was, however, short-lived. It was his affection and respect for his grandmother, I felt sure, that had prompted his surrender, not the superiority of our arguments.

Feeling restless after the midday meal, I went outside and walked around the courtyard, keeping to the outside path, enjoying the wind on my face and admiring the gardens. The morning's sunshine had given way to clouds heavy with the promise of rain. The *parterres* were orderly collections of tamed flowers and coloured gravel, sculpted in the French manner to prove man's mastery of the natural world. It was a faked sort of beauty, like a woman with dyed hair and a painted face, and I found myself thinking that, if I were rich, I'd let Mother Nature have a greater say in her garden.

From the wall overlooking the steep embankment, the normally placid Marne looked dark and swift and treacherous. Or perhaps I had come to view all rivers with trepidation after my swim in the Seine. I shuddered and descended the shallow steps to sit on the edge of the dolphin fountain, soothed by the sound of water trickling into the pool. I had to know what had happened with the baby. Had it been an accident or . . . or had it been violence? As soon as I was alone with Alex—a rare occurrence, except at night—I would ask.

I no longer wondered why he hadn't divorced me long ago. I thought I knew. Married, he had complete control over me and anything I possessed. Divorce would involve the courts, legal issues, and the newspapers, especially for the renowned Alexander DeSequeyra of Le Mans fame. He would be too much in the public eye to dispose of me or take his revenge as he planned. Worse, he would be publicly embarrassed at having been bested by a woman, something he seemed to dread more than his own death.

Still, I had to ask myself about his unnatural obsession with a few paintings. Here was a man with pockets full of money and as many paintings as a museum. Four had gone missing. And it was such a calamity that he had hired private investigators to hunt me down? For five years? I understood the paintings were valuable, but the cost of recovering them must surely have exceeded their value by now. I could only surmise that ego was driving this quest. He had been humiliated. By a woman, no less. And one beneath him in rank. It was more about revenge than art.

One of the kitchen servants opened a door and shoved Charlot outside. He trotted over to the fountain, lapped up a drink, and sat at my feet as if to say, "We are a pair—no one wants me either." I looked about for a stick to throw for him but in this highly disciplined garden, no such intruders were tolerated. I walked back up to the stone wall overlooking the drop to the river. It was a short wall, not even as tall as my waist, and beyond it was the untended embankment and scrubby bushes that fell off to the river—and some sticks. Keeping my eyes off the river and fixed on the ground before me, I sat on the rounded coping of the wall and swung my legs over.

"Careful, there!" Jean-Claude had just emerged, pipe in hand, from the chateau. Quickly he approached the wall, but I had already eased back over into the courtyard.

"I was careful. I was after this." And I threw the stick a short distance. Delighted, Charlot dashed after it.

"Just take care you don't toss that stick near *Grand-mère*'s flowers," he warned, "or there is no pardon that will save you from Madame la Guillotine."

I laughed. Being around Jean-Claude was good for my spirits. The clattering sound of tools thrown into a wheelbarrow turned my head. "Look, here comes the gardener to make it even lovelier." The man looked older than Moses but his step was spry. Following him today was a helper, a much younger man with dark hair almost hidden under a wide brim hat. Ignoring us, they began weeding.

Dark purple clouds bruised the sky above the river. Jean-Claude evaluated them as he drew on his pipe, giving me my silence. He was not one to fill the space between two people with a lot of empty words. It was rare, that sort of empathy in a man.

"Did you enjoy the aperitif?" he asked at last. I said I had. "It was a demi-sec. Women prefer it. Chateau Denon champagne has always been the driest, the Brut, and I don't plan to cut back on that. But a demi-sec would, I think, be a strong seller. That was the purpose of my trip to Dijon, to discuss with our distributor whether he thinks there is a market for a Denon demi-sec."

"I didn't know you could determine the sweetness in wine. I supposed it happened by itself."

"Nothing happens by itself in wine-making. Would you like to see our winery? I would be delighted to give you a tour of the caves and bottling facility, and the vineyard itself if you like."

It sounded like the beginning of an escape plan, except that I was not yet strong enough. "I should like it very much," I said. "Perhaps in a day or two."

A movement in an upstairs window caught my eye, and in the second before he drew back, I made out the figure of a man. Had

Alex been at the window, watching me? Watching us. I had the eerie feeling he knew what I had been thinking. Or was it merely Thonet, the butler? Had Alex left for Reims already?

"Ah, I meant to give you this," Jean-Claude continued, pulling the creased Dijon newspaper out from his large coat pocket. "Can you read French as well as you speak it?"

"Flatterer. My French isn't very good, but I think I can make out a newspaper if I go slowly. I'd like to read about that political demonstration, thank you very much."

"It looks as if the wind is chasing the clouds away." He pointed to the west where the sun was breaking through. "It seems there will be no rain today, after all. And that means I have work to do. *Au revoir, madame.* A pleasure to meet you."

He made a little bow and strode through the archway toward the fields. Newspaper in hand, I made my way to a wicker chair that had found its way back outside, and I settled in to read about the women's vote in France. Soon I was lost in the effort of translating.

By the time I finished the entire eight pages of news, the sun had burned off all the clouds and the afternoon had grown warm. My chair sat in the shade of the south wing beside the rose trellis that spread across the wall like a Chinese fan opened wide. I was quite comfortable. I may even have dozed a little. With a sigh, I leaned back, catching my hair on the thorns of the fragrant pink blossoms and disturbing a bumblebee at its labours. The angry insect menaced my face. Gingerly I waved the newspaper to frighten him away, but he was a persistent pest. His buzzing grew louder, his flight more threatening, when all of a sudden he attacked my head and became tangled in my hair.

In a panic, I dropped the newspaper, jumped up, and ran toward the fountain, swirling my hair about wildly and swatting at my head, trying to dislodge him without getting stung. I meant to duck my head under water as a last resort.

There was a crashing sound behind me that I was too busy to heed, so absorbed was I in the bumblebee melodrama. With a final shake of my hair, he and I were free. Immensely relieved, I glanced over my shoulder to see what had caused the long, loud clatter.

A cloud of dust surrounded my chair. Or what was left of it. My eyes lifted to the roof, then back down to the wicker chair. A number of heavy slate shingles had come loose and fallen from the roof, four stories above the ground. If I had been sitting there, they'd have killed me.

Shaking off my horrified stupor, I looked about the deserted courtyard. There was no one in sight. I continued to stand as motionless as a statue at Versailles, my mind replaying the crash again and again like a skipping record. I was nearly killed. I had just missed Death—a second time. If it hadn't been for the bumblebee, I'd be dead. Eva Johnson, Claire Smith, whoever she was, killed in a freak accident. At that moment, Lianne emerged from the kitchen with a pastry in her hand. Adding the pile of broken slate to my shocked expression, she came up with the right answer, squeaked, and rushed back inside. Moments later she emerged with the cook.

"Are you quite well, *madame?*" the cook asked, her eyes wide with worry.

I had stopped shaking by then. "Yes, yes, I am quite safe."

Thanking the cook for her concern, I made my way back to my room and lay down on the bed to think.

Later that evening, Jean-Claude came to inspect the damage. "The last time slates came loose, it was many years ago, during a fierce storm. I shall have the entire roof inspected," he told me. "Nothing like this must happen again."

Everyone was relieved I had not been hurt in the unfortunate accident.

The business in Reims must have taken longer than Alex anticipated, for he did not return to the chateau that night. I lay in the bed awake and alone for hours, listening for the sound of his footsteps, wanting to hear his side of the story about our lost baby. It was inconceivable that I could not remember such a momentous thing. Eva and I could not be the same person. Yet the evidence to the contrary overwhelmed me, and my persistent denials only fed the belief that I was delusional, or worse, schizophrenic. I longed for some way to learn more about this newly discovered illness of the brain. All I knew was that Swiss doctors were leaders in experimenting with treatments. And Switzerland was just over the border. It would be a simple thing for a husband to have his wife committed against her will.

The steady rain did nothing to improve my mood. Determined to build my stamina, I decided to walk indoors, through the dank corridors of the chateau, and call it exploration. Cécile had come and gone, so I changed from my dressing gown and slippers to a comfortable two-piece jersey knit that stretched a bit at the hips and waist. Then I took the lowest heels from my wardrobe and put them on. They were quite loose on my feet.

It dawned on me that this was the third pair of shoes that was too large. It was one thing to explain away a pair or two of stylish shoes that didn't fit very well; it was quite another to contemplate an entire wardrobe of shoes—at least fifty pairs, I estimated quickly—that were all too big. I snatched the closest example, a silver pump with glittering rhinestones, and slipped it on. Too big. The iridescent snakeskin pair beside it was too big. So were the mahogany leathers and the mauve velvet spikes and the sable boots. Either they had been made for a different foot, I thought grimly, or I had lost weight in my toes.

But how was I to interpret this new evidence that I was not Eva against the mounds of incontrovertible proof that I was? Make two columns, one for Eva, one for Claire, enter tally marks for each bit of evidence, and let the highest score win? That would clearly be Eva. But not one of my memories related to anything Alex had told me about my life. It was true that, as yet, I could recall only my childhood until my mother's death, but the doctor in Paris had been right—every day brought the return of more details. I thought about this until my head hurt, then I filched a pair of Alex's socks to make the low-heeled shoes fit, and set off to explore.

In the turret overlooking the Marne I found a circular staircase, its limestone steps well worn by centuries of clogs going up, clogs going down, hauling endless buckets of water, armloads of fuel, trays of food, and stacks of linens. Enough daylight seeped in through the leaded glass windows to warn me of the uneven steps. Still, I stumbled several times as I climbed to an iron-banded door at the top. Locked. Peering through the bars I could make out generations of debris piled high beneath massive arched beams that, like Atlas's shoulders, supported the weight of the roof. Crates, trunks, barrels, and hampers stacked high, mysterious shapes covered with old linens—I stood for long minutes imagining the treasures that lay forgotten in the midst of the junk, wishing myself beyond the iron grill where I could open and search and unpack and hunt through all that was there. Where did I get such a curiosity about old junk? An image of my father flickered into my head and disappeared again just as quickly.

Much of the top floor consisted of a maze of tiny rooms no longer occupied by the army of servants that once had been necessary to the smooth management of a country chateau. With beds made, floors not exactly clean but swept occasionally, pictures and fabrics faded but intact, and fireplaces that hadn't seen coal in decades, they looked like abandoned stage sets from the last century waiting patiently for the actors' return.

I wandered downstairs until the flowery scent told me I had reached the living quarters of *Grand-mère* and Cousin Pauline. I found myself in a delightful sitting room made cheerful even on this dreary afternoon with bouquets of fresh lilac and jasmine, potted plants, bright Turkish carpets, and everywhere family photographs framed in gleaming silver. The paintings on the walls drew my eyes. Scores of imperious Denon progenitors watched as I dared examine their faces for a resemblance to the current generation. Haughty noblemen, ladies, children, entire families, even beloved horses and dogs had been preserved for posterity by the artist's brush. I could see little resemblance to the current occupants until I came to a prominently placed portrait of a woman whose snapping eyes and sardonic smile reminded me of Alex. Then I realized I was looking at *Grand-mère* as a young woman. She had been very beautiful, very proud. She was still.

The Denon portrait gallery rivalled those of the Louvre. Landscapes, still lifes, religious paintings, sporting scenes, historicals, and even some of the more recent Impressionistic works that Alex had referred to when he talked of his mother, all the paintings that had not been destroyed by the Germans, hundreds of them, some probably collected by Madeleine in her artistic heyday. I bent closer to see if any were signed by Madeleine herself.

A cat's curiosity pulled me into a room off the corridor that was no larger than a dressing room. It was a peculiarly unstable room. The colours sparred with one another like roosters in a cockfight. None but a deranged mind, I thought, could have purposefully hung maroon toile draperies next to burnt orange wallpaper in a room with pink upholstery and a blood-red settee. To test the idea that had appeared out of nowhere, I turned up a corner of the drapery fabric and stretched apart the hem. Yes, I was as clever as Sherlock Holmes! The maroon colour had faded from a more pleasing red. I turned over a chair to look for a bit of protected fabric, found a piece unexposed to light that had once been a good deal darker. Time and a southern exposure had faded the entire room. Once everything had been red. I knew that dyes turned for chemical reasons as well as from sunlight—white always yellowed, madder turned from red to brown. Greens, the least stable colour, often slipped to blue. What colour had this hideous orange wallpaper been when it had first been pasted to the walls?

My eyes swept the room for a mirror or a picture or a whatnot cabinet behind which a pristine piece of wallpaper might hide. Even from a distance I recognized the painting in the corner as a Durer. It was a portrait, small but very fine, by Albrecht Durer, the greatest German artist of the Renaissance, painted sometime in the early 1500s. It captured my attention for several minutes until I remembered my purpose and lifted it up to check the colour of the wallpaper underneath.

"Planning your next heist?"

I jumped a foot in the air, which only made me look more suspicious. The subdued lighting did not obscure the grim lines of Alex's face, or the hard set of his jaw. "That one will bring you quite a sum."

"I-I-I have M-Madame Denon's p-p-permission to look around. I'm d-doing nothing wrong." My scarlet face turned even redder with fury that he could still make me stutter. I had conquered the affliction, conquered it completely, except when Alex was around to aggravate me.

"How else would you fund your escape? Oh, I know what you've been thinking; you're as transparent as clean glass. Grab some jewellery, tear a few paintings out of their frames, bribe your way out the gate—or will you show some imagination this time? Perhaps something more dramatic involving knotted sheets and windows—and you can run to your friends." I tried to push past him but he caught my arm in a tight grip. "As husband of a runaway wife, I have legal rights your silly suffragettes haven't dreamt of, plus the heartfelt sympathy of every man in France. I also have your passports, even the fakes secreted in the lining of your valise, and you can't get a new one without your husband's permission. You aren't going anywhere until I'm finished with you."

"And what then?" I asked, pulling out of his hurtful grasp.

"That depends on my mood at the time."

"What if I never remember where the paintings are?"

"You will."

"I don't think so. I'm not convinced I am Eva." He rolled his eyes and turned to go. Stung by his unjustified slander, I grabbed his sleeve and pulled him back. "Wait! I'm not saying it makes sense, only that something is very wrong. Just listen to me, once, without interrupting!" He glared at my hand until I dropped it, then folded his arms in a paradigm of boredom and stared at one of the landscapes behind me. "Like the doctor said would happen, I've remembered a lot over the past week. None of it—*not a single piece*—corresponds with anything you've told me about Eva."

"Nothing conflicts either."

"Everything conflicts! Eva was an orphan; I had a happy family. I remember my home, my parents, my school, my pony."

"As I've said before, it's possible your orphan story was a lie. Or that these memories are from films."

"I've been living in London and working for the suffrage movement," I protested.

"That's credible. You grew up in London. Now we know where you've been for at least a few of the past five years. As for the suffragettes, you would find their views on Free Love appealing."

"But none of my regained memories are of you or Lianne or Brazil or Paris."

"Absence of memories proves only that there are still memories to regain."

"But I speak French and Eva didn't." I folded my arms defiantly. Let him explain *that!*

"You've had five years to learn it."

"In London?"

"You've been in France a good part of those years. In the south. I have proof of that."

I pulled out my trump card and played it with a flourish. "And my shoes don't fit." I got nothing but a blank stare. "I mean, they are too big. I'm certain they were made for someone with a larger foot than mine."

"Now you're being absurd, Eva. Because some of your shoes have stretched out, you're concluding that you aren't my wife?"

Stretching. I hadn't considered that. Shoes could stretch. He saw the doubt in my face and said with a cajoling voice, "Eva, be reasonable."

"I am being reasonable. Some shoes could stretch, yes, but not all of them!"

"And have you tried all of them?"

"Well, not yet."

"So the few you tried seemed slightly too large?"

It sounded absurd when he phrased it like that, but I wouldn't back down. My returning strength enabled me to mount a more spirited defence, and I switched tactics again. "Think, Alex, did Eva have any sort of identifying mark, a mole, a birthmark, a scar, that would prove to you I am someone else?"

I saw him consider my question briefly and then shake his head, irritated that he had indulged me even that far. "Look here, Eva—"

Hearing that name again was the last straw. I flared up like a roman candle. "Once and for all, d-don't call me that! My n-name is C-Claire!"

"Look here," he said again, softly, like a doctor trying to calm a lunatic. "The cause of this confusion is not so hard to understand. You have lived with so many lies and so many aliases for so long that your mind has twisted fact with fancy. In your current state, even *you* don't know what is true anymore. Some people believe that each of us has an exact double in this world. I do not. But suppose it is true, suppose Eva is your exact double, or your twin sister. Why were you wearing her wedding ring in Paris? Why were you carrying her handbag, staying at her hotel, and using her passport?"

I felt dead. It always came back to those incontrovertible facts.

"Do you remember what you said to me in the hospital, about the playing cards?" I nodded. "Tell me again."

"It was nothing much. Only that the four kings are named for great kings in history, and one of them is Alexander the Great."

"Those were your exact words when we first met in Monte

Carlo. When we were introduced at the Casino, and you heard my name, you called me Alexander the Great and flipped the King of Clubs across the baccarat table. No one has ever said that to me in my life. In the hospital last week, similar circumstances triggered a similar retort. When you made that remark a second time, I started to believe in your amnesia. The strawberries were the final proof."

I sank into a chair and dropped in face into my hands. "We met at Monte Carlo?" I asked, unable to raise my eyes from the floor. "In April of 1923."

It was not a pretty story. He enjoyed telling it.

We had been introduced in the Casino, where I made it plain that I was available for the asking. Within hours, I was drunk and in his bed, a pattern that repeated itself daily for the next two weeks. I gathered it was nothing unusual for modern girls to throw themselves at the rich playboy who drove a flashy motorcar. He certainly thought nothing of it.

Then he left, making the South Atlantic crossing from Bordeaux to be home for his sister's wedding. When I learned I was pregnant, I followed him to São Paulo, demanding a large sum for an abortion or, if that offended his Catholic sensibilities, an even larger amount to bear his child and surrender it to him. After a doctor had pronounced the pregnancy genuine and the probable birth date within the correct time frame, Alex decided he did not want his son or daughter raised by a trollop and her lover *du jour*. He opted for marriage to make the child legitimate. The family honour was at stake—DeSequeyra men had for generations held firmly against the begetting of bastards, which I gathered translated not to abstinence but to the selection of one's lovers from the large pool of married women. There was a private wedding in the tradition of morganatic marriages, where the marriage is legal but unofficial, the child is legitimate but has no claims on the family's titles or fortunes, and the lower-class wife remains in the background. Alex's unspoken plan was to pay off the wife, annul the marriage, and bring up the child in comfortable seclusion at *Casa DeSequeyra* in Brazil while he continued his fast-lane life of racing and gambling in Europe. If, however, there were reasons to doubt his paternity, an annulment would follow and the offenders would be shipped back to France on the next boat. Steerage, no doubt.

"You left a month later, shortly after I had the doctor give you a blood test and you learned what it meant."

"What did it mean?" I had never heard of such a test.

"It is a new way to determine paternity. Scientists discovered that there are four types of blood. They are called A, B, AB, and O. I am type O, as are you. When the blood type of both parents is known, that of the child can be predicted. Our child could only have type O. If you bore a child with any other type blood, I could not be its father. I have no doubt you read the writing on the wall and ran off before the tests could confirm paternity. I expect you had several lovers at the same time—perhaps you honestly did not know which of us was the father, and I was merely the best prospect. Your decision to leave was financially astute—you stole as much or more than I would have paid you had the child been mine."

I absconded. There had been no miscarriage—that was the story he had told young Lianne who had expressed great concern about the whereabouts of her little brother or sister. "She was too young—and still is—to know of such things as abortions." I had waited until Alex was away at one of the distant *fazendas*, snatched the jewellery, pried the paintings out of their frames, and fled. During my stay in São Paulo, I had managed to alienate Lianne, *Grand-mère*, brother Manuel, and every servant on the estate, so there was no great grief when I was discovered missing. By the time a maid noticed that four of the frames hanging in the ballroom were minus their canvasses and Alex had checked the jewellery chest, I was long gone. Private investigators had been on my trail ever since to recover what they could of the art.

"And the baby?" I asked.

"At the time, I presumed you had rid yourself of it, as it could not profit you." His eyes narrowed. "Is that not true?"

I shook my head numbly. I remembered nothing of this. And yet, deep in my head was a glimmer of memory, something about a little boy.

"The investigators traced you to Paris a month ago, straight from a posh London hotel, and had only just discovered your name in the hotel register when the police arrived, inquiring about a woman who had been assaulted on the *rive gauche* the previous night. I came immediately from Lausanne."

Profoundly humiliated, I returned alone to my room. Theft, extortion, lies, baby selling, promiscuity, abortion . . . my list of transgressions was long. How could I have done such shocking things? I lay on the bed against the pile of pillows and stared into the cold fireplace while I tried to make sense of my circumstances.

Yes, escape from Chateau Denon had been my plan, but escape was out of the question until I was stronger. The confrontation with Alex had left my limbs trembling like jelly. And not to be overlooked were the bald facts that I had no money, no friends or relations to borrow from or stay with, no job, and no home. I didn't have coins for bus fare to the nearest city, let alone cash for a train ticket or meals or a hotel room. London may as well have been the moon, and I couldn't remember the name of a single acquaintance there. If I could get as far as Paris, I could throw myself on the mercy of the British embassy, but without a passport, I couldn't even prove I was English. Maybe I wasn't.

From my window I could see a bit of life in the village. The rain had stopped but a brisk wind had come up from the south. A boy ran home with several *baguettes* clutched to his chest, a dog snarled at a thin cat in the main square, the French flag at the *mairie* whipped against the pole so hard I feared it would tear. There was no police station in Ranton-sur-Marne—I knew that from Cécile. No place to go for help, even if I could get out of the chateau. Thoroughly dejected, I watched two women fill their tin pails with water at the fountain, gesturing loudly with their hands as they waited. In a village like this, too small for a police station, problems would be petty ones and the inhabitants would handle them according to tradition. If only there had been a police station, I could have made my way there, somehow.

Suddenly I straightened. There was no police station, but there was a *mairie*. I studied the flag for some time, my heart pounding, thinking that every French village, no matter how insignificant, had its town hall and a government functionary of some sort. If I could get to that flagpole, I could ask them to call the police for me. Surely if any place in Ranton had a telephone, it would be there. Surely someone at the British embassy could locate William Smith. And any day now, I would remember more that would help find him.

I had only to escape from the chateau walls.

4 THE VILLAGE

"Bonjour, mesdames." Jean-Claude hailed us as he strode through
the shade of the archway into the full spring sun of the courtyard
where Cécile and I were enjoying the morning. Yesterday's rain
had continued through the night, leaving the air smelling as damp
and clean as laundry on the line.

"You have worked wonders, Madame Renaud. Your patient
blooms like a flower."

Cécile nodded solemnly. After they had agreed that today's
sunshine was an agreeable improvement over yesterday's storm
and that the fields had received just the right amount of moisture to
sustain growth for another week, Cécile resumed her knitting—a
red shawl for old Madame Flohr—and Jean-Claude addressed me
in his formal way.

"Would it please you this morning to make an excursion to the
winery?"

Cécile responded for me. "Madame DeSequeyra is not to leave
the courtyard."

"Yes, I understand," he replied, with a look that told me he did.
"But it is a short walk to the winery, and I take full responsibility.
Of course, the invitation extends to you as well, *madame*." She
pursed her lips, then stuffed the knitting into her satchel. It meant
yes.

Elated at the prospect of piercing the ramparts of Chateau
Denon, I took Jean-Claude's arm.

We made an odd-looking trio as we passed old Lucien at the

gate: Jean-Claude in his boots and baggy blue trousers streaked with dried mud and Cécile in her clogs and dark, indistinguishable layers of blouse, tunic, and skirt could have stepped out of a Brueghel painting, while I, waltzing along in my fur-trimmed couturier ensemble and alligator pumps, felt absurdly miscast. Not for the first time, I wished I had some practical clothes. And some larger sizes—I was eating my way out of my wardrobe. If I didn't find a seamstress who could make alterations, I'd soon be going about in my dressing gown.

Dirt streets packed hard by centuries of horses' hoofs, thick cart wheels, and coarsely shod feet had been transformed by yesterday's rain to a minefield of muck and mire. Jean-Claude held on to help me navigate the gentle slope and around the puddles.

"Gallant as Sir Walter Raleigh," I teased, and when he did not know the story, I told him of the English nobleman who laid his cloak across the mud for Queen Elizabeth.

"What? And ruin a good cloak? Why did he not just pick her up? I don't want you to destroy your shoes. They look quite fine. Is that the new style, wearing them with men's socks?"

I laughed. "Chic, isn't it? But it's the only way I can keep them on my feet. I seem to have lost weight in the most unlikely places. And I'm gaining it in the worst places, my waist and my . . . uh, never mind."

He grinned like a little boy. "The price of our chef's fine cooking is your flapper figure, eh? Not to worry, I don't think men care much for the flapper figure." It occurred to me I had no idea what sort of figure Alex fancied in a woman. Did he find me more attractive now that I was gaining a little weight, or was he the sort who favoured the flat-chested, boyish look so popular with the fashionable set? Guiltily, I slammed the door on my thoughts, embarrassed at the direction they took when left to wander on their own. I cared nothing for that crude man's opinion. Nothing whatsoever.

As we rounded a corner Cécile announced that she had seen enough winemaking in her lifetime. "Old Madame Flohr lives just down this lane. I think I will stop in and see if she needs anything, then run home to pick up some more yarn. I'll meet you back at the chateau."

Jean-Claude promised not to keep me out too long—an hour or

so would be enough to see the winery and the fields. She nodded and set off down the middle of the lane, heedless of the mud. The moment we entered the chilly warehouse, I wished she had left me the red shawl she was knitting.

"The temperature varies little inside, summer to winter. You see, the rooms here are cut into the hill, into the rock." For the moment, I forgot the cold, looking about in amazement at the amount of work it must have taken to hack out such large underground chambers from solid rock. Jean-Claude assured me it was quite common. "Limestone is everywhere in this region. It is in the chalky soil that grows the best grapes for making champagne. Much of the winemaking and storage goes on under the ground because of the constant temperature. This tufa rock is soft, not too difficult to cut out. There are miles of these caves in Champagne. Even those of us who grew up here do not know them all."

He slipped his jacket over my shoulders. Its warm tobacco scent mingled with the aroma of acrid fruit that permeated the building. "You are seeing everything backwards, I'm afraid. This is the end of the process that starts in the fields. Here in the front where the light is good, we do the bottling and corking. That machine is where the man fixes the wire coverings to help hold the cork against the pressure of the champagne."

"To prevent it from popping out until it is opened at the restaurant?"

"Exactly. As you may know, the same black pinot noir grape that produces the noble reds of Burgundy also produces champagne, but in this part of France, it yields a more acidic wine suitable for blending and sugaring." I must have looked lost, for he asked, "Do you know how wine is made?"

"I thought white wine came from green grapes and red wine from red."

He laughed, but it was an affectionate laugh, not a mocking one. "When the grape skin pulp is left with the juice during fermentation, the resulting wine will be red; if the skins are removed, the wine will be white. The grapes are harvested in September and the new wine is stored in barrels, here, for three or four years." He held up the lantern and I could see a large cave with oak barrels stacked to the ceiling. The pungent moist scent of fermenting grapes overpowered my senses, and the eerie shadows danced as our lanterns moved. "There are many other storage caves like this, full of barrels or bottles, some empty, most full." He pointed to the back of the cave, where I saw an opening to another cave beyond this one. And another beyond that, no doubt, like a giant honeycomb. I shivered, and not because of the cool temperature. There was something darkly sinister about these caves that made me want to run back to the sunshine.

We made our way into a side grotto where the rough-hewn ceiling would force most men to stoop. Everywhere were wooden racks, so close together only a thin person could squeeze between them without touching the bottles.

"Here we put the bottles neck down, and shake and tilt each one every day."

"All these bottles? Every day?"

He nodded. "Then comes the *dégorgement*. This is the trickiest part. A man must be highly skilled to ease off the cork, one bottle at a time. This permits the sediment to shoot out like a bullet from a gun, then he adds a liqueur of wine and sugar to sweeten the contents."

We retraced our steps, stopping to peer into each lonely cave until we arrived back to the front rooms where windows made the lanterns unnecessary. Absurdly glad to reach the daylight, I extinguished my lantern. "Where are all the workers?"

"Tradition calls for bottling to begin at the first full moon in March, so it is finished now. This is a slow time in the wine-making business, the time for me to tend the office and for the men to tend the fields. I am ordering new labels that vary slightly from our previous design, and there is always correspondence to catch up and orders to fill."

"You need a secretary."

"Shall you be one for me?"

"Not I!" I said hastily. Something flickered in my mind like a scene from a film. I didn't want to be a secretary. I didn't know how to take shorthand or use a typewriter. I didn't want to work in an office all day. It was not the career for a bachelor girl like me. I had said so many times before. I tried to capture the thought but it trickled away like water through my fingers.

We stepped outside, blinking in the bright sunlight, and I handed Jean-Claude back his jacket, wondering briefly that so charming a man had not married. "If you don't mind, I'll visit the fields another day."

He looked closely at my face and seemed a bit concerned at what he saw. "Of course. I do not mean to tire you." As we walked slowly back up toward the chateau, he chattered like a tour guide on holiday, pointing out the village school, the original Gothic bell tower, the *boulanger* where the best *brioches* in all of France were made, the marketplace that was filled two days a week with farmers from the outlying countryside, the *Café de la Paix* where men gathered to share the news, and the water fountain where women gathered to gossip. Seen through his eyes, the shabby village took on the glow of quaint tradition, like a much-loved antique cradle that had rocked generations of children.

"Oh-ho! So the men *share news* but the women *gossip*?" He grinned, and I knew he was deliberately baiting me. If I had a brother—did I have a brother?—I would want him to be like Jean-Claude. When we reached the moat, I thanked him for the excursion.

"It was my pleasure."

"I don't know what you've been told . . ." I began awkwardly and when I faltered, he took up the sentence without the slightest embarrassment.

"About you and Alex? Only that you had left him years ago with some items that were disputed, and that he has found you now. I hope the issue will be settled to everyone's satisfaction."

"He's waiting for my memory to return so I can tell him where the paintings are."

"These paintings are very valuable. Especially his mother's."

"I supposed that one to be worth relatively little."

"In money, yes. Madeleine was good painter, not a great one, or so it seems. But valued in sentiment, it is priceless. It shows her two oldest sons, Philippe, who died in the war, and Alex, playing on the beach at Deauville, where the family spent holidays in happier times. And it is one of only three by Madeleine in existence. Unfortunately, the rest of her work was destroyed by the Germans when they burned the Denon chateau on the Aisne River."

"I had not realized that." Or had I? Had I taken that painting by mistake as Alex thought, or because I knew it would hurt his heart rather than his pocketbook?

"Perhaps the wrong is not all on one side." He spied a piece of broken bottle glass on the ground and made a great deal of picking it up. "The DeSequeyras are hard to love. What will you do?"

"When I've recovered, you mean? I'm sure Alex will give me a divorce as soon as I remember where the paintings are. I'm still hoping I'll remember more about my family or some friends, so I have someplace to go while I look for a job."

"Not a secretary's job?" he grinned. I shook my head. "If you need money, I have a little."

The unexpected kindness brought the sting of tears to my eyes. "Thank you, Jean-Claude. You don't know how much that means to me."

And there was that versatile Gallic shrug that said, *It's nothing.*

We crossed the drawbridge, nodded to Lucien at the gate, and entered the courtyard when the church bell rang ten times, which meant it was probably no later than half past ten. I said goodbye to Jean-Claude and watched him return to his desk.

I rested by the fountain for a while, breathing the perfume and watching two scrawny cats chase through the garden. From outside the walls, the scrape of a cart's wheels on stone pavement and the clip-clop of a dray horse's hooves grew louder until a wagon rounded the corner and pulled into the courtyard. It was the ice delivery. I wandered toward the kitchen wing and watched the driver throw back the canvas cover, drag a large block of ice off the wagon bed, wipe off the sawdust, heave it onto his back, and disappear into the kitchen. I looked around the courtyard and saw no one.

A few moments later, the iceman reappeared. Without glancing at me, he hauled out a second block, wiped off the sawdust, and carried it inside. I looked up at the second floor windows and saw no one.

It was too soon, I wasn't well enough, and if I thought about it for more than a second, I'd lose my nerve. So I didn't think. I climbed onto the cart, burrowed beneath the canvas, and squeezed between the chunks of sawdust-coated ice where I could not be seen.

Just in time. Seconds later, the iceman returned. He tucked in the edges of the canvas, swung himself up onto the wagon's seat, and with a slap of the reins and a click of his tongue, coaxed the horse into a slow walk toward the arch. My heart was pounding so hard I didn't even notice the chill. I was surprised he couldn't hear it over the horse's hooves.

It all happened so fast, I had no time to consider what I was doing. It had been my plan to have a plan. I had nothing.

In no time, the iceman reached his next customer downhill from the gate. He lurched to a stop and flung back the edge of the canvas. With a grunt, he dragged out the nearest block of ice, wiped off the sawdust, and heaved it onto his back. I heard a gruff voice greeting him, and a door slam, and I scrambled out of the cart.

I was free. It had been shockingly easy.

I stood at the foot of the hill, looking up at the chateau perched on top of the village like the decoration on a wedding cake. I could not see the *mairie* but its flagpole with the tricolour fluttering guided me through the narrow streets. I made my way quickly, nodding to a bent old woman in black. I could feel her disapproval at my uncovered head, bobbed hair, and bright lavender skirt hemmed short. The odd foreign woman would not go unnoticed in Ranton.

"*Bonjour, monsieur*," I greeted the lone *fonctionnaire* in my best French as I stepped over a dusty dog baking in the sun. I tried to appear calm so he would not think I had escaped from a lunatic asylum, but even my abbreviated story sounded like something from a lurid novel. I needed the police, I told him. I needed them at once.

The nearest police station was in Troyes, said the small man behind the large desk. A motorbike could bring the policeman within the hour if it were necessary.

I told him I was English and afraid for my life. I had been kidnapped by a man who mistakenly thought he was my husband, and had been holding me prisoner in the chateau. I needed the protection of the police and the help of the British embassy in Paris while this was sorted out. "Please call the police at once," I begged. "There is no time to lose. I shall soon be missed."

His face betrayed no emotion as he listened to my improbable tale. His eyes raked over my clothes, then searched the dingy room as if looking for directions written on the walls. Decision-making, I gathered, was not his *forte*. Would *madame* please wait in the other room? *Madame* would not. I wanted to hear him make the phone call.

Reluctantly, he reached for the handset. I heard him contact the exchange operator, then ask for the police station in Troyes. After a moment, he spoke with someone there, requesting an officer. He listened a while, spoke again, and returned the handset to its cradle. "Now, *madame*, there will be a policeman soon. You can wait here."

I sat awkwardly on the hard bench, swatted at a persistent fly, and watched the clerk as he went back to work at his typewriter, click-click, click-click, laboriously with two fingers, as if each click cost him a week's wages. Typing was not his *forte* either.

Time crawled. My nerves were stretched taut. Nearby the church bell rang once, which was absurd since it couldn't possibly be one o'clock—it had just rung ten times no more than an hour ago. The parish priest, as if sensing my exasperation, swung on the bell cord eleven more times, which meant that it was either eleven o'clock or noon, depending upon whether you counted the first chime as part of the whole. The bell was obviously intended to signal the break in the school day, for within minutes, the shouts of students could be heard as they swarmed out of the schoolhouse like bees from a hive.

Within moments, a blue smocked youngster of about ten bounded noisily up the steps into the office. Giving me a curious stare, she kissed the clerk, called him Papa, and babbled something I couldn't catch about her teacher. With his hands full of papers, he could not give her the hug she expected, but he accompanied her to the door, pledging to be home for dinner as soon as the English lady was taken care of. The child skipped off. Soon enough I realized he had used the diversion to hand her a typed message, and that she had delivered it to the chateau.

Alex arrived shortly thereafter.

He really was the consummate actor. Not by the slightest expression could anyone but me tell Alex was livid. An easy smile and gracious manner reassured the lowly clerk that he had done exactly the right thing. Poor *madame* had been much confused ever since the terrible blows to her head in Paris—see her broken arm and the scar above her eye?—and although she was improving every day, there was still, alas!, the occasional relapse. By this evening, when she felt more like herself, she would call him to apologize for the trouble.

He gripped my arm tightly and steered me out of the *mairie*. The narrow streets were deserted—Ranton's population had retreated for the midday meal—but windows and doors stood open all day during good weather. He spoke in English, in words that spat like machine gun fire, sharp and deadly. "I can only imagine what favours you granted Jean-Claude to persuade him to look the other way!"

"What a filthy mind you have! Jean-Claude knows nothing about this! I came out—"

"Yes?" he asked, looking as if he would like to choke me.

I clamped my lips shut.

"Never mind," he said. His jaw was clenched; so were his fists. "I'll find out soon enough, you damned fool."

At that, he raised one fist and slammed it into the palm of his other hand. Instinctively, I flinched. My loose shoe caught in the gluey mud and I slipped forward, stumbling against a stone doorstep, trying to protect my broken left hand as I fell on it. Alex grabbed my good arm, nearly wrenching my shoulder from its socket.

"D-Don't t-touch me!" I shouted in panic, pulling away from him hard. Surprised, he let go and I landed on my knees in the mud, trapped against a dirt-spattered wall like a cornered fox as the hounds closed in. I looked wildly up and down the lane, hoping against hope for a burly farmer, the parish priest, an earthquake, a miracle. "If you so much as lay a finger on me, I swear I'll scream blue murder until the whole town comes out to watch."

Alex looked at me through narrowed eyes without moving a muscle, without blinking an eyelash, as if he were seeing me for the first time. As I watched, the examination turned inward and it seemed he was no longer aware of my presence, that he had slipped into some distant place where he was as vulnerable to emotion as the rest of us. A pained expression passed over his features, and in that instant, I thought I caught a glimpse of a man with a capacity for tenderness and humility. The loud slam of a door down the street called him back. Slowly, without lifting those obsidian eyes from mine, he extended one hand, palm up.

"A thousand pardons, *madame*. May I help you up?" he asked softly.

Disoriented by his sudden transformation from tormentor to gentleman, I could make no move.

"I am sorry my intentions were misunderstood. I'm not going to harm you, *madame*. I was only trying to help you across the mud."

Was it true? Had I misread it all? Had I really seen that flash of compassion? He had meant to steady me, not hit me? Perhaps so. After all, I assured myself cynically that if Alexander DeSequeyra were planning to beat his wife, it wouldn't be in broad daylight in a public square. He'd have ample opportunity once inside the chateau's thick walls. I swallowed hard and nodded. He helped me stand up and sluiced off the clumps of filth from my skirt. Heedless of the mess, he lifted me into his arms and continued, his face carefully expressionless, up the hill to the chateau.

"You won't get away with this," I blustered. "The police will find me. They are on their way from Troyes."

"No, they aren't."

"The clerk in the *mairie* telephoned to send a man for me."

"No, he didn't."

"I heard him place the call."

"That was a ruse. He lifted the headset but his finger remained on the cradle. It saved your life. The police are the last people we want to see at present."

"Speak for yourself."

"I am speaking for you. You are wanted for murder."

Confusion greeted us in the courtyard.

A sporty Delage skiff was parked against the pair of lion-rampant statues that guarded the main entrance to the chateau. Its top was down, but the wind hadn't dared rearrange even a hair on the head of the fashion model who was posing beside it like an actress in a motorcar advertisement. *Grand-mère* was standing at the foot of the stairs, leaning on her cane, beside a beaming Cousin Pauline. Lianne was skipping around the little vehicle, begging to drive it *just* a little ways if she promised to be *very* careful. The gardener rested on his hoe, his face shaded beneath a floppy-brimmed straw hat. Charlot bounced about in the excitement, making little yips.

"Good God," said Alex. "It's Danielle." Instead of putting me on the ground, he tightened his grip and walked closer, as if he could not quite believe his eyes.

It could not have been coincidence—she was dressed to match the Delage. Both wore a dark green and beige costume, sleek and stylishly cut, only the motorcar's top was down while her's—a dramatic cloche hat festooned with blowsy ostrich plumes—was perched firmly on her head. She looked like somebody's pampered mistress. "Somebody" looked surprised to see her.

Sauntering toward us, she stripped off her driving gloves in a manner that could only be described as provocative and gave a catlike smirk. "Alex, darling. I'm none too soon, I see." She took in my appearance, her pencilled eyebrows arching delicately as she raked me from messy head to muddy toe. "Any later and you'd have done away with her again. *Ciao*, darling, I'm Danielle. You mustn't let him bully you like this. Learn to fight back. I did."

Alex made no move to put me down or to explain why I looked as if I had just finished a hard day digging potatoes. "What are *you* doing here?" he demanded, his voice heavy with suspicion. Evidently the man treated his mistress no better than he treated his wife. For a moment, I felt sorry for her. The moment passed.

"Such an effusive welcome! I'd shake hands, but you look rather . . . ugh." She wrinkled her nose in distaste. "I heard you had recovered your extraordinary wife, and I seized the chance to have a look before she vanishes again. I postponed Lisbon and motored over to see for myself. Aren't you going to introduce us?"

"Excuse us," he said curtly. Manoeuvring past Danielle, he carried me into the chateau, up the staircase, and directly to our bedchamber. Never mind the woman, I fumed. It was the earlier bombshell that was still exploding inside my head. The moment we were alone, I erupted.

"You made that up to intimidate me! Admit it!" He did not deign to respond, merely set me down, looked askance at my filthy clothes, and began rummaging through my wardrobe. "Very well, tell me about this supposed murder! I don't believe you anyway, but tell me!"

"Later. It's time for dinner."

"I am not going anywhere until I know."

He closed the drawer and spun around to face me, his lips grim with suppressed fury. "Last February, my people learned of a Madeleine Denon painting of a beach scene for sale at an insignificant art gallery in Marseille. It was 'Memories.' Our investigation led to a woman who was disposing of several paintings she inherited from her elderly father who had been killed during a burglary the previous autumn. He was at his villa in Cap Ferrat when it was broken into and had the bad judgment to confront the intruders. There was a struggle. He was killed by a blow to the head. The police investigation revealed that you had sold the painting to him over a year ago."

"And how does selling a painting make me a murderess?" I demanded indignantly.

He paused to take a cigarette from a gold case and light it, then began pacing as he inhaled deeply. "The police have now noticed a number of similar art thefts along the Riviera over the past few years. Seemingly unrelated crimes, all had a common detail—an art purchase from one Eva Johnson, or one of your aliases, some months before the burglary. And while the police are not interested in domestic disputes, they are very, very interested in homicide."

My initial anger deflated as rapidly as a balloon, to be replaced by a profound uneasiness that tightened my throat. "I don't understand," I whispered, fearing that I understood all too well.

"The French police understood. You and your lover infiltrated the Riviera's society once again, as you had done when I met you. Your purpose was clear—to work a swindle. You could not sell my paintings to knowledgeable art collectors without arousing suspicion, so you decided to target wealthy people who knew little about art. Where better to find an international array of wealthy people? You became friendly with the buyer, visited his home, and learned the location of his valuables. Months later, when the connection between you and a robbery would be too distant to be remarked, you broke into the house and stole back the original painting along with other objects that could be sold in turn to the next victim. The police believe you did this at least four times during the past five years. It could have continued unnoticed indefinitely if you hadn't made the mistake of breaking into Monsieur Daudier's home while he was there."

"I don't believe you. The police came to see me when I was in hospital. They knew my name, and they could have arrested me there if I were wanted for questioning."

"Ahh, the French police . . . well-intentioned, poorly equipped." He tapped his temple to demonstrate where the equipment was lacking. "Back at the hospital, they were thinking of victims, not criminals. Poor *madame*, the delicate English woman, attacked in the streets of Paris. Paris is a big city with a big police force. There is probably one office for homicides and another, far away on a different floor, for robberies. No one would think to check the name of the victim of an assault against the list of wanted criminals. Eventually someone might have stumbled onto the fact that there was an Eva Johnson on two different desks. I had to get you out of Paris before that occurred, or I would lose you to the police who care nothing for the recovery of my paintings. If it were not for the information locked in your head, I would have identified you myself and let the police deal with you." He pulled a dress from the armoire, a frothy creation with slashed sleeves and silk roses pinned to the shoulders and around its loose drop waist. "Come, I'll help you change."

I felt sick to my stomach. "That won't be necessary. I'm going to bed."

"The hell you are. You'll come down to dinner."

"You've gone mad. Dinner with the family, as if this whole escapade had not happened? Sorry, I'm not that good an actress. I can't pretend to be friendly at a table where everyone's tittering about me." He came closer. "No!" I said sharply, realizing with mounting alarm that he was going to do exactly what he wanted, he always did, never mind anyone else. Having an excess of money and celebrity made people think they were superior to those with less.

But he stopped an arm's length away. "Eva," he said, pausing between each word for emphasis. "Let me help you change from these filthy clothes."

His manner was firm but gave me to understand that he would not touch me without my permission. In the time it took me to draw two calming breaths deep into my lungs, I reasoned that it was better to hold my head high and face whatever was thrown at me than to cower in my room like a frightened lamb among wolves. "Very well," I said softly, lifting my chin a fraction. "I'll go." It could well have been my imagination, but I thought I detected a spark of admiration in his eye.

I stood quietly while he unbuttoned the back of the expensive dress that Coco Chanel never expected to see clotted with muck from some remote village street and let him guide me into the bathroom. I sat on a bench in my underclothes while he unfastened my laddered stockings from their garters and gently washed the mud off my legs, pretending I felt nothing when his warm fingers brushed against my thigh or when his palm rested on my knee. The intimacy unnerved me more than I cared to admit.

"Is your hand hurt?"

I jumped. "What? Oh, my hand, yes." I examined the dirty splint. "No, I think not." I could not meet his eye. My skin tingled and an army was marching through my head.

He got the dress over my head and fastened the tiny hooks, then helped me with a new pair of silk stockings.

"I trust you can do something with your hair. I am no help in that capacity."

I made some response and edged toward the dressing table. As he changed into a beautifully tailored dinner jacket, I did the best I could with my hairbrush and one hand, and applied a little confidence to my cheeks and lips. He regarded me from behind through the mirror, waiting until I was finished before asking, "What you told the clerk at the *mairie* about me intending to kill you, that was exaggeration, was it not? For sympathy?" I remained silent enough for that to be an answer in itself. He gave a deep sigh and continued softly. "You are not in danger of physical harm, Eva. I have never struck a woman in my life. I don't intend to begin now. You must believe me?"

"I have no reason to believe you or not believe you. I've only known you a fortnight."

He stiffened. "*Tiens*, Eva, if I wanted you dead, you'd be dead. I've had plenty of chances. Don't be melodramatic."

"I didn't think you were trying to kill me, at present. You'd lose any chance at recovering your property. It's what happens afterwards that concerns me, after I've given you what you want and I am worth nothing to you."

He considered what I had said for several moments. I believe it was the first time he had made any effort to understand my position here.

"Perhaps I should apologize. I did not mean to frighten you in this manner. Or perhaps I did, but that was before I believed your amnesia was real and your stutter not an act. I didn't understand that you . . . had changed. You must not leave *le chateau Denon,* do you understand? You are here for your own safety, until you are well. After I know where the paintings are, I will leave you with money to get to London or Rome . . . but for God's sake, don't go to the police with your story or neither of us will get what we want."

My freedom for his paintings. A simple enough bargain if he held to it. I had neither choice nor leverage at my command.

"So you think I'm a murderer, as well as a thief?"

"To be honest, I don't think you're strong enough to bludgeon a man to death—even an elderly one—by yourself. More probably it was your lover who struck Daudier, with your help or connivance. But the police are not apt to make such fine distinctions and you were undoubtedly an accomplice. The guillotine is the fate of murderers, my dear, and France, unlike your native land, still enjoys public executions."

The family had already gathered when Alex and I entered the room. Lianne squatted on a low stool as she tried to teach Charlot to shake hands, and Jean-Claude was talking earnestly with Danielle. I had forgotten Danielle. The talk of murder had driven her right out of my mind. Her eyes met mine. The rivalry I expected to find in them was not there.

As if he had not seen her in the courtyard only half an hour earlier, Alex greeted her with three quick kisses to the cheek, then introduced me with all the old-world formality of a courtier making a presentation to the queen.

"Danielle, may I present my wife, Eva? Eva, my sister, Danielle Blanchard."

Fortunately everyone was looking at Danielle for her reaction, and no one noticed my jaw drop in astonishment. So she was not, after all, his mistress *du jour*. Why had I jumped to that conclusion? I pressed my lips together, feeling absurdly relieved. Danielle turned to Alex and, carelessly knocking the ashes from her cigarette into an eighteenth-century Limoges vase, said, "Not Blanchard, darling. I've lost the mean little beast forever. I've reverted to DeSequeyra—until I bring down my next quarry."

Other than dark hair, there was little resemblance between brother and sister. Looking very smart in her dinner costume, a grey pleated sport suit with feathered shoulders and enormous pearl buttons across its double-breasted front, she examined me through narrowed eyes that had seen it all before. A few years back, when ingénues were all the rage, Danielle had no doubt affected a wide-eyed naiveté, but now that no modern woman would dream of looking innocent even in her coffin, she was a chic personification of all the vices. Transferring her long ivory cigarette holder from her right hand to her left, she blew a cloud of smoke out the corner of her mouth and bestowed on me a rather limp hand to shake.

"And who shall have the honour of being number three?" Alex did not trouble to disguise the sardonic twist of his lips.

"I'm in hot pursuit of a Portuguese this time. My first two husbands queered me for good on Brazilians and Frenchmen. God, the world is full of ineligible men. Every one of them seems to have more money than brains or more brains than money. The war robbed us of all the best."

Grand-mère frowned but said nothing.

"What brings you home, Danielle darling?" fluttered Cousin Pauline.

"Why, to see you two dears, of course," she replied. "And to meet my *belle soeur*, Eva, before she disappears again. My dear, you are easily the most intriguing person in the family. I can't wait to hear how Alex recaptured you in Paris!"

Grand-mère's frown deepened. Alex showed no inclination to share the story with his sister, at least in my presence. It made no difference: Lianne would fill in the details of my depravity as soon as my presence no longer inhibited the free flow of conversation. But Danielle wouldn't leave it alone.

"I heard you had recovered 'Memories,'" she said to her brother.

Alex grunted an affirmation.

I must have looked like a carp with my mouth opening and closing so often. This time Alex noticed before I could react. Of course, he would have purchased his mother's painting back from the art gallery in Marseilles as soon as it came available. I should have assumed that without being told. The cost would not have been great; it was sentiment that made this particular painting valuable. It was the other three that were worth untold thousands of pounds.

"Would you like an aperitif, Danielle?" asked Jean-Claude as the butler appeared. "Last year's *brut* is one of the best we've ever produced."

She pulled a last drag on the cigarette and shook her head as she exhaled. All this smoke was starting to make my head ache. "No, darling, a cocktail, *s'il te plaît*. A martini. Does Thonet know how to mix them?" I was surprised Danielle bothered with the butler's name and disgusted with her manner of speaking through him as if he were too stupid to answer for himself. Servants were not people to the rich. The thought no sooner lodged in my brain than I recognized it for what it was: a telling bit of prejudice that effectively excluded me from ever having been a member of the upper class. No duke's daughter here—it was rather more likely that I had worked as a parlour maid in some posh household. That would explain my resentment as well as my familiarity with fine furnishings and antiquities. Uncomfortably, I realized it also lent support to the theory that I was an orphan, since most orphans were trained to go into service.

"Yes, I'm sure he does," replied Jean-Claude, "don't you, Thonet?" Somehow I knew, although Jean-Claude's face showed no sign, that he was disappointed in Danielle's choice.

"I'll have champagne, please," I said, and then felt silly. It was not as if I could make up for Danielle's slight with my own selection.

"So Alex found you in a hospital, nearly dead. Lianne says some sailors fished you out of the Seine, and you can't remember a thing. Such an exciting story—and so very convenient."

Lianne gave her father a guilty glance. He didn't seem bothered by her gossiping with Danielle, but I was. I didn't like these people knowing more about me than I knew myself. I didn't like them talking about me behind my back. *Grand-mère* had been painfully aloof since the moment I met her, no doubt she and Cousin Pauline considered me a viper in their midst. It embarrassed me. More than that, it angered me. Eva was a horrible person. I simply could not be Eva.

"Both her wounds and her amnesia are quite real, Danielle," said Alex. I looked at him with an unexpected surge of gratitude for having taken my part.

"Are you certain, brother? You, who were gullible enough to be fooled twice before by this . . ." and here she paused to rake her eyes contemptuously from head to toe, "this con artist."

"I am no con artist, Danielle, and if I could remember anything helpful to the recovery of your family's art and jewellery, I assure you, I would share it at once and leave here forever."

"Then why don't you tell us where you have been these past five years and what you have been doing. Even with genuine amnesia, you must remember some of it."

"I have remembered some things," I said, conscious that I sounded defensive and a little shaky. "Quite a lot, actually. And more every day. But not a single recollection involves Alex, or Brazil, or Monte Carlo, or paintings, or jewellery."

"The thief remembers everything except the theft," she sneered. "What a coincidence."

"There's no coincidence about it." I looked at Jean-Claude who, of all the people in the room, was watching me with sympathetic eyes. I continued as if I were talking to him alone. Jean-Claude would believe me. He would not dismiss what I had to say. "So much doesn't fit. Eva was an orphan. None of my childhood memories are of an orphanage. I remember parents. Their name was Smith. My name was—is Claire. And Eva's shoes don't fit me. Not just one pair—all of them are too big. Do sick people lose weight in their feet? And I am left-handed, but I think Eva was right-handed. In the photograph Lianne showed me, she was holding a tea cup in her right hand."

Alex interrupted with a snort and raised high his champagne glass as if proposing a toast. "*Mesdames et messieurs, attention, s'il vous plaît,* I am holding this glass in my left hand, yet I am right-handed."

I didn't trouble to reply. "Eva had red hair, mine is brown, even at the roots. More importantly, Eva did not speak French."

"But this is fascinating, darling," said Danielle before Alex could intervene. "You think you are not Alex's wife? Do tell us more about this great mystery." I was out in the open now, an inviting target for all who cared to shoot.

When his murderous glare did nothing to derail his sister's dogged pursuit of scandal, Alex turned toward me. He crossed the room to my side, no doubt hoping that towering over me would give his warning a more menacing impact. "This isn't worth discussing now, Eva, we've been through—"

"But I haven't heard any of it," protested Danielle. "Do go on, this is better than the theatre." She was baiting me, I knew that, and needling her brother at the same time. I felt on trial. Alex was the prosecutor, Danielle and the others the jurors. I was my only defence.

"No one here has seen Eva for five years. Five years is a long time to remember someone's features exactly, especially when no one knew Eva very well to begin with."

"So you are her secret twin?" Danielle's voice dripped with sarcasm.

Alex stood by my side, twisting the large ring on his right hand until he could restrain himself no longer. "Come now, all this can readily be explained. I don't want to be cruel, but if your hair is naturally brown, then the red I thought genuine was dye. And you've been living in France much of the past five years. Learning the language is no shocking feat."

All eyes turned to *Grand-mère* as she cleared her throat, set her glass on the japanned table, and folded her hands in her lap. "Eva speaks schoolgirl French," she said with the forceful calm of a judge pronouncing the verdict. The room was silent as we waited for the explanation she felt unnecessary.

"Yes, she does," agreed Alex with a lilt to his voice that encouraged her to continue.

"She did not learn her French in France. It is not the idiomatic French that one picks up in the streets; it is precise, regimented French. The verbs conjugate straight from the textbook. The subjunctive flaunts itself at all the right moments. Orphans are taught to be servants, not to speak French. This young woman learned French from a schoolteacher."

"Forgive me, *Grand-mère,* but that only proves Eva lied about being an orphan."

Charlot stood up and wandered over to where I was standing and put one paw on my knee. I patted his head, grateful for the show of support, even from a dog.

"Eva hated dogs," Lianne piped up excitedly. "Remember Prince in Brazil? She wouldn't touch him or any of the other dogs." A quelling look from her father caused her to shrink back into her chair, but the point was made.

"How *drôle!*" said Danielle. "Frankly, my dear, I'd stick with the amnesia excuse if I were you. It plays better than denial."

"Look, I don't care what any of you think, I'm not a criminal. I didn't steal anything. I didn't murder anyone!"

This last bit was news to some. Tersely, Alex was forced to recount the events at Cap Ferrat. Lianne's eyes grew as wide as saucers. Clearly, the next letter to her chum Helen would be a long one.

Danielle eyed me with new respect and leaned forward eagerly. "I know what happened! I can explain everything! Listen to this. Last month at a house party in Paris, I met a man who knew hypnotism. He was a marvel, kept putting guests under his powers and making them do things they wouldn't normally do. He hypnotized me that evening and made me—"

All at once her eye fell on Lianne, trying to blend into the upholstery.

"And he made me do something I would *never* have done had I been in possession of myself. Afterwards, everyone kept telling me what I had done, and like you, I had no memory of any of it. I think you must have been hypnotized during that time."

"I don't believe hypnotic suggestion lasts for months," Alex said sardonically as he resumed his pacing. "There is another, more probable explanation. Of course the initial diagnosis for Eva's case was simple amnesia brought on by the blow to the head, but as time goes on and her memory loss continues, it is increasingly possible that other psychological factors are involved. I refer to the work of the French doctor, Pierre Janet, whose studies in schizophrenia and split personality relate very well to Eva's circumstances. I am starting to think that there may, indeed, be a Claire as well as an Eva, two personalities inhabiting one body, each knowing nothing about the other. Dr. Janet believes that split-off parts of the personality can become capable of independent thoughts, actions, and identities without the knowledge of the other parts. Dr. Sigmund Freud is starting to study split-consciousness as well."

Danielle lit another cigarette. "So you're saying she's crazy."

"I'm not!" I looked to Jean-Claude for support, but he was studying his champagne glass as if he'd never seen one before.

"I'm only saying that what we thought was simple amnesia is looking more and more like an example of split-consciousness. I've been talking with the director of the Kreutzer Institute in Switzerland where they specialize in treatment of psychiatric illnesses such as this. He said that a traumatic experience is the usual cause of the split—"

"—her attack in Paris," interrupted Danielle.

"Exactly. And she could be repressing certain memories and mannerisms in favour of other, more appropriate ones that aren't as threatening to her as the other . . ."

He droned on in a cold, clinical way, a professor with rapt pupils hanging on every word, but I no longer heard him. A crescendo of noise like radio static filled my head and suddenly I knew that if I stayed with these horrid people another minute, I would faint like some tight-corseted Victorian. As I turned to flee the drawing room, I thought I heard *Grand-mère* say, "Nonetheless, Alexandre, you must hire people in England to search for these Smiths."

The next morning, after a large English breakfast in my room, I did the cowardly thing and set out to find a book. I had slept badly. Overwhelmed by conflicting emotions and plagued by unanswerable questions, I needed to lose myself in someone else's trials and tribulations, to break out of the endless cycle of my own fears and into a well-organized plot that resolved itself neatly on the last page. A good novel would, I hoped, distract me at least long enough to fall asleep at night.

The library was small, and the leather-bound volumes packed from floor to ceiling reduced the sunlight to what could squeeze through two narrow windows, but my eyes adjusted quickly. Most of the books were ancient tomes of tedium: sermon collections, philosophical discourses, scientific books, and military works, but these were intermixed with pristine collections of Moliére comedies, the plays of Racine and Corneille, and other treasures in German, Latin, and even Greek. All looked valuable. None had been dusted in decades.

My foot bumped against a basket of magazines. I flipped through the titles and saw that, unlike the books, these were all dated within the past few years. As I leafed through the top one, I came to a page with the corner turned down, marking a large picture of Alex escorting a bare-shouldered flapper to someone's *soirée.* The magazine beneath it had several photographs of Alex, wearing scantily-clad women on his arm like costume jewellery, his eyes glittering, his smile all teeth. The third one did not need a folded page to mark Alex's picture—he was on the cover, surrounded by adoring *ingénues* and holding high a trophy. Disgusted, I dropped him facedown into the basket and turned away, but he called me back. I resisted as long as I could, but the urge to inspect him more closely, to look as long as I liked without his knowing, was too strong to withstand.

The realization, when it came, hit me hard: I was looking at a happy man. Of course a racing victory would make any man happy, but it was more than that. Here was Alex before the scowl lines had etched his forehead, before soft lips had thinned with anger—a wholly different person who radiated a pure, uncomplicated *joie de vivre.* One I would have been keen to know. The sparkle in his eyes made me smile in spite of myself and, with a jolt, I realized I had not seen this emotion reflected in his face as long as I had been with him. For the first time, I considered Alex's role in our miserable drama of theft, murder, and betrayal, and wondered what it was costing him. So accustomed was I to being the victim that I had overlooked the fact that it was Alex who had initially been deceived, robbed, and humiliated, and now I knew the cost had been dear. I could see it reflected in his face and in his character.

Approaching footsteps caused me to drop the magazine back in the basket and move hastily to the nearest bookshelf. My hand fell on a collection of nineteenth-century military works as the door swung inward. Alex appeared at the threshold, his face shadowed by the light from behind.

I sighed at the inevitable conclusion he would draw. "No, Alex, I am not plotting my next heist. I am looking for something to read."

"Yes, of course you are," he said, coming closer. He looked deep into my eyes like a gypsy trying to read the tealeaves and then followed my arm to the shelf. "*Experiences sur les Poudres de Guerre.* Experiments with Gunpowder. That should prove entertaining, especially with all its mathematical tables."

I refused to be baited. "I was hoping to find something light, a novel perhaps."

"You won't find that here. I doubt anyone has opened any of these books since the Franco-Prussian War. But we are not philistines—remember that only *Grand-mère* and Pauline live here the year round. Their books are in their wing. And there are current magazines in the morning room."

"So what brings you into this book morgue?"

He hesitated, then indicated an antique desk positioned in the light by the window. "The telephone," he admitted rather sheepishly.

"I didn't know there was a telephone in the house!"

"A good thing, that. You might have tried to call out."

"And who would I call?"

"Your lovers, your partners. You don't work alone."

Arguing with this man was an exercise in futility. I turned to leave. He grabbed my arm. "Don't run off." I looked pointedly at his hand and he dropped it.

"What sort of reading material would you like? I can call Paris and have English books sent here by tomorrow if you like."

The kindness was so unexpected, I'm afraid my face showed my surprise.

"Shocking, eh? Take advantage quickly before I revert to type." The slightest hint of a smile punctuated his words.

Names of popular authors popped in my head like Guy Fawkes fireworks. I was keen on British authors like E. M. Forster and H.G. Wells and the mysteries of the American Mary Roberts Rinehart. I wondered whether orphans typically had such tastes in reading. If Alex thought it odd, he gave no sign. While I stood beside him, he telephoned Paris and arranged for a parcel of books to be delivered.

"And now, I'll take you to the morning room to see if any of the magazines will interest you," he said, steering me out of the library. "And I apologize for the earlier remark. It's hard for me to remember that you are not yourself."

"I'm not insane."

"Confused is the more accurate word. Two very different personalities cohabiting one body. By the time Lianne and I have sailed for Brazil, you'll have reached the end of the memory quest and we can begin your treatment."

I froze. "By having me committed to some sanatorium?"

"It might well be the best thing for you, undergoing treatment at a reputable psychiatric hospital."

"And you would commit me if I refused to go?" A chill crept up my spine.

"If it were best for you."

"Your concern for my health overwhelms me."

"Your cooperation would indicate that you didn't need treatment. It would persuade me to put you on a ferry to England instead of a train to Switzerland."

"Believe me, Alex, if I could end this nightmare by telling you the location of your paintings, I would do so like this," and I snapped my fingers contemptuously.

"Whatever the state of your mind, my dear, you are involved in this up to your pretty neck. One way or another, you'll lead me where I want to go."

We were walking through a gloomy centre passageway I had not travelled before and my sneezing told me more about its decoration than my eyes did. At last we turned into a sunny gallery with a pair of overstuffed toile chairs. It would have been a delightful place to pass the time of day had Danielle not been there before me, curled up on a fainting couch like a sleek cat in the sun. I knew if I stayed the claws would come out.

"Good morning, you two." She set down her coffee and letters. "Bad news from home—the price of coffee fell again. Manuel says there is too much being grown all over the world and he is taking my *fazendas* out of production. If things don't recover soon, I'll have to sell myself on the marriage market." The poor little rich girl sighed.

"We're looking for reading material," Alex said, pointing out the stack of magazines beneath a table. I helped myself to two recent issues of *Marie-Claire*.

"What a charming room," I said for something to say. "It must always have been a favourite in the morning, with its eastern and southern exposures." From where I stood, I could see the changeable Marne, reflecting the blue of today's cloudless sky. It was beautiful, but I shivered nonetheless.

"The sun is harsh, though," said Danielle, "and it fades the fabric. Look." She turned over a cushion to show the contrast between the original multicoloured toile and the exposed side. "*Grand-mère* needs to have draperies installed, or Venetian blinds."

"But that would defeat the room's purpose," I replied. "A thin gauze curtain would filter most of that, and still let in the light."

Danielle looked thoughtful. "That's so. I'll speak to Thonet about it. But I doubt *Grand-mère* will make any changes unless you ask her, Alex. She's swimming in money but won't modernize." She rolled her eyes. "*Grand-mère* prefers life as a pauper to cheat the Germans. The old dear thinks they are going to return and destroy everything once again. The coffee's hot—would you like some? Join me a while, things are frightfully dull here." She yawned and stretched to display her ennui.

I was about to reply that I preferred the courtyard when Alex asked, "Thank you, but we're touring. Eva has an interest in draughty old chateaux."

"Wait for me," said Danielle, uncoiling her legs and slipping her feet into shoes with toes so pointed they looked like weapons.

"You really are bored," said Alex dryly. "Come if you must, then."

Incredibly, we spent nearly two hours walking through the antiquated chateau, re-visiting some rooms I had already seen and entering others by routes so circuitous I would never have found them on my own. An ancient chapel boasted an altarpiece by Titian—or at least, by one of his students—that glowed as if beneath a celestial spotlight. The furnishings fascinated me, but I discovered Alex and Danielle could answer none of my questions about any of them in spite of the fact that they had spent part of their childhood within these walls.

"It must all have been collected early in the last century by your ancestor, Vivant Denon," I concluded. "The things he didn't send to Napoleon's Louvre."

"Surely not those chairs," protested Danielle.

"Or course, you're right, the upholstered pieces like those are recent, but most of the furniture is Louis XV or Louis XVI, or Directoire at the latest." In my excitement I forgot what conclusions Alex and Danielle would inevitably draw from my analysis. All I could think was that I knew a good deal about art and old furniture, and I reflected once again on what it might mean. I could not have grown up around such valuables, as I was certainly no aristocrat or heiress, and the parlour maid idea seemed just as improbable.

By the time we reached the minstrel's gallery overlooking the reception hall, Danielle had grown tired of me and the Denon antiques. She squeezed herself into a stone window seat where she could gaze out over the courtyard. It was nearly noon.

"Alex, darling," she said. "Were you expecting the police?"

Alex stiffened at once. Four great strides took him to the window where he could see for himself. I knew instantly. They had come for me.

For days I had schemed for ways to escape to the police. For days I had prayed for exactly this to happen, for the authorities to come rescue me from Alex and deposit me at the British embassy to be sent home to England. That was before I knew about the murder charge. How did the old saying go? *Be careful what you wish for, lest it come true.* My own wish was going to bring me down. My saviours had turned into my executioners.

"I'll take care of this," he said, turning smartly on his heels.

"Stay out of sight."

No sooner had Thonet admitted the two *gendarmes* and gone off in search of Madame Denon than Alex reached the top of the *grand escalier*. Danielle and I watched through the crack of the green velvet curtain that separated the minstrel's gallery from the adjoining room, looking down into the hall as Alex glided down the staircase like the lord of the manor. I forgot to breathe.

Perhaps they were from Troyes. Perhaps the *fonctionaire* had called the police at Troyes after all, and they had come to see that the mad Englishwoman was not in danger from her husband. Alex would call me down, I would explain that I had been delirious with fever, and they would leave. Perhaps I had no need to panic.

"Good afternoon, gentlemen." Alex's clear voice floated up from the hall. "I am Alexandre DeSequeyra, at your service." His imperious manner belied the courteous words; his expression that of an aristocrat displeased to have been disturbed in his home. My heart beat faster. Go softly, I wanted to warn him.

Their voices were not distinct, we were too far above them for that, but I strained to make out the conversation. Alex deliberately positioned himself so that the men had to turn their backs to the gallery but even so, I did not dare pull back the curtain more than a crack. I could see nothing but their backs, two toy soldiers in identical blue uniforms with identical pillbox hats. They introduced themselves. They had come from Paris. "We are seeking Madame DeSequeyra," one of the men began. I could not tell which one was speaking.

"You are not the only ones," replied Alex.

"She is not here?"

"I regret she is not."

"Where is she?"

"I have no idea." He turned his palms up to signify that he was as confounded as they were.

"You left the hospital Notre Dame du Bon Secours with her on the morning of June 8, is that correct?"

He nodded his agreement. "I drove her to *L'Hotel de Crillon,* as I informed the doctor. I planned to remain there until she was recovered from her injuries."

"The *Crillon* has no registration record for you on June 8."

"It would not. Before I had the chance to register, she slipped away. I spent the rest of the day looking for her, then gave up and came here to my grandmother's home."

"Is it not remarkable, sir, that a woman as badly injured as the doctor says Madame was, that such a woman could, ehhh . . ." and he waved his fingers in the air, "just slip away?"

"I'm afraid my wife is an accomplished liar, gentlemen, as well as a thief. She had convinced the doctor and me that her injuries were so severe she could not move without aid, so we were not on guard to an escape. I am ashamed to admit that I left her unattended in the Peugeot while I entered the hotel to register. I have hired detectives to continue the search." Alex folded his arms across his chest and tilted his head. "May I ask, gentlemen, what is your interest in my wife's disappearance? I have been searching for her these past five years, and the police have refused to become involved in what they termed a domestic dispute."

"Monsieur DeSequeyra, when we arrived I asked your butler if Madame DeSequeyra was at home. Your man said she was."

"Thonet said that?" Alex asked slowly. He paused, as if puzzled. He was stalling, trying frantically to think his way out of the trap they had sprung. So much for the stupid policemen. He looked about the room as if searching for Thonet. Seconds ticked by. The *gendarmes* waited, letting him dig himself deeper if he would. My hands were shaking. I could not see their expressions from where I stood, but I imagine they were gloating. "Perhaps you misunderstood," Alex said slowly.

"There was no misunderstanding, *monsieur*."

"He probably thought you meant Madame Denon, my grandmother. I shall summon him and clear the matter up—"

"That will not be necessary." Of course not. They knew full well that a servant would change his story with a look from the master. They would arrange to question him further alone, where he could not be coached by silent signals.

But a sound at the top of the *grande escalier* stopped them. All three men turned to see Danielle start down the stairs. I had been straining so hard to hear them that I didn't realize she had left my side. "Here I am, gentlemen. Thonet said you were asking for me. How can I help you?" She reached the bottom of the stairs and nodded haughtily to the *gendarmes*. My hand flew to my mouth. It would never work. We bore no resemblance to one another, and they must have had a description of me from the doctor.

The policemen exchanged glances. "You are Madame DeSequeyra?" one asked.

"I am Danielle DeSequeyra." Marie Antoinette must have looked like that when she faced down the rabble that screamed for her death: proud, imperious, and utterly disdainful of their authority.

I expected the men would wither at the force of her contempt. They did not. "You have papers?" one asked calmly.

"In the Delage."

One policeman turned to the other but before he could speak, Danielle interrupted. "Wait here," she ordered, conveying the unmistakable message that she didn't want peasants pawing about her precious sports car. "I'll fetch them."

One of the men jerked his head indicating that the other should accompany Danielle. Her vehicle was berthed beside the gate and it was only a matter of moments before she dug her identity papers out of the glove box and returned to the hall. Without a word, she handed them to the man she judged the senior of the two.

"This gives your name as Danielle Blanchard."

"That *was* my name. I've divorced the handsome face with nothing behind it and taken back my maiden name. No doubt that is why Thonet persists in calling me *Madame* DeSequeyra. *Mademoiselle* just doesn't fit a woman with my record."

"Record, *madame*?"

"Two divorces in four years. Criminal, eh?" In case her impatience to conclude the interview had not communicated itself, she folded her arms across her chest and tapped her foot smartly on the marble floor.

I could not tell if they believed her, but it was clear she trumped them. There was no point in questioning Thonet again. No way would he stumble a second time. Relief made me weak. Perversely, now that I was safe, my knees gave away and I sank to the floor.

But the policemen were not finished. They exchanged glances again, and the senior man continued, unmoved by Danielle's theatrics. "And you have been at this house how long, *madame*?"

"Goodness, I have no idea. A few days. I arrived—when did I arrive, Alex—Tuesday? Wednesday? I'll be leaving soon. This place is a crashing bore."

They could still ask to search the chateau until they found a woman's belongings in Alex's room. They could still question the servants, one by one, until someone let something slip. But no, they seemed entirely taken in by Danielle's deceit. They were listening to her account of her brother's marital misfortune. "No, I've never met the wretched girl. How could I? They were only together for a couple of months in Brazil. My poor brother," she looked pityingly at him as if he were years younger and none too bright, "was duped by a clever con artist. The paintings have never surfaced, so naturally we believe she has them still, and we hope he will recover them in the end. Why the interest now, may I ask?"

The police explained what Danielle already knew, in part at least, that Eva Johnson DeSequeyra was wanted for questioning in a murder. Someone in the Paris headquarters had finally linked the Englishwoman in the hospital to the art thefts on the Riviera, and they were in pursuit of both Madame DeSequeyra and her accomplice, a smooth Italian who claimed petty nobility. Police in Monaco had him in custody a month ago, but he escaped while being transported to Nice for trial. Danielle feigned surprise at the news; Alex was impassive, playing it both ways.

Danielle noticed the butler before anyone else. "Ah, there you are, Thonet. Explain to the police that you meant me when you spoke of Madame DeSequeyra."

My heart turned over but the butler didn't miss a beat. "Of course, *madame*," he answered gravely, bowed, and addressed the policemen. "I was referring to Madame DeSequeyra," he said gravely. "And now Madame Denon will receive you in the drawing room."

The two men followed him through double doors. I had no idea what would occur there, but if they were not convinced, they would search the house. The first place a man of any brains at all would look would be the master's bedroom, where my belongings put Danielle's statements to the lie. And these policemen had plenty of brains.

I flew through the hallway and up the stairs.

In minutes I had emptied the contents of my armoire onto the bed in a heap and scooped out all my undergarments from their drawers. Gathering the ends of the coverlet together, I dragged the load down the hall to Danielle's room where I heaved it on her bed. They wouldn't search her room. If they did, she would come up with something clever about packing or unpacking.

I ran in stocking feet back to the top of the staircase and listened to the silence. The double doors remained shut. I hadn't been through the entire chateau, but if there were secret chambers behind the panelling or underground tunnels cut through the tufa limestone, I was unaware of them. I had just about decided on a chest in one of the desolate third floor bedchambers when the drawing room doors swept open. The two *gendarmes* herded Alex and Danielle toward the stairs.

Not until that very moment did I remember the dressing table with its vials of perfume, pots of make-up, and bottles of nail lacquer. Stifling a cry, I dashed back into the bedchamber, swept everything into the wastepaper basket, and grabbed the jewellery case that was sitting on the table like a blood-stained murder weapon. By then, they had reached the top of the stairs. I had only seconds to hide.

The wardrobes were the first place they'd look. The linen closets would be second. That left the space under the bed. A child's solution, but I had no choice. With the wastepaper basket under my good arm, I crouched to slide beneath the bedstead only to be stopped by empty suitcases. I shoved them away to make enough room for myself, hoping they didn't protrude from the other side. If the policemen looked under the bed—as surely they would—odds were they would look from the other side, the side closest to the door, and see only luggage.

I had no time to arrange myself comfortably. The wicker basket dug sharply into my side, my foot was twisted against one suitcase and my bad arm was crushed against another, but I lay like the dead as they entered the room.

I could feel Alex's surprise in his silence. Everything was still for a long moment. Someone yanked open a wardrobe door, then pulled out a couple bureau drawers. Empty, or filled with masculine paraphernalia.

Sweating profusely, I could hear the ticking of Lianne's clock growing louder by the second. At last one of the men said, "And next to this room?"

"My daughter's, then my sister's." With a grunt, they moved on.

I had no idea how long they would search—a few minutes? Several hours? From my hiding place, all sound was muffled and I would not be able to hear them leave, so I would remain where I was no matter how cramped until someone sounded the all clear. It seemed like days passed before I heard Alex calling, "Where are you?"

I struggled out from under the bedstead, the wastepaper basket embedded in my ribs. I was stiff as a wooden doll. I took a deep breath and managed to make enough sound to draw Alex into the room.

"My God, you were *here*, in this room, all along? I thought they looked under . . . ah, I see, the valises blocked their view. Come, you need some air." Talking as much to himself as to me, he moved to pick me up.

Now that all danger had passed, I began trembling with cold, as if I had been standing naked in a wintry wind. I dearly wanted strong, warm arms around me, but pride made me shake my head before I knew what I was doing. I intended to shout, Yes, hold me tightly and keep me safe, but someone else answered stiffly in my voice, "No, thank you, I can walk, just slowly."

With unexpected compassion, he put his left arm around my waist to help me hobble through the door and down the staircase. "They left some time ago. I've been searching for you in the most devious places, only to find you hidden under the bed, like Charlot from the thunder."

"It's all I had time for."

"It was perfect. You were remarkably quick. And Danielle deserves the *Croix de Guerre*. There I was, ready to feed the police a lame story about Danielle's clothes being stored in my room because she didn't have enough closet space, when I saw what you had done. When we came to Danielle's room and found them piled on her bed, she said something about getting back to her packing. They swallowed the whole thing." This time, he did not call them fools. "They learned nothing from *Grand-mère*—she feigned senility while Aunt Pauline rattled on about the *Bosch* shelling their home—then she felt a heart murmur and sent Thonet off for her medicine, and he warned the staff. When the search was finally finished, I apologized for their wasted trip, handed them money for a midday meal, and recommended a good *auberge* in the next town

. . . hoping they wouldn't tarry in Ranton to question the villagers."

"Did it work?" I asked, looking anxiously about me as we stepped into the courtyard. It was empty save for the two gardeners who were engaged in a vigorous attack on the weeds in the vegetable garden: Henri, the old retainer, and the younger fellow also dressed in the traditional blue worn by labourers. They gave us a glance and returned to their chores. With his arm still firmly around my waist, Alex guided me to the fountain and sat me on the ledge where I could splash the cool water onto my arms and face.

"I watched from the tower until I saw their automobile heading west from Ranton."

I looked up at him and, for the first time, saw an ally. I was safe. I closed my eyes and laid my head against his chest. Had I not been a modern English girl, I would have wept.

Lianne was furious to have missed the excitement. She had been down in the barn playing with the kittens when the police paid their call. She glared at me through dinner as if I had conspired to keep her from the fun, and kept asking Aunt Danielle to tell again what she had said to fool the police. Jean-Claude marvelled at her quick thinking. Danielle basked in the praise. I tried several times to attract Alex's attention, but he avoided looking in my direction. Madame Denon watched everyone with discerning eyes.

That night, I went to bed before Alex. I fought against sleep while I waited for him to no avail. When I awoke the next morning, his side of the bed was undisturbed. Nor did he appear for breakfast.

"Where is Alex?" I asked at last, remembering the old saw about the wife being the last to know.

"He slunk out early this morning," said Danielle, her dark eyes gleaming with malice, "muttering something about someone in Paris. When I pressed, he told me whose business I could mind, so I refrained from asking why he was sleeping in an upstairs bedroom by himself."

She did not really expect a reply to that, and I did not give her one. I finished my breakfast and went out to my favourite place in the courtyard to enjoy the fine day with one of the books Alex had ordered. It was a good read, but my mind wandered. Who was Alex meeting in Paris, and why had he left without telling me? When would he return? Why had he been so distant during dinner? And why had he not come to our bed? Every night I had wished he would sleep in another room, and last night, when he finally did, I was sorely disappointed. *Be careful what you wish for* . . . Damn Danielle!—she was like a mosquito bite that never went away. I knew what she was hinting, and I told myself sternly that I didn't care—other women meant nothing to me. Nothing at all.

The soft strains of a Debussy piano sonata greeted me the following day as I passed the morning room. Jean-Claude was there drinking coffee.

"A new record?" I asked from the doorway.

"An old favourite," he smiled. "Please, come in. Sit." He poured me a cup and we talked comfortably of vineyards and village, like friends who had known each other all our lives. It was peaceful—a far cry from the tensions that flared whenever Alex and I were in the same room. Suddenly Jean-Claude snapped his fingers with chagrin. "Ah, I forgot to bring the newspaper to show you! A piece about your Mrs. Pankhurst. She has died in England at the age of seventy."

I felt curiously empty, unsure whether I had known the suffragette leader personally, but certain I was somehow involved in her battle for women's rights. Her willingness to spend time in prison had brought public opinion around enough to pass laws mandating equal pay for equal work and giving women equal rights in divorce. More recently her daughter Christabel had become the leader in the battle for the vote, and the more I said her melodious name—Christabel, Christabel—the more I felt there was something waiting for me just beyond the edges of my consciousness.

"Yes, thank you. I should like to read the article very much. Perhaps it will shake loose some memories."

"Why don't you come back to my house now?" he said, rising from his seat. I saw nothing improper in the invitation, and I accepted at once.

But we had gone no farther than the archway when Lianne bounded after us, braids bouncing on her back as she ran. "I'm going to feed the kittens. You must come." She grabbed my hand and tugged.

"Where are they?"

"In the barn, this way."

"A higher calling," said Jean-Claude with an indulgent nod of his head. "Go on, Claire, I'll bring the newspaper later." So I let Lianne pull me along through the meadow toward the old stone barn.

Some years earlier, at Alex's insistence, a portion of the original stables inside the chateau had been converted to garages, motorcars having replaced the horse and carriage for those who could afford them. Alex's vehicle sat there now, with Danielle's Delage, *Grand-mère's* touring car, and a battered Citroen that belonged to Jean-Claude, all with keys in the ignition ready to go—more motorcars under one roof than existed in the whole province, I suspected. The few horses that were left had been moved, with the carts and farm wagons, out of the chateau and into the barn.

Lianne pushed open one of the immense oak doors and peered cautiously inside, as if she expected to see someone waiting for her. "What is it?" I asked.

"Yesterday Henri said gypsies were spotted at the edge of town. He and some others ran them off, but you never know where they might be hiding."

I shook my head and smiled. Lianne was so fanciful. We made our way through the round bales of hay to the stalls at the far end where I met several horses, one cow, and four small grey and white kittens on a brown blanket bed. Lianne had named them all, but her names changed daily, and I thought it safer to call them Kitty until the matter was settled.

"I come to feed them every day. I am their mother," she announced. "If I hadn't heard about them, they would have been drowned. I saved them. I can't believe anyone could do such a cruel thing. They are so cute!"

I had to agree.

"I have to tell you," she said suddenly. "Even if the others don't believe you, I think you are Claire Smith and not Eva. I don't think you can be both at the same time, like Father says."

"Thank you, Lianne." Her words buoyed my spirits a little, but in the end, it made no real difference what this mercurial child thought. Tomorrow she'd have another opinion.

"*Grand-mère* and I were talking about you . . . about Eva."

"Oh?" I would dearly love to know what *Grand-mère* thought of me, since she was one of the few people who had any influence over Alex, but I had to think how to ask without my intention seeming obvious.

Lianne went on, "Eva was mean. You're not mean. And Eva smoked. All the time. You don't smoke."

No wonder Alex was always offering me cigarettes.

"You must be twins, though, you are so exactly alike. You'll soon remember her."

"I'm afraid that won't happen, Lianne. I do remember my childhood, or enough to know that I grew up an only child, like you."

"But it could be that you don't remember your twin sister because you were separated at birth. It could have been like this: two babies were born but one was stolen away by the midwife and given to another mother whose baby had died. Neither of the mothers knew about the switch. Really, it could happen! I read a story like that in a book and it happened very easily. Or maybe your mother had two babies for a walk in the pram and while she was looking in a shop window, an old gypsy woman came by and snatched up one of the babies. Gypsies do that all the time! Everyone knows that."

"If you please, Lianne, I appreciate the sentiment, but if a baby had mysteriously disappeared in a small English town, it would have been discussed at tea for the next two hundred years. Let's talk of something else."

Lying in the fragrant straw, I closed my eyes and savoured a scrap of a memory that pierced the fog surrounding my childhood. For a moment, I was young, much younger than Lianne, lying in the straw in a shed that served as a small barn behind our house, listening for my mother to call me in for tea. Nothing more, but it was a warm, wonderful memory that I savoured as long as I could. Reluctantly I returned to the present where the silence magnified the quiet sounds around me, the nickering of a horse, the swishing of a tail, a creak of the rafters, a scurrying in the loft. My heightened awareness picked up something else, the spine-crawling sensation that I was being watched.

My eyes flew open and I tensed. Lianne was beside me, completely absorbed with the kittens on her stomach. I sat up and glanced about the barn, toward the open door and up at the loft, where I thought I had heard movement, a scraping sound, a noise too loud for a mouse to have made. Not wanting to alarm Lianne, I held my breath and listened carefully. Gypsies?

There it was again.

"Lianne," I said, making my voice sound casual. "I'm thirsty. Let's go back to the kitchen and ask for some lemonade."

"No, I want to stay—What?" I put one finger to my lips and pointed upwards. She followed the motion and frowned in confusion. "What's—?" I put my fingers on her lips and made a soft "Shhhh" sound.

"Come on," I said loudly and cheerily, pulling her up from the straw with my good hand. "I have something to tell you as we go."

We walked to the barn door in awkward silence, my ears straining for any other sound. I heard nothing. But I was certain I hadn't imagined it. Someone was in up the loft, spying on us.

With pulses racing, we exited the barn, pushed the big door closed, and made our way around the barn, Lianne at my heels, scared silent. As we turned the second corner, I nearly collided with Jean-Claude.

"Oh, Jean-Claude, you startled me!"

"My apologies. You look as if you have seen a ghost."

"I, well, I was frightened. I think there is someone in the loft."

Lianne squeaked, "Gypsies!"

"I heard noises . . ."

Jean-Claude looked grim. "You go back to the house. I'll have a look." And he strode around the corner toward the barn door.

In unspoken agreement, Lianne and I stayed where we were, hearts pounding, and listened as Jean-Claude pulled open the big door with a thud. Then we heard nothing, no matter how hard we listened. Minutes seemed like hours as we waited. Finally, I could stand the suspense no longer and I retraced my steps, arriving at the barn door just as Jean-Claude came out.

"You young ladies have big imaginations," he said, brushing

some straw off his shirtsleeves. "I searched the barn floor and then the loft and found no one. You probably heard a mouse or bird. Small creatures make more noise than you think."

I gave a self-conscious laugh. "Well, I'm very sorry to have bothered you. Ever since the police visit, I have been jumpy."

"It is no bother. I had to come back this way anyway to bring you the newspaper. I see your kittens are doing well," he addressed Lianne.

As the three of us walked around the other side of the barn, the side facing the river, I glanced up and noticed there were several windows at loft height. The ground below one of them was disturbed, the soft soil pitted and the grass crushed. The height was not so great as to make a jump dangerous, and there would have been sufficient opportunity for someone to escape from the window in the several minutes that lapsed between the time Lianne and I stood up from the straw and Jean-Claude climbed into the loft. The Marne River was close and its banks were thick with vegetation. Someone could have jumped from the window and hidden in the bushes. It would not have been easy but it would not have been impossible.

But who? Gypsies? What did I care if gypsies sneaked into the barn? What would they do—steal a horse or a hen? A shame, but nothing to do with me. Or was it? Should I point out the crushed grass and explain my theory? It would only make me look paranoid. The last thing I needed was more evidence that I was mentally unstable. After all, Lianne had heard nothing at all.

"I want to take them home to Brazil with me," Lianne was saying, "but Papa won't allow it."

"I need the cats here to keep the barn free of field mice," said Jean-Claude.

"You won't drown them when I'm gone, will you?"

"No, no. You will find them here next autumn when you return." He looked at me and smiled.

"Thank you for the newspaper, Jean-Claude," was all I said. I couldn't risk losing my only friend, the only person who was trying to help me, with his offer of money and his other kindnesses. I said nothing about my observations. "Come on, Lianne, let's pick some of those wildflowers on the way back to the house."

The three of us arrived back at the chateau laden with wildflowers only to be met by Thonet with bad news.

"Excuse the interruption, sir, but Madame Denon has suffered a fall and twisted her ankle."

Jean-Claude tensed.

I gave a soft cry of dismay. "The poor dear. Where is she now?" I asked.

"I carried her to her bed."

"Did you telephone for the doctor?" asked Jean-Claude.

"I sent for Madame Renaud, sir. The doctor would be at least an hour arriving." And I read the unspoken message that Cécile Renaud would know better than the doctor what to do.

"I'll go to her at once," he said, and at that very moment, Cécile appeared with her satchel in hand.

"I want to see her too," said Lianne.

Jean-Claude sent me a silent plea. "Come, Lianne," I said. "Let's put these flowers in a vase for your grandmother. Then we can stop by her room in a little while, after Cécile has had the chance to see her patient."

Within an hour, Cécile had *Grand-mère* resting comfortably with her foot propped up on a pillow, neatly bound and iced. Thankfully, it was not broken, but because of *Grand-mère*'s advanced age, even a sprain would take a good while to heal.

"She must not put weight on it for a while," ordered Cécile. "Perhaps several weeks, I am not sure." At this point, she eyed my arm critically, and I knew what was coming. "*Enfin,* I had planned to come tomorrow to see about your hand and make you a new splint."

"You may as well do so now," I finished for her. I had been looking forward to the day I would graduate to a smaller, less cumbersome splint, and I led the way to my room. It took only a few minutes for her to unwrap the gauze and sticks, examine my poor hand, and bind it again.

"*Voilà,*" she said, surveying her work with satisfaction. "It has been three and a half weeks since your injury. The young mend faster than the old."

"How much longer, do you think?"

She pursed her lips. "Three more weeks if you are very careful, four would be better."

"Your Chateau Denon patients are keeping you busy."

She nodded. *"Pauvre Madame.* She will chafe against her confinement. I am sure I remember an invalid chair, one used by old Monsieur Denon after the Prussian War. If I can find it, she could leave her bed and be wheeled easily from one room to another." She dried her hands on a linen towel and packed her satchel. "I will go to the attic to search."

"May I come? I can help you look." The prospect of rummaging around among the cast-offs in that mysterious, padlocked attic piqued my interest.

Doubt was plain as her eyes raked my bias cut ivory frock, raw silk with beaded embroidery and a handkerchief hemline. I didn't care for the dress either, but it had virtues I could not afford to ignore, such as a straight waist and some flair at the hips. A pair of ladies' trousers would have been ideal, but I had no doubt that the sight of trousers on a woman would send these people into shock.

"Never mind my dress. I would really like to have a look about the attic."

I followed her down the hall and up the stone steps to the locked door. It took some jiggling of the skeleton key to shake loose the bolt, but we were in. A strong sense of *déjà vu* came in with me.

Most of what the Denon family decided to store away was nailed inside great wooden crates or locked trunks that perched one on top of the other like giant building blocks, but not everything was inaccessible. Curiosity would not permit me to pass through a room without lifting the linen dustcovers for a peek at what was underneath—empty gilt picture frames by the dozen, wardrobes stuffed with out-of-date ball gowns, wire birdcages, an intricately carved settee that had to be worth a small fortune, rolls of hand painted wall paper, and a small flax spinning wheel of the sort that Americans were buying up by the boatload and sending home. It was a graveyard of cast-offs that could be dusted and sold for a great deal of money—but then, what did the Denons need with money? I could hear their languid voices in my head, *"Oh, la la,* I don't know, just take it up to the attic."

"There it is!" Cécile pointed to a Bath chair several yards away, squeezed between two dressmaker's forms and an old marble sink. It took ten minutes of moving furniture and brushing away spider webs before we could reach it. "Thank goodness it is in good condition." And she whipped out a rag and attacked the dusty caning.

While she worked, I glanced behind me at the narrow dormer, the source of our light. The diamond paned window that led onto the roof had been opened recently, for the grimy film on the glass had been disturbed by someone's fingers. On the floor at the foot was a stack of slate tiles. Reminded of my recent brush with death, I shuddered. This must be the spot, near this dormer window, where the slates had come loose and crashed onto my chair. I peered at the stack more closely. A century ago, judging by the thick layer of dust and cobwebs on them, someone had stored extra slate here in the attic for use in future repairs. The top few at one end of the pile were clean of dust. Sherlock Holmes would have approved my deduction: that the workmen Jean-Claude had hired had already come, taken up some slates from this pile, and repaired the roof. Good. I hoped they had also inspected the entire expanse for other loose spots.

The Bath chair protested fiercely as we rolled it to the door, but Cécile was sure a few drops of oil would silence the squeak. It was not one of the new, lightweight versions, but a clunky model that took the two of us to manoeuvre downstairs. Cécile was pleased. She pushed it toward Madame's rooms while I washed my filthy hands.

"Thank you, my dear, for finding this chair," said *Grand-mère* when Thonet wheeled her into the parlour that evening.

"It was Cécile who remembered it," I said. "I merely went along with her to see what was in the attic."

I knew how that would sound to those who insisted on branding me an incorrigible thief, and sure enough, Danielle said, "There's nothing of value up there, just a lot of old junk that ought to be tossed onto the midsummer bonfire." She gulped the last of her martini and held up the glass in a silent command. Thonet hastened to refill it.

"We used to play up there as children," said Jean-Claude, turning to me, "until they caught us trying to climb out onto the roof and put a lock on the door."

"Speaking of the roof, have the fallen shingles been replaced?" *Grand-mère* asked.

I opened my mouth to answer in the affirmative but Jean-Claude was faster.

"Not yet, *Grand-mère*. Thonet sent word to the usual man only to learn that he died last winter. We'll have to ask in Troyes for someone who can do that sort of work. Never fear, I will not forget."

The conversation continued around me but they could have been speaking Chinese for all I understood. For a few moments, I counted the number of attic dormers in my head, then counted again to be sure. Without a word, I set down my drink and rose from my chair. Jean-Claude gave me a puzzled look but no one said anything as I left the room. Quick steps took me to the entrance hall where I threw back the massive bolt and slipped out into the long shadows of early evening. Walking rapidly, I crossed the courtyard to the kitchen side, turned, looked up at the roof, and counted off four attic windows from the left until I came to the one where the spare shingles were piled. My eyes dropped to the ground directly below. Exactly to the spot where someone had placed my garden chair. The air was warm but I shivered.

Immediately I climbed the stairs to the attic. Cécile had not relocked the door so I entered easily and made my way through the debris, counting the windows that overlooked the courtyard until I came to the one with the slate pile. The fourth one. I had not been mistaken.

When the workman from Troyes came to make repairs, he would find no damage on the roof. There was nothing to repair. The slates that had almost killed me had come from the replacement pile, not from the roof itself.

Who would do such a thing? Who wanted to hurt me—no, kill me—so badly that they would stage this "accident?" I had not asked anyone to bring me a chair that day; my chair was already there. Someone had placed it in the exact spot below the fourth window and waited for me to sit down and be killed. And dead I would surely be had an aggressive bumblebee not been making his morning rounds that day.

Who could have done it? Not Alex, he was gone that day. Or so he said. Could he have positioned the chair, pretended to leave the chateau, and waited in the attic until I sat down? It was possible. But why, when I hadn't yet led him to the paintings? If not Alex, who else? Certainly not his grandmother or Cousine Pauline. Certainly not Lianne. She had come out of the kitchen shortly after the slates fell. Certainly not Jean-Claude. He was my only friend and besides, he was not inside the chateau then. Danielle had not yet arrived. Who else but the servants were on the premises?

I would have to go downstairs and find something pleasant to say, all the while pretending I had not just learned that someone had tried to kill me. I decided not to tell anyone about my discovery in the attic. Not yet. Not until I knew whom I could trust.

I had no word from Alex for several days, and my spirits flagged. No one heard from him, or if they had, they did not tell me, and I was too proud to ask. I slept and ate, played cards with Lianne and Cousin Pauline, helped tend to *Grand-mère*, threw sticks to Charlot, read my books, and avoided Danielle as best I could. I wanted to know what Alex was doing and whether it had anything to do with me. If he were indeed my husband—a prospect that managed to seem both probable and absurd at the same time— should I not be troubled by his unexplained absence?

"Am I interrupting you?" asked Jean-Claude. Dinner was over and I had retreated to the morning room where I was curled up with the last of my English books.

"Certainly not, please come in." He closed the door behind him as I swung my feet down from the sofa to make room for him beside me. For a few minutes he spoke about one of the village men in his employ who had broken his leg in the fields this morning. Cécile had set the bone and said all would be well in a few months.

After a moment, he held up his pipe. "Do you mind?"

"Not a bit."

I settled back and waited quietly, recognizing this delay for what it was, a thought-gathering interlude. With only one arm, the routine might have been very awkward but ten years of practice had condensed the motions until I think he took no more time than a

two-handed man to fill the pipe, tamp it down, and light it. When
he had finished, he offered me a cigarette, which I declined.

"You've been keeping to your room a good deal since Alex
left."

"Has someone complained?"

"No—"

"I thought not," I said drily.

"—but I thought I'd—I wondered whether there was something
wrong. You miss Alex?"

"No!" I protested, a little too sharply. "It's only that I am a little
restless." Faced with Cousin Pauline's discourse on the decline of
lace-making in her native Brittany or Lianne's fourteenth rendition
of *Für Elise* on the piano, I was starting to find even Alex's acidic
conversation appealing, that was all. Perversely, I was glad he was
gone and wished him here at the same time.

"He'll be back soon." He looked at me more closely. "Denons
and DeSequeyras can be over-proud people, wedded to their
opinions and slow to change them. They could not be expected to
welcome Eva back after what had passed. You faced an army of ill
will when you arrived yet, in spite of that, Lianne has come to treat
you like a big sister and follows you about—"

"She's very bored."

"—and Danielle admires you—"

"Only because she can add a murderer to her collection of
acquaintances."

"—and *Grand-mère* has come to respect you—"

"As she keeps her eye on the family silver."

"—and I like you." The finality in his voice challenged me to
dismiss his affection as I had the others. I blinked back hot tears.
"You are discouraged."

"Not so much about that. Mostly because . . ."

I paused a long while and it struck me how patient he was. "I
feel so empty. I'm afraid that this is it. That I've remembered all
I'm going to. Yes, my hand will heal and my scars will fade, but
I'll leave here and get a job in a shop somewhere and live
blindfolded for the rest of my life."

"After the war, doctors found that the mind took longer to heal
than the body." As he puffed on his pipe, I understood what he was
trying to tell me, that he had suffered injuries both physical and

mental, and had overcome both in time. And I knew it had not been an easy road for him either, but he had persevered.

"What if I never learn for sure whether I am Claire or Eva?" I asked morosely.

"You mean, which one is genuine and which is made up?"

"So you think I am both?"

"It seems the only logical explanation."

"It means I'm mad."

"No, it means you are confused after a blow to the head."

I considered what he said. Jean-Claude was the only person I trusted. Moreover, he had no stake in this sad affair. He was an insider with an outsider's perspective, a man whose personal sense of honour would always come before blind loyalty to family or faction. In another world, another time, when life had not been derailed by a war to end all wars, that rare combination of impartiality and involvement would have made a compassionate judge or a principled politician. If Jean-Claude thought dual personality was the only explanation that fit the facts, it must be so. As we sat there in companionable silence, a sense of calm settled over me and I fancied I could feel my two halves come closer together, merging into one. But which one would it be? Please not Eva. I would cling to Claire with all my might.

At last Jean-Claude broke the quiet, but he did not get far. "Perhaps Alex will return with some new—"

The door burst open. Danielle stood there, arms akimbo and a snarl on her lips. "Well, now, isn't this cosy?" She focused her dark Portuguese eyes on me and hissed, "With your history, my dear, we expected no less. But you!" She turned on Jean-Claude with the fury of a woman scorned. "One would have hoped you could keep your trousers buttoned around your cousin's wife. Alex will be very interested to hear of this when he returns."

Jean-Claude got to his feet, his face scarlet. "Danielle! You disgrace yourself. Apologize at once and leave us." Amazingly, she did as he ordered. For several moments after the door slammed behind her, he stared at the space she no longer occupied, as if she were still there. "I am sorry for that," he said softly, distracted by his own thoughts. "Danielle does have her good qualities, although after that childish performance, you cannot be expected to agree."

"He will believe her. He already accused me of—well, of

playing up to you the day I went to the *mairie*." It shamed me to even speak those words. I hated to admit that Alex could think such despicable thoughts about either of us.

I supposed he hadn't heard me, so deep in concentration had he fallen, but finally he regarded me with a puzzled frown. "Yes, I know. He confronted me as well. Odd, isn't it?"

Odd, yes. And then I knew. I should have known earlier, when he had said something about DeSequeryas being hard to love. Jean-Claude was in love with Danielle. He had probably been in love with her since they were children. Meanwhile she merrily moved from husband to husband, oblivious to his feelings. Had my presence sparked some change in Danielle? Was this jealousy on her part?

"Look, Jean-Claude, I don't want to come between you and Alex. Blame this on me. I can't drop any lower in his esteem," I said, bitterly aware that I had only just started to rise a bit in his regard, and this would destroy what little I had accomplished. "I'll be gone soon, but he's your family forever."

"Do you know the French poet, Jacques Delille?"

"I don't think so."

"'Fate chooses our family, we choose our friends.'"

The next morning I returned to the library. I had finished the last of my English books and hoped to find something else to read among the hundreds on those shelves. Even if I didn't, the prospect of investigating the old volumes drew me like a moth to a candle, and as I squinted over their titles in the dim light, I felt like an archaeologist making out faded hieroglyphics in an Egyptian tomb.

The telephone bell erupted in its harsh ring, startling me so much I nearly dropped a heavy volume of Clausewitz on my toe. It jangled rudely three more times before I concluded that Thonet was not coming. I picked up the receiver. "*Bonjour*," I said cautiously. French phone etiquette was not a subject I had mastered.

The operator jabbered something unintelligible and after several loud clicks, put through the call. "Hullo, hullo," came the voice on the other end, unnaturally loud, the way people raise their voice

when talking to foreigners. "Does anyone speak English there?"
"Yes, I do."

I could feel his relief through the wires. "I am calling from London for Mr. Alexander DeSequeyra."

"I am sorry; he is not here at present. May I take a message?"

He was an Englishman with an accent much like my own, and he sounded so everyday ordinary that I felt a sudden affinity for this faceless person—the first countryman I had spoken to since my swim in the Seine.

"My name is Jack Marsh and I'm calling with information about the orphanage. He said it was urgent, so I'm—"

I froze on the word orphanage, but only for a heartbeat. "Mr. Marsh, I am Mrs. DeSequeyra. What information have you found?"

He heard the tension in my voice and backed off. "Well, now, I've been hired by Mr. Alexander DeSequeyra, and he didn't say anything about—"

"Yes, quite. But your investigation is about me. I know all about it," I lied. "You were to look for information about Eva Johnson and Claire Smith, were you not?"

"Well, yes . . ."

"I'm sure he told you about my head injury, and my amnesia. I—we have pinned our hopes on your abilities to discover some clue about my early life. What is it you've found?" I was gripping the telephone receiver so hard it's a wonder it didn't snap in two.

I could almost hear him thinking on the other end, what harm could there possibly be in speaking to this woman who knew about the investigation anyway, and I willed him to talk with all my might. Balancing the receiver between my shoulder and chin, I rummaged messily with my good hand through three desk drawers before finding a pencil and some blank paper.

"Well, I looked in all the London orphanage records, and I didn't find a whisper of the name Eva Johnson. Or Claire Smith neither. But I didn't stop at that, not me. I heard about one or two orphanages that were all closed up, one of them the Ragged School on Copperfield Road. I went to have a look. It's a factory today, but I asked around and learned that they kept the records at a bishop's house. This was really good luck since lots of 'em never kept records at all or threw 'em out when the orphans left, so I went to the bishop's and got a look through the files. Sure enough, there

139

you were in black and white."

"Who was there, in the files? What name?"

"Why, Eva Johnson. No parents named, but it says they're dead. Seems a neighbour brought in little Eva when she was two, in 1906, and she was adopted soon after by a couple, name of Winston. Mrs. Winston died and Mr. Winston couldn't work and take care of a little one, so he brought Eva—you, that is—back to the Ragged School when she—you—were five. Do you remember anything like that, Mrs. DeSequeyra?"

Crushed, I responded weakly. "No, I'm afraid not. Please continue."

"Well, there's nothing written like this but I can figure for myself that a five-year-old isn't as likely to be adopted as a babe, and one of the priests tells me that what they did back then was keep orphans until they were about ten or twelve, then send them to Canada or New Zealand to have a chance at a better life than the London slums. But when Eva was ten, another family, name of Tennant, came 'round and took her. Took you, I mean. Sounds good, right? But a few years later, there's this note on the page that says Tennant was arrested for thieving, and it seems the family was not so reputable, if you know what I mean. So the orphanage people were wanting to find Eva to bring her back, but she was fifteen then and not much they could do about it, was there? So that's the end."

It all sounded like a bad piece of fiction. There was no earthly chance that this was my story.

"What about Claire Smith? Did you find that name in your search?"

"No, I did not. It's a common enough name, now, isn't it, but I didn't see it anywhere in any of the orphanages, not this Ragged School, not any of the others. I'm sorry if that isn't what you wanted, but that's the truth about what I found."

"Thank you, Mr. Marsh. I don't doubt your word. I was just hoping that there would be something about Claire Smith too."

"Nary a scrap. Now, you'll be passing this information along to Mr. Alexander DeSequeyra for me, I know, but I'll be writing up the particulars and sending everything off to the Paris address with the bill for my services."

A careful man, Mr. Marsh. And not altogether trusting. A

necessary trait, I supposed, in his line of work. "Yes, thank you, Mr. Marsh. You've been a great help."

I set down the receiver and burst into tears.

After recovering my wits, I gathered up the tear stained pages of notes and attempted to straighten out the mess I'd made of folders and papers that had fallen to the floor in my clumsy search for writing material. That's when my eye chanced upon a French newspaper clipping. I wouldn't have given it a glance had it not carried a large photograph of Alex above the headline, "DeSequeyra Kills Government Minister; Avenges Brother."

I sat back down and started to translate.

The clipping had no date, but judging from the picture, it couldn't have been more than a few years old. I couldn't make out all the words, but I got the gist of it. A mid-level war office employee named Yves Calvet had died of gunshot wounds, killed by Alexander DeSequeyra a few days before the start of the annual race at Le Mans. Calvet had been the hapless *fonctionnaire* who had signed DeSequeyra's brother's orders to the front where he had immediately been killed in battle. In revenge, DeSequeyra had tracked down Calvet and shot him. The rest of the article dealt with whether or not DeSequeyra would be permitted to compete in the race and, concluding that he would, moved on to discuss the merits of his vehicle. I replaced the article and closed the drawer.

Vigorous walks about the courtyard improved my stamina. The rich food restored my curves even as it diminished my clothing selection. In desperation one day I took up needle and thread and managed to save two of my frocks by moving the buttons back an inch. In doing so, it came to me that the only time my wardrobe had fit me was when I had come out of hospital after a two-week fast.

I searched until I located my light yellow dress—the one I was wearing when the Polish sailors fished me out of the Seine—crushed into the back of a drawer. The nuns had done admirable work mending the tears at the neck and replacing the missing buttons with ones that almost matched, still it looked pitiful against the natty custom-made clothing hanging in my wardrobe. I slipped it over my head and gasped at my reflection in the mirror. It was too large, even now. There was no way the girl who had worn this dress could be the same as the girl who fit into the expensive designer costumes from the Champs Elysées.

What was I to make of this? Just as I was trying to reconcile myself to the logic of Alex's dual personality premise, along comes another piece of evidence to insist it was nonsense, that I could be no one but Claire. Claire fit the yellow dress. Eva fit the fashionable wardrobe. I could hear Alex scoffing at my conclusion as clearly as if he had been standing beside me: "You haven't tried on a tenth of the clothing that followed us from Paris," he would say in that dismissive manner that so exasperated me. "Doubtless you will find that sizes vary to accommodate changes in your weight." I would be forced to admit that, theoretically, that was possible, and also that a few of the straight-waist, loosely styled items did indeed fit me now. His logic would carry the day, but I would remain conflicted.

And yet, he had hired a man to investigate my claims. I fancied I had *Grand-mère* to thank for that but on some level, he must have believed that my suspicions were valid and that somehow, something was rotten in Denmark.

The family departure to South America was fast approaching, and my anxiety grew with each passing day. Brazil sounded like the end of the earth. I emphatically did *not* want to accompany them, but I was afraid Alex would insist if he believed the whereabouts of his paintings were still lodged in my unconscious brain. Even if I convinced him somehow that I was not Eva, he was sure to think that I was in league with her in Paris, working together on some grand swindle. Had I been in London—had I possessed some money—I could have mounted my own investigation, placing notices in the *Times* and searching the ranks of the suffragettes for women who had worked with me and knew me. To my intense frustration, no one in the house but me would see any of that as productive.

Alex returned from Paris. I heard his voice as I was passing the parlour and my pulse quickened. I was eager to tell him about Mr. Marsh's call and about my latest idea for tracing my parents, the Smiths.

"Alex!" I blurted cheerfully from the doorway. "You're back!"

He acknowledged my interruption with a cool, fleeting glance and returned to his conversation with *Grand-mère*, Cousin Pauline, Danielle, and Lianne. I stood awkwardly, feeling like an intruder at a family gathering until *Grand-mère* patted the seat beside her and motioned for me to join them.

"No, thank you," I said, my exhilaration plummeting. From the look of the scene, he'd been home for some time. Foolishly I had assumed he would seek me out the moment he returned. Now I feigned indifference, pretending I had not been cut to the bone. "I'll wait until you're free, Alex, to tell you my news. Excuse me."

It was evening before he sent Thonet to request my presence in the library. He was alone. I told him at once about Jack Marsh's call. To my surprise, he already knew of it, from Marsh himself who had managed to reach him just before he left Paris.

"I think Marsh's report speaks for itself," he told me. "You will have no objection, I trust, if we cease investigating the fictional past of your Claire Smith alias?"

"Actually, I have had another idea. I've been thinking about the English suffragettes."

One sardonic brow lifted. "That's right, I forgot. You are a moral crusader."

I refused to rise to the bait. "The name Christabel Pankhurst keeps teasing me, repeating over and over in my head like a cuckoo clock, and I believe that I know her personally—or more to the point, I believe she knows me. Mrs. Pankhurst was old. Her daughter Christabel must be closer to my own age. Of twenty-four," I added pointedly.

"Yes, it seems you were right about the year of your birth." He demonstrated his indifference by taking out his pipe, filling the bowl with an aromatic blend, packing it solid, lighting it with a gold lighter, and drawing several contemplative puffs—all at a speed not generally associated with race car driving. Duelling silences concluded, he went on. "Having never before encountered a woman who lied about her age to make herself seem *older*, I did not believe you when you told me in hospital that you were born in aught four. After giving the matter some thought, I believe I understand what occurred. When you took aim at me in Monte Carlo, you were astute enough to realize that I would have sent an unmarried girl of nineteen away with a slap on her bottom. You inflated your age by just enough to maintain your eligibility."

Frankly, I found a claim to such scruples hilarious in a man who would take to bed a woman he had met hours earlier, but I refrained from telling him so.

"I've seen a photograph of Christabel Pankhurst," he continued, leaning back in his chair and folding his arms in that superior way of his. "She must be fifty if she's a day, and if a more unattractive harridan exists, I have been fortunate enough to remain unaware of it. You are far too young to consort with such an Amazon."

"Not friends, then, but acquaintances. Perhaps we worked together on the vote. In any case, I thought that I might write to her, asking whether she recognizes the name Claire Smith."

"And what do you propose to use for an address for this preposterous woman?"

"I thought to ask Mr. Marsh to deliver it. And telephone me with the reply."

"A waste of time, but I can see you will not be dissuaded." He went to the delicate Louis XV escritoire beside the window and took out a sheet of engraved stationery, a matching envelope, a gold fountain pen, blotting paper, and a bottle of blue ink. "Here. When you have finished, I shall post it for you." Alex left me alone. Elated to have my way for once, I sat down and started to compose a short letter to Miss Pankhurst.

As I wrote, my spirits rose. This was as solid a lead as I had ever had. My best hope for success, short of the complete recovery of my memory. I was certain that my attachment to the suffrage movement would prove to be the key that opened the lock to my identity.

I finished the letter and waited awhile in the library for Alex to return. I waited awhile upstairs in our bedchamber, thinking that tonight he would surely sleep here, and I waited awhile longer in bed until I fell asleep, alone.

5 THE HANDFAST

The next day, Lianne found me in my room. She had wind in her hair, dirt under her fingernails, and excitement all over her face.

"It looks as though you've been gardening again," I said. Gardening now rivalled the kittens as her favourite pastime, although I suspected that the new assistant gardener had more to do with this than a sudden appreciation for botany. I had only seen him from a distance, but he looked to be dark and handsome.

She tried to brush off the soil that clung to her skirt but only succeeded in making it worse.

"Yes, gardening. Wait 'til you see who has come! Some friends of Danielle's. They are so *drôle*. Papa told me to get you. Didn't you hear all the car horns when their caravan pulled in? It sounded like a wedding! And they are staying the night! I must go and clean up before Papa will introduce me," she said, and she dashed out of the room.

I went downstairs.

We were introduced by first names only, a faddish custom among the idle rich that only made it harder to converse. The entourage—six people plus the requisite number of maids, valets, and chauffeurs—was on its way to the Riviera to a house party that would last the better part of a month. Everyone switched effortlessly between English, French, and Italian, and I was left to follow as best I could. They seemed like carbon copies of Danielle—brittle, bored, and cynical. Before I could slip away, someone turned on the gramophone and the gathering became a party.

"My, you are a fetching thing." Taking notice of me for the first time, Artie was mincing my way, his hazel eyes raking me from head to toe. "Has anyone ever told you you're a dead ringer for Clara Bow? Lovely, just lovely. Look at her, Mary," he called over his shoulder to a plain woman wearing trousers and a pinched-waist man's jacket who ignored us both. "Now she's blushing, isn't that charming? Who knew anyone could blush these days? I must paint you, my dear. Watercolours, I think. How long are we staying, George?"

"Just the night, Arthur," replied George, a titled English ex-pat if ever I saw one.

"Damn, and it's already getting dark, isn't it? Need sunlight to paint. Lovely complexion. Such fresh innocence. How did an old *roué* like Alex end up marrying a child like you, eh?"

Forcing a smile that did not mask his annoyance, Alex chose this moment to join us and, without comment, draped one arm around my shoulders in a proprietary gesture that sent Artie scurrying to the bar for a refill.

Before I could protest that I had done nothing to lead Artie on, Danielle approached with a thin, pale, blond man in her wake. "Claire darling," she began—she had taken to calling me Claire, I thought, only to vex her brother—"do you know what I just this moment realized? Remember the other evening when I was telling you about the man at the party who hypnotized people? Can you believe the coincidence—that person is Bobby! What fabulous good luck for you! Fate, I should say. Isn't it true, Bobby darling, that hypnotism can sometimes cure amnesia? It's not just a parlour trick, is it?"

Bobby nodded. "Some doctors have used it in treatment of people who cannot remember parts of their past, but it is not always successful."

"Claire has a touch of amnesia, darling. Perhaps you can root around in her subconscious and dig up the missing brain cells?"

"No, thank you very much, I'd rather not," I said. Danielle's remarks some days ago about the embarrassing things she had been led to do under hypnosis convinced me that this was some trick of hers to humiliate me in front of her friends.

"But you must!" she persisted. "Hypnotism is such fun!"

Fun for the observers. I shook my head firmly. "I'm not going to provide the evening's hilarity, barking like a dog or taking my clothes off."

"Madame DeSequeyra," began Bobby in that patient voice one uses to calm a child's tantrum. "Have no fear. No one can make another person become hypnotized. The subject must want to become hypnotized for the procedure to take effect, so you are in no danger of being tricked into anything." Deprived of her entertainment, Danielle drifted sullenly away as Bobby muttered something to Alex that I was not meant to hear. Alex tightened his hand on my shoulder.

"Listen," Alex said at last, turning me to face him, holding me close against him with both of his hands on my waist. His coal black eyes held me still. "Bobby has offered to try the hypnosis with you privately, to see whether the technique can help you remember anything. You will not be ridiculed. You will not even be observed by anyone."

And after I was firmly under the influence, he would summon the troops and everyone would have a grand time at my expense. "No, thank you."

Alex followed my thoughts. "I was thinking to arrange for a hypnotist from Paris to meet with us before we left. It is a legitimate treatment for amnesia—by allowing the patient to relax completely, it can bring back buried memories. Sometimes it fails entirely. Is it not worth the chance to try this technique? You have my word that no one else would be in the room the entire time." Without turning his head he asked Bobby, "How long would it take, old man?"

"Oh, ten minutes if it isn't working. Longer if the memories are returning."

"There you have it. In ten minutes you could know the answers to the questions that have been torturing you for the past weeks. Is it not worth that small effort?"

I looked down at his shirt buttons so he couldn't see I was wavering. "Would you be in the room as well?"

"I'd have to be, to ask the questions. Just the three of us." With one finger he lifted my chin so I was forced to meet his eyes. "Trust me."

Funnily enough, I did. In this matter, at least. Danielle was the one looking for cheap laughs at someone else's expense. Alex was looking for information. As was I. No one noticed the three of us leaving the room.

"I warn you in advance," said Bobby as we made our way to the morning room, "not everyone can be hypnotized, even if they want to be. And if you have reservations, your subconscious mind may resist." I assured him I would try to cooperate. Nervous, I began to bite a fingernail.

Bobby settled me into my favourite place by the windows. The hands of a small shelf clock pointed to 10:15. Alex stood behind my chair where his presence would not distract me. Bobby pulled another chair up and sat before me almost knee to knee. He talked calmly for a few moments about nothing, but I noticed that his voice had dropped in pitch and evened out into a gentle monotone that resonated like the notes of a Gregorian chant.

"You probably think we use a watch and chain, and wave it about before your eyes, and I usually do for the parlour tricks, but it isn't necessary. It is only necessary that you concentrate on my voice and let your body relax into the soft cushions and listen to the ticking of the little clock grow louder and louder . . ."

Time lost its meaning. The only reality in the room was the liquid voice that soaked into every thirsty pore of my body and the endless ticking that grew slower and slower . . . and slower.

I blinked and looked about, a little disoriented. Why had we stopped? "Oh, did you change your mind? Was I not doing it properly?"

"Not at all." Bobby patted my knee and stood up. "We're finished and you were splendid. How do you feel?"

"Fine." In truth, I did feel splendid. Rested, serenely content. A glance at the clock told me that only eighteen minutes had passed. "What happened? It didn't work?"

Alex held up his notebook. It was blank. "You went under very quickly. But you could not answer any of the questions."

"None?"

"The basic ones, things we already know like your name, your age—"

"Did I say my name was Claire?"

"Yes."

"What did you ask? Besides the location of the paintings."

"About the orphanage, about Monte Carlo, the hotel in Paris, your assailants. None of it came back."

"It's not your fault," said Bobby gently. "I didn't realize that you had suffered a severe blow to the head. When your husband told me that, I brought you out of the trance. Hypnosis can help you remember what your subconscious mind is hiding. It can get behind the barricades people erect to shield themselves from painful experiences, but it is of little use in cases where there has been actual damage to the brain."

I blinked back tears. To have my hopes raised so quickly and dashed so fast seemed the cruellest trick of all. My disappointment was keen.

"Shall we rejoin the others?" asked Alex, looking more pensive than discouraged. But then, it was my life that was missing and only his paintings.

"I believe I'll retire now," I said rubbing my temples.

"Come," he said, taking my hand in his. "I know you are disappointed. So am I." But he was smiling now, and he didn't appear disappointed at all. As I looked from Bobby to Alex, an uneasy feeling swept over me that I had, indeed, said something significant, something the two men were concealing from me. But why would they do that?

Alex poured on the persuasion. "Come back with me for a few minutes for form's sake, then slip away if you must."

In truth, I didn't feel a bit tired—the hypnotism left me energized beyond all logic—but it was the sincere note in Alex's request that decided me. We returned to the others together.

Lively, loud, and unfamiliar music was blaring from the gramophone—someone had brought along new records—forcing the conversation to rise above it to be heard. Our brief absence had not been remarked. Feeling livelier than I had in weeks, I picked up a glass of champagne from Thonet at the bar and listened to the banter of the two glamorous females in the group.

Suzie and Elise, who between them wore enough ropes of pearls to stock Cartier's cabinets, were talking about a jazz club in Montmartre where crowds thronged to see the celebrated Josephine Baker, an American Negress who had danced her way into the hearts of Parisians. Elise had seen *La Baker* perform just last week in a costume made entirely of snakes—a fashion I did not think likely to catch on—and was wild to twirl her pearls and demonstrate the latest version of the Charleston. "Oh, do hurry and give George another drink so he'll play us some jazz!"

George demurred gallantly, then heaved a sigh of resignation and lifted the top of the grand piano. Awestruck, I watched his beautiful fingers dance across the keys, releasing Gershwin's *Rhapsody in Blue* from the ebonies and ivories that had held it prisoner until this moment in time. Without a breath, he moved through half a dozen American ragtime numbers I knew to a couple of soulful jazz pieces I had never heard. The audience, affectionately disrespectful, called out favourites and George obliged.

Too timid to shout out a title, Lianne raised her hand like a dutiful schoolgirl and waited to be noticed. "Do you know 'Yes, We Have No Bananas?'" she asked.

"Only if you sing the words."

"Oh, no, I couldn't."

"Very well then, come sing it with me. A duet." George strummed the opening chords and sent her an exaggerated wink, and in a flash she was there, beside the piano, belting out the nonsensical words to the song. The applause was generous, the ice broken, and in no time everyone was singing like happy Christmas carollers. George entertained next with the popular "I'm Just Wild About Harry," but substituted Mary's name for Harry, and I realized the two were a couple. Next he returned to some lively jazz so Elise could show everyone the new style Charleston she had learned at the *Revue Nègre* and in moments, Danielle and Lianne were trying it on for size. Jean-Claude came up and asked me to help him prove that one-handed people could do the Lindy Hop.

The amount of champagne I had consumed helped overcome my aversion to the spotlight but I couldn't shake the persistent feeling of being followed by disapproving eyes. I looked toward Alex who had adopted a sullen Byronic pose against the fireplace mantel while Jean-Claude and I danced. A drink in one hand, he was glaring at Artie who was holed up in an armchair with a large sketchpad on his lap. Near him slouched Danielle, dressed in a sensational blue beaded flapper dress that revealed a good deal of her fine figure, balancing a martini glass in one hand and a long cigarette holder in the other. Between dances, I managed to snatch a look at Artie's sketchpad. It was a pencil drawing of me, shoulders up. Amazingly enough, it was an excellent likeness. Suddenly I was ashamed at my earlier prejudice against these rich friends of Danielle's. Before I had bothered to know them, I had written them off as well-heeled hedonists when they were, in truth, no better or worse than anyone else.

Artie scrawled his name below my shoulders with a flourish worthy of Pablo Picasso and ripped the sheet off the pad. "*Avec mes compliments,* Mademoiselle Clara Bow. Save it. It will be very valuable one day when I am recognized around the world as the twentieth century's greatest artist!"

"A good likeness," came Alex's voice from behind me. He reached for the sketch and examined it closely. Then he placed it on a table and took up my hand. "May I have the honour?" he asked.

Matching George's downshift in speed, Alex took me in his arms for a slow foxtrot and laced the fingers of his left hand firmly through the fingers of my right. He danced as he drove—accurately, effortlessly, and in complete control. Being held as close as that made my pulse race and my heart pound so hard I was afraid he could feel it, and I tried to ease my self-consciousness by doing what women all over the world are taught to do when presented with an awkward moment: I asked him about himself.

"I heard Artie talking about the race at Le Mans. You didn't enter this year?"

The chuckle that rose in his throat told me he had seen through my tactic but would play along for a while. "I retired after the two wins. Although it might be more accurate to say that my partner retired, and I did not want to start over with a new one."

"I'm afraid I don't know anything about racing. D'you drive with a partner?"

"Le Mans is an endurance race, *ma petite,* not the Grand Prix. It is as much a test of racing cars as of men. The car is driven for 24 hours at the highest speeds possible around a circuit of about ten miles, a route that winds through the city of Le Mans and a few outlying villages. There are two men to a team."

"They change when one becomes tired?"

"And fewer changes save time."

"I see. Did you have a favourite in this year's race?" I swallowed hard and gave him what I hoped was a guileless look, so he would not suspect that his nearness was causing havoc with my nerves. Breathing evenly required my steady concentration. I should not feel any attraction to this man who had threatened me and bullied me for weeks, but I did.

"While I no longer drive, I still compete. I sponsor a team. They came in third which was commendable since they were not expected to place. Your compatriots, as it happens, won the race in an English Bentley. Good friends of mine. I intend to write to them with my congratulations."

"That must have been bittersweet, watching your own car come in behind your friends."

"Alas, I did not see the race. I was unable to attend this year."

"Why ever not? I thought racing was your chief passion." Poor choice of words. I bit my lower lip and hoped he would not notice.

"Because I had a telephone message about a woman in the Seine."

"Oh."

"Besides, I have other passions than mechanical ones." And he tightened his arm around my waist as he said it, pulling me closer against his body until I could feel his warm breath on my ear. "The timing was unfortunate in several ways—I missed Lianne's performance as well as the race—but it was more important that I be at the hospital, with you."

I winced as George eased from a perky version of "Tea for Two" into the soulful "You Made Me Love You." Alex and I moved together well, like a couple who had been dancing partners for so many years that their thoughts were synchronized, and it did not seem possible that I had known him only three weeks. Being circled by Alex's arms felt good. More than good. And somehow very normal, as if it had happened many times. I had to admit he was an attractive man, one who, but for my presence, would have aroused our female guests, Elise and Suzie, to blows by now.

If I had just met him today, I might have joined them.

George ended his number with an arpeggio flourish and Alex spun me gently around and bent me backwards towards the floor in an exaggerated pantomime of romance. I was sorry the dance ended. Alex's hand on my back brought me up to face him. He was going to kiss me. My heart raced. I wanted him to kiss me. A faint smile played about his lips and his left hand lifted my chin a little until his eyes could bore into mine. Searching for answers he could not find anywhere else? We were both looking for answers. What had he already discovered? The sharpness of unexpected desire caused my breath to catch in my throat.

"My turn to cut in, old chap," said George, with a tap on Alex's shoulder. "Time for the gramophone to take over so I can have a chance at the ladies." And he led me away before I could gather my wits to decline.

After a brisk foxtrot, I pleaded the need for a drink of water. George fetched me a glass, and I drained it. I very nearly dropped the thing when I heard the hall clock strike two. Lianne?—there she was, curled up on a sofa against the wall, fast asleep beneath all the noise as only a child can do. Alex had given in to her pleas to stay up with the adults but she had succumbed to sleep in spite of her best efforts. It was time for me to be similarly occupied. If I left now, while Alex was talking earnestly with Artie and Mary, I could slip away without his notice, before he claimed me again. I thanked George for the dance and meant every word. I had been disappointed at first; now I was relieved. He had cut in not a moment too soon. My life was complicated enough without letting a temporary physical attraction get the better of me.

For the hostess to leave her party before her guests is a social sin of the most grievous magnitude, but as these were Danielle's guests and she the party's hostess, I let people think I was going to powder my nose and escaped, thoroughly unrepentant, to the hall.

"May I help you up the stairs, *madame*?" Thonet's disembodied voice bounced from frescoed ceiling to the chessboard floor, echoing inside my head as I made my way rather circuitously toward the staircase. Startled, I turned too quickly and might have lost my balance had not the butler's long arm reached out to steady me. The room tilted on its axis.

"No, thank you, Thonet, I'm fine. Truly I am. I was just going to my room. The Michelin guide scenic route, as you can see." Paying no mind to my protestations, he guided me to the stairs and set my hand firmly on the banister.

"*Voilà, madame.*"

"Good night, Thonet."

The bathtub beckoned. A hot soak with some of Cècile's herbs and a soft pillow would make a perfect end to what had turned out to be a pleasant evening indeed.

Half an hour later, I danced out of the bathroom, buoyant as a soap bubble, wearing nothing but my splint and humming the popular Maurice Chevalier song that would not leave me alone. I did a neat pirouette around the clothes that were lying in a puddle in the middle of the room, wondered vaguely why they hadn't put themselves away, and then paused to wrap my dressing gown around me before continuing on to the fireplace to drop a few more lumps of coal into the grate. I let my bare feet Charleston their way across the rug while I sang.

Haven't got a lot, I don't need a lot,
Coffee's only a dime,
Living in the sunlight, loving in the moonlight,
Having a marvelous time.

I'm right here to stay, when I'm old and gray,
I'll be right in my prime,
Living in the sunlight, loving in the moonlight,
Having a glorious time.

Heedless of the cool night air, I threw open the casement window and leaned out to find the crescent moon sailing above the darkened village. Maybe I would see a shooting star to bring me good luck. Small birds fluttered erratically against the night sky. I had only to close my eyes to feel Alex's arm around my waist again and his hand holding mine as we whirled our way through the music. "I'm so happy, happy-go-lucky me," I sang. I was tipsy, I was happy, I was "having a wonderful time," I would hold onto that euphoria for as long as I could, thank you very much, and I would not ask why. I switched to "My Blue Heaven," even though the sky was black. It seems I had no trouble remembering song lyrics!

"A fetching view."

Startled, I bumped my head on the side of the window as I spun around to find a grin at the door. "Ouch!"

"The scene would remind me of Rapunzel, but your hair is too short to climb."

"Look what you made me do, sneaking up on me like that," I

pouted, rubbing my head.

"A thousand pardons, *madame*," he said with a dip from the waist that passed for an old-fashioned bow. It was then that I noticed he held a bottle of champagne in one hand. And two glasses in the other. He set the glasses on the table and began twisting off the wire. "I carried Lianne up to her bed and realized you, too, had retired. I thought I would bring the party up here. A special bottle. Vintage 1923. The year we met."

"I was looking at the moon and watching the birds."

He laughed. "Birds? *Chérie,* the birds are long ago in bed. Those are bats."

"Oh." Feeling dumb as a post, I gave the window a nervous glance, hastily latched the shutters, and pulled the thick draperies across it.

"They live in the caves and come out at night to feed on insects. You aren't afraid of them, are you?"

"Certainly not," I said with more bravado than conviction, thankful I hadn't encountered any bats in the wine caves with Jean-Claude.

"They are harmless creatures. They never attack people or get tangled in your hair as they do in films."

"If you say so."

"My, you are agreeable tonight. Have we a truce?"

The cork gave a resounding pop and Alex caught the foam neatly in one glass. He filled both slowly, halting at the precise moment when another drop would have sent the white froth cascading down the side. Not knowing how to respond, I changed the subject. "Has everyone retired?"

"Just us. And Lianne, of course. I should have sent her up hours ago. Here." He handed me a glass. It sparkled cool and fresh on my tongue.

I heard the song lyrics again in my head. "There is no harm in staying up late once in a while. She was having a wonderful time."

"Mmmm," he grimaced. "And learning things I would rather she not learn."

"You can't prevent her from growing up."

"I'm trying, though, aren't I?"

I couldn't help my smile. "Well, yes, but I suspect that's what fathers do."

"Were you enjoying yourself?"

"I was, actually."

"Why then did you leave?"

Why *had* I come upstairs when I did? Suddenly I was self-conscious in my dressing gown. I wrapped it more tightly around me and tied the belt with clumsy fingers. "The lateness of the hour."

"Is that all?" No, it was not. I could not meet his penetrating gaze. My eyes wandered about the room and it came to me how long it had been since he had come in here. I wondered whether his clothes were still in the drawers. We hadn't shared the big bed since his trip to Paris.

I thought it best to change the subject again. "So . . . the party continues without us?"

"The party has reached the shrill *dénouement* that predicts a rapid decline. With duelling a relic of the past, I expect Bobby and George have resorted by now to insults at twenty paces while the ladies wound one another with rapier-sharp compliments. I escaped in the nick of time."

I laughed. He refilled both glasses, held his up, and locked his eyes to mine. "S*anté.*" He drank. I did the same. It was impossible not to. I looked deep inside those Valentino eyes, searching for a spark of emotion, and found his thoughts. I knew why he had come. I had sensed it downstairs in the steady stare that shot across the room and drilled through my defences. I had sensed it in his arms when we shared a dance.

His intentions exposed, Alex set his glass down, crossed the distance between us with three easy steps. He reached for my shoulders. I tried to swallow the panic that was rising in my throat. Instinctively my palms pressed against his chest, my lips parted to say no—then closed tight.

My hands made him pause. He studied my face through narrowed eyes. Slowly, he kissed my cheek, then thoughtfully kissed the other like a man making sure everything was equal. I couldn't stop myself from brushing my fingers along his jaw and that was all it took.

I awoke the next morning beside a man I knew far better than I had the previous night.

Before I could open my eyes, images from the night before rushed back into my head, bringing a flush to my cheeks and a sigh to my lips. An emotion I did not recognize sent shivers down to my toes. I wondered if it was love. Unsure how to break the silence, I turned to look at my husband. He was lying with his head propped on his elbow, watching me, his brow creased with a frown. With a tenderness I would never have expected, he brushed a strand of hair back from my face. Then he spoke the last words I expected to hear.

"I am so sorry," he said softly. "I apologize." He was *sorry*? Surely I had misunderstood. I could only stare at him in utter bewilderment as he continued softly, "I am afraid I lost control of myself. The drink . . . but that is no excuse. Can you forgive me?"

I was speechless. What meant so much to me had been a careless mistake to him? As if he had stepped on my foot during a dance, he wanted forgiveness? *Pardon, madame, excusez-moi. De rien, monsieur.* It was nothing. I couldn't help it—tears of humiliation burned my eyes. I tried to turn away before they spilt down my cheeks but his arm stopped me, and held me fast against him. He was *sorry*.

"I should never have been so rough with you. I forgot about your injuries. I should have been more careful." When I understood his meaning, I gasped, then nearly wept with relief. *That* was what he was sorry for. Now it was his turn to misunderstand, and he held me tight, his lips against my hair. "Ah, little one. Did I hurt you very much? I am a beast. It won't happen again, I promise."

When I leafed through the jumble of images from last night's interlude, a few instances of uncomfortable physical excess did rise to the fore. I, too, had been drinking champagne all evening, and the details were hazy. There were fresh bruises on my upper arms and some soreness in other areas, but my splint was intact. "I am not some fragile porcelain figurine that breaks with handling, you know."

"Not normally, but under the circumstances—oh, never mind." He kissed me until I was thoroughly aroused, then demonstrated how things should have gone between us had we both been sober. It was a wondrous improvement.

When we had untangled ourselves from the sheets, Alex insisted on leading me into the shower where we played like children, soaping and spraying one another until we were drenched from head to toe by the nozzles aimed from our knees to our shoulders.

"My splint!"

"Nurse Renaud will be here soon and she can make you a fresh one."

The thought of Cécile's imminent arrival sent both of us rushing to dry and dress until I noticed the clock. "Ah, look," I said. "No need to hurry. It's nearly noon. Cécile will have checked on *Grand-mère's* ankle and left hours ago."

"And she left your medicine," said Alex, opening the bedroom door and finding a tray with a glass of cider on it. "Finish it. This is the last of the restorative. Shall I get you more?"

"I don't . . . um, what is it?" I took the glass from his hand.

"Some American medicine called Valentine's Meat Juice, intended to strengthen invalids. Has it helped, do you think?"

I could hardly confess that I'd suspected him of trying to poison me and had been pouring it down the sink every chance I got. Heartily ashamed of my foolish suspicions, I only said, "Well, I am feeling much stronger than I was a few weeks ago, but I think I've had enough."

I pulled back the draperies and opened the window, flooding the room with sunshine. Alex looked about the room with some puzzlement, noticing the surroundings for the first time since he had moved out. "The furniture—you've been redecorating?"

"Oh, yes," I confessed. "The arrangement was awkward so I moved the sofa to face the two chairs, and found that table in the hall. And the lighting was poor so I borrowed those lamps from upstairs and the *torchère* from the attic. Cécile wouldn't let me lift anything but the vase." He still had said nothing, so I continued a little defensively. "I can always return the objects if . . ."

"No. Heavens, no. It looks quite nice, and I approve of anything that makes you happy. But right now, I'm starving. I'll order us something to eat and send word to Cécile about your bandages." At the door, he paused and looked back at me. A playful grin tugged at the corner of his mouth. "I believe I can manage a short separation, *chérie*, but I am not sure I can wait until tonight to have you again."

Such blunt language turned my cheeks red. Alex just laughed and kissed me until I was breathless. "I shall spend the time thinking up new ways to make you blush."

As it turned out, our late breakfast marked the first appearance of Danielle and her guests as well. Lianne joined us, then sulked through the meal when Alex declined to take her riding afterwards. As the only person in the room who knew what Alex wanted to do afterwards, I fixed my eyes firmly on my plate. No sooner had we waved the entourage and their caravan out through the archway, than he turned to me.

"Would you care to take a walk?"

It was not what I expected, but the suggestion appealed. "One problem," I ventured, looking at my feet. "I can manage with these on smooth floors but they will not do for countryside rambles." I stepped out of my calfskin pumps to show him how loose they were. "Even if I were to wear socks, there is nothing in the closet except evening shoes and stylish daywear that would fall apart after a dozen steps through the brambles."

"Why didn't you say something, Claire? Just change into something suitable, and I'll take care of the shoes."

He called me Claire. A slip of the tongue or was he trying to placate me?

Alex was lounging at the edge of the courtyard fountain, the epitome of a European gentleman dressed for a saunter around the estate in his tweed coat and beige flannel trousers that were no less Bond Street for their casual cut. He reached for my hand as I approached and kissed my lips. There was no one to see but a serving girl carrying a load of bed linens into the laundry and the two gardeners stripping the kitchen garden of lettuce and early peas, nonetheless, I blushed at such an outward show of affection. Fingers clasped tightly, we left the chateau with Charlot at our heels.

"One stop before we begin," said Alex mysteriously. My curiosity piqued, I said nothing as we made our way through the narrow village streets. We passed the *boulangerie,* its shelves almost empty of bread this late in the afternoon, and the *épicerie* with its sausages dangling from the open window, and crossed the well-worn threshold of one Monsieur Daumier, a balding shopkeeper cum shoe repairman who lived, as they all did, behind his business. Wiping his hands, M. Daumier emerged from the workroom to assist us and within minutes, I was the proud owner of a pair of new lace shoes. Sturdy, brown, asexual, and without a hint of style, they had probably sat on his shelves since the Great War. I loved them. Slipping out of my delicate pumps, I stepped into my sensible new shoes and tied them tight.

Our trek took us along a path that followed the River Marne, crossed some rusting railroad tracks, skirted fields of grapevines, and snaked past a thatched farmhouse and another small village that could have been a twin to Ranton. Alex kept up a steady commentary about the days when he was a child and had visited here intermittently with his brothers and sister. I heard about the fish they caught, the trees they climbed, the rabbits they trapped, the imaginary Germans they shot—for even in those days before the Great War, Germany had been France's sworn enemy. At the edge of the river he pointed out an old *lavanderie*, a stone hut built along the river at a point equidistant between the two villages where women still gathered to launder their clothes as they had for centuries. A breeze from the river kept the sun from scorching our faces. The scent of roses and the sound of bumblebees filled the air. Charlot dashed to the edge of the woods and flushed out a covey of plump quail.

"Look at him!" I laughed. "Look at Charlot, he's quite puzzled that his humans are making no attempt to shoot them out of the sky."

Alex picked one overblown pink blossom from a rose bush that grew at the end of a row of grapevines, pinched off a thorn, and stuck it through my buttonhole. "Here, take the scent with you." And he kissed me in the warm sunshine. "You must tell me if you become tired so we can turn back."

"Are we going far?" Wrapped in the romance of the moment, I felt I could walk forever beside this man, that I would never tire of the sound of his voice or the feel of his lips on mine.

"Just a short distance more," he said, but he looked about with puzzled eyes. "It seems yours is not the only faulty memory. Ah, there it is now."

We turned off the main path through the field, manoeuvring between the rows of wheat. What my eyes had dismissed earlier as an outcropping of stone now appeared to have shape.

"Do you know what *hunebeds* are? I don't know the English word; perhaps it is the same?" I shook my head to both questions. "Never mind . . . no one knows much about them anyway. Prehistoric stone structures, some say built by Celts, some say by Druids. There are hundreds across northern France."

It was a simple structure, two massive upright stones with a flat stone laid on top like a roof or a table. A fourth stone at the back made it into a little three-sided shelter. On the ground inside were the remains of a recent fire. A chipped cup lay in the corner.

"Dolmens. We have such things in Britain. Everyone knows of Stonehenge, but there are many smaller circles of standing stones and some like this."

Alex took out his pipe and began the ritual of lighting it. "In France too. Stone circles. In fact, there is a small stone circle near the village that I'll show you another time. As children, we came here often to play."

I walked around it. A green lizard chased its mate out of a crevasse and across the tabletop. The stones were cool to the touch, in spite of the strong sun. "What d'you suppose it was?"

"A sacrificial table, an altar to their gods, a burial place, a primitive dwelling. A mystery forever. One time my brother Philippe took some pig's bones from the kitchen and buried them here for us to find." Ah . . . that was the same Philippe who had been killed in the war, whose death Alex had so heartlessly avenged—no, I was not going to let such thoughts ruin my mood. "And Manuel used to pull Danielle up on the top," he continued. "and tell her he was going to sacrifice her to the gods."

"I am jealous of your memories," I remarked.

"Don't be. They aren't all so pleasant. And yours will return when you least expect them. I think it is best that you not strain yourself overmuch trying to force memories until they are ready." I smiled to myself, thinking, *This from the man who has been plaguing me for weeks to recover my past!* "Come," he said, taking my hand for the walk back.

The next couple of days brought all the euphoria of a honeymoon. Turning aside any thoughts of the past or the future, I focused myopically on the present where my handsome, attentive husband courted me as if I were the season's prize debutante. Whenever my memory problem threatened to intrude into my idyll,

I reminded myself of the soldiers, the lucky British Tommies and French *poilus* who had returned to their farms and shops from the horror of the trenches to resume the ordinary life they had nearly lost. They had to put behind them the years of unimaginable deprivation and the acts too ghastly to speak of that they had committed against their fellow man, and learn to appreciate again the ordinary world where birds sang, children laughed, and dinner was served on a clean white plate at a table. Like them, I had to lock up the past few years in a dark closet in my mind and throw away the key. Whatever I had done as Eva, whatever the reason, it was over and done with, and no good would come of bringing it to light. Recovery, I realized, lay not in remembering but in forgetting. I had to live in the present. I was not sure what would happen when it was time for the family to leave for São Paulo, but I was convinced Alex would allow nothing to come between us now. He had not mentioned my memory or his paintings since that night of the party, and I played the ostrich with the buried head and was blissfully happy.

The only hair in my soup, as the French would say, was Lianne. She had been willing to befriend me when her father despised me but no sooner were his affections engaged than hers evaporated. I tried to include her in our evening card games, our walks through the countryside, our visits to the little village market, but she would not come. When he was not with me, Alex spent long hours in the library writing at his desk and talking on the telephone to Paris.

I asked about my letter to Miss Christabel Pankhurst but Alex said that Mr. Marsh had received no reply. I invented reasons for the delay—she could be away from home or even under arrest—to avoid the more likely conclusion, that she didn't know Claire Smith from Eve.

"Wake up, Claire."

I came awake slowly. The hands of the clock were not visible but I could make out Alex standing beside me. "What is it?" Without answering he wrapped me tightly in a blanket and carried me, like Cleopatra rolled in her rug, down the travertine steps where his motorcar was waiting. As the Peugeot purred through the sleeping village, I picked out the stars in the Big Dipper shining like the dot-to-dot puzzles in a child's play book, then watched as the eastern glow extinguished them one by one.

Enjoying his little mystery, Alex pulled over to a small hill near the river and carried me to the top. Without a word, he walked into a circle of standing stones, and sat down with his back against the largest, facing east toward the Marne. "Am I to be sacrificed at dawn?" I teased.

"Today is Midsummer's Day," he whispered, settling me between his legs and leaning me against his chest so I could feel his words as well as hear them. "The summer solstice. The longest day of the year." His cheek was rough against mine; his arms tight around me. "Are you cold?"

I shook my head. It felt wonderful wrapped in his embrace. As we waited, I heard the quiet approach of others, villagers coming to stand against the largest stone, to watch for the sun that today would rise exactly between two pillars. The only sound came from the crickets in the wet grass and the frog chorus throbbing lustily beside the river.

If Stonehenge were the great pagan cathedral, this was the small parish church. I counted thirteen grey stones in the circle, none taller than my shoulder, marking the journey of the sun through the endless cycles of the seasons. Images of prehistoric sacrifices, funeral pyres, and sun worshippers filled my head, and I could almost hear the cadence of chants swirl in the mist above us. I shivered. Alex tightened his hold.

"The *Feux de la Saint-Jean* comes tomorrow night," I began. "What have midsummer bonfires to do with St. John the Baptist? I don't see any connection."

"When Christianity replaced the old religions," he said softly, his mouth at my ear, "church leaders wisely laid Christian holy days atop existing pagan celebrations so people would not have to abandon the old ways, only adapt a little to include the new. Their ceremonies were all connected to fertility. As the centuries passed, the Catholic Church grew less tolerant and tried to wipe out the old customs, such as bonfires and handfasting, but they persisted in secret."

"Handfasting?"

"A temporary marriage, solemnized at Midsummer to last a short while. No wedding, no divorce. Very modern," he teased.

Then the sun rose between the pillars as it had for thousands of years, lifting the river mist. It happened much faster than I thought it would, so fast I could actually see the movement of the sun through the stone markers. Even Alex, who must have witnessed this a dozen times as a child, sat spellbound. When the sun had at last escaped the stones and the countryside was bright with daylight, we looked around us for the first time. We were alone. The villagers—if villagers they had been and not ghosts—had vanished.

Not a soul did we see as we returned to the chateau. We were back in bed shortly after five, but we did not sleep.

"It isn't what it used to be when I was a child," said *Grand-mère*. I envied her her long memory. "Days before the *Fête de la Saint-Jean,* the boys and men would build a bonfire as high as a house, vying with neighbouring towns for the biggest. When the sun finally dipped below the horizon, we would look toward the closest village to the east and watch for its bonfire to light the sky. That was the signal to light ours. Then we turned to the west to see the next village set its fire. I wanted to be a bird so I could fly high above and watch all the fires sending greetings to one another, east to west in a great chain, like stars fallen to earth."

"Why don't we do that now?" asked Lianne.

"Perhaps we have other ways to send greetings now," said Alex. "Telegrams and telephones."

She pouted.

"I remember the gypsy women coming to the village," added Cousin Pauline. Such is the trick with memories and old people that she who could not remember what she had done this morning recalled every detail of the celebration seventy-five years ago. "Nowadays they are chased off, and it is probably for the best, they are such thieves! But we miss their magic."

"What magic?" Lianne was ravenous for tales of the olden days, and I found myself eager for the answers too.

"All the girls knew that the bonfire brought love magic," said Pauline, lowering her voice mysteriously. "Through the fire's power, young girls would find out about their future husbands."

"How?" Lianne fidgeted with excitement, her eyes as big as dinner plates.

"Those who had a silver coin paid the gypsies for their fortunes. Others gathered St. John's wort, mugwort, dwarf elder, yarrow, lilies, vervain, and orpins to make garlands for the neck. At midnight on the Eve of Saint John, they walked seven times around the church sowing hempseed and chanting 'I sow hempseed, Hempseed I sow, Come my true love, Appear before me now.'"

"Then what happened?" she asked breathlessly.

"Then they would turn," she paused for effect and turned her head slowly to see behind her, "and look over the left shoulder, like so. And they would see the one they would marry. Or his spectral image, if he were far away."

Lianne quivered with excitement. Her thoughts were as plain as if they had been written in black ink across her forehead, and I knew where we would find her tomorrow night at midnight.

"Come with us, Lianne," I said. "Your father and I are going to see how the boys are doing with the bonfire." I thought the word "boys" would bring her along if nothing else, but she ran off toward the gardening shed.

"Gardening is in her blood," Alex remarked. I did not tell him my hunch that it was the new gardener, not the garden, that drew Lianne.

Tradition placed the bonfire on the small hill next to the stone circle. Village boys had built a pile with dead tree limbs, scrap lumber, and a rotted wine bottle rack. As the boys went about their work with purposeful zeal, Jean-Claude rolled up his contribution: a few petrol-soaked logs.

"It should burn well," he said with an impish grin, "with these."

We returned to the chateau by way of the fishpond where I picked an arm full of poppies and daisies that grew wild along the edge of the fields. At the archway Alex went to check to something in the garage, and I continued into the house to find an empty vase for my flowers. As I passed through the entrance hall, my eye fell on a small brown paper packet on the table. On it was written in bold letters was my name. Wrapped in a piece of clean linen and held together with a straight pin was some sort of dried herb concoction I knew at once came from Cécile. The note confirmed it. "Make a tisane of these herbs and drink after dinner." I stashed it in my pocket and went up the stairs to ring for some hot water.

The vases in our room were already filled with yesterday's blossoms, so I went into the spare bedroom beside Lianne's where Alex had slept those nights he did not stay with me. Although he had not slept there since the party, some of his clothes still lay about on the bed and chairs, waiting for a servant to brush and fold them away. I glanced about and spotted a china pitcher perched on the shelf of an étagère high above the fireplace. Dragging a chair across the room to stand on, I accidentally knocked onto the floor Alex's grey flannel jacket that had been draped across the back. When I picked it up, an envelope dropped from its pocket.

It was my letter to Christabel Pankhurst.

Rage replaced shock, but as I stormed from the room to confront him, self-preservation held me back. Trembling, I collapsed onto a settee and forced myself to think dispassionately.

Could it have been a simple mistake? Had he forgotten to post my letter?

If that were the case, he would not have lied about Mr. Marsh's supposed response. But that is what he would say if I confronted him—a simple mistake, my apologies—and he was so glib I had no doubt he would make it sound persuasive. I would learn nothing, and he would learn that I knew. But why *not* post the letter? What harm could come of it? What could Christabel Pankhurst possibly say that he didn't want me to hear? I thought he wanted to know the truth about my identity. Did he know already and intend to keep it from me?

My gullibility made me sick to my stomach. Ever since he had returned to our bed, I had been putty in his capable hands. I actually fancied myself in love with him! That romantic charade had served him very well indeed, lulling me into a passive acquiescence when all along it had been nothing but play-acting on his part. I was like one of those actresses so caught up in her role that she couldn't leave her character on stage. It was time to stop playing the role of adoring wife and return to reality.

I had trusted him. I had believed all his nonsense about split consciousness. I believed him when he said I was Eva and Claire at the same time. I believed his explanations of the discrepancies. He made the facts fit, but he did it by pounding the stubborn pieces into the jigsaw puzzle with a mallet. Forced into place, the pieces fit—barely—but the picture made no sense.

He knew something about me that he wasn't sharing.

I returned to my bedchamber in a daze. I took my yellow dress from its drawer and held it up against me before the mirror. This is who I was. The girl in the yellow dress. Too plump to fit into Eva's chic clothing. An English girl who worked for a living, somehow, somewhere. Why did he want me to believe what wasn't true? And why did he no longer press me to remember the paintings? Yesterday evening, when I told him I had just remembered some things about my past, he had changed the subject. For no reason, I heard Cécile's voice in my head. "Pierre Lebrun gets spots instantly."

I hurried down the staircase and across the entrance hall, threw back the bolt, and stepped into the courtyard. I crossed to the kitchen garden. Without much searching, I found the strawberry plants. The season had passed but I was sure to find one or two late-ripening fruits clinging to the vines. I popped the few I found into my mouth and went to sit by the fountain. I was so still that a brilliant green hummingbird sipping water from the spray took me for a statue and almost came to rest on my hand.

Of course nothing happened.

Mary Miley

6 THE CAVE

Ever since the Armistice, *les Feux de la Saint-Jean* had started with a picnic in the courtyard of Chateau Denon. All two hundred inhabitants of Ranton-sur-Marne turned out. The Denon family provided much of the food—foie gras, country pâté, grilled saucissons, slices of dried Ardennes ham, and casks of wine and cider to wash it down—the priest provided the prayers, and the villagers provided the gaiety.

The residents of Ranton did not come empty-handed to the *fête*—to do so would have shamed them. Every housewife who climbed the hill would bring along a basket of bread, a tart made with apples, rhubarb, quince, or grapes, a Madeira cake, a crock of red pepper cornichons, a cherry clafoutis, or a plate of tangy goat cheese to set on one of the long trestle tables that the gardeners were busy assembling this afternoon. I don't know how long I sat beside the fountain, frozen in the afternoon sun. By and by I became aware that the courtyard was busy with villagers and servants making torches for the parade, and setting the tables with earthenware plates, bunches of lavender, and fragrant beeswax candles.

Cécile passed me with a perfunctory greeting and laid a dish of poached pears on one of the tables. Instinctively my hand went to my pocket. "*Bon soir*, Cécile," I answered, thinking of the packet of herbs I was supposed to have taken. "I forgot about your herbs. What are they for? I no longer need anything to help me sleep."

She peered at the packet as if she had forgotten it as well. It was a bit of clean white linen, a scrap from an old shirt or napkin, folded around the prescribed herbs, and held shut with a straight pin. She took it from me, shook some of the flakes into her hand, stared at the concoction intently, and sniffed it. "Where did you get this?"

"It is the packet you left on the table in the hall."

"I left you nothing."

She sniffed again, then put a pinch on her tongue and made a face.

"But the note—" I stopped. Had the note actually been signed? Or had I assumed it?

"What note?" She spat on the ground.

"There was a note saying to make a tisane of these herbs and drink it after dinner. I forgot."

"God is watching over you, *madame*. Someone made a serious mistake. This is foxglove. Easily mistaken for comfrey—the leaves have the same hairy surface and the same shape. But foxglove leaves have tiny teeth edges. The edges of comfrey leaves are smooth."

A cloud passed over the sun. "Is it poison then?"

Cécile took her time, weighing the packet in her hand like a merchant considering the price. "Many things are poison if used incorrectly. This would make the heart beat very fast, upset the stomach, and cause confusion. Perhaps worse." She gave me a speculative look. "I would like to know who prepared this. They must be taught the difference. A little knowledge is a dangerous thing."

I promised I would ask around and let her know. I knew I would do no such thing. "Please don't mention it tonight," I added. "No need to bring unpleasantness to the festival." She gave me another sharp look, but I took it to mean agreement. When I reached for my packet, she hesitated. "I need it if I am to ask where it came from."

She nodded and reluctantly surrendered the herbs. "Take care, *madame*."

The time for taking care was past. Claire Smith would leave tonight during the festival when her absence would not be noticed for many hours. She could not afford to wait until tomorrow. Someone was trying to kill Claire Smith—for something she knew or would remember, for something she had done or would do, for reasons she would probably never work out. Alex was in on it somehow, with his failure to mail her letter, his sudden change in personality, his unexplained trip to Paris, his phone calls, his calculated seduction, all aimed at preventing her from learning the truth about herself. Blinded by my own problems, I'd neglected to delve very far into Alex's motives. Why was this rich man so concerned with the loss of four paintings? Especially after he had recovered his mother's "Memories," the one that mattered most. Of course, the missing three were valuable but he had dozens more, maybe hundreds for all I knew. His pride had been wounded, yes, I understood. Still, to have spent five years searching for me so he could recover three paintings? It seemed a quest out of proportion to the prize.

There was too much I couldn't comprehend here. Too much I wasn't meant to comprehend. So tonight, Claire Smith would borrow some money from the one person she trusted, tie up a few things in a bundle, walk through the night until she reached a town large enough to have a cart to hire to get to a train station, and work her way north to the Channel.

Ten minutes of searching Alex's desk in the library turned up a red leather pouch containing five passports: the English one for Eva Johnson, two Italian ones for Maria Nunziante and Chiara Agostino, and others for Switzerland and Canada. No French passports—no, naturally not, Eva could not speak French. And Claire could not speak Italian, so I chose the Canadian document and replaced the others, hoping the missing one would not be noticed among so many. As I left the library, I nearly collided with the butler on his way to the wine cellar.

"Thonet, *excusez-moi*." I pulled the herb packet from my pocket. "D'you remember seeing this packet and a scrap of paper lying on the table in the entrance hall this afternoon? I am looking for the paper."

"My apologies, *madame*, I thought you were finished with the note. I threw it away." I followed him to a wastepaper basket in the maid's closet, from which he quickly produced the crumpled paper. Cécile's signature was not there.

It was a long shot, but I asked anyway. "*Regardez,* there is no name on the note. I am wondering who left it for me. Did you by any chance see anyone?"

"*Oui, madame.* It was Monsieur Denon."

"Jean-Claude?" I uttered in disbelief and looked again at the handwriting. That crude penmanship could not be Jean-Claude's, could it? But I had never seen his writing, so I did not know for sure.

"*Oui, madame.*" A worried frown creased the butler's forehead. He wanted to ask, but it wasn't his place.

"It is nothing important," I reassured him. "Thank you very much." With a stiff bow, he left me.

My heart would not believe what my head was telling me. Jean-Claude was my friend. He could not have been involved in this second attempt to kill me. Nor could he have dropped the slates on my chair. He was not in the chateau when that happened. Jean-Claude could not have been involved in any of this. Probably he was only examining the packet, and Thonet drew the wrong conclusion. Yes, that was it. I could see him now, curious, was it perhaps for him? He would pick up the packet, read the note, and set it back where it was. I had to believe in Jean-Claude. Without borrowed money, I could not leave. And if I could not leave, there would surely be a third "accident" coming my way.

No, said a voice inside my head, a fourth.

All at once, the assault in Paris took on new meaning. The police, the doctor, the nurses, the Polish sailors, everyone had come to the wrong conclusion. They thought the motive of the riverside attack was robbery. A bag-snatch and a woman shoved into the Seine in a moment of panic. No one asked why a common bag-snatch should become attempted murder. Or why thieves who already had the purse should want to kill the victim. The answer was simple. Because the motive had not been robbery. The motive had been murder.

Mine.

The priest pulled the bell cord eight times before climbing the hill to the chateau, his black robes flapping like a crow's wings as he passed through the archway. He was a short man, spare and prematurely balding, a man who hadn't laughed since he had returned from the Great War to answer God's call. Even his rare smile seemed forced, as if he were wearing it to reassure others but wasn't fooling himself; however he made his lips turn up when he came into the courtyard and saw his flock gathering like lost sheep into the fold.

"*Bon soir, madame.*" He opened his arms to embrace the multitude. "Sundays bring half the town to church, but holy festivals bring everyone," he said. From different lips, the words might have sounded petulant. Ranton's priest sounded grateful.

Jean-Claude had not yet appeared. I nibbled on my fingernails as I watched for him. At my feet, tucked under the scrolled lip of the stone fountain where it was scarcely visible, sat a pillowcase from the linen closet that held barely more than a change of clothes and my hairbrush.

At last Jean-Claude strode through the archway. Not for the first time, I was struck by his quiet authority and self-possessed manner. This was his land; these were his people. I started toward him but others reached him first, and after a while it became clear I would have to wait to speak to him privately. Every moment that passed was one fewer step on the road toward London. And there was Lianne—I knew Alex could not be far off.

He came up behind me as the nine-man band started to play *La Marseillaise,* a song identifiable only by its thumping tempo. I was grateful that we were in full view of a crowd—he would never do anything so vulgar as to show affection in public, and I was afraid I would recoil at his touch. "Good evening," he said softly. "Lianne and I had a nice ride this afternoon. I must thank you for the suggestion."

"*De rien,*" I choked. Only a few hours ago, I would have tingled with pleasure at his praise. Only a few hours ago, I had thought myself in love with this man. Now being near him made my stomach cramp. He leaned against the fountain beside me, and our hands touched. I forced myself to hold still.

Near the kitchen door, boys threw firecrackers and whistled innocently as they exploded in the dirt. Alex flinched as if in pain. Most men ducked. One poor soul dropped to the ground and covered his head. The ensuing silence was filled with self-conscious chatter that covered up the sound of the lads' mothers thrashing them soundly.

"It never goes away," said Alex, looking not at me but out over the townspeople. His voice was soft, contemplative, intimate, drawing me in. I tried to resist. "You think it is past, you think you can forget or put it behind you, but it stays with you forever, haunting your dreams and troubling your waking hours. We none of us dare to look too close at it for fear of what we'll find." He studied my face. "Experiences change people. I am a different man than I was before the War. You are a different woman than you were when we first met in Monte Carlo. I think this time we will do very well together."

He was very convincing. I was almost convinced. When I said nothing, he continued. "The crossing will be a short one, six days. The *paquebot* leaves from Bordeaux. One of my father's sisters will join us, along with her daughter, my cousin, who is not much older than you, and her family."

He thought I was going with him. I let him believe I was.

"Let's eat," he said.

Anxiety had robbed me of my appetite, but I thought it best to eat as much as I could, considering the uncertainty of my next meal. During dinner, Jean-Claude came over to our table and stood behind us, his hand resting affectionately on Alex's shoulder. "*Tiens, mon vieux*, will you take charge of lighting the *flambeaux*?" The pile of thick sticks wrapped in tar-soaked rags waited near the archway for someone to set them alight as they were claimed. Alex nodded and I breathed a sigh of relief—he would be occupied as the procession formed. I could slip away unnoticed.

There was nothing I could do to let Jean-Claude know of my need to speak to him, so I chewed on my fingernails and tried to still my hammering heart as I waited for the signal to come that would drain the courtyard of people. The gay mood mocked my fears. The music and laughter grew louder as the wine disappeared.

One by one I studied them, the DeSequeyras and Denons, wondering which one was trying to kill me. Who had a reason? Certainly not *Grand-mère* or Cousin Pauline, they were too old and feeble to heave slate out a window even if they despised me, which I did not think the case. I reconsidered that day in the courtyard and remembered Lianne had been there when the slates crashed to the ground . . . but no, there was a lapse of time between their fall and her appearance . . . time enough for her to dash down from the attic and pretend shock? Probably, but that was unthinkable. Lianne was just a child! Moreover, her jealousy had not come until later. Despite what Thonet had said about the foxglove, I couldn't suspect Jean-Claude. I didn't know where he had been when the slates fell, but he and I had never even met before this month. What possible motive could he have to kill me? In some mystery novels, the butler did it, but to suspect Thonet or the other servants was ridiculous. That left Danielle and Alex. Danielle didn't like me, but not liking is a long way from wanting to kill. Alex had been in Paris when the slates were dropped, not that absence precluded involvement. Murder for hire was not unknown, especially for a man with unlimited resources who took special care to establish an unshakable alibi. But why now? I was still his only link to his paintings, unless . . .

. . . unless he had found them and no longer needed me. Accidental death was an easy way to dispose of an unwanted wife.

Finally, *monsieur le curé* lifted a large wooden crucifix and gestured to the motley group of musicians. These men and boys— evidently it was unseemly for women to play band instruments— clustered behind him and started slogging through their repertoire. I lost Alex as he went to man his post, lighting tar-soaked torches and handing them to those who wanted to carry one.

The priest marched through the archway. All of Ranton followed.

Jean-Claude went in the opposite direction toward *Grand-mère* and some other widows, motioning to a stable boy for the landau that would carry the old ladies up the hill. Dismayed, I watched as he climbed up to escort them. Without a word, Alex handed me a torch and I blended into the crowd. I would have to catch up to Jean-Claude at the bonfire.

Although neither Lianne nor I had ever participated in *les feux de la Sainte-Jean,* we had heard enough to know what to expect. Every year, the procession snaked through the village streets to the bonfire where the priest led the people in prayers for a bountiful harvest, exhorting everyone to work hard and trust in God's mercy. During the last rousing chorus of *la Marseillaise,* eager boys would throw their torches to the top of the bonfire and everyone would cheer as it burst into glorious flame. The music would start up again. Pretty girls wearing wildflower crowns would dance circles around the fire, breaking away every so often to seize a boy and try to pull him into the frolic before his friends could pull him back. When the priest wasn't looking, some would toss messages into the flames asking for special blessings; others would gather around old widow Fontville whose Tarot cards predicted the future—at least until *monsieur le curé* drew near and she had to scoop them into her pocket. Men planted their torches into the earth and sat on the ground drinking. Mothers knotted together, keeping close watch on the young ones. Some would walk home after a couple hours. A few men would be found the next morning snoring beside the fire.

Lianne sidled up to me as the procession oozed through the village. Like most of the girls, she wore a crown of flowers. "Here," she said. "This is for you. I made it."

"Why, Lianne, that's lovely!" Using daisies, small roses, and lavender, she had twisted together a floral wreath for me. I was absurdly touched. And thankful that her jealousy had given way to her excitement about the *fête*. After tonight, I thought with a pang, she would no longer have to share her father with me. With effort, I dragged my attention back to the girl skipping beside me without a worry in her head. "Thank you very much, Lianne."

"I am going to have my fortune told. Father said I could. He gave me this coin to give Madame Fontville."

"How exciting!"

"Do you know what else I'm going to do?" She lowered her voice. "I'm going to the church at midnight." I had no doubt that most of the village girls would come, and the boys too, jostling to be seen or not seen when a certain girl opened her eyes after her seven circuits around the church. I wondered if Lianne's young gardener friend would be there as well.

"Just don't leave with anyone afterwards." I tried not to sound like a mother hen, but she hadn't been raised to have a care for her own safety, and I was a little concerned.

"I won't." A dark-eyed village girl ran up to us, grabbed Lianne's arm, and giggled something in her ear. *Thank heavens*, I thought with some relief, *she'll go off with her friend now*. Lianne's unexpected company would spoil my plans. To my dismay, Lianne waved her companion off.

I gave an exaggerated sigh. "We're moving so slowly. I think the interesting part is up front, with the band. Why don't you run on ahead with your friend?"

"No, no, I want to stay by you. I have something to show you."

"What?" I asked, a little too sharply.

She gave me a puzzled look, then a mischievous expression came over her face. "It's a surprise. We're almost there. Here, come this way." She indicated a narrow lane that branched off from our street and hugged the hill. In the dark it was hard to tell, but I supposed it to be the way to Jean-Claude's winery and caves.

"Oh, no, Lianne, I don't want to miss anything at the bonfire."

"It won't take long." She grabbed my hand and tugged.

"No, honestly, I'd rather continue with the others. You go on if you like."

"Oh, I'll stay with you, then, until after the bonfire. We'll go then."

I needed to see Jean-Claude *alone*. I needed to return *alone* to retrieve the bundle of clothing I'd left behind the bushes by the archway. Until I rid myself of my young shadow, the entire plan was in jeopardy. This time my sigh was genuine. "Very well, Lianne, what is it? Will it be quick?"

"Yes, very quick. Come, come!" The noises and singing faded behind us as we cut left along the buildings, mostly abandoned, that were tucked against the side of the hill. Lianne led the way, our footsteps echoing up the walls, our torches throwing enough light that I could see boards nailed over the windows and shutters sagging in disrepair. This was not the way to Jean-Claude's winery but it looked quite similar, although deserted. When we stopped at one dilapidated building and she shook open the rickety door, my curiosity peaked. What in heaven's name was she going to show me here? More kittens?

"Lianne, what is this all about?"

"Just come!" she said, dancing on her toes. "It's a surprise." We stepped over the threshold onto a dirt floor. My torchlight fell on a broken chair, some mysterious machinery that had all but turned into rust, staves of broken casks, and a great heap of empty wine bottles that could have been lying there since before the Great War. Cobwebs brushed across my face and the smell of decay hung in the air. Lianne passed through this room and into another, her feet, and then mine, crunching loudly on something round that popped as we stepped.

"What *is* this?" I asked, but my light was too dim to see more than what appeared to be round white pebbles. The temperature dropped. We were into the hill now, into the space that had been hollowed out of the soft tufa rock, crushing thin glass balls with every step we took.

"Oh. They are *escargots*. Don't think about it." Appalled, I halted in my tracks, only that seemed worse. Snail shells, thousands of them, carpeting the floor in a monotonous mosaic. Only the French could be so cavalier about snails!

"I think I've seen enough, Lianne." A cold frisson of disgust shivered up my spine and my mouth turned dry as dust.

"Just two more steps and you're out of the snails."

Faced with two steps forward versus six steps back, I swallowed hard and went on, refusing to contemplate the return trip. I stretched to take two long paces, wincing at every crunch, trying not to think about the slimy slugs squishing beneath my shoes. Smooth, clean dirt never felt so good! I took deep breaths of dank air to calm my stomach and steady my wobbly knees.

"*Ciao, bella.*" The male voice spun my head around so fast I dropped my torch. It clattered to the floor and went out. A man standing in the corner, hidden by the pitch blackness, leaned over and scratched a match hard against his shoe.

"Who's there?" I gasped, straining to make out his features in the flickering flame. He bent and lit a tin lantern at his feet and as it flared up, I could see dark, baggy clothing and a white scarf tied about his neck. Our shadows loomed onto the rocky walls in weird, threatening postures.

"At last, our touching reunion," he said, his smooth voice drenched with sarcasm.

My heart pounded in my throat. I swallowed hard. I had never seen this man before in my life. Was he someone from my past, or just some village lout who had drunk too much wine?

"Who are you, young man?" I demanded in the most disdainful tone I could muster, hoping to intimidate him with a display of aristocratic hauteur.

"Shaving my moustache was a good disguise if even *you* did not recognize me, *cara mia*. Of course, I took care to keep my distance—and my cap on my head." A wave of gooseflesh rose on my arms as I analyzed our position. Lianne and I were in a troglodyte building with some dark-haired gypsy. The entire village was a mile away making noise enough to wake the dead. No one knew we were here. No one would hear us if we screamed at the top of our lungs.

"Come, Lianne," I bluffed haughtily. "We are leaving at once."

With a speed no drunken man could have managed, he moved between me and the way out. "I think not, *cara mia.* I shall have to insist on the pleasure of your company. After all, we have so much to say to one another."

"How dare you!" I blustered, hoping my voice did not reveal the cold fear that had me in its grasp. This was no village oaf. The accent was wrong. "Who are you?"

"*Basta!* There is no need for pretence, *cara*, she knows about us." He jerked his head in Lianne's direction. "You thought you would go tomorrow, did you? You thought you would leave me behind. As you did in Monte Carlo. As you did in Cap Ferrat. A thousand pardons, Eva, but I am calling the shots now, and I will be obeyed."

"Look, *monsieur,* I don't know who you are but I—"

"He's Luca, your lover come to rescue you!" Lianne's childish voice rang out with exasperation, bouncing against the rock walls and low ceiling until the words came to rest on the cold floor.

"—but I am not Eva."

He held up the lantern and moved a few steps closer. It was the young gardener, less young than I had supposed. Tiny flames danced inside the pupils of his eyes, as dark and as empty as a bottomless pit. Without warning, his hand came up and struck me hard across the face.

Lianne screamed. I staggered but did not fall.

"You set me up, you worthless whore. Left me for the police—it was you who tipped them, wasn't it? And bolted with the paintings. Don't deny it, I know you better than that." He struck me again, the blow coming so fast I had no time even to throw up my arms in self-defence. This time, I fell to the floor, at the edge of consciousness, the blood slamming in painful strokes inside my head. "I had a little revenge, though. I confessed to the *flics* that it was you who killed the old man, and then I escaped, very cleverly, like that time in Le Touquet, remember? I traced you to Paris. You thought I was in prison for life, so you were fool enough to stay at our usual hotel."

"You . . . it was you who attacked me by the river, not common thieves!" I spared a glance at Lianne who remained frozen in position toward the back of the cave, and I struggled painfully to my feet, holding the wall for support.

He shook his head regretfully. "No, *cara mia*. Not my style. Although you seem to collect enemies wherever you go, do you not? When I arrived, you were in hospital and that fool had reached you first. I learned where he took you by frequenting the salons— you know how eager everyone is to welcome a title. Fortunately, DeSequeyra's sister was in Paris. When I met that little trollop, I told her about you and her brother, how you had disappeared off the face of the earth. I made sure she was *very* curious and then I followed her here. I have been watching you for days now, waiting for the right moment. I want the paintings. And to tell you the truth, I find I am no longer satisfied with my share. I want them all. I deserve them all. Here is what you will do, and quickly: tell me where they are, and we will go together to retrieve them. Then I will leave this country for good and go somewhere far beyond the reach of the *flics*. If you are good to me, you can come along. Or I can work just as well with another."

"I can't help you. I don't know where the paintings are."

He came closer. I scrambled backwards until my shoulders hit rock. He thrust his face in mine. It was contorted with fury. "You have told *him* already, haven't you?" he hissed.

"No, I promise you. I haven't told anyone because I don't know."

The anger drained from his face, replaced, eerily enough, with a dreamy smile. "The amnesia trick is a clever one, Eva, but not with me. Where are the paintings?"

Lianne chose that moment to bolt for the front door. She was not quick, and Luca had little trouble snatching a handful of her hair before she had taken four steps. As she screamed, he dragged her backwards and threw her headfirst against the wall. The child slumped to the floor, dazed and sobbing wildly.

"Don't hurt her!" I cried and tried to move toward her. Luca grabbed me, missing my short hair but catching a fist of my blouse and tearing the fabric from my neck to my shoulder. He shoved me back against the wall and seized me by the throat. "She's just a child," I gasped. "Leave her alone!"

His expression changed to confusion and he eased his grip on my throat without letting go. I took it to mean I had touched his conscience. "I swear to you, this is not a trick. There is still a lot I can't remember, but I remember enough to know I am not Eva. I look like her, perhaps somehow we are related, but I am not Eva, and I don't know where the paintings are."

He stared at my bare shoulder for a long moment, then with one violent movement, tore the remnant of my blouse from my body. But for my brassiere, I was naked to the waist. Releasing my throat, he seized the lantern and held it up to my face while his fingers grabbed my hair to hold me immobile. He studied my features, pulling harder on my hair until my eyes watered and I cried out in pain, "I don't know!"

Seconds before he would have torn my hair out by the roots, he let me go. I collapsed on the ground. His fingers clenched and flexed as he stared into the black oblivion of the cave.

An eternity passed. He looked down at me, his face all dreamy. "Two summers ago, in June, we went sailing off Capri. The weather was beautiful, the water as clear as crystal. You could see all the way to the bottom." He was smiling and talking in the mellow voice one uses for pleasant reminiscences. The change in his personality was so irrational, I wondered if he were mad. "You had an accident. Very unpleasant, lots of blood. I took you to the local hospital where a young doctor stitched you up. You never flinched. You only cried when he was finished, because he said you would always have a scar. On your shoulder."

Now he was friendly, even charming, as he crouched beside me and smiled like a mischievous little boy. "You are not Eva! I can hardly believe it, but it is true. The scars were deep and ugly. Your shoulders are smooth as silk." He caressed my shoulder with his fingers, and I steeled myself not to flinch when he dropped a moist kiss on my flesh.

"Such scars could not disappear in a hundred years. And your face, now that I study it, your face is different. How could I not have seen this, even from a distance? Your face is fuller, your eyes are not the same, and your teeth—Eva does not have that little space between the front teeth. Her teeth are perfect. She is prettier than you. Yes, sisters, twins, you must be. So alike. But I never heard of a twin. She would have told me if she had known of a twin, I am sure of it. She told me everything."

Lianne moaned from her corner. He looked at her thoughtfully and rubbed his chin.

"Go now," I rasped, my throat sore from the abuse. "We won't tell anyone about this. You can get clean away." I hoped he wouldn't realize that our bruises and torn clothing would demand explanation even if we tried to remain silent.

He replied with a scornful glance. "I shall have my paintings."

"I told you, I don't—"

He lifted his arm to strike me again. I threw my arms over my head but the blow never came. When I peeked out, he was chuckling silently and I knew without a doubt that he was mad. "I shall have my paintings. You will get them for me, just like always. The lowly gardener has not seen *all* the riches of the chateau, but he has gossiped with the servants, and he knows what is inside."

While he talked, he edged toward Lianne who was cowering against the opposite wall. He squatted next to her, stroking her hair as if she were a beloved pet. It made my skin crawl. "There is no time to waste. You will return to the chateau at once, *cara mia*, take six of the most valuable paintings from the walls—none of the recent junk the Denons favour, just the old masters. The old ladies' jewellery, you'll get that too, then bring one of the motorcars down here to me. The Peugeot, I think. I like it best."

Appalled at the prospect of leaving Lianne in this man's clutches, I gasped, "I can't do that!"

"There is no one left at the chateau. You will have no trouble. Do you understand?"

"Yes, but—"

"People work best with incentive, don't you think?" He lifted Lianne's chin. I watched in mounting horror as he gently wiped a tear-streaked cheek with his thumb, then cradled her face in one rough hand while he stroked her neck with the other. His back was turned, and I might have made a dash for the door if it hadn't meant leaving Lianne with this sadist. He turned his glittering eyes toward me and snarled, "I said, *don't you think?*"

"Yes!" I would say whatever was necessary to protect Lianne.

"I thought you would agree. Now, what would provide adequate incentive for you to return quickly?" His voice teased like a naughty child who knows the answer but wants to be cajoled into telling. I bit my lower lip so hard it began to bleed. Luca stroked his chin in a pantomime of reflection meant to torment me. His eyes glittered. "Ah, I know! Return to me within twenty minutes and little Lianne can keep her fingers!" He pulled a blade from his boot. "One minute late, I cut off her little finger. Another minute, another finger. And so on, until ten minutes have passed and I shall be forced to find something else to cut before I leave. Sweet little Lianne." She whimpered in fear and he hushed her like a father would a beloved child. "Shhhhh now, little one. There is nothing to worry about. Eva—or whatever her name is—will not fail you."

"I—I need more time than that. And I don't have a watch."

"That is so." He pulled out his pocket watch and pretended to think awhile, smiling as he enjoyed himself. Horrid boys who burnt the tail off kittens would have that look about them, I thought with a queasy stomach. "Well, shall we then say, return before the church bell chimes eleven? That gives you even longer—about twenty-two minutes, if you start now."

"But, the priest—he isn't accurate with the bells! He often—"

"Then you had best hurry, hadn't you? And pray while you run that he doesn't ring them early tonight."

Without another word I leapt up, clattering over a length of lead pipe and several wine bottles and crunching across the snail carpet on my way to the door. Half-naked and clammy with fear, I ran through the silent streets in two minutes, counting to myself, one thousand one, one thousand two, one thousand three, as children count to estimate the distance of the lightning in a thunderstorm. I raced across the deserted courtyard and up the grand staircase, planning my itinerary as I ran, counting, so I would not waste any of my precious seconds.

I reached four minutes.

In my own room at last, I snatched the pillowcase off my pillow, dumped the contents of Eva's jewellery box into it, and grabbed the first blouse I saw from the wardrobe. It wasn't modesty that drove me to cover myself; it was how suspicious I would look if someone saw me in this state of undress.

Six minutes.

I headed toward the Madame Denon's rooms where I had seen all the paintings so many days ago. No servants roamed the halls;

no sounds but echoes of my own making followed me as I ran, out of breath but without pause, through the dark interconnecting corridors and down the stairs.

Racing into the Red Room, I seized the painting hanging above the Chinese chest. I had admired it that day when I went exploring, when Alex accused me of "casing the joint," as the mobsters would say. The irony would have amused me under other circumstances. It was small, Durer's delicate Venetian girl. I tried to separate it from the frame but it was too firmly attached. In frustration, I stepped on it, but it would not break. I slipped the whole thing into the pillowcase, realizing I would have to find some way to extricate these paintings from their frames or I would not be able to carry all that Luca wanted.

One thousand fifty-eight, one thousand fifty-nine, one thousand sixty. Eleven minutes. One thousand one, one thousand two, one thousand three.

I dashed back into the corridor, passed the bamboo tables and whatnots crammed with figurines, snatched up a Breughel winter scene with a gold leaf frame that was loose at the corners, knocked it off, and thrust the canvas into the pillowcase. The David horse portrait was too large, so was the Delacroix battlefield scene, but there was a smaller Ingres nude whose frame I smashed with a strong kick. A Gericault soldier was much bigger than the pillowcase, but the frame was sagging and practically fell off in my hands when I lifted it from the wall. I ripped off the canvas and rolled it up. How many was that? At least six, he had said. I had been counting seconds, not paintings. No time to think. Just grab something else. In *Grand-mère's* bedchamber I found an unsigned still life that could have been painted by a Dutch master. Never mind, no time to decide. Put it in the bag. One more.

Fourteen minutes.

I was reaching for a Madonna with a crumbling gesso frame that looked like a Tiepolo but probably wasn't, when a noise from behind spun me around. It was Danielle, a cigarette between her fingers and a smirk on her face.

"Well, well, well. *Carpe diem*, eh?"

"Oh, God, Danielle, no time to explain, it isn't what you think. A man has Lianne and is going to kill her if I don't bring him paintings, quickly, you've got to help me—"

"You wretched little thief. You may have conned gullible old Alex again, but you're mad if you think I'll swallow that drivel. Give me that." She took the pillowcase as I was trying to pry the Madonna loose from her gesso frame. In a flash she had dumped its contents onto *Grand-mère's* bed, a mountain of sparkling jewellery mixed with the paintings. "Dear God!" she exclaimed.

She grabbed my wrist, thinking, I suppose, to stop me. I didn't have time to argue. Without considering what I was doing, I picked up the pillowcase and pulled it over her head, knocking her cigarette to the floor and pinning her arms to her sides. Danielle was one of those women who thinks no one is as clever as she, so it was a simple feat to rout her. Before she could decide to struggle, I had shoved her inside one of *Grand-mère's* large wardrobes and turned the key on her outrage.

Ignoring the pounding fists and muffled threats describing exactly what she would do to me when she got out, I threw the last painting onto the bed, pulled the four corners of the spread together to make a bundle, and hoisted it on my back like a peddler's pack. A cold horror swept over me—the struggle with Danielle had made me forget to count. I had stopped on sixteen. Had one minute passed? Two? I could not possibly lug this bundle back to Luca in time. A motorcar was my only chance.

Through the corridors, down the staircase, out the door, across the courtyard, to the garage I ran, dragging the bundle on the ground behind me when it proved too heavy to carry, until I could thrust it into the back seat of Alex's Peugeot. Climbing into the front, I reached for the key in the ignition, feeling so sick I was shaking. Then I remembered something.

I did not know how to drive.

Think! my brain screamed. *Hurry! How hard could it be if even Lianne could do it?* Lianne. Panic threatened to paralyze me.

First you turned the key. I did. Nothing happened. Pedals. One was go. One was stop. The other was called the clutch. I pushed them one at a time while turning the key. With the clutch depressed, the engine roared to life. When I let it go, the engine cut off. That brought to mind something important—letting out the clutch was supposed to be tricky. I breathed deeply and began again. Half a minute of experimentation revealed the basics of using the two pedals together, and I lurched forward out of the stall as the gears protested. Praise God, I was securely in first gear. I didn't know how to get to second, but first would do.

Aiming the hood ornament toward the centre of the archway and paying no heed to the scrape of the front wheel bumper against the stone, I chugged through the opening and turned the wheel to the left. I neglected to un-turn, ran onto the grass, but managed to right the vehicle before it tipped into the dry moat. I had neither the time nor the inclination to locate the headlamps; the quarter moon provided glow enough to see shapes and buildings. No need to watch for other motorcars—there were none in Ranton.

Only then did I realize that the priest was not likely to ring the bell at all tonight. He was probably still at the bonfire.

Still, that madman had a watch and I didn't underestimate his depravity. With two turns I found the right lane, coasted down to the bottom of the hill, and braked in front of the abandoned warehouse. The vehicle bucked like an unhappy horse when I took both feet off the pedals at the same time. Dragging the bundle of loot behind me, I burst through the door.

"I'm here!" No sound greeted me from the dark interior. I hurried across the snail carpet into the back room, frantic that I might be too late. "I'm back! I'm back! Don't—"

A hand grabbed me from behind. The arm around my throat strangled my words.

"Good girl," he said, pushing me toward the cowering lump that was Lianne. She moved. I gave her a hug meant to reassure and then pulled her to her feet, holding her shaking body close against mine. Luca spread the coverlet and surveyed the contents.

"Very well, now we'll go," I said in the most matter-of-fact tone I could manage.

"The hell you will." He turned over one of the paintings and grunted. Unrolled another, then spread apart the knot of jewellery with the toe of his boot. I had no idea where *Grand-mère* kept her jewels and trusted he wouldn't know mine from hers. Only now did I remember that he might very well be acquainted with Eva's finery, especially if he had bought any of it for her. Or stolen it. I held my breath, but if he recognized it, he said nothing.

"You don't need us—"

"Shut up. I'll decide what I need." And what he clearly didn't need was the bulky coverlet. After stuffing the jewellery into deep pockets, he took up the three paintings with frames still intact and pried them apart with the tip of his blade. "You know what is funny?" he asked pleasantly, changing personalities as fast as a tennis ball changes direction. "I was jealous! I, Luca Morosini, son of a nobleman, grandson of a duke! When I saw you with him, holding his hand, looking into his eyes with that lovesick expression plastered over your face, I wanted to kill him. But more, I wanted to kill you. If I couldn't have you, I vowed, no one shall. And I forgot about the paintings, and tried to kill you, but then I would remember the paintings and rejoice that I had failed. I decided to kill you after I had the paintings, not before."

I remembered the chair placed so carefully in the path of the slate avalanche. "So it was you who pushed the slate on my head."

"I got the idea when I went to the attic for pots with old Henri."

"And the foxglove." With his attention on the loot, I edged cautiously toward the door, holding Lianne's wrist in a grip that Death itself would not dislodge.

"Is that what it was?" he asked idly. "I bought it from some filthy gypsies. I was going to give you a helping hand into the river, but you never came outside the chateau without the brat." He glared at Lianne, who buried her face in my shoulder and clung to me for dear life. Luca laughed and shook his head. "Just as well. How does that old saying go, about things working out for the best in the end?"

I put another yard of distance between us. "The Peugeot is out front. You'd better go quickly, before someone sees it sitting there and starts to wonder."

"Oh, I'm not worried. I'll have my insurance policy." A length of rope appeared in his hands as if by magic.

"Wh-what are you going to do?"

"Where's your imagination?" He held up the rope for an answer, dangling it playfully like a boy playing with a cat, his voice teasing. "But never fear, someone will hear your cries eventually and come to untie you. She comes with me."

"No!" I protested. Lianne gave a scream of terror and nearly went limp on me. She seemed close to collapse, and I struggled to keep her on her feet. If she fainted now, we'd lose any chance of making a dash for it.

"I don't believe you're in a position to issue orders, *cara*. With little Lianne along, my own safety is assured. I'll not rape her—God knows I have no taste for fat little girls. I'll leave her somewhere public when I'm through with her."

With her throat slit.

"No, don't take her! Take me instead."

"Surely you jest, *cara mia*. DeSequeyra may find you good between the sheets, but I'm quite sure his only child will prove a more valuable insurance policy than his mistress. Besides, think about it. If I leave her here, she'll tell him you aren't Eva, and if he knows that you can't help him find his paintings, you're finished. You haven't deluded yourself into thinking he would have any interest in a low-class slut like you?"

I twisted away from Lianne and let her crumple to the floor, figuring he couldn't carry the loot and Lianne at the same time. And she was clearly going nowhere on her own power. The child clung to my leg like a ball and chain, sobbing.

"No, she won't tell him a thing! She hasn't absorbed any of this. Look at her—she's rigid with fear. Listen to me, I'll go with you quietly, no trouble. I can help you. She'll be nothing but a giveaway."

"Forget it." He came at me with the rope, his violent intent reflected in his eyes.

"Wait! You said it yourself: everyone thinks I'm Eva. Even the police. If you take me instead of Lianne, you could turn me into the police and the heat would be off you. Eva is the one they want for the Cap Ferrat murder—you made sure of that. They'd quit looking for you!"

That stopped him cold. I could see his brain clicking through the possibilities like an adding machine and totalling the results. It was *almost* enough. But not quite. Predator eyes locked onto mine and he approached with the smooth movements of a wary panther closing in on a cornered doe. He feinted to the left and grabbed me when I went opposite, as he expected. Taking a leaf from his own book, I seized a handful of his dark curly hair while I tried to knee him in the groin. I prayed Lianne would pick up a wine bottle and break it over his head.

I was no match for Luca. Within a heartbeat he had me pinned to his side, one arm around my neck and the other fumbling with the rope.

Our scuffling and grunts did not cover the sound of a shoe on snails.

Luca grabbed his knife and held it to my throat. "Show yourself or I kill her!"

He did not have to threaten twice. Alex stepped out of the darkness into the halo of light from the lantern.

"Ahhh, the lord of the manor. Better than a burglar alarm, those snails."

Alex held his empty palms out. "I am not armed."

"A pity for you. I am."

At the edge of the flickering light, I could just make out Alex's lithe form, his face white as porcelain, his posture tense with uncertainty. I could sense his fear, not for himself but for his daughter whom he was powerless to protect, and I knew he had stepped into a terror far greater than any he had faced on the Western Front. I was ecstatic to see him and horrified at the same time. I wanted to be rescued, but I was too realistic to think any unarmed man could go up against Luca's deadly knife and survive the fight. Alex was in as much danger as we were.

At the sound of her father's voice, Lianne started to struggle to her feet. "Don't move!" Luca barked, brandishing his knife in my face to back up his words. She ignored him, so strong was her desire to get to her father and safety, and I was sure Luca would slit my throat in reprisal.

"Stay there, Lianne," Alex ordered sharply, and then more softly so as not to frighten her further. "Stay there, *minou,* sit down. You're safe now." After waiting until she had obeyed, he turned to Luca, waving his hand toward the door like a maître d' at Maxim's. "You may leave with my belongings, but not with my wife and child."

Luca gave a falsetto laugh that echoed weirdly into the depths of the cavern, like an India rubber ball bouncing off the walls. "Your wife? She's in this with me. Aren't you, *cara?*"

With his blade pricking the thin skin of my throat, I'd agree with anything. "Yes, of course," I rasped. I had stepped into a surreal painting, a crazy de Chirico landscape from which there was no escape.

A sudden command came from behind us. "Put down the knife or I'll shoot!"

Jean-Claude materialized from the darkness behind us, from inside the ancient cave that connected to all the other corridors and rooms in anthill fashion. "Put it down," he ordered again. I heard the menacing click of a hammer as he cocked the pistol and held my breath. Even if mortally wounded, Luca could still cut my throat as his final act.

Luca turned enough to keep both men in his sights. "You're bluffing, comrade," he said to Jean-Claude in a genial tone, as if they had just met at the local café for beer. "You don't dare take the risk that you will miss, or that even if you hit me, I still have time to kill her. No, I think it is you who will drop his weapon," he said calmly. "Now."

I wanted to scream, "Shoot him, for God's sake!" but Luca's arm pressed so hard against my windpipe that even breathing was impossible. Horrified, I watched Jean-Claude bend down and set his pistol on the ground.

Luca began edging toward the door, chuckling to himself as we passed within ten feet of Alex. My fingernails dug into the flesh of his arm as waves of sickening darkness washed over me. I gasped for air. If he didn't ease up on the pressure, I was going to die of asphyxiation before we reached the Peugeot. At the door, Luca paused.

"Now get up, Lianne, and bring the gun over here."

I could just make out the gun, its pewter grey barrel silhouetted against the darker earth. Lianne looked to her father. He gave a curt nod of his head and she complied. Slowly, Luca returned the knife to its boot sheath and held the gun to my head instead, letting go my neck in the process. I had been waiting for some sort of movement from him, anything that would give me one last chance to break away before he forced me into the motorcar and deposited my corpse in some farmer's field beside the road to Paris. I decided that he would never be quite so full of himself as he was at that moment, secure in his superiority of fire power and brain power, so I brought up my good arm and knocked his gun hand aside as I tried to twist free.

Alex sprang. Luca pointed the gun squarely at his chest and pulled the trigger. My scream remained trapped in my throat.

The gun gave a dull click inches from Alex's heart. The two men grappled briefly, giving me the chance to scramble out of reach. Before Jean-Claude could come to his cousin's aid, Luca landed one hard blow on Alex's jaw, knocking him aside long enough to bolt through the door. The next sound we heard was the Peugeot engine roaring to life as it pulled away into the darkness.

When Alex put his arms around me, I was coughing and shaking uncontrollably. Then my stomach turned over and I vomited on the snails.

An hour later found us in the parlour, Alex, Jean-Claude, Lianne, Danielle, and me, soaking up the warmth of the fire as eagerly as if we had just been pulled out of a snowdrift. We had been six but Cécile Renaud had gone home at last. Summoned to attend to our wounds, she had cleaned our cuts and scrapes with lavender oil, patched them with comfrey poultice, and left us with a pot of scalding tea made from chamomile, valerian, and hops that she guaranteed would put the wide-awake fast asleep. Alex had already administered his own brand of medicine—a stiff shot of Scotch whisky all around.

"Shock," he told me bluntly. "Drink this. You'll be fine; you're strong." No sooner had it reached my empty stomach than the chills and trembling ceased. He saved his kinder words for Lianne. I prickled at that; then, listening to him fuss over her, I realized I would have revolted against that sort of condescension. I was not a little girl. He was not my father. He was my—no, he was not that either. I knew, at last, with utter certainty that I was not Eva. I was Claire. It was an incredible relief.

Lianne's hiccupped confession confirmed what I had surmised. It had been a simple thing for a sophisticated ladies' man like Luca to dupe a romantic girl into helping him rescue his long lost lover. He was astute enough, too, to pick up on her jealousy, to notice that the more interest Alex showed in me, the greater her resentment, and to use that as a lever to pry open her trust. If Lianne could be rid of me through Luca's efforts, she would remove a rival for her father's affection. Could she have been his courier for the foxglove?

Jean-Claude was saying something to Alex about the gun. "You knew?"

Alex nodded. "Once you laid it down, I saw the indicator and understood."

Jean-Claude gave a grunt of assent. When nothing more was forthcoming, Danielle asked him the question that was on my lips, "Understood what? Why didn't you shoot?"

"No round in the chamber. It's a Savage combat issue from the War, one of mine that *Grand-mère* keeps in her room. She doesn't keep it loaded. I had no idea where she kept the shells—she couldn't remember and there was no time to mount a search. I've a loaded gun at my house but it was too far, so I took this one with me and hoped the threat would suffice." He gave a rueful grin. "I am a poor poker player."

So Alex had known the gun was not loaded when he rushed Luca Morosini. It was ungenerous of me—it shouldn't have mattered—but the brave gesture that had seemed so noble an hour ago now looked a little less daring. I pushed the thought aside. "How did you know where we were?" I asked Alex.

Jean-Claude answered. "*Grand-mère* had seen enough of the *fête* and I was bringing her home. You nearly ran us down in the Peugeot. In the dark, I couldn't see the driver but I could tell it was someone who did not know how to drive—I could hear the engine straining to escape from first gear—and since I hadn't seen you at the bonfire, well, I guessed it was you. I couldn't see the car when it stopped, but I heard the engine cut off and knew you were near the old Gasquet winery. Just then, young Vioget passed by on his way to do some mischief, so I sent him running back to the hill to tell Alex while I took *Grand-mère* to her room."

I had forgotten all about Madame Denon. "Where is Madame now?"

"She is in bed. She knows everyone is safe. She wants Lianne to sleep with her tonight so that, if she wakes up frightened, she will have her great-grandmother to comfort her." Lianne brightened at the prospect. "Danielle was making noise enough to bring down the rafters above our heads," he continued with a fond look in her direction. "She told us what you had said about Lianne." She had told him as well of her own conviction that I was stealing the paintings, I was sure, and he had no doubt seen the wreckage of the frames on the floor, but for some reason, he hadn't believed it. I was absurdly grateful. "I hadn't seen Lianne at the bonfire either, and that was odd, so I grabbed the gun and ran to the cellars. There is an underground passageway to the old Gasquet caves that I knew from our childhood and I remembered it well enough to come up on you. I knew I would have the element of surprise. Sadly, it did no good."

"I wouldn't say that." Lianne and I were safe and not seriously harmed.

"I mean, the man escaped."

Danielle and I locked eyes. An unspoken message passed between us. She didn't apologize for misjudging me; I didn't apologize for manhandling her into the wardrobe. Nonetheless, I sensed a grudging respect that hadn't been there before. She snapped open her gold cigarette case and, with a silent gesture, offered me one. I shook my head and she lit her own.

"I saw the Peugeot leave," she said, "from the gatehouse window. I didn't know who was in it then."

"Did he go west?" asked Alex. She nodded. "Toward Paris." With a great sigh, he stood up. "Come, *minou,* finish your tea and I'll take you up to *Grand-mère* before you fall asleep here." Lianne hadn't said much since the tea and whiskey, and her eyelids were heavy. I hoped that by tomorrow, it would all seem to her like a bad dream.

"I'll call the Paris police," said Jean-Claude. "They can intercept Luca in a few hours when he reaches the city."

Alex lifted his daughter and faced me. "I heard what you said in the cave, when you tried to protect Lianne, when you tried to persuade him to take you hostage instead, and I . . ." His voice broke. "I thank you for my daughter." He turned to Jean-Claude. "Let him go. If the police pick him up, he'll only tell them Eva is here. Anyway, he won't reach Paris tonight. There wasn't that much petrol in the tank. I'm not sure how far he'll get before he has to abandon the Peugeot, but it won't be Paris."

"I'm not Eva. Luca admitted as much. There is no longer any doubt."

Alex stopped at the door but did not turn around. "He also said you were his accomplice. The man is clearly deranged. Excuse me. I'll take Lianne upstairs and come back for you. We'll talk then."

Jean-Claude refilled my teacup. Swallowing was painful but the hot liquid felt good on my throat. I sipped it slowly while I listened to him talk about the intersecting passageways between the wine caves and how he had come upon us, hoping there would be only one man, hoping he could stall until Alex could arrive. Absently I rubbed my bruised neck, staring at the fire, wrapped in thoughts that would not leave me alone.

So I had a sister. A secret twin. The thought filled my head, crowding out even the awareness of my surroundings. All I could think of was this sister. My sister Eva. And how no one in her life knew about her twin—me.

My childhood memories included no recollection of a twin sister. But I must have known about her. Why else was I in Paris, wearing her ring, carrying her bag and passport? Eva was in serious trouble, a short step ahead of the French authorities, her vengeful husband, and the Italian lover she had betrayed to the police. Had I come to Paris to help her elude her pursuers? Or was I there to help her set up yet another swindle? I must have been pretending to be Eva that night on the riverbank, substituting for her for some reason, when I chanced to be robbed. Were the men trying to kill me that night? Or were they trying to kill Eva? There was still much to learn.

Danielle knelt on the floor among the paintings that had been forgotten until now. Carefully she spread them out, one beside another and examined each.

"Are they ruined?" I asked, not caring very much if they were or not.

"A little damaged perhaps, but nothing serious."

"How fortunate Luca forgot about them in the confusion."

She shrugged. "They're only paintings." Not exactly the DeSequeyra family motto, I thought wryly. "This one I don't remember," Danielle said with a puckered brow, picking up the Durer portrait. "Where did it come from?"

"From that small dressing room off the corridor. Where the fabrics and paper have faded over the years. Originally everything was red."

She leaned back, resting on her elbows, and stretched her slender legs out until she was nearly prone while she examined me like someone squinting at a particularly nasty specimen through the microscope. "Is this an English trait, this obsession with household

194

furnishings?"

"Pardon me?"

"This preoccupation of yours with draperies and old furniture. You ask tedious questions about dreary antiques and nasty old curios—at first I thought you were planning to nick them, and then you started rearranging the furniture when no one was looking."

"Oh, I've always had an interest in furnishings, that's why I went into interior design work." The words spoke themselves, as though my lips knew something my brain did not. For a moment, I sat, stunned, as an avalanche of images tumbled through my head: a mean work room crowded with assistants' desks and drawing boards, a fabric sample closet in its colourful disarray, shelves of furniture catalogues and vendor lists with the stern notice, "Return each catalogue to its proper slot," taped to the top. I remembered the coveted assignment to do the prep work for the Paris home of a rich Italian contessa whose name would not come to me. The familiar headache attacked with a vengeance but I refused to let go of my concentration. What was her name?

"Castiglione! That's it! The client in Paris!" I leapt to my feet and started pacing the room. At long last, I had something concrete, something to pursue. Like that children's game where you followed a tangled string all the way to the prize at the end, I had a direct line to my identity.

Danielle and Jean-Claude looked at me as if I had lost my sanity. Jean-Claude rose to get me some more whiskey and tried to coax me back into my chair. I struggled to explain.

"The Contessa Castiglione could verify my name. She could tell me what firm she had employed for her renovation. I can return to England where my employer and co-workers will identify me and probably my family." Perhaps they were searching for me still. Perhaps they were holding my job in anticipation of my return. More likely, I'd been sacked after I disappeared in Paris but surely I could explain everything and be reinstated. I was Claire Smith. The countess would point us to proof that even Alex couldn't deny. Consumed with my thoughts, I forgot about Jean-Claude and Danielle, who continued their conversation in hushed tones. I forgot all about my bundle hidden in the bushes near the archway. There was no need for it now.

The minute Alex returned, I told him that I was not going with him tomorrow. I was going to Paris where I would learn the rest of my story.

"Don't be ridiculous," was his response. "You're still in shock. Come, we will discuss this upstairs."

"I am not going to South America. The answers are here, in France and England, and I shall find them if I have to walk to Paris and swim to London."

"Whatever you decide, Claire," Jean-Claude said, "my offer still stands." Alex's eyes travelled from Jean-Claude to me, but he was too proud to ask what this offer was and all at once I was too exhausted to explain. The younger man said goodnight with a kiss to my forehead and a long hug for Danielle. Was I the only one who recognized it for what it was? Danielle escorted Jean-Claude to the door, leaving the two of us alone as the porphyry mantle clock struck one delicate chime that lingered in the air for long seconds.

Alex stood over me, gripped by a rare moment of indecision that he covered up by moving away and poking about the fire. He was angry, or maybe jealous. I didn't want to let it fester. From miles away I heard my voice saying, "He offered to lend me money to return to London."

"My wife doesn't need to borrow money from another man."

"I'm not your wife. I ate strawberries. There is no scar."

He replaced the fire screen then turned in time to see me wipe the tears off my cheeks with the back of my hand. "You're incoherent. Everything will look different after a good night's sleep."

I opened my mouth to answer, then gave up. He was right, even talking was too much effort. Without another word, he scooped me up from the sofa and headed to the stairs. I remember my face, warm against his neck, and the precious feeling that I was safe.

"Wake up," said Alex brusquely, wrenching open the draperies to let the early morning sun stream in. I blinked stupidly and groaned as I saw the clock. "Michelle and Julie are here to pack your wardrobe. We'll have the larger trunks sent on ahead and bring the smaller one and your valise with us now. We need to hurry if we are to reach Bordeaux tonight. *Le Mosella* sails in the morning."

He did it on purpose. Brought in the maids so their presence would constrain my protests. Before I could speak, they were pulling the suitcases out from underneath the bed even as I was still in it. I would not be cowed. "Alex," I began, switching to English for privacy. "Alex, I am not going with you to Brazil."

"Rubbish," he said, handing me a robe. "Get dressed."

"I shall go with you as far as Paris and arrange there for transportation to London. I know what to do now. I know how to find the last pieces of the puzzle." He seemed not to hear me. Turning to the maids, he gave them some instructions so colloquial that I could not follow the French. They bustled from drawer to wardrobe to trunk, lifting and folding my clothes. No, not my clothes, Eva's. Eva's shoes that were too big for me.

I didn't notice that he was holding something in his hand until he tossed it on the bed. The bundle I had stashed near the gate. Lifting my chin, I met his eyes with a degree of calm I didn't feel. I said nothing. Let him start the conversation. After our silent battle had raged for several moments, he yielded. "Explain this."

I had been in France long enough to attempt my own version of the Gallic shrug. It was, I think, a fair imitation. "Surely it is obvious to a man of your abilities."

"Of course it's obvious," he snapped. "It should have been obvious from your distant behaviour last evening, but I thought we had come to an understanding."

For a moment, he sounded hurt and I felt a pang of guilt. But no, a voice inside me argued. Don't turn sentimental now. This was Alexander DeSequeyra, the international playboy, the bee to every flower in the garden, and I reminded myself that while he seemed interested in our relationship, he was not, by all accounts, the monogamous sort. Still, for reasons I preferred not to examine too closely, I did not want him to think me completely unaffected by our relationship during the past week. As much as I did not want to care for him, I had to admit that I did. Very much.

"Yesterday—" Gad, it seemed a year ago—"Yesterday, several things happened to make me think that you might be trying to kill me and I—" He made a sharp noise in protest but I held up my hand to stop him and continued. "It was Luca, but I didn't know

197

that then. Luca dropped the slate on my chair that day. He admitted it in the cave. And it was he who left a poisonous tisane for me to drink." Alex's eyebrows flew up at that revelation. "I was meant to think it came from Cécile. Lianne left it on the table for me."

"You didn't drink it?"

"There are times when a faulty memory is an asset. Look, you won't believe me, but my suspicions have all been correct. I am not Eva Johnson. Luca confirmed it. He said my teeth were different, and I didn't have a scar on my shoulder where Eva had been injured."

"And I have his word for this? A man whose list of crimes begins with murder? This is not reassuring. How do I know this isn't something you two planned to persuade me to release you?"

"Lianne was there and heard every word. She'll tell you—"

"I've already asked. She was too frightened to have paid any attention to anything you were saying. I admit that, from the beginning, there have been some puzzling inconsistencies in your story, but the fact remains that you were found wearing my wedding ring and a passport stating your name as Eva Johnson."

"I cannot explain those things either, but I'm trying to find the answers. You're trying to prevent me. Why?"

"I'm trying to keep you out of prison."

"The only proof that will convince you is for me to find someone who knew me as Claire Smith. The Contessa Castiglione is such a person. From her I will learn the name of my employer in London and from him, my address and the name of my parents. If you will lend me some money to get to London, I shan't forget to repay you."

He swore. "And if I don't, you will get it from Jean-Claude!" He seized me by my upper arms and would have shaken me had maids not been in the room. One would not have to speak English to understand there was an argument going on here. The maids directed the full force of their attention to laying tissue paper between the folds of my clothing and pretended to be deaf. Alex's lips turned up in an unconvincing smile. He began to pace the floor. It was, perhaps, the first time in a long while that the celebrated King of Clubs wasn't getting his own way.

"Look, Alex, let me explain."

He waved my words away and I stopped, defeated by his

stubborn refusal to consider the facts. Nothing I said was going to convince this man. No matter what I told him about scars or teeth or strawberries or shoes, he was not going to believe that Claire and Eva were different people. The real Eva could stand beside me and he would say it was a trick with mirrors. Why could he not bend enough to acknowledge that what I said might be true? Because he could not possibly have been wrong? Or because his vanity would not let him admit that he had been duped again by Eva, and possibly with my help?

"No, let *me* explain. The unpleasantness of last night has made you forget the urgency of your situation. You cannot go to Paris. Within hours of your arrival, you would be arrested for the killing of the old man in Cap Ferrat. Every policeman in the city will be on guard for the pretty murderess, not to mention the hoteliers, taxi drivers, and train station attendants. They don't even need to distribute photographs. All they have to do is put the word out that their culprit looks like Clara Bow! That is why we are driving to Bordeaux and not taking the train. You cannot cross the Channel; all the ferries will be watched. You cannot stay here. As soon as that damned Italian is picked up, he will attempt to free himself by using you as a bargaining chip. Even if he eludes the police, his anger over the paintings may well cause him to call in an anonymous tip. He may have done so already. There is no time to lose."

I went to the window. The road to Paris lay like a pale yellow ribbon between green fields, empty save for a rickety *charette* headed out to collect bundles of winter wheat. *Les paysans.* The French word sounded so much more dignified than the English "peasants." Soon now the entire village would be dissecting every detail of the previous night's adventure, adding morsels of what had been overheard at the butcher's shop, passing around the facts gleaned at the *lavanderie,* stirring in the learned opinion of the schoolmaster, and seasoning it all with a good dose of self-righteous indignation. *They* would not have been taken in by such a charlatan. *They* knew better than to trust foreigners. Hadn't *they* said right from the start that the Italian was a bad one? Gardener, my left foot! Hadn't Madame Fontville predicted trouble with fire? Dark as a gypsy, that Italian. As a matter of fact, hadn't he come in with the gypsy caravan last week? It had been a *feux de la Saint-*

Jean the village would not soon forget.

"I must go to Paris. I shall take the risk."

"I cannot permit that." He folded his arms across his chest and stood, legs apart and eyes blazing, lacking only the flowing Arab robe and a scimitar to double for Valentino's sheik.

"Then you will have to lock me in a tr—" I glanced at the empty trunk uneasily. I put nothing past this man. Our eyes locked and I thought I detected a gleam of amusement behind the frustration.

"How do you suppose I was planning to smuggle you on board *Le Mosella*?"

"Be reasonable, Alex. If you will just leave me at the nearest train station I can make my own way to Paris. I'll go in disguise."

He could not hide the emotional struggle raging inside him: his teeth were clenched, his fists were a bloodless white, and the muscles in his neck stood out like twisted cables strained to the breaking point.

"Very well, then, damnit! You are the most obstinate female that— Get dressed!" He flung the words at me and stalked dramatically through the doorway.

"What does that mean?" I called after him.

He would not stop or even turn around. "It means we leave for Paris in half an hour."

7 THE TOWN

We found a suitable inn at a remote crossroads north of Paris. After a respectable meal of rabbit and salad and a glass of local wine, I collapsed into bed and slept like the dead without a thought for Alex or where he would sleep. Early the next morning we were going to take the paved road to Paris, slip into the city, find the Contessa Castiglione, and learn some answers to my identity.

I awoke when the innkeeper's wife knocked with fresh bread and coffee. Alex was on her heels, wearing the same clothes he had worn the day before. He helped himself hungrily.

"Paris is too dangerous for you," he said in his blunt fashion. "No, don't argue with me. I have already obtained the information you wanted. Last night, after you went to sleep, I drove into Paris and located the Contessa Castiglione."

If he'd said he'd flown to the moon for tea, I could not have been more surprised. Only then did I notice that the corners of his eyes were creased with wrinkles and the pillow beside mine was not. "It was a better road than we had seen all day, and I made good time. *Madame la Contesse* was good enough to see me."

Madame had had little choice in the matter. I could imagine Alex arriving at her door in the middle of the night, apologizing for the ungodly hour, explaining to the servants his dishevelled appearance, and asking to be received on a matter of utmost urgency. I remembered the Contessa. An imperious woman in her sixties who made up for her small stature with ramrod posture and a haughty stare.

"A young woman matching your description was there for two days last month. The Contessa did not remember her name, only that she measured the floors and windows and drew plans of the three floors slated for redecoration. What she did remember very well was her anger when this young woman disappeared without notice. She was so furious that she sacked the interior design firm in London. But I got what I went for: its name and address."

"What are you saying? That you believe me now, that I am Claire Smith and not Eva?"

"I make no rush to judgment. I am proposing to take you to London, now, today, to investigate."

I leapt to my feet as if to leave that very second. "Someone there will know me, and have some record of where my family live!"

He grunted. "Unusual people, *non?* People who don't report to the police when someone goes missing? Their employee disappears, their daughter disappears, their friend disappears, and there is nothing in the newspapers, no call for information, no police investigation? Explain that!" He drained the last of the coffee in one large gulp. "I managed to place a telephone call to Jean-Claude. The police paid them a visit shortly after we left."

"Luca's revenge. What did Jean-Claude tell them?" I started to bite my fingernail. Alex noticed. I stopped.

"Actually, Jean-Claude wasn't there. He had taken Danielle and Lianne to the train station at Troyes. I spoke with Thonet who let the police believe we were all on that train. They will board it in Bordeaux, expecting to find you there. Danielle can handle them. Thank God she agreed to chaperone Lianne as far as the ship. Our aunt will take charge of Lianne from there."

"How will we cross the Channel? They will be watching the ports. I had thought a fishing boat, perhaps?"

Alex shook his head. "Have you ever flown?"

Engine noise made all talk impossible. I would have watched the pilot for reassurance, but he rode outside in an open cockpit, so I stared hard at the chair in front of me as the DeHavilland biplane charged down the packed-earth airstrip with lightening bolt speed. I knew that regular air service had been available from Paris to London for several years, but to actually fly in an aeroplane—well, that was something I had never contemplated. But if Amelia Earhart could fly an aeroplane across the Atlantic Ocean, then by God, I could ride in one across the English Channel!

That particular segment of the Channel is relatively narrow and before many minutes had passed, the white-flecked waters were behind us and we were cruising over the green fields and pastures of England's south coast at the unimaginable speed of ninety miles per hour. I could make out farmhouses and barns on the ground, all intersected by roads and rivers and sewn together like pieces of a patchwork quilt, and I felt glorious, like a hawk soaring over the land. And although I had never seen my country like this, it looked familiar.

A sporty-looking Bentley met our aeroplane at a deserted private airfield much like the one we had just left. A light rain fell. My ears were still ringing from the noise. "Where are we going first?"

"To the offices of Blake & Forrester, Interior Design." It didn't sound the least familiar.

"We're less than an hour from the City."

Having battled our way through the traffic that choked London's streets, we arrived at an attractive three-story building in the Basinghall Street district where every business seemed to involve textile manufacturing, leather working, and furniture building. Blake & Forrester had an understated, unobtrusive entrance, but then, the firm did not cater to the street. Designers waited upon upper-class patrons in their homes.

A thin woman dressed in a severely cut fawn suit greeted us without a flicker of recognition. I was sick with disappointment. I didn't recall the firm's name, I didn't recall the building, I didn't recall the clerk in the front office. Claire Smith didn't belong here. There had been some dreadful mistake.

"What can we do for you, sir?" she asked with the distant courtesy of an employee who would rather not be interrupted.

Alex gestured in my direction, stepping aside at the one time I would have appreciated his habit of taking charge. "D'you know me?" I asked her. "I was employed here. Recently. I stopped in to see some—to get some information. My name is Claire Smith."

Her eyes widened. She knew the name if not the face. "I'm new here. Two weeks ago. But I've heard your name, miss." And it hadn't been coupled with compliments, if her pinched mouth was any indication. "Let me tell Mr. Forrester you are here."

Alex planted himself in the corner. I was too much on edge to sit. My eyes wandered about the large room, finding nothing familiar. At last, they landed on double doors with frosted glass panels and all at once, I knew that behind those doors was the large workroom that I had remembered two days ago. I think I would have gone through those doors if they hadn't at that very moment opened and released two young women, each carrying an armload of files.

"Claire!" said the redhead with a touch of confusion but not much surprise. Her pleasant, lilting voice betrayed her Scottish heritage at the first word. "Whatever are you doing here? I thought you had left for Canada weeks ago." She sent a worried glance in the direction of the door that the receptionist had passed through a moment ago. "Better get along before Himself comes through!"

I gathered my wits. "Moira!" It was my friend, Moira, who had worked with me for many months. My heart raced. I was remembering! "It's so good to see you. I've had an accident. I've been in hospital and have had trouble remembering some things. I came back to see if I could find some information. Did you say I was going to Canada?"

"It's what we heard, wasn't it, Lucy?" She turned to the blond girl beside her for confirmation, and I remembered her name as well—Lucy. "A secretary position with some big corporation. Odd, we thought, didn't we, Luce? You always said you'd never be a secretary, sitting at a desk ten hours a day."

"We weren't here when you told off old Forrester," said Lucy with another of those looks at his door, "but we heard plenty from his secretary."

"I don't remember. Tell me what happened." Faced at long last with a source of information, I was ravenous for every morsel.

"You really don't remember? Well, you came back from Paris after three days. Just marched right into his office, didn't give notice or anything, just left on the spot. They say Mr. Forrester went purple! Wish I'd seen that, don't you, Moira?" she giggled. "But you don't want to see him again, he's not going to believe you've forgotten all about it and—you haven't come for your job back, have you? Because he won't give it. You cost him that Contessa woman, your leaving like that. She hired another firm."

"No, no, I don't want my job back. I only want some information. D'you know where I come from?" They exchanged glances like two people humouring a mad woman. "The village where my people live. D'you know the name?"

"Well . . . you talked about a village in Sussex, but I don't remember which one, do you, Lucy?" The door behind me opened and closed. Moira remembered her errands. "We'd better get along, Lucy, before Sanders' closes. Lovely seeing you again, Claire. I hope you, well, feel better soon." The girls eyed Alex as they edged toward the door making their exit before I could say anything more than goodbye.

The receptionist delivered her verdict. "Mr. Forrester cannot spare the time to see you, miss. He is certain that you and he have nothing further to discuss, and wishes you a good evening—excuse me, sir. You can't go in there!"

But he could.

Before Miss Hardy could bar the door, Alex was through it and into Mr. Forrester's office. She and I trailed behind in his wake.

I recognized Mr. Forrester at once. Charming to his clients, he was a tyrant to his employees whom he milked for ideas like a farmer milks his goats. But he was a famous interior designer, the best in London—in the world, were you to ask him—and we kept on with him for the experience. Besides, jobs didn't grow on trees, and who would hire a female interior designer?

As soon as he heard Alex's name, Mr. Forrester promptly exhibited his inborn talent for grovelling to rich European celebrities: within seconds he'd surrendered my employment records along with his dignity. Claire Smith had been hired in April of 1924 from International Fabrics where she had worked the two previous years. Before that she had worked for William Smith, her father, at his antiques shop on the High Street in Morefield, Sussex. Her assets included a knowledge of fabrics, especially imports, and antiques. Her weekly wages had been upped twice in the four years, the second time when she took on the training of new girls. The clients she had worked with were listed on the following page. Her birthdate, London boarding-house address, and days off were also recorded.

I was on paper. I was real. I was Claire.

I left Blake & Forrester in a daze, hardly aware of Alex beside me. Before we had crossed the street to the waiting taxi, a voice behind me called, "Claire! Wait!" I turned to see a young woman, tall and gangly, following us out to the street. "I heard you were here," she panted, pulling her green cardigan close around her shoulders. "Ever since you went to Canada, I've been hoping you'd write to someone so I could have your address."

"What is it?" I struggled for her name. V--, Victoria? Vivian? No. "What is it, Violet?"

"I wondered if you could tell me . . . that is, after you left for Paris, your brother came by to find you. He didn't know you had gone to Paris and was disappointed to miss you. He—well, we—I hope you don't mind, but we stepped out that night. He took me to the pictures and dinner. Such a nice gentleman, he was." She pushed the spectacles up on her nose and moistened her thin lips. "He gave me his phone number at the office and told me to ring him up the next week when I knew my schedule, and I did, but I'm so stupid, I know I wrote it down wrongly." Another push to the spectacles. She misinterpreted my astonished stare for disapproval. "You don't mind, do you? I didn't want him to think I was giving him the brush off . . ."

"No, Violet, it isn't that." I looked helplessly at Alex.

"Excuse me, Miss—?"

"Treadwell," she supplied. "Pleased to meet you, I'm sure, sir."

"The honour is mine, Miss Treadwell. I am Alexander DeSequeyra." The charm offensive had commenced. He smiled engagingly and made a stiff bow. Violet Treadwell blushed and bobbed half a curtsy. "Miss Smith is recovering from a serious accident and her memory is confused. You say her brother came here looking for her? When was that?"

"Why, just a day after she left for Paris. I remember because I said what a shame it was he had just missed her by one day. Back from Edinburgh, he said."

"What was his name?"

Now she looked at me incredulously. "You don't know your own brother's name?"

"Violet, I don't have a brother. At least, I don't think I do."

Here eyes narrowed. "Ohhhhhhh, I see how it is. I'm not good enough for your precious—"

Alex calmed her ruffled feelings with a condensed version of my memory loss and managed to learn that my "brother" was named Gerald, that he was about thirty, a smart dresser, had brown hair and brown eyes, and sported a John Barrymore moustache.

"And he asked for me by name?"

"Right as I left the building for lunch, he did. Said he was waiting for you but you hadn't come out, so I told him you'd gone to Paris for some fancy client and would be back in a week."

"Did you tell him anything else?"

"What else would I know?"

"Violet, I am certain I don't have a brother." Of course, last month I was certain I didn't have a sister. From Violet's expression, she was less than certain that I was telling the truth.

"Honestly, Violet, I'm going now to Morefield where my father lives. I'll ask about a brother, or half-brother, and if I have one named Gerald, I shall write to you with his address. I promise."

"Oh, very well then." She sounded unconvinced. "Sorry to have bothered you."

Thick traffic slowed our cabby's progress to Victoria Station and made me tap my foot with impatience.

Now I was sure I had a twin. I had known it since the night of the bonfire but now, even Alex would have to concede the fact. Someone looked enough like me to walk into my employer's office and left my job without raising his suspicions. No wonder Mr. Forrester had not notified the police of my disappearance! I had not disappeared. I had quit. While I lay in a Paris hospital, my double had given notice and cleared out my belongings. Gone to Canada. Or so everyone thought.

But what of my father? Twins might fool acquaintances but it was quite another thing to fool a parent. If I had a twin sister who grew up in an orphanage, I must also be adopted. No one would give away one child and keep another. Or would they? Perhaps that was part of the past I had not yet remembered. Perhaps it was kept from me. Perhaps I had a brother too. My thoughts raced ahead. As soon as I reached my father in Morefield, I would know.

Fortunately my feet knew the way home because my head was busy trying to see both sides of the street at once.

"There! That's my father's shop," I pointed eagerly to the two-story frame building with a window full of furniture. "We lived upstairs when I was a little girl. That window on the corner was my bedroom—the bedroom in my dream. And that's my school, around the corner, and that is our butcher's." I must have sounded like a tour guide, pointing out landmarks that Alex could not possibly have cared about, for all that he made the occasional supportive remark. Exhilaration surged so strongly inside me that I couldn't stop myself from showing off every memory. After so many weeks of not knowing anything, at last I could remember!

The sun hovered above the horizon when we turned into the short lane that led to Rose Cottage, a modest house of uncertain years set behind a tangled profusion of pink and yellow roses. We reached the front door. I swallowed twice, cleared my throat, and rapped the knocker.

The woman who opened the door was a complete stranger. It was the last thing I had expected, and I stared at her, all speech knocked out of me. She was tall, taller than I, gaunt in the way of older women, her grey hair was pulled into a severe bun on the top of her head, her spectacles bounced on her bosom at the end of a chain. She put them on with one hand and squinted.

"Oh. It's you. What happened?" Surely this was not my mother. The woman turned her head. "William! It's Claire. With *a man*."

A man with thinning hair came stiffly to the door. I flew past the stranger into my father's arms and clung to him for comfort as I had when I was a child frightened by thunderstorms. "There, there, darling. This is a surprise, isn't it? Hmmm? We weren't expecting to see you for some time, were we Edna? It must have been a quick trip, eh? And who is this you've brought with you?"

"I am Alexander DeSequeyra, Mr. Smith. Honoured to make your acquaintance."

"Oh? Well, Mr. Dessick—ah, any friend of my daughter's is a friend of mine, eh? Come in, now, no need to stand on the porch all evening. My, my . . . what a surprise this is. A nice surprise."

Sensing my confusion, Alex turned to the woman and inclined his head. "Mrs. Smith, I presume?"

"And who else would be living here, I ask you?" she said in a huff, her large bosom rising in indignation at the perceived slight.

Before we had settled in the parlour, enough of my composure had returned for me to realize that this was my father's wife. Evidently my father had remarried but I had no recollection of my stepmother. It took only a few minutes to regret the end of that blissful ignorance. I let Alex handle the explanations.

If it had been any tale but my own, I would have found it entertaining to hear Alex tell it, every time with a different slant. Like a playwright, he gave each audience the facts it needed and no more, deftly serving up a version that would appeal to their sympathies in the fewest words possible. Since he was addressing my father, he was careful to mention the presence of servants at the chateau in Champagne and to speak lovingly of his grandmother, sister, and daughter. His narrative omitted anything about marital difficulties with Eva or their five-year separation, making it sound as if he were searching for a woman who had recently disappeared. My battered face and bandages had caused him to mistake me, briefly of course, for his missing wife, and he thought that helping me solve the mystery of my identity would help him find Eva.

Horrified at my brush with death along the Seine, my father determined to write to the Paris police tomorrow to demand they catch the criminals at once. His concern for my physical wellbeing was surpassed by his acute distress at my partial loss of memory, and it was all I could do to reassure him that I had very nearly regained it all.

My stepmother made no comment through this exchange, but her eyes travelled annoyingly from Alex to me and back again. Her lips were pressed together in a tight smirk that said more clearly than words what she thought of this chaperone rubbish. It didn't help that my cheeks reddened so readily.

"Eva always told me that she had grown up in a London orphanage," Alex said by way of conclusion. "Is it possible that Claire could have a twin sister?"

At that, my father stiffened his back like a preacher confronted with sin. "What are you suggesting, young man?"

I stepped in to smooth his feathers. "I'm wondering—after all, this—it's the only logical explanation . . . was I, by any chance, adopted?"

"You? Adopted? No, certainly not! How could you think such a thing? Or maybe you're thinking we had twins and gave one to the orphanage, eh? Bah! You are our very own girl." He took out his pipe and pouch. The familiar routine seemed to soothe his ruffled feelings, and he continued in a calmer manner. "If there is another who resembles you, then I can't account for it. Coincidence. You know what they say, every person in the world has an exact double."

"I didn't have a sister? A cousin, perhaps?"

"No, my dear, no close relatives on either side. You must not have gone to Canada, then, what with the accident and your time in the hospital, eh?" My utterly blank look made him continue. "We heard from you, oh, let's see, it was over a month ago, wasn't it, Edna? We got a letter. Must be you don't remember. You said— where is that letter, Edna? Do we still have it?"

"No, I threw it out." As it well deserved, her tone implied.

"Never mind. It was a short note. It said you were going to Canada for a job and would write more when you arrived."

"The handwriting looked like mine?"

"It was written on the blue stationery you save for special, with the initials engraved at the top. And postmarked London. You saying you didn't write it?"

"I don't remember."

"Were you planning to stay here tonight, Claire?" asked Edna abruptly. "If so, I must go get the bed made up. There's only your old room, of course, so one of you would have to sleep on the sofa."

"That is most kind of you, Mrs. Smith," said Alex, "but we don't wish to put you to any trouble. Claire and I plan to return to London tonight."

"Last train left half an hour ago," said my father. "We'll fix up an extra bed—"

"That won't be necessary. I noticed an inn beside the train station as we came into town. I'm sure they will have lodgings."

"Now if there are no rooms at the inn, you must come straight back, Alexander," said my father. "I may call you Alexander, mayn't I? It's easier said than the second name, isn't it? And easier remembered. Alexander, like the cards. The King of Clubs was Alexander the Great, you know."

I looked from my father to Alex. "Like the cards?" I echoed stupidly.

"Yes, dear, don't you remember that either? We used to play cards at night, your mother and you and I, and we called the kings and queens by their names. Tradition, you know," he turned to Alex, warming to the topic, "says that the Kings had names: Charlemagne, King David of Jerusalem, Alexander the Great, and Julius Caesar. Not many people know about that but those of us in the antiques business, it's our job to keep the old tales alive. Ah, those were happy days, eh Claire?" His wistful smile gave me to understand he had gone back in time for a moment, at least until Edna's harrumph brought him back to the present. "Right, well, here you go, darling, don't forget your purse. And remember, it's no trouble at all to have you here—we've plenty of room, eh Edna?"

We exchanged goodbyes and promised to stop back in the morning. Automatically, we retraced our steps, engrossed in our own thoughts, my disappointment threatening to erupt into tears of frustration at any moment. How could I not have a twin? It was the only explanation left!

We had just turned the corner when I heard my father behind us. The lane was so quiet and the air so still that his soft voice echoed to the far end of the High Street and back, ricocheting off the buildings.

"Claire, wait," he said, breathless from hurrying. "This must have fallen out of your purse. I found it on the floor by the chair." He handed me a lipstick and pushed the strands of white hair back from his forehead. I recognized the ploy for what it was: he'd filched the lipstick so as to have an excuse to run after us. We stood awkwardly as I waited. "Claire, dear . . ." He swallowed hard. "I need to tell you the truth. I know what I said back there, but it wasn't true. You must know that I love you like you were my very own, but . . . but the truth is, you *were* adopted, just like you said."

Astonished, I could only ask, "But then . . . why did you just tell me . . . ?"

"I had to. See, Edna . . . well, she's a great girl, Edna is, I don't know what I'd do without her. She practically runs the shop herself, while I do the picking and deliveries."

"Yes. It's odd, but I don't remember her."

211

"Well, that's probably because you left home not long after we got married." A squeeze on my elbow told me that Alex knew exactly why I had left. My father shifted his feet, cleared his throat, and said in a rush, "Before you were born, Claire, your mother and I lived in Cheapside. I worked for an auctioneer, she taught at a school. We wanted children. Six of them, she used to say. When ten years passed with no sign, we went to Doctor Barnardo's. You were just starting to walk. The prettiest thing I ever saw in my life. We brought you home."

"Why did you never tell me?"

He looked at his feet and cleared his throat uncomfortably. "I promised your mother I wouldn't. She said if people knew, it might go hard on you later in life. That's why we left Cheapside and came here, where no one knew you weren't our very own. We never talked about it. We never thought about it."

"So I was adopted."

He couldn't bring himself to say the word. "We brought you home. But there wasn't a sister. We would never have taken one and not the other. There was no sister."

Unless she had been adopted first.

"Don't say anything about this to Edna. She's a great girl, she is. I don't know what I'd do without her. But she's . . . well, two women in the same house just doesn't work, does it? It was Edna who found you your first job in London with her brother's fabric shop, so very kind of her. Just don't let on to Edna about this. She has daughters and, well, she wants some of the business for them. I tell her it's yours when I die but if Edna knows, well, she'll say you aren't any blood relation, and that blood is thicker than water, and I won't hear the end of it 'til I'm cold in the grave. Your mother was right. Some people will make it harder for you if they know. I hope you understand, Claire darling. We couldn't have loved you more if you had been born to us . . ."

He wiped his eyes with a clean, white handkerchief, creased from the iron. Edna took good care of him. He was weak and she was strong. My mother had been the strong one too, making the decisions, running the business. For the first time I realized how lost he must have been when she died. I threw my arms around him. He smoothed my hair and kissed my cheek, then remembered Alex beside me. "Excuse me, sir, for such a display. What will you be thinking? I thank you for looking after my daughter. You're a fine man to take the trouble. I'd best be getting back now."

We hugged goodbye a second time. I watched him through tears as he walked back in the direction of Rose Cottage, but he had only gone a few steps when he turned once more.

"Claire, darling, the real reason we didn't tell you, your mother and I, was . . . well, we never, ever thought of you that way. As adopted. And that's God's truth. You *are* my very own daughter, and any man says otherwise will have me to deal with!"

Alex and I picked up our bags at the train station and headed across the street to the Grey Swan. "It has been a long day." He said it carefully, like a surgeon probing for a bit of shrapnel, trying not to cause the patient pain. "I see now why Jack Marsh didn't find your father. He was looking for a William Smith on the high street. He would not have paused over a William and Edna Smith, and Rose Cottage is not on the high street."

"The store is. That's what I remembered."

"And, of course, Marsh wasn't looking for a store."

"Nor did he find any trace of me at the orphanage. Perhaps he isn't very skilled at his trade."

"Even the best can make mistakes. The orphanage files might bear further investigation. We can look into that aspect tomorrow."

We headed in the direction of the Grey Swan, its sign rendered colourless in the fading light. Alex carried both bags. The scent of meat and potatoes made my stomach rumble and I realized how long it had been since we had eaten. The street was empty. Regular folks were home with their families. I had found my father and the town where I had grown up. Why did I still feel like an orphan with no family and no real home?

"So Lianne was right after all," I said with an attempt at levity. "I do have a twin sister, but it didn't involve the gypsies." Alex remained deep in thought. "I wonder if I knew about her. She certainly knew about me. How did that come about, d'you suppose?"

"I think I can guess. You were adopted into a family that moved away from the city. She was adopted before you, obviously, or your parents would have taken both girls, but things didn't work out and she came back. She was also old enough to read, so could easily have rifled the files to learn about her own background and by doing so, found yours. Somehow she learned who you were and where you lived."

"She might have known about me for years."

"Or she might have just come across the information while she was in London this spring. If she learned you lived in Morefield, she could have contacted your father with some story about trying to find an old school chum. He would have been proud to tell anyone who asked that you had moved to London and worked for Blake & Forrester. It would have been simple enough to send one of her lovers around to find you there. Only he didn't find you because you had just been sent to Paris. He selected Violet, unattractive, unappealing Violet, who was so flattered to be asked to dinner with the handsome "brother" of her friend that she had no compunction about telling him where you were, including, presumably, the name of the hotel in Paris."

"She wanted to find me, so I could switch places with her. Which I must have done gladly, as there I was with her purse and ring, walking along the Seine."

He gave me a long look. "Not exactly."

"What are you suggesting?" I cried, agitated at the direction his thoughts were taking. "We switched places for some reason, and I was set upon by men who mistook me for her, or perhaps it really was just a random crime that had nothing to do with anything else."

"I know Eva and you don't. She was getting desperate. After five years, her Riviera art-theft scheme had been cracked, the French police were after her, my agents were closing in, and one of her lovers turned out to be a possessive madman. Think about it from her point of view. How can she get rid of the maniac lover, the French police, and the vengeful husband all at once? By dying. Tell me it hasn't occurred to you that those men on the quayside were interested in something more than your purse?"

I could not deny it.

"She follows you to Paris, gets a hotel room and a Clara Bow wig and makes sure she is seen. She hires some thugs to do the dirty job, never dreaming you would survive. They crack your skull, throw to the ground Eva's purse with her hotel key in it, and force her wedding ring on your finger, breaking your hand in the process. They push your unconscious body in the Seine, which by all rights should have killed you in minutes if you weren't already dead, and are chased off by some Polish sailors. Eva checks out of your hotel the next morning and returns to London with your baggage, your passport, and your identity. She leaves your job, empties your bank account—oh yes, I'm sure that when you remember the name of your bank, you'll find the account closed—goes to your boarding house, and uses your monogrammed stationery to write to your father—never mind about handwriting, the stationery will predispose anyone to think it is from you—to write about leaving the country. No one reports Claire missing because Claire isn't missing. She has gone to Canada for a job."

My mind was reeling. That there were people evil enough to plot such wickedness, I did not doubt, but my own flesh and blood? My own twin sister?

"But I didn't drown." I pointed out rather unnecessarily.

"I doubt very much Eva knows that," he mused, trying to suppress his elation at reaching the end of the maze. He put me in mind of a hunter who has finally broken through a briar thicket to find himself in a clearing with his unsuspecting quarry in full sight. "She would not have waited around to see what happened after her men did their job. And I kept it out of the newspapers for obvious reasons. She probably left Paris at once."

"And went to Canada."

"And went anywhere *but* Canada. I suspect she made arrangements for a letter or two to be sent to your father from Canada, then nothing. When he tried to investigate, the trail would be stone cold. Claire Smith would have disappeared without a trace."

"So where is she?"

"That is the question, isn't it? Knowing Eva's penchant for the glamorous life style, I strongly doubt Canada would be her choice of refuge. Too dull. Australia and New Zealand would lack sophistication. So would the United States, except perhaps New York. India might appeal to her. Very exotic, India, and very far away. South Africa and Rhodesia perhaps, for the same reasons."

The clean night air gave way to the smell of cigarettes, pipes, and beer as we entered the panelled oak pub at the Grey Swan. "Order me whatever you choose while I see about our lodgings."

By the time he returned there were two pints on the table. Alex drained his without a word and motioned to the barman for another. "I've got two chicken and potatoes coming," I said. "I thought you'd prefer that to steak and kidney pie."

He grimaced. "One day you English will learn how to eat. Probably not in my lifetime."

For the first time in days, I smiled. "You must be exhausted. You had no sleep last night."

The shrug. Yes, I am. No, I'm not. Never mind. It was as much as he could manage before refuelling, and I couldn't blame him. I felt drained myself, a motorcar running on fumes. I knew I should plan what to do next, but I was unable to focus my thoughts on anything beyond the here and now.

Pub food had never tasted better. The food and drink revived us both and we talked very little as we ate. The stout proprietor approached our table and apologized for the interruption. Alex had a telephone call. "I'll be right back," he said.

No one but my father and Edna knew where we were staying, and they had no telephone. I waited for a moment before following Alex.

The Grey Swan telephone booth was wedged at the end of a narrow passageway behind the coat racks, next to a side door that patrons used to enter directly into the pub without passing by the reception desk. The booth door was missing, and I suspected there was no need to replace it in a town where everyone knew everyone else's business anyway. I could stand around the corner without being seen and hear most of Alex's conversation.

"Yes, as was I . . . use locals . . . you know her modus operandi by now . . . no . . . the other three . . . I don't care about them, I want the boy . . . not before 25 May . . . right, our big chance . . . she doesn't know, she will have let down her guard . . . the timing's ideal."

I slipped into my seat seconds before his return. He was going to hope I didn't ask. He should have known me better by now.

"Who was that?"

"Jack Marsh. I put the call through when I registered. I needed to pass along the recent leads."

"You haven't given up on finding her, then?" My heart sank.
"No, I never give up."

"Those blasted paintings! You are obsessed with them. Surely by now you have spent as much as they are worth on investigators!"

"Not even close."

"What is it about a boy?" Startled, he met my eyes. "I overheard you say something to Marsh about a boy."

"It is not important." His denial only served to convince me it was. He put his hand over mine. "None of this need concern us."

No, why should it? None of this had anything to do with me, the Innocent Bystander Extraordinaire. What matter to me that my twin sister had tried to have me murdered, that her cast-off lover had continued the effort, and that the French judicial system was eager to separate my head from my shoulders?

"Come, we are finished. A hot bath will be the thing for you."

We climbed the narrow steps at the end of the passageway. Alex unlocked the door to a well-proportioned room situated above the pub. The floorboards creaked under my feet, and I could smell the smoke that filtered up between the cracks. The noise filtered up too, but that would not last long; no one in Morefield kept London hours. I looked about the room furnished with country-made pieces that had probably been there since the eighteenth century.

Alex tossed his jacket over one chair, laid his wallet on the table, removed his shoes, and disappeared into the tiny bathroom. I waited for him to come out.

"Who is the boy?"

He threw the towel onto the back of the other chair and feigned surprise, although I was sure that my question was not unexpected. Folding his arms, he looked deep into my eyes for a moment, deciding whether or not he could skate past me with a trumped up tale.

"The truth, please," I added.

"Very well. You shall have it. The truth is, I am searching not only for the paintings, but also for a boy. Eva's child."

"I thought she rid herself of the child after she left."

"So did I. She did not."

"But the child isn't yours. Why do you care?"

He dug into his jacket for his cigarette case, retrieved a

cigarette, then a lighter, and lit it, all to buy time to marshal his thoughts. He still didn't entirely trust me.

"When the doctor tested Eva's blood, he unfortunately explained the system to her. Shortly thereafter, she disappeared. I drew the obvious conclusions. However, I was proved mistaken. A year later, the detectives charged with tracking Eva and the paintings unexpectedly came across a hospital in France where Eva had been admitted. She had given birth there to a son. The date was within the expected range for a child of mine. A little early, perhaps, but some babies do come early. Lianne was, herself, three weeks early. Logic said the boy was not mine—why would she have run off if she knew I was the father? No, she would sell the baby to me for a great sum. Nonetheless, I must know beyond the slightest doubt. The date is right, so I want to see this child, to see if there is a family resemblance. And to have his blood tested in the new manner. That will let me put this issue to rest for good."

"Why did you not tell me about your search for the boy?"

"Because you knew nothing about it."

"You never asked me."

"But I did. I asked you when you were hypnotized."

I could feel the distance between us lengthen, almost as if I were on a small raft drifting away from shore, watching this man I had cared for growing ever smaller, less significant. What else had he kept from me?

When I made no comment, he said, "And now, we are both tired. Let us go to bed."

"I want my own room."

"*Tiens, cherie,* we have been through a lot. I have not held you in my arms in two days." Fastening his deep, dark eyes onto mine, he crossed the room and put his hands on my shoulders. "I need you tonight. And I think—I know—you need me."

I tried not to let him see that he was right. There was nothing I wanted more at that moment than to lie in his arms and feel his body on mine. He read the answer in my eyes and lowered his lips to mine. My response led him to believe I had acquiesced.

"We're both exhausted," he said, his mouth brushing my ear with his words. "Let's just go to sleep now and see how we feel in the morning, hmmm?"

Four mornings of waking up beside this man had taught me

exactly how I was going to feel—warm, soft, drowsy, and very receptive. I put both palms flat on his chest and leaned away.

"I want my own room."

His eyes flashed with ill-suppressed annoyance. "Don't tell me—you're having an attack of morality. Nothing important has changed, yet suddenly this is wrong?" He kissed me again with hard urgency to show me exactly what "this" was.

"Suddenly you're married to my sister. There's no longer any doubt. You can't go on denying that I'm Claire."

"I'm not denying it. I've known it for some time."

"You *did* hear Luca in the cave, didn't you?"

"No, I'm afraid I crunched onto that scene after he had discovered your scar, or lack thereof."

I felt a chill. "So . . . when did you know?"

He ran his fingers through his wavy hair, a gesture I had come to recognize as his favourite stalling technique.

"I should have realized it sooner than I did. I should have been suspicious when I saw you in the hospital, before you were even conscious, lying in that narrow bed bandaged like a mummy. I saw your fingernails bitten to the quick. Eva would have chewed glass before she bit her fingernails. And Eva smoked. Constantly. But these things hardly registered. Like your shoes that were too big, there was always a reasonable explanation. After all, shoes stretch, people do stop smoking, and worry can make them start to chew their fingernails. But no, it was after our first night together that I was certain you were not Eva. There was no longer any doubt."

I stopped breathing. I knew what he was going to say. He could tell the difference between us because Eva was better in bed than I. She was prettier and thinner and sexier—Luca had said virtually the same thing as soon as he got close enough to realize we were two different women. I couldn't bear to hear Alex say it too. Full of brass, I squared my chin and beat him to the punch. "That inept, was I?"

"You could call it that. It was perfectly natural, though, for a virgin."

I gaped at him, stunned to silence. He had known. I had not. The possibility had never occurred to me, thinking as I did then, that I'd had lovers and a husband. And the details of that night had been lost in a haze of drunkenness. But Alex had known. And he hadn't said anything. All this time, he had accused me of deceiving him when in the end, he had been deceiving me. It was the classic card-cheat strategy—accuse your opponent of cheating to distract him from the card up your own sleeve.

"There is a very powerful attraction between us, Claire. And I flatter myself that it has you in as tight a grip as it does me. We are in love, are we not? We belong together, you and I, tonight and always, but especially tonight when all the illusions have been shattered like so much broken glass."

"And what do you propose for the future? Will you divorce your wife and marry her twin? That would get your name onto the front pages, wouldn't it? And make you the laughingstock of Europe."

He looked uncomfortable. "Claire, I cannot divorce Eva until I have settled the question of the boy. That has always been the reason, not the paintings. If he is mine, I must prove to be his legal father, or I could not take him. Besides, none of this has anything to do with us. You are a modern woman. We can go on as we have begun, for the time being anyway. Come home with me to São Paulo. No one will know you are not my wife."

We are in love, are we not? I had not heard that word from him until that moment. We had only been living as man and wife for a few days, and I was so caught up in the physical expression of love that I thought the words were understood. Well, he was right about one thing: my illusions had certainly been shattered.

"Why the charade? Why did you pretend to have doubts after you knew?"

Again, the fingers through the hair. "Because I wanted to give us time, time for you to see what it could be like, the two of us together. It was good, wasn't it?"

My emotions, frayed after the whiplash of the day's events, lurched once more. Yes, it had been good. But it had all been based on a lie.

What I felt was beyond tears, a kind of emptiness and betrayal mixed with shame. I remembered that first night at Chateau Denon when I had wanted my own room and he had refused. I had no recourse then. Now I did. I could ask the innkeeper myself or go to my father's house. I could tell from the expression on his face that he followed my thoughts.

"I want my own room."

"Well, well, Miss Hypocrisy! Where are those modern values you suffragettes are so keen on—free love, birth control, equality of the sexes? Never mind, have it your way tonight, I'm too tired to quarrel with you." He turned, took a deep breath, and went downstairs.

The absurdity of my position would have made me laugh if I hadn't been so close to crying. He wanted to pursue Eva to the ends of the earth, recover his precious paintings, get his revenge. That's what really mattered. This story about the boy, it was fairy tale. He had the advantage now and would hardly give up the chase. Eva would grow careless. She felt safe and flush with success. She would relax. She would not be expecting Alex's agents to be looking for her any longer, now that she was officially dead. She would live the high life until the money ran low, then rekindle the Riviera scheme. If she were resourceful enough, she could probably handle the scam without a partner, simplifying her life and doubling her take. Maybe she would settle down one day with a rich widower and give up larceny . . . Sooner or later, Claire Smith's name would appear in the newspapers, linked with some wealthy scion of American industry or some stuffy plantation owner in British India, and Alex and his men would pounce like cats on a complacent mouse.

Alex was in love with me? That he could say that and in the next breath offer me a life of pretence, masquerading as his wife, made me ill with shame. With Eva wanted in Europe and me posing as Eva, I would have to remain hidden away in his São Paulo kingdom while he continued the playboy circuit with his European friends, paying his mistress in Brazil annual visits as he did his French grandmother. I would love him and he would use me. It sounded like an amusing novel—most men kept their wives at home and pursued their mistresses but Alex would do the opposite! He didn't love me. He was *in love* with me, or more likely, intrigued with the mystery of twins. It was a temporary state of affairs, one that he could easily fall out of when the novelty wore off. A handfast. I was naïve for believing that it was anything more than that.

Why had he insisted on coming with me to England? Not for my sake, I felt sure. Rather, by helping me search for my past, he expected to find something that would lead him to Eva. I was still the link to his paintings, to Eva and the boy. Through me, he hoped to get to them. That was the crux of his continuing interest in me.

I needed to leave him. Now, while I was strong enough. I was honest enough to admit my own weakness—I did love Alex, heaven only knew why—and I knew beyond a shadow of a doubt that tomorrow morning he would wear me down. I could disappear among London's eight million people but there were no trains until morning. However, I could, if there were a very early train, be gone before Alex woke up.

I heard footsteps in the hall. In a flash, I snatched up the wallet Alex had left on the table, pulled out half the money, and slipped it in my pocket. I was a thief after all, just like Eva. Some would say it was in the blood, and I couldn't argue with that. Alex would discover what I had done only if he took all his cash out and counted it, but I gambled that he would not do that, at least, not until he went to pay for our lodgings in the morning. By then it would be too late.

"I took the room at the end of the hall." He set the iron key on the table and picked up his wallet at the same time, slipping it into his breast pocket. "You're right, it's better this way. We'll both sleep well and save your father from Edna's malicious tongue when she learns, if she hasn't heard already, that we took two rooms instead of one. We'll catch the 10:05 in the morning. That will give us plenty of time for another visit with your father if you like. In London, we can go have a look at those orphanage records, perhaps, or maybe we can find your boarding house to see if any of your belongings remain, which I doubt."

It felt odd hearing these plans being made for me, knowing I wasn't going to go through with them. He was putting a good face on the matter, jollying me along, as my father would say.

"Good night, then." I should have tried to stop him from kissing me, but I couldn't summon up enough will power to refuse when he took my face between his hands. It would be the last time.

"*Tiens,* no one kisses like you, *cherie,* with your whole body," he whispered hoarsely, his breath warm against my ear as he held me in an embrace so tight I could not tell whether the thundering heartbeats I felt were my own or his. At length, he pulled back, and I could read the cost of the separation in his face. He cleared his throat with difficulty. "If you change your mind, my room is number 4. What time do you want to wake up?"

"I'm very tired. I'd like to sleep as long as possible."

"Half past eight, then. *A demain.*" Taken literally, it meant until tomorrow. But there would be no tomorrow. The English word was more accurate: Goodbye.

I gave him enough time to settle into Room 4, then I crept down the stairs on silent feet, through the passageway to the front desk. A light bulb dangled over the empty desk, glowing weakly. It was late. Even the proprietor had retired. I pulled open the desk drawers one by one until I found a copy of the train schedule. The first one came through Morefield on weekdays at 6:15. Alex's choice, the 10:05, was next. I was about to replace the schedule when I noticed something I wasn't expecting. There was a late train to London, tonight, at 11:35. My father had said there was no late train, but he was often forgetful. A glance at the clock behind the desk told me I had twenty-five minutes before that last train came through. Having had no rest the night before, Alex would surely fall into a deep sleep at once, so deep the train's arrival and departure would not register. I had to gamble on it.

Fifteen minutes later, I crossed the street to the station and waited on the platform, alone, in the dark. I boarded the train to London at 11:35.

Mary Miley

8 THE CITY

The longer I lived in London, the more I remembered it. Two days after I'd arrived, I answered an advert at Christie's, the city's oldest auction house, and obtained a position there as an appraiser's assistant. On some days, like today, the boss sent me on a job by myself.

"Need some help with that parcel, miss?" The street urchin appeared out of nowhere as I left the building.

"Not today, thank you, Tommy."

Undeterred, the boy scampered alongside me as I hurried along King Street, matching each of my steps with two of his own. "Where you headin' this morning, miss?"

"Regent's Park."

The boy tugged the notebooks out of my arms. "Dover Street Station, then, would be best, miss, getting' off the tube at St. John's Woods. I'll go along with you—you'll be needin' help with the liftin'. Looks like rain, miss. Good thing you brought your brolly."

I suppressed a smile. "Don't you have one, Tommy?"

He answered me with a scornful look that said umbrellas were for girls, not Soho street toughs who, if the truth be known, probably supported more than himself with the tips he earned hustling around Christie's. Boys made themselves useful when clients drove up with a trunk or table to unload, and they made themselves handy with us employees too when it came time for carrying.

"I shan't be doing any lifting, Tommy. Christie's sends men and a lorry when I've finished with my part of the job."

"Finished what, miss?" Clearly, to Tommy, if it wasn't lifting, it wasn't work.

"I'm an appraiser, the person who decides how old things are and how much they're worth."

"Can you really tell how old things are, miss, just by looking?"

"There's nothing magic about it. I grew up in the antiques business. You develop a feel for different styles after a while. See that house on the corner? And the one across the street? Which one is older?"

"Pooh, that's easy, miss. The corner place is almost new. The other is old."

"How d'you know that? You didn't see them being built."

"It's as plain as day."

"But why?"

"Well . . . He squinched up his face in thought. "Old houses don't have them big windows, and well, I don't know how, but I can just tell. I'm right, ain't I?"

"Exactly right. And it's the same with furniture. I can tell when a piece was made because of certain features that were common during certain times."

I liked my work. And I was proud that the supervisor said I was the best he had ever seen for my age, *man or woman*. For the past three months, I had put in six long days a week at Christie's and spent every Sunday with the suffragettes, distributing leaflets to educate women about their new right to vote and canvassing working class neighbourhoods until my feet throbbed. The vote had been won, but there were miles left to travel before equal rights were achieved. No one at Christie's knew about my Sunday work. It wasn't wise to talk about one's unpopular causes.

Suffrage work occupied more than my hours; it filled the hollow inside my chest and gave me something more important than myself to dwell on. Last month we had a visit from Christabel Pankhurst. Of course, she did not know me—I was a foot soldier and she was a general. But we were introduced, and exchanged a few sentences. I couldn't help but remember the letter that Alex never mailed because he had not wanted me to learn my true identity. Ironically, it wouldn't have mattered if he *had* sent it—if she had replied, it would only have been to deny any personal

226

knowledge of me and that would have played straight into Alex's dual personality explanation.

I tried not to think about Alex. I tried a hundred times a day not to think about Alex. I should have been content with my life: I had a career with promise and a cause I believed in passionately. I was Claire Smith, a modern Englishwoman beholden to no one. Like one of Jean-Claude's bottles of champagne, I kept my pressurized emotions tightly corked and bound with wire.

In July, about three weeks after I left Alex, I learned I had nothing to fear about any effects of our brief interlude. I was hugely relieved and achingly disappointed at the same time—the perfect mixed-up patient for that famous French psychiatrist Alex had threatened me with!

Shortly after I'd taken the position at Christie's, I made a point of seeking out the orphanage records Jack Marsh had mentioned in his report. I retraced the private investigator's steps from the Copperfield Road orphanage—Jack Marsh was right, Dr. Barnardo's old orphanage had been turned into a factory—to the nearest Church of England bishopric where the records were being stored. It was my great good fortune to have passed, however briefly, through an orphanage where administrators thought it important to keep records on their young charges. That these records had been saved even after the demise of the orphanage was nothing short of a minor miracle. I was determined to learn what I could, especially why my twin sister was listed among the orphans and I was not. Had my file been lost? Or stolen?

All over the world, who has not heard of Doctor Thomas Barnardo, the philanthropist who gave up his early ambition to be a foreign missionary when his medical work in London's slums made him aware of the great numbers of homeless children in the cities of England? With help from wealthy patrons, the good doctor established more than a hundred orphanages throughout England where children were fed, clothed, educated, and trained for a useful trade, most becoming domestics, farmers, or seamen. His most laudable success was to give orphans a chance at a new life in Australia or another of the Commonwealth countries where effort mattered more than birth. In the endless nature-versus-nurture debate, Dr. Barnardo scorned nature, convinced that orphans from the slums could succeed because environment counted for everything, heredity for very little—sheer heresy to the upper classes! I never knew him—he died the year after I was born—but I felt spiritually aligned because we shared the same philosophy. I believed firmly that it was who *you* were, not who your parents were, that mattered in life.

I had been admitted to the bishop's offices by a grey-haired woman with thick spectacles.

"I've come to examine the records from Dr. Barnardo's orphanage on Copperfield Road."

"Yes, we get your sort, now and then," she muttered, clicking her tongue in the judgmental way of older people to show how much she disapproved of meddlesome folk with the effrontery to want to know something about themselves. "Come this way."

What had once been a stately home now served as the offices for the diocese as well as the residence of the bishop. Faded banners emblazoned with military insignia and escutcheons hung mute and limp above our heads. Someone had arranged an ancient collection of crossbows, pikes, axes, and halberds in geometric patterns to cover the walls in a glorification of medieval violence I found incongruent in a church building. Strains of *"Onward, Christian Soldiers!"* marched through my head. The clicking of typewriters and the ring of telephones ushered me out of the Middle Ages as my reluctant hostess opened a door and turned on a weak ceiling light.

"You will return each item to its proper place, you understand?" She pointed to a bank of grey filing cabinets and left without waiting for my reply.

My fingers were trembling with anticipation as I wrenched open the filing drawer marked "S-Z." The system seemed simple—there was a single sheet of heavy paper for each child filed alphabetically by last name. There was a profusion of Smiths, naturally, and the tension mounted as my fingers walked through Carol, Catherine, Cecily, Charles, Christopher, then a rush of disappointment as I continued through Collin, Constance, and Cynthia. I sat back on my heels in exasperation. Come now, Claire, did you really think you would find your name neatly filed in alphabetical order when a trained investigator had failed? My file card might have been misfiled. I would have to look through thousands and even then, there was no guarantee I'd find myself.

I turned to a drawer that I knew contained answers. Johnson, Eva. Unlike the other cards, Eva's was covered front and back with entries made in many different hands, starting neatly enough in the upper left hand corner but becoming more cramped and terse as the years of her life unfolded in unhappy sequence. The blue ink of the first entry contained the standard information: "Eva Johnson, born 10 May, 1904 in East London; brought in by neighbour 8th March, 1906; mother dead, father unknown; underweight, otherwise healthy." No mention of a twin sister.

I read on. Black and blue ink alternated randomly with pencil, giving the report a sense of history in the making. Eva had been adopted within days by Muriel and Charles Winston. That event should have marked the end of her file, but she had been returned three years later by Charles Winston when his wife died. Unemployed and unable to care for a child by himself, he left her with promises to return when he found work. Older children had little hope of adoption, so five-year-old Eva was sent to the Ragged School with the goal of a life in Australia or Canada after she had learned a trade. It was a system that had worked well for decades, and every indication suggested that Eva would turn out the way 95 percent of Dr. Barnardo's children did: as decent, productive citizens of the British Commonwealth.

Shortly after her tenth birthday came bad luck disguised as good fortune. A couple named Giles and Adelaide Tennant adopted Eva. Five years later, in 1914, she came back—someone at the home had sought out Eva and persuaded her to return. As I read on, the reason became clear: Giles Tennant had been sent to prison for grand larceny and those at Copperfield Road believed Eva's interests would be better served back in school. She lasted only a few weeks before she took off. No doubt they could have found her again, but she was beyond the age where they could compel her to return and, Lord knows, there were too many children who wanted help to waste time chasing after one who didn't.

Tennant. Why did that name fairly dance in my head? I knew no one of that name. But there was something about Tennant . . . and Winston . . . something wrong . . . something I should remember.

In a blinding flash of intuition, it came to me. No questions are more difficult than the ones with obvious answers: *The orphans were filed alphabetically under their original surnames.* Eva was not filed under W for Winston or T for Tennant—her adopted parents' names—but under her birth name, Johnson. And Jack Marsh had been told to search for Claire Smith, my adopted name, not Claire Johnson, my birth name.

Not daring to breathe, I stood up to reach the higher file drawer and flipped backwards from Eva's card. Emily Johnson, Ellen Johnson, Edward Johnson, Doris Johnson, Dennis Johnson, David Johnson, Cyrus Johnson, Colleen Johnson . . . and there it was. Claire Johnson. Precisely where it should have been. My knees wobbled. I pulled out the file.

The first brief notation was penned in blue ink by someone with an elegant slanted script. It contained the same information as Eva's entry but the wording differed slightly. "Claire Johnson, born East London, 10th May, 1904. Brought in by neighbour 11th March, 1906. Father deserted family. Mother dead. Healthy."

Three days separated my arrival at the orphanage from Eva's. What could explain that?

There was one other notation, dated the 27th of July of the same year, written in a different hand. "Adopted by William and Marjorie Smith." I pictured my father and mother visiting the orphanage, asking to see a young child rather than an infant, asking whether there were any siblings, and being told the truth. There were no siblings. My twin sister was long gone and who could remember the details of one small child among hundreds, especially when the child had been there such a brief time?

I was so engrossed in what I was doing that when the door opened behind me, I jumped a foot. A plump woman bustled in carrying a load of papers. "Excuse me for interrupting, my dear. I heard one of the orphans had come looking for information and I always—" She squinted at me in the dim light. "Oh, my dear! Eva!"

I had been told I was Eva so many times, I almost said yes. "No, I'm her twin sister, Claire."

"Oh, my dear." She took a few steps toward me and put on her spectacles to get a better look at my face, then sank into a comfortable wing chair and pulled them off again, letting them fall onto an ample bosom. "My word, child, you certainly are her double."

"You know Eva?" I had one blood relative in the world. She

was, no doubt, a thoroughly wicked person, but she hadn't started out that way, and I wouldn't apologize for wanting to know more about her. Still clutching my file card, I sank weakly into the nearest wooden chair.

The woman nodded. "I worked in the office at the Copperfield Road home, and when it closed, I was sent here along with the files. Life being what it is, I made myself useful and stayed on with the Bishop. Usually they tell me when one of Doctor Barnardo's children comes by. I'm Elaine Travers. I knew Eva had a twin—I was the one who told her so one day."

"Could you—could you tell me what she was like back then?"

Mrs. Travers patted a stray hair back into its bun as she warmed to her topic. "Oh, she was a willful one, she was . . . more trouble than a barrel of boys. Still, I always had a soft spot for the girl. She came back here after Sister Angeline saw in the paper about that horrid man being sent to prison. Sister Angeline went looking for Eva and coaxed her back. About fifteen she was then."

"Had Mrs. Tennant died?"

"'Twern't no Mrs. Tennant, just some trollop he lived with. And he was no carpenter! A housebreaker, more like it. Like that Fagin fellow in *Oliver Twist*, you know? Teaching innocent young things how to steal. He would pick the locks of fine homes and wait outside while the children went in and loaded up on silver and jewellery. If they got caught, they being children, the law wouldn't come down as hard on them. But he got caught finally . . . and got put away for years. But Eva wouldn't stay with us. She would mock me. 'Why work for a few bob a week when I can get a year's wages in one night?' She was used to flash by then and knew how to get what she wanted out of men. The director wanted to send her to Canada right away, but she was of age to make her own decisions. She refused to go. Dear me, I am always sad thinking about Eva."

We shared the silence for a long moment, she shaking her head with regret for what had been beyond her power to effect, I trying to picture a childhood so very foreign to my own ordinary upbringing. Suddenly she snapped her attention back to me. "Here, now, have you seen her? What's she doing now, mended her ways I hope?"

I had to admit that I hadn't seen her, that I had only just learned of her existence a short time ago. "And this confirms it," I said, holding up the two file cards. "But it doesn't say here that we were twins."

Mrs. Travers slipped on her spectacles and studied the cards. "No, it surely does not, not in so many words, but you see, I noticed the same last name and birth date. What else could explain that?"

"We were brought in on different days. D'you know why?"

"No, dear, I wasn't working there until some years after. But it says a neighbour brought you in. Could be she had thoughts of keeping one, then changed her mind. Could be she had a long ways to come and two was just too much to carry so far, and she had to make the trip twice."

I nodded and was quiet for a while. Whatever the explanation, that short delay meant two different women were on duty when my sister and I came to Copperfield Road, neither of whom made the connection between the two sisters. Yet it had made all the difference in both our lives. I roused myself to ask, "You said she knew about me?"

"Ever since she came back the second time, yes. I caught her searching the files one day, looking for her own family she said, and I told her then about a twin sister. She was so excited, I fancied it would make a difference to her having some family. She wanted to find the sister, and she did. I don't know how, but that one had connections. She found out where you lived—"

"Morefield?" I could not have been more astounded. Eva had come to Morefield, and I hadn't known of it?

"I don't know how, she never told me. But she disappeared for a few days and when she came back, she was meaner than ever. Used to smack the little ones until one of the matrons gave her a good thrashing herself and, well, that's what made her run off. I'm sorry, dear, I hoped . . . well, I guess that was foolish." She pulled out a handkerchief and blew her nose.

"You mean that Eva came all the way to Morefield and left without making herself known?"

"Bragged that she dressed up like a boy so no one would recognize her. I don't know quite what went on, but she told me she found you and that you were a—well, she said some unkind things, so angry she was."

"But why?" Surely she had come to Morefield intending to meet me. Why hadn't she knocked on the door of Rose Cottage?

"Don't you see, dear? You had everything she didn't and . . . well, sometimes envy eats at people from the inside out until there's nothing left but hate."

She hated me. From the first time she saw me, my sister hated me. She never made contact. She kept the knowledge of her twin festering inside her until one day last spring. And then she had acted to replace me, to take my life, in every sense of the phrase, and become me. Alex had been right. It felt like the cold outside air had poured into the library through an open door.

After the revelation that day, I threw myself into my work at the auction house. I tried to keep my thoughts from straying overmuch to Eva and the Copperfield Road Ragged School, but the questions kept swimming around in my head like a great whirlpool. What if the Winstons had caught sight of me that day instead of Eva? What if it had been I whom they adopted and then returned to be adopted again by the Tennants? Would I have turned out a thief? A woman of easy virtue? A coldly selfish human being capable of murder?

And if Eva had been there when Dad and Mum came, if they had taken her home and brought her up in Morefield in my room, in my school, in my chair at the table, would she have been me? Would she be working in London today while I lived the fast life in some faraway city? Could I have stolen and killed to keep myself in baubles and pretty clothes? Could I have had my sister murdered to save myself from being caught? Surely not, and yet . . . and yet . . . if Doctor Barnardo was right about the ascendancy of environment over birth . . . I would have turned out like Eva and she like me. Inconceivable as it seemed, I would not exist as I was today.

October arrived and the days grew shorter. I kept an eye out for Tommy or one of his cohorts as I left the office and made my way to Marlborough Street, but even the street urchins had gone home for the night. I passed St. James Palace and entered the park with the brisk walk and bold stare of a no-nonsense matron. I had not yet had the occasion to cross the park after dusk, but I was not one of those timid spinsters frightened by the dark. Mice and spiders didn't give me the vapours, and I had never swooned in my life. Girls today were far better equipped to take care of themselves than were the girls of my mother's generation. Nevertheless, as I started into the Park, my confidence wobbled. After dark, the Park is silent and cold. Thoughts of the Seine intruded.

"Nonsense!" I spoke to the trees. If the Park were dangerous at night, the police would have bobbies on patrol. The few dark shapes I passed moving in the opposite direction gave me as wide a berth as I gave them. Twenty minutes saw me home.

I had just removed my coat in the front hall of the hostel when Mrs. Price, my landlady, approached.

"There you are, Miss Smith. There is a call for you on the telephone."

Alex, I thought. Ridiculous, I corrected myself too late to stop my hands from going cold as ice. Who would telephone me? In three months at Price's hostel, I had not received a single telephone call.

The telephone was located in a closet off the dining room to give some semblance of privacy, although as anyone nearby could tell you, privacy was a polite myth that only the stone deaf believed. Mrs. Price lingered in the hall as I picked up the receiver.

"Claire, is that you?"

"Yes, Dad, what is it? Whatever is the matter?" Never before had my father telephoned me, and I knew at once that it must be life and death.

"Nothing wrong here. I just wanted to be certain that you were still in London."

"Of course I'm in London. I just came in from work." I had the sense that he was holding something back, something he was reluctant to tell me.

"But it is you, my little Claire, isn't it?"

"Yes, of course it is," I replied, my worry and my impatience mounting. "What is the matter?"

"I'm afraid the police are going to be paying a call soon," he said, sounding older than his sixty-five years.

"Me?" Disjointed thoughts jumbled through my brain. Alex. Something happened to Alex. No, Alex had traced me. No, the

French police had traced me. I took a deep breath to calm my panic and reminded myself sternly that I had nothing to fear from the French police. Now that I could prove I was not Eva, they were no longer a threat. "Dad, what on earth is this about?"

"I told them there had been a mistake. The police, they came 'round the house today to bring the news. They said they were sorry to inform me that my daughter in New York had died. I nearly had a heart attack, but then thought the better of it and told them there was some mistake, that my daughter lived in London."

"It's Eva," I said, keeping my voice expressionless to protect against the wave of emotion that would engulf me soon.

"I told them that. I had to explain everything, and right in front of Edna too! I told them she had taken your passport and was masquerading as you. I said I didn't know why and that's the truth. I don't know what sort of mischief was going on there. I just know that you weren't involved in anything illegal. Were you?" Perhaps it was the telephone wires that made his speech sound so querulous and unsteady, almost as if he were trembling with cold.

"No, Dad, never. It was Eva."

"Well, I knew that, not my little girl. But they are keen to send a detective from London to see you. Probably tomorrow. I just wanted to warn you. And I wanted to tell you about your sister. It's a shame, it is, even though she must have been a bad 'un. Nobody deserves to die so young. She might've straightened out her life if given half a chance. If only your mother and I had come sooner to Dr. Barnardo's, we could have taken Eva too and given her a good home, poor little mite."

As I realized I would never have even a slim chance of meeting my sister, the wave I had been holding back crashed over my head at last. I'd lost the only person in the world related to me by blood. More than that, we'd shared the same womb. Part of me was gone, and I felt the loss keenly even though I hadn't known her. My eyes stung. I swallowed hard and struggled to speak. "How did she die?"

"They asked me the questions, not the other way 'round."

What my father knew of Eva was only the bare minimum I had told him after my examination of the orphanage files many weeks ago. He would have had little to offer the police by way of information. No doubt they had worked that out and were coming after me for the rest. I thought again of that day the French police paid their visit to Chateau Denon and again reminded myself I had nothing to fear. I had done nothing wrong. But I stayed home sick the next day so they would have no reason to track me to my workplace and embarrass me there. I couldn't afford to jeopardize yet another job, not one that paid 2£ 15s a week.

The next day at half ten, I ushered two policemen into the hostel's front parlour. Neither wore uniforms.

"My father told me to expect a visit," I told them. The one with the old-fashioned moustache showed me his badge and introduced his partner as Detective Inspector McDaniel. I was too rattled to catch his name.

"Then you know why we are here." The man with the moustache did all the talking. "Can you show us some identification?"

Having never replaced my passport or applied for a driving permit, the best I could do was to produce a library lending card. I could also have shown them my membership certificate from the suffragette society but that would have been like waving a red cape in front of two bulls. I knew very well what the London police thought of uppity old maids who didn't know their God-given place in society.

"The usual embassy channels brought word from America," he began, "that a British citizen was dead in New York. She was identified as Claire Smith from her passport and some correspondence found in her flat. She was traced through the embassy to her address in Morefield where we learned there was some question as to her identity. Can you clear this up?"

Like a penitent in a church confessional, I began my story with my hands folded in my lap and a contrite look on my face. Both men took notes as I talked without interruption about the attack in Paris, my memory loss, and subsequent investigation into the orphanage records. I told them what I knew about Eva's criminal activities and that she was wanted by the French police.

"So Eva needed to disappear," I concluded. "Her solution was to become me. She learned about me the same way I learned about her—through the orphanage files. I'm sure she thought I was dead after the bag-snatch, which she set up so as to leave *her* bag at the scene and *her* ring on my finger in case the body was recovered. If she were pronounced dead, the police would stop searching for her."

"So she travelled to New York, assuming the plan had worked and that you were dead, carrying your passport? And she lived there under your name?"

"That seems to be the case. I know it all sounds a bit far-fetched . . ." I couldn't work out whether he believed me or not.

"I've heard a lot of strange stories in my time," said the moustached inspector in a manner that gave nothing away, "and I can usually smell the frauds. Just a few more questions, if you don't mind, Miss Smith."

I kept my hands clasped tightly in my lap while the two clarified some details and duly noted the names of the Contessa, the hospital, and the Parisian doctor who had treated me. They would contact the French police for verification as to Eva's arrest warrant and notify them of her death. They would check the orphanage records and speak to Mrs. Travers at the bishop's office. I couldn't bring myself to tell them about my own relationship with Alex. It had no relevance to the case, I told myself. They were here to clear up the identity confusion, that was all. And what would I say? That I fell in love with Eva's husband, a man who held me in such high regard that he proposed to sequester me in South America as his mistress while he continued the playboy circuit of racing cars, casinos, women, and wine?

When I saw them put away their notebooks, I spoke up. "Can you please tell me what happened in America? I never met Eva, but she was my sister, and I should think I have a right to know how she died."

Typical policemen—all questions and no answers—they stood to leave. "We aren't involved in that," said one. "I saw the report from New York, something about a wealthy young woman murdered in her flat. Few details."

"Murdered?" I gasped. The two inspectors looked surprised at my surprise. "I heard she died," I continued weakly. "I thought . . . a traffic accident or illness. But *murder?* No one said anything about murder."

"Strangled. But they know who did it. They have witnesses who heard them arguing about some paintings. And he was seen running out of her flat. It's the electric chair for him when they catch him."

I thought of Eva's penchant for lovers with ties to the criminal world. She had finally come across one as ruthless as she was.

"He's still at large then?"

"They probably have him by now. If not, they soon will. They know who he is."

"Who?"

"Her husband. It's usually the husband, isn't it?" He tipped his hat. "Good day, miss."

Funnily enough, I was surprised. I shouldn't have been. Alex's demented quest for his paintings had passed beyond the point of sanity long before I'd come into the picture. So he'd finally caught up with Eva. Surely she didn't have the paintings with her. Had he forced her to tell him where they were before he killed her? He had got off the first time he killed someone; no doubt he thought he could do so again. I remembered his words on that long ago day: "Murder gets easier each time."

"Miss Smith, a change in your assignment tonight, if you please." I looked up from my desk to see my employer standing beside me, clipboard in one hand, pencil in the other. It was Friday, a major auction night in the Great Room, and I was to stay late, as usual, to help with the proceedings. The other girls in the room fell silent so they could hear whether I was being singled out for special favours. "I need an appraiser to make a call. I know it's late, but the client requested haste, and it involves only the dining room. Shouldn't take you but an hour, and you needn't return to the auction afterwards. That's a good girl." He handed me two keys and a bit of paper with an address on the other side of St. James Park. I began to gather up what I would need for the job.

No sooner had he left the room than the gossipy chattering resumed exactly where it had left off.

"So I decided to make sure," said Florence, "that I would be in the reception hall at 11:00 to break a string of pearls the moment he walks through the door. I've done it before—works like a charm. No gentleman can resist stopping to help a girl pick up her pearls."

Rebecca gasped. "You'd risk losing one!"

"They're not real pearls, goose. What do you think, Claire?"

I jerked my head up from the papers I was assembling. "I beg your pardon, who are you talking about?"

"You know, the gent from Wednesday. The one you practically ran over as he was leaving the office."

"Oh, right." It was quite the office joke: Claire Smith brushes against the handsomest man in London in the vestibule and doesn't notice him. My lack of interest in men was starting to draw comment.

"It's so very exciting." Florence clasped her hands against her breast and sighed. "Ever since he first came to the office last week, I've been dreaming glorious dreams and he's been in every one. He's such a mystery!"

"He is? I thought you knew his name."

"We do," said Rebecca. "Diego de la Vargas. But we can't find out anything else about him."

"He sounds Spanish," I offered.

Rebecca rolled her eyes—that conclusion had been reached long ago over coffee. "Josephine and I have scoured the *Times* for mention of a Spanish nobleman visiting London but nothing has turned up."

"You think he's a nobleman?" I asked. It was certainly possible. Many of Christie's clients were titled. A few were royal.

"Or a diplomat. Who else would have come so far to dispose of an art collection?" said Florence.

"He's definitely rich," said Rebecca.

"Or so greatly in debt that he has to sell his art collection," I added in a futile attempt to douse the flames of passion that were raging throughout the office. "And he's probably married as well."

"I love his curly hair. And that moustache! It's so . . . so . . . manly," she sighed.

I rolled my eyes as I located the last of my notebooks. As if some rich Spanish don was going to glance at—let alone marry—a silly little English clerk. They had read *Cinderella* when they should have been reading *Tess of the D'Urbervilles*.

I, however, was well acquainted with poor Tess, cast off and ruined forever by her upper-class lover. Life was not so hard on modern women. I certainly didn't consider myself irrevocably ruined, quite the contrary, I had a respectable job with a good future. Women today could lead decent lives without marriage or children. They had no choice, what with the terrible shortage of men killed or maimed in the war. Nevertheless, I didn't like hearing the girls rattle on about their handsome Spanish don. It aroused memories of Alex, memories I could suppress only by burying myself in my job and my suffragette work. Never mind their silly prattle, I told myself as I left the office. I was putting the past behind me very well now. My memory was almost completely restored and my peculiar stutter had vanished. Alex intruded on my thoughts far less often than he used to do. Sometimes an entire hour passed without me thinking of him at all.

A dense fog mixed with the soot of a thousand thousand coal-burning fireplaces and factories thickened the night air, bringing a grimy, foul-smelling darkness unknown in rural parts. I longed for a deep breath of clean Morefield air as I headed out into the murky city. In the thick gloom, I heard more than saw other pedestrians on the opposite side of Marlborough Road. The sound of a cough reached my ears, an aimless whistle, a walking stick tapping the pavement, a dog's bark, but the London fog plays tricks on those it ensnares, teasing the senses by confusing the direction of the sound so that the noise you believe is behind you actually comes from the front. I worked my way toward St. James Palace and the Park, watching over my shoulder and peering into every alley for Jack the Ripper, hoping Tommy or one of his Soho mates would materialize out of the haze and skip up to my side tonight—as they had last night—with an offer to carry my parcel. I would gladly pay a whole shilling for that service now.

But there was nothing to be concerned about. This wasn't Paris. London was perfectly safe. Or at least this part of it was. There had been no mention in the newspapers of citizens being accosted at night in St. James or any other park where bobbies made regular rounds. I would have to conquer this rampant imagination or admit that women *were* the weaker sex!

I first noticed the footsteps when I crossed the street into the Park, as if someone had been waiting for me around the entrance. Ridiculous, I told myself. An over-stimulated imagination. But my pace picked up as I made my way toward the footbridge in the centre of the park. The footsteps drew closer. I walked faster until I was almost running on my toes, quietly so my pursuer wouldn't hear me and increase his own speed. Surely the edge of the park was not far now!

For a moment, I thought I'd become lost in the fog but just in time, the bridge appeared before me, suspended in the air above a river of dense fog like a vision out of the Peter Pan book. My thoughts jumped quickly to the Seine River. I stumbled as my feet hit the wooden arch, caught myself with my hands, and panicked. Looking backwards over my shoulder for my invisible stalker, I scrambled over the hump and down the other side. I could not see him and the blood pounding in my ears obscured the sound of his approach, but I could feel him gaining on me.

I collided with an elderly gent on the other side. "Whoa, there, young lady," he cried, steadying my shoulders with his hands and preventing me from dragging us both to the ground.

"Oh, excuse me, sir!" I said, but before I could step away, a very large dog trotted closer and wrapped my ankles with its leash. The more I turned, the more tangled I became, until the owner finally spoke in a firm voice—to me or the dog, I wasn't sure— "Now be still, and we'll straighten this out in no time."

Dog and I obeyed. At that moment, to my left, my pursuer emerged from the gloom and overtook us on the other side of the bridge. Dressed in a neat greatcoat with a copy of the *Times* folded under his arm and an umbrella in the other hand, he did not look like Jack the Ripper, although his face was obscured by the rakish angle of his bowler. I nearly melted with relief.

"Here, miss, step out now." The old man held the leash away from my legs so I could extract myself. The dog sniffed at my shoes.

"I'm terribly sorry," I said. "This fog is thick as pea soup and the footbridge so steep . . . I'm afraid I was in such a hurry I didn't see you until it was too late."

"No harm done, lass. Steady as she goes now, let's set our sights on Birdcage Walk, shall we?"

I had the impression he was walking toward me when we collided, but I must have been mistaken. Now that I knew he was heading in my direction, I was glad for the escort. An elderly man like him wouldn't be much protection if I were to be threatened, but not many people would try to molest someone with a fierce-looking dog. "Is your dog friendly?"

"Rufus is a good dog," he said, tightening up on the leash. Which didn't answer my question, but I left it.

With a spry step, he led the way through the foggy park, putting me at ease with his conversation. He introduced himself, a retired colonel with thirty years service in India, and he proceeded as we walked to regale his captive listener with comparisons of life in Calcutta to London. The occasional "You don't say," was all that was required from me until, ten minutes later, we reached the street I was looking for. "This is my street. Thank you very much for the escort—and Rufus too."

"Oh, fiddlesticks, it was my pleasure, lass. Can't have you young things running about the streets at night unaccompanied, can we? No. I'll just wait here until you get inside," he offered delicately. And he stood at the corner with his dog until I had located the right building, pulled out my key, and let myself in. When I turned to wave, they had disappeared into the fog.

The absentee client whose appraisal couldn't wait until tomorrow lived on the third floor of a contemporary building where mahogany panelling and polished brass gave the lobby the feel of a posh ocean liner. Surprised to find no doorman on duty behind the telephone stand or inside the lift, I punched the number three button myself. For a new building, the lift took an interminable amount of time grinding its way to the third floor but at last the door opened and I found number 34 at the end of the hall. My second key opened this lock.

The flick of a light switch transported me to a mandarin's palace in the heart of feudal China. From the sculpted rugs on the floor to the silk-tasselled kakemono scrolls on the wall, everything had come from the Orient of dynasties gone by—surely the owner here was a Chinaman! And a very wealthy one at that. I inhaled the soothing scent of sandalwood, set my notebooks on the dining room table, and went straight to work. Within seconds, I was wholly absorbed in the identification of a pair of Meiji period

Satsuma vases, not old but beautifully decorated that had to be worth—

Footsteps on the parquet floor spun me around. In the shadows of the adjacent room stood a man.

Measured steps brought his face into the light and I stopped breathing.

"Good evening, Claire."

"Wha—what are you doing here?" I croaked. My mind raced. He must have waited for me to leave the office. He must have followed me here. I must have forgotten to lock the front door behind me. And now I was alone with a murderer and nothing sharper than my lead pencil. "What d'you want?"

"Come." Alex motioned me into the parlour. "Sit down and talk to me. I'm sorry I startled you." I didn't move a muscle, just stared at him with wide eyes. "You are white as a sheet," he said, sounding puzzled, and he moved to take my arm. I snatched it away.

"Very well, then, I apologize." He held his hands up like a surrendering soldier. "Perhaps this wasn't the best idea, but I did not think you would respond to an engraved invitation." He gave a lopsided smile that nearly melted my fear. Horrified, I realized that what I wanted most was to throw myself into his arms and sink into the soothing fiction of his love.

"Why did you follow me?" I lifted my chin and stood tall, making myself stare directly into his eyes so he would find no trace of fear in my attitude.

"I didn't follow you. I was upstairs when you came in." I still didn't understand. "Come, Claire," he said, "you're quicker than this."

I looked around me with disbelief. "This is *your* flat?"

"My brother Manuel owns it, to be precise." He looked around ruefully. "His wife decorated the place . . . a bit excessive, I'm sure you'll agree."

"It was a ruse, then?" I stammered. "This job. To get me here."

"It seemed the simplest way to have you to myself, without any outside interference. I have important news for you. And I was in a bit of a hurry."

I should think he was! But in a hurry where? Where in the world could he go and not be pursued by the police? Brazil, maybe?

"How did you get here so fast?"

He raised his eyebrow at the question but answered calmly enough. "By aeroplane, as before."

"Not from France, I mean across the Atlantic."

"*Paquebot,*" he said. Steam ship. He must have jumped on the first ship out of New York to get to France in so few days. I wondered if he disguised himself or stowed away. Maybe he hired on as crew. He was examining me closely, taking in every detail of my face and figure. All at once, I understood why he had gone to all the trouble of tracking me down. I knew why he was here: to get the answer to a vital question before he disappeared forever beyond the reach of the authorities. Like his father, Alexander DeSequeyra was not a man to leave a trail of bastards in his wake. After all, he had married Eva for the child he believed was his.

"I am not carrying your child."

"So I see. A great disappointment to me. I had been hoping a child would cause you to reconsider your position. But I have another way to persuade you to return with me."

He didn't know that I knew. With his disdain for police intelligence, he would never think that word of Eva's murder would reach England or be investigated so quickly. I flung the truth in his face.

"You must be daft to come here! You think they don't know yet? You think they can't trace you here? Two police detectives questioned me just *two days ago*. The British Embassy has certainly notified Scotland Yard by now—nowhere in Europe will you be safe."

"What in the name of heaven are you trying to say?"

"*They know!* They have witnesses! They're hunting for you now!"

My half-French-half-Portuguese former lover seemed as English as the King as he stood before me, cool, unruffled, and unflappable. "I'm honoured, I'm sure, but would you mind sharing with me the reason for all this attention?"

"They know you killed Eva!"

He recoiled as if I had struck him. "Eva is dead?"

"Save it for the courtroom, Alex. I know everything. More to the point, so do the American police. And by now the British and French police."

He turned his head toward the window but I had the sense that he was seeing nothing, inside or out. "What happened?" he asked softly. "And when?"

"Brazil may be your only haven. You'd better—"

He was on me before I knew it, seizing my upper arms and giving me a sharp, angry shake. "I swear to you, Claire, I don't know anything about Eva's death. Tell me what happened." He could see the fear pounding in my throat. I took a deep breath, looked pointedly at his hands, and met his fierce gaze. He released me.

"You needn't lie to *me*. The American police know you murdered Eva. There were witnesses who heard you arguing over those blasted paintings, witnesses who saw you running out of her flat. They have your description; they know your name and that you were married to her. I don't know how you slipped out of New York—"

"So she went to New York," he muttered.

"—but they traced her passport to my father's address where they learned that she was Eva and not Claire Smith."

"When did it happen?"

I wanted to protest, *Don't play this game with me, you know very well when it happened,* but prudence suggested I jolly him along before he turned violent again, at least until I had put a good distance between us. "The police didn't say. Perhaps a week ago." Time enough for him to slip away from New York and get to Europe on a fast boat.

Alex paced the room, rubbing his chin, reviewing his options as I reviewed mine. I was trapped in a room with a man who had already murdered two people—would my refusal to come with him make him turn to force? I could not out-run him. I could not reach the lift and wait for it to arrive before he caught up with me.

But stairs? Had I seen stairs? In new buildings the law required a staircase next to the lift. I was fast on the stairs. When I was in school, I used to make a game of descending the stairs very fast, two at a time—even three. The trick was to turn sideways so your feet would land parallel to the tread. Could I out-run Alex on the stairs? If I reached the doorman—surely he had returned by now—would I be safe?

"Look, Claire," he ran his fingers through his hair in that

familiar gesture I had thought never again to see. "I did not kill Eva. I don't know how this all came about, but I swear to you that I did not kill Eva. I did not even know she was living in New York!"

I didn't believe a word of it. Not this time. Not ever again. I had been deceived and manipulated by this man because I let love blind me to his motives. I was not blind now. I needed to get away.

"Then your private investigators are overcharging you."

"I called off the detectives last June. Sit down. Let's talk this out. It isn't what I had planned to discuss, but I see we aren't going anywhere before we've settled this." He reached for my arm and drew me firmly to a chair. "I think we could both use a drink. Would you like something? Whisky? Sherry? Tea perhaps?"

"Yes," I replied calmly, thinking fast. There was a bar in the corner, so asking for liquor would not take him out of sight. I played my high card. "Tea would be lovely."

"I'll put some water on to boil. Sit down and relax. I'll be right back."

I bolted for the door. I opened it as quietly as I could, then ran for all I was worth toward the sign next to the lift.

I tackled the steps sideways as if they were on fire, clattering down two at a time, pulling hard on the rail at each turning, making so much noise I could not have heard a brass band thundering after me.

"Help! Help!" I shouted as I reached the lobby but the words echoed as if in an empty tomb. I would have to keep running. There would be bobbies patrolling somewhere near the Park. I would head that way. By the time the door slammed behind me, I was in the empty street running toward the park as if all Hell's demons were nipping at my heels.

For a full minute, I rushed ahead blindly, hearing nothing but my own footsteps pounding in time with my heart. In the smelly fog, I could see nothing ahead of me or behind. The lack of visibility made every step treacherous. I narrowly missed knocking myself unconscious against a wrought iron street lamp, and twice stumbled where kerb met street. I made the mistake of calling out "Help!" once, but only once. There was no benefit in giving away my position. I turned twice, retracing the path I had come earlier. I paused at Birdcage Walk and looked both ways for traffic or pedestrians. Or a bobby.

Only I was not at Birdcage Walk, and the footsteps behind me muffled in fog meant I could not stop to figure out where I had gone wrong. I ran straight ahead, coatless but heedless of the damp air, following the row of anaemic street lamps as if they were lighthouse beacons, telling myself that if I were lost, likely so was he. Surely I knew London better than a foreigner who came here once a year. In a moment I would come to a busy street where I would be able to flag down a motorist.

That moment did not come soon enough. I had two steps worth of warning before he was on me, seizing me around the chest with his right arm and covering my mouth with his left hand so I couldn't scream. With the fog for cover, he dragged me forward, not back the way we had come but across a narrow street and into an alley. One arm was pinned against me but I lashed out with my other. It did no good. He was behind me, out of reach. All I did was flail away at his greatcoat.

Another street lamp. We had passed out of the alley and onto a major thoroughfare. I heard vehicles splashing through puddles, the slam of a car door, the sound of a klaxon and a squeal of tyres as someone braked too quickly, and far in the distance, the agonizingly sweet sound of a bobby's whistle. I tried to make some noise but he only pressed his hand harder against my face until I could barely breathe.

All of a sudden the pavement turned to grass. We were in the park, heading someplace remote where he could dispose of me without any danger of witnesses. I twisted hard, clawing at his hand over my mouth and trying to kick his shin but managed only to lose a shoe. His arm was like a steel band. His bulky clothing protected him against any stray blows I could inflict.

He dragged me down a small incline. When my feet touched cold water, I understood everything. I was back in Paris at the edge of the Seine, and I remembered everything now. The note that had brought me out that evening, the men accosting me from nowhere, snatching my purse, pushing a ring onto my finger, and dragging me to the edge of the river. It was all happening again, the story repeating itself. Only this time it would look like an accident or worse, suicide.

I redoubled my efforts but he forced me into the lake. The water came to my knees. The mud sucked off my remaining shoe. His hand was still smothering me, and I fought for air. If I could fill my lungs before he pushed my head under water, I might have a chance to outlast him.

Suddenly, a giant's blow pushed us both off balance, wrenching me sideways, half in and half out of the lake, tearing me out of his grasp. The motion thrust me deeper into the water. I caught myself before my head went under. Choking and gasping for breath, I scrambled up the bank. My wet skirt caught between my legs and tripped me onto the grass. A few feet away, two men were locked in a deadly embrace, rolling against one another in a silent, fatal grip. I couldn't even stand, let alone run. On my hands and knees, I watched them, shrouded in fog, as they pummelled each other, grunting as the blows hit their marks.

Like a poorly synchronized film, I saw the flash before I heard the shot. One hand held a pistol, two hands tried to rip it away. One man fell back onto the ground, pulling the other on top of him and throwing him over his head. The gun went flying toward me. With the grace of a wounded elephant, I clambered over to it.

"Stop!" I called out.

In a Hollywood film, this would have brought instant results. Both men would have lifted their arms above their heads in weary submission, I would have pointed the gun at them and tied Alex to a tree. A platoon of bobbies would have trooped over the hill to the tune of a gay military march and my rescuer would kiss me as the picture reduced to a spyglass fade.

Neither man paid me a bit of attention.

No sooner had I thought about firing the gun than it went off on its own accord, knocking me down with the unexpected recoil. I gave a scream of surprise, then prudently froze, as afraid to let it go as I was to hold on. There was no pause in the fight.

A powerful blow to the head knocked one of the men flat on his back. The other, who seemed to know he'd delivered a knock-out punch, fell backwards and sprawled, his breath coming in rough gasps, beside him. I stood and squinted into the dark to see which man was left standing. I told myself I was not afraid, no matter who it was. After all, I had the gun.

He caught his breath and held out his hand to me. "Give me the gun, Claire," said Alex.

"You're insane." He stood up a little unsteadily and took a step in my direction. "Come any closer and I'll shoot. Don't think I won't." I swear I only *thought* about the trigger, but thoughts alone seemed enough to fire this gun. Startled, I screamed again as the bullet fired harmlessly into the ground in front of me.

"For God's sake, Claire, don't move a muscle. That gun has a hair trigger. I'll get it—"

"No! Don't come any closer!"

"Gently, now. Stay calm." He looked back at the other man, unconscious or dead, took a deep breath, and wiped his brow with his sleeve. "I see. You think—" He motioned to the body a few feet away. "Claire—" His words broke on a harsh laugh that came out like a dog's bark. "Hell, I confused you with a thief. Why shouldn't you confuse me with a murderer?" His voice sounded very, very tired.

I didn't see his feet move but he seemed closer now, close enough that I could make out his eyes glistening like those of a predatory animal, fastened onto mine by some invisible lifeline that he would not break. And I could not. I took a step back. "Stand still, Claire. I'm going to come over and take the gun from your hand, very carefully . . ."

"No."

". . . before you kill the both of us."

"No." I took another step backwards.

"Don't move!" he shouted tersely, and seemed immediately to regret the outburst. He continued in a low monotone, like the voice Bobby had used when he tried to hypnotize me that night at the chateau, as he moved inch by inch in my direction. "I know what you're thinking, Claire. You're confused. You think I was the one who attacked you. You think I was the one who tried to pull you into the lake. No. He was the one who dragged you here," he said, nodding his head toward the man while keeping his eyes glued to mine. "I came after you when you left. I followed you and found you struggling with him here. He can't hurt you now. I'll take his gun now and you'll be safe."

I looked at the gun in my hand. I looked at Alex. I had to admit, what he said made some sense. But no, if this other man was my attacker, how had he known to find me at the Chinese apartment?

"Only two people knew where I was," I flung the accusation at Alex. "My employer and you. No one followed me to that address."

249

"He did," replied Alex, keeping one eye on the mystery man who was trying, without much success, to roll over. "And so did one of my men."

Could someone have followed me without my knowing? I didn't think so. I had been careful. Of course, there was that kindly old colonel, but he hadn't followed me, he had only accompanied me part of the way. The figure lying prone on the black, wet grass had not fought like an old man, nor was he dressed like the colonel. Beset by doubts, I lashed out at Alex. "Everything with you is secrecy and lies. Why should I believe you?"

"I can't honestly think of a single reason you should. But I am telling you the truth now. Believe me, Claire."

He was closer now. He could have reached me in one leap, but the gun's volatility precluded sudden moves. The man on the ground groaned. Alex never unlocked his eyes from mine. "Only the truth between us, always."

I stood like a statue, mesmerized by the force inside those eyes, until he was inches away. The gun was loose in my hand, barrel pointing to the grass. He could have snatched it from me. He held out his hand.

"Trust me, Claire. Give me the gun."

I laid it in his hand and sank to my knees, hot tears streaming down my face. Above me I heard the click of steel on steel as Alex removed the remaining bullets. From the distance came a shout.

"DeSequeyra! Where are you? Blast this fog! Go on, boy!"

"Over here!" Alex answered, unruffled and unperturbed.

I felt the pounding of footsteps in the soft earth as he closed in on our location, drawn by Alex's voice. A dog's wet nose nudged between my folded arms. Startled, I looked up to see Rufus unleashed. His master was not far behind.

"Bring the torch," commanded Alex.

"You all right, young lady?" asked the colonel, patting my head as he would Rufus's. "Dear me, you're shaking from cold." He shrugged out of his greatcoat and draped it around my huddled form, tucking it under my feet like a father bundling up his child in bed. He brought his light to Alex who was turning the unconscious man on the ground face up. "Let's see who this chap is," the colonel said with the cheerful curiosity of a man flipping over the winning card at a baccarat table. "Well, well, well. No surprise there. Diego de la Vargas. The man at Christie's."

Alex took Vargas' shoe, filled it with water, and threw it in his face. He sputtered to life, wincing in the torchlight. Rufus growled an unmistakable warning. "What do you mean, 'man at Christie's?'" asked Alex.

"This was the chap who walked into Christie's last Wednesday with paintings to sell." The colonel took some handcuffs out of his coat pocket and jerked the man's arms together behind his back. "Here you go, laddie, some nice jewellery for your collection. Sit, Rufus, good dog. I was keeping an eye on the young lady like you told me, sir, and right when she walked in, he walked out. Nothing strange there, but when he hid in a doorway for two solid hours until she came out again, I told myself, this one's up to no good. I sent a couple of the boys to escort her, and I followed him. I knew he was no nabob, sir, if you know what I mean, though he dresses the part, he does. He was staying over a pub in Soho where it happens I know the owner who told me the man asked where rich folk go to buy fine paintings. My friend told him Christie's or Sotheby's. What I couldn't figure out was why he's been trailing the missus—ah, the young lady—since then."

Alex came to my side and eased me to my feet. Wrapping his arms around me, he held me tight against his chest as if he would never let me go. Far away in the fog, I heard a policeman's whistle. Two bobbies hurried onto the scene, sheathing their batons and pulling out their own torches when they saw the excitement was over.

"Here's your man, boys," said the colonel, pointing with his torch. "Done your job for you we have."

Alex guided me to Vargas. While the bobby's torch shone in the man's face, Alex said, "Do you recognize him?" His hair was longer and he sported a flourishing moustache, but I would not soon forget Luca. "I thought so," he said and turning to the colonel, who had shed decades along with his coat, he continued. "I think I can explain. This man is Luca Morosini, come to London to sell some stolen art. By chance, he chose Christie's, not realizing Claire worked there. When he saw her, he panicked, thinking that even with the moustache, she would recognize him from Chateau Denon. And she would have, given a good look. He's wanted by police in France for murder and art theft, and in Britain too, no doubt.

Because he couldn't reclaim his stolen property from Christie's without raising suspicion, his only recourse was to get rid of the one person who could destroy his scheme."

"And he's been on her like a leech, he has, waiting for his moment." And he looked like a leech at that very moment, a dark, spineless slug that had fed all his life off the blood of others.

Suddenly, my addled brain made the connection. I knew where I had heard that voice. The retired colonel with the gruff accent had been a disguise. And while my memory was still wobbly for the distant past, it was excellent for the last four months. After all, I had once spoken with Jack Marsh on the telephone.

Without further ado, Alex slung one arm under my knees and lifted me off the cold earth.

"If you have no objections, constable, my man here will answer any questions you have. I need to get my wife home at once but we will both be available tomorrow for—"

"Wife!" Luca Morosini exploded into high-pitched laughter, the first sound I had heard from him. "*Your* wife? She is my wife! *E mia moglie!*" His tirade was nearly incomprehensible as it pitched wildly from English to French to his native Italian, all of it punctuated with hysterical cackling and coughing and cursing that revealed a highly disturbed mind. "You think she—ha! ha! Money is all you have for her—she always comes back to me, I am the only man who can give her what she needs." He spat contemptuously at Alex's feet and let loose with a string of Italian profanity. "She thought to run away from me—she can hide from you for years but not me. I have brains enough to find her. C*ette une grande ville,* New York, but I found her! She will not run from Luca Morosini again! The paintings are mine now. *Sono le mei!* Whatever is hers is mine—that is what wife means, *non e vero?*" He kicked at Alex as the policemen dragged him to his feet.

"Enough of that, now, come along," said one, prodding Luca in the back with his baton.

In seconds I was bundled into the back seat of a police vehicle on our way back to Manuel's mandarin palace. Luca's words played through my head until I had puzzled out what was behind them. He had finally caught up with Eva in New York. They had a row, he had turned violent—and I knew all too well the depth of Luca's sadism—and he had murdered Eva in a fit of passion. Her husband, Luca Morosini, had killed her.

Alex thanked the constable for the ride home and carried me through the lobby, now staffed by a blue uniformed doorman who whisked us up to the third floor with an admirable lack of curiosity, as if barefoot, muddy, bedraggled women were carried through the building on a daily basis.

He took me directly into the bathroom where in short order, I was stripped of my filthy garments and helped into a hot shower. The sharp stream of water felt like it penetrated my skin, warming my numbed bones and reviving my senses, but I was wrapped in a heated towel before I became aware that Alex had been beside me the entire time. In the blink of an eye, he had lit a fire in the fireplace and sat me on the plush hearth rug to dry my hair while he disappeared. It felt so good to be warm and safe, I couldn't move a muscle for fear the bubble would burst. The room, the fire, and the whole world seemed small and far away from my very large body, as if I were a giant peering through the wrong end of opera glasses.

"Here, drink this." He was beside me, dressed now in soft dry clothes and holding a glass of something. Whiskey, his all-purpose cure. Obediently I sipped it as I watched him out of the corner of my eye. The fire threw flickering light on his face as he stared unblinking into the flames, like an old fortune-teller trying to read the future from glowing embers. His hair was wet, his chin dark with the shadow of a beard, his jaw was clenched. His lower lip was swollen. There was a cut on his mouth and a nasty lump on his cheekbone that would turn purple by morning.

"How could you believe I had murdered Eva?" he asked, throwing down the last of the whiskey.

"The police told me you did it. They said Eva's husband killed her. I didn't know she was married to Luca. Besides, you threatened it often enough. And you have killed for revenge before."

"What do you know about that?"

"Only what I heard from others and read in a newspaper clipping."

"And like most people, you think I got off because of my connections."

"That's what people say."

"I got off because the judges ruled it self defence."

I said nothing. What was there to say?

He leaned back in the chair opposite mine and sighed. "During the war, a great many military orders passed across the desk of one man, Yves Calvet, a greedy bureaucrat who quickly grasped the possibilities. He made a business of changing orders for a large fee. His mistake was in making his proposal to the honourable Philippe DeSequeyra who refused and then began collecting enough proof to expose the man. Calvet heard about this and quickly altered Philippe's orders, sending him to a dangerous section of the front where he was killed two days later. I knew nothing of this until the nurse who had cared for Philippe in his last hours forwarded to me his effects, including a letter to me telling me about Calvet. As soon as the war was over, I began to build enough evidence to destroy Monsieur Pompous and Rich Calvet—I hoped he would receive the death penalty but public disgrace and life on Devil's Island would have been almost as satisfying. Someone warned him what I was doing, and he confronted me at Le Mans after a practice. He had a gun but little experience using it, and his shot missed me. I wrested the gun away. I did not miss. I killed Calvet, yes, but it wasn't murder."

He stopped and waited for some reaction from me. I hardly knew what to say.

He filled the silence. "The judges ruled it self defence. You can verify all this in the court records or the newspaper accounts."

Still I said nothing.

"You aren't afraid of me, are you? I suppose I can't blame you if you are, not after the way I bullied you and threatened you. No wonder you believed me capable of murder."

"You deceived me. You knew I was Claire yet you let me go on doubting myself and everyone around me."

"Only for a few days! I meant only to buy enough time for you to see me as something other than a vengeful monster, as someone who loved you. I had to change tactics in the middle of the battle, to stop trying to make you remember and start trying to prevent it. At first it seemed impossible that you were not Eva, then I blinked, and it seemed impossible that you were. You looked like her, you wore her rings and had her belongings. Eva had played me for a fool before, how was I to trust you? The minor discrepancies were easily explained away. Then after our first night together, the first night we made love, I knew the truth. I didn't understand it, but I knew you were not Eva and that I loved you."

His face softened and the lines disappeared. For a moment, I was looking at the younger, happier man who had once graced the cover of popular magazines. "I planned to take you to Brazil where life is slow and the outside world is far away and you would belong to me. After a certain time, I would have continued the investigation and let you discover who you were. And like the race at La Mans, I came *that close* to winning before my car broke down short of the finish line, and I lost you. Do you understand what I'm trying to say? I apologize for my mistakes. I am trying to beg your forgiveness for my unforgivable behaviour. Come back with me. I swear you will have no regrets." He searched my eyes for some sign of assent.

"What about the paintings? If you think I can help you find them, you are sadly mistaken."

"I don't care about the paintings. No, that's not true. And I promised you the truth, didn't I? The truth is, I've been chasing those bloody paintings for far too long. So I let them go."

My astonishment showed in my face. "But they're worth a great deal of money!" And after working at Christie's for the past three months, I knew just how much that was. More than that, they were the symbol of his humiliation. A woman—his inferior in every sense of the word—had made a fool of him.

"I don't need money. I don't need paintings. I need you. I went away to forget about you. You were all I thought about."

Speechless, I studied him, noticing for the first time a cautious, hesitant posture so uncharacteristic of this man. His shoulders hunched forward as he rested his elbows on his knees, twisting and clasping his hands with a rhythmic, nervous energy. It was a side of Alex I had never thought to see. Hi face was creased with anxiety as he struggled against emotions that the masculine half of society had decreed must never be shown.

The fire popped and hissed like an angry cat. I wasn't ready for this, not yet. I was too vulnerable, too confused. I wished he had told me of his doubts when they first appeared. But to be honest, if he had, would I have allowed myself to become attracted to him? Would I have gone to bed with my sister's husband? I did not think so.

It was safer to talk about canvas and I clung doggedly to that topic. "Maybe some of the paintings Luca put up for sale at Christie's are yours."

"If they are, they will come back to me of their own accord. I have stopped pursuing them. I have only started pursuing you."

A war waged inside me. "Alex, please don't. We wouldn't suit."

"I remember four nights that suited us both very well."

"You were married to my sister."

"I was *not* married to your sister. She was already married to Morosini. I had a two-week affair with your sister in Monte Carlo that did not resume when she came to Brazil. And I obtained an annulment from the bishop in Brazil last August. A great joke on me, eh? I finally get an annulment only to learn that I was never legally married in the first place." He refilled his glass, and came to sit beside me on the hearthrug.

"With Eva gone, you will never find her son," I said. "You will never know if he was yours."

"*Au contraire.* I did find him, just last month. This is what I wanted to tell you. When we learned Luca's surname was Morosini and that his family came from Milan, we were able to find his birthplace, a small village outside Milan. He claimed nobility—ha! His father was a grocer. He and Eva had left the boy on a pig farm to be raised by a distant cousin, a woman paid to board him. The boy had not the look of a DeSequeyra, but a fist full of lira persuaded her to let me take him to a doctor in Milan for a blood test."

"And?"

"He was not type O."

"So you were correct. The boy is not yours."

"But he is yours."

"What?"

"He is your nephew. Eva is dead. Morosini will be executed for murder. I wonder what will happen to the boy. The farm wife is unable to keep him without the annual payments. But never mind, there are orphanages in Milan."

An orphanage? The word made my blood run cold. It had been my great good fortune to end up at one of Dr. Barnardo's institutions—few were as progressive as his—and to have been adopted by good people. Fate had not been as kind to Eva. What would Fate do to a five-year-old boy in an Italian orphanage? Would he be sent to school? Or, more probably, hired out as cheap labour as soon as he was strong enough? Would a life of crime be Eva's legacy to her son?

"Look," said Alex, pulling a photograph out of his breast pocket. "I had this taken in Milan to show you. His name is Matteo. A thoughtful boy, intelligent. He has your eyes and your impossibly long lashes. He was quiet but unafraid and quite brave at the doctor's when they stuck the needle in his arm. Think of it: he is the only person in the world related to you by blood."

The image was startlingly familiar, like looking at an old photograph of myself as a child. Matteo. Matthew. A handsome lad, yes, but it didn't take a mind-reader to see the nervous tension in his raised eyebrows and tight lips. He made me think of a skittish rabbit ready to bolt at the slightest sound. Poor little thing. Was he doomed to follow his parents or was Dr. Barnardo correct that nurture trumped nature? If only I could have him. But that was impossible.

Alex seemed to follow my thoughts. "The woman will give him up for a significant consideration."

"How much?'

He named a sum equal to ten years of my salary.

"I—I can't afford—"

"But I can. Come with me to Italy and see the boy. You will love him on sight. You will want to have him. The old woman will give him up for money, especially if he is to go to a relative. Marry me, Claire. Marry me and I will buy Matteo from the old woman and adopt him as my own son. Come to São Paulo with me. I believe you will fall under the spell of Brazil and love it as much as you love me."

"I—I never said—"

"Ah, but you did. And most convincingly. That night you were hypnotized, I had Bobby ask if you loved me. Un-gentlemanly, to be sure, but was it not an Englishman who said, 'All's fair in love and war'? I was having trouble reading you—you are not as transparent as most women—and knowing you were in love with me helped me decide what to do later that night. I was surely in love with you."

He had obtained an annulment and abandoned his quest for the paintings before he even knew of Eva's death. He'd found Eva's boy, then he came back to find me. My throat was dry. I swallowed hard and turned toward the fire to sort out my confusion. Marriage? I had thought all along that Alex wanted a temporary liaison, something that would last as long as it pleased him, at which point he would give me a large emerald and passage home. He had shown such contempt for Eva whose low-class birth was identical to mine. It had never occurred to me that he might want to marry me.

Overwhelmed, I could hardly find my tongue. That he would do that for me—adopt the son of a woman he hated and a man who had nearly killed his daughter—could only mean what he said was true. He loved me.

"I thought . . . I thought . . ."

"No, don't start thinking again! Just agree quickly, before you come up with some other fool objection." He stood up now, all traces of uncertainty gone, and with arms akimbo, glowering in a typical Alex effort to bully me. Typically, it didn't work.

"I thought you wanted something temporary."

"A handfast? We had our handfast in June, did we not? This time I shall settle for nothing less than forever."

He stood up, plunged one hand inside his trousers pocket and dug around. Taking my hand in his, he turned it palm up and dropped a kiss into the centre of my palm. He pressed a gold band where his lips had been. It was delicately etched on the outside, and it gleamed as I held it up to the firelight to make out the words engraved on the inside.

For Claire, with my heart, Alexander.

EPILOGUE: 1945

Old Cécile Renaud woke early to the sound of raindrops tapping softly against her shutters. Humming to herself, she tossed a few coals on the grate, pulled on her quilted underclothing and brown woollen shift, and threw open the shutters to assess the weather. The sun would not appear on time today, if, indeed, it broke through the thick clouds at all. She smiled broadly. It was a great day.

She made coffee—the pleasure of having real coffee again had not yet dimmed—and drank it with a breakfast of yesterday's bread and strawberry jam. Wrapping her favourite shawl around her shoulders, she was into her clogs and out of her door in one step, walking briskly along the narrow street that curved up the hill toward the *mairie*. She noted with satisfaction that no one else was in sight.

Turning the corner, she looked up at Chateau Denon, empty since the filthy *Bosche* had been driven out in early spring. The second great war had ended. The long Nazi occupation was over. *Collaborateurs* had been executed, and Frenchmen who had been hauled away years ago for slave labour had returned home from Germany at last . . . some of them anyway. Life would be hard for a while, as those like Cécile who had survived the first war knew all too well. But they were hardy folk and they would grow strong again. Soon the DeSequeyra family, Alexander and his English wife and their four children, would return for visits as in the days before the war.

She arrived at the *mairie* and stood alone under the dripping eaves, waiting for the *fonctionaire*. He would arrive soon, at the usual time, haul up the French tricolour as he did every day, and unlock the door as always. But this was not any day. This was October 21, 1945, and Madame Cécile Renaud had come early to the *mairie,* determined to be the first woman in the history of Ranton-sur-Marne to cast her ballot.

Suggested Book Club Questions for STOLEN MEMORIES

1. The story is set in France and England in the Roaring Twenties. How did French and English life in the 1920s differ from the American experience?

2. Were American women ahead or behind the French and English in the area of women's rights?

3. When does Eva/Claire begin to question her identity? Why does she initially explain away her doubts?

4. Dr. Thomas J. Barnardo was a real person who died in 1905. Was he correct, that heredity counted for very little and environment was everything? Would Eva have become Claire and Claire Eva if they had been adopted by the other's parents?

5. Clearly, both heredity and environment (nature and nurture) play a role in every person's development, but how would you rank the importance of each?

6. Did you have a grandmother or older relative who told you about the first time she voted?

7. Did you recognize any of the other characters in the book, beside Dr. Barnardo, as being "real people?"

Roaring Twenties Mystery Series
by Mary Miley

The Impersonator (2013)
Winner of the Mystery Writers of America/Minotaur award for Best First Crime Novel

To Jessie, a young vaudeville performer who occasionally finds herself on the wrong side of the law, the stranger's proposal spells Trouble. But desperation drives her to accept a major role in his inheritance scam, impersonating a long lost heiress for a cut of the fortune. The charade convinces everyone—except the one person who knows what really happened to the heiress and now must kill the impostor. With help from a handsome bootlegger, a mysterious Chinese herbalist, and a Small Time comedian, Jessie deduces the identity of the murderer. But it's a standoff—exposure of either destroys them both.

Miley shows a deft touch and sets a blistering pace . . . Leah Randall/Jessie Carr leaps off the pages in the Roaring Twenties period piece that drips with bathtub gin, truck-size cars, outsize personalities, money, high stakes and enough twists, turns and sleights of hand to keep one reading late into the night. . . Simply put, this book is FUN. –David Baldacci

Miley has delivered a tale that lures us into the dangerous underworld of Prohibition: rum smugglers, bootleggers, and the glamorous lost realm of vaudeville . . . a realm so real that we can almost smell the greasepaint." The Impersonator is an exciting debut! –Katherine Neville

Miley's lively debut . . . The story is engrossing, the characters satisfyingly larger than life, and one can only hope for an encore from the smart, feisty, and talented heroine. –Publisher's Weekly, starred review

Compelling characters, an engaging story line, and a heroine with lots of moxie make this a thoroughly enjoyable read. –Library Journal

Verdict: Miley's clever historical debut successfully portrays an intricate puzzle featuring multiple cons. Her protagonist dazzles us with her fearlessness. – Booklist

Silent Murders (2014)

In the second Roaring Twenties murder mystery, Jessie trades her nomadic vaudeville life for a modest but steady job in the silent film industry. She quickly learns that all Hollywood scorns the Prohibition laws: studio bosses rule the police and gangsters supply speakeasies everywhere with bootleg hooch and Mexican dope. When a powerful director is murdered at his own party and Jessie's waitress friend is killed for what she saw, Jessie takes the lead in an investigation tainted by corrupt cops. Soon tangled in a web of drugs, bribery, and greed, she finds herself a prime suspect as the bodies pile up.

Miley captures both the elegance and the absurdity of Hollywood in the Jazz Age. And Jessie truly is a honey.
–New York Times

Readers will enjoy the novel's taut climax, cameos by famous and future stars, and a resourceful heroine who uses her acting skills in investigating and escaping from trouble. –Publisher's Weekly

A brisk, knowing adventure whose self-reliant but vulnerable heroine takes big risks for her Hollywood boss and stops just short of romance with two men who couldn't be more different. Only the sequel will tell which one she chooses and who she'll be next. –Kirkus

Renting Silence (due in 2016)

The third in the Roaring Twenties mystery series takes Jessie from silent films back into the world of vaudeville to track down a performer with something to hide. At the request of her silent film star boss, Mary Pickford, Jessie calls on her vaudeville talents to investigate the murder of an extra by a Hollywood actress who has already been sentenced to death after a fair trial. Her inquiries lead to the discovery of a blackmailer and more than a dozen actors facing ruin or even death if their secrets are exposed. As one suspect says, "You don't buy silence; you only rent it. And the rent keeps going up."

Murder in Disguise (due in 2017)

Someone has shot a theater projectionist, run up into the balcony, and vanished. In the course of her investigation, Jessie discovers several other murders that occurred in a similarly theatrical manner, and she attempts to learn what the victims had in common and how the man could have escaped from such public places. Meanwhile, a young deaf relative of Jessie's roommate comes to stay while her mother is off looking for work. When the girl's mother fails to return, Jessie has another mystery to solve.

Made in the USA
Middletown, DE
31 May 2016